A Decent Killer

Everyone liked Max Follett in the small artistic community of Bay Cove. So when he was fatally electrocuted in the shower everyone assumed it was an accident. He had just sent his second novel off to the publishers and had attended a party for him given by wealthy Leona Morgan.

Max had said an attempt had been made on his life but no one had taken him seriously. It didn't take Detective Carl Pedersen long to conclude that some one didn't want Max to see the publication of his second novel and that among the decent, likeable members of the artistic community lurked a murderer.

Lament for Two Ladies

They couldn't have been more different. Ann Koppleman was an attractive widow who lived alone in her beautiful Californian home. Euge nie was a bag lady who slept rough, grabbing the odd empty bed in a nearby hospital. Everyone turned a blind eye to her.

Yet on the same night both ladies were murdered in an identical fashion: by a slender knife effectively plunged into the heart. What could they possibly have in common? Detective Carl Pedersen sets to work fitting the jigsaw together.

JEANNE HART

A Decent Killer

Lament For Two Ladies

Diamond Books

An Imprint of HarperCollins*Publishers*

77–85 Fulham Palace Road

Hammersmith, London W6 8JB

This Diamond Crime Two-In-One edition
published 1994

A Decent Killer © the Estate of Jeanne Hart Schrager 1991

Lament For Two Ladies © Jeanne Hart 1991

The Author asserts the moral right to
be identified as the author of this work

ISBN 0261 66461-1

Cover photography by Monique Le Luhandre

Printed in Great Britain

A Decent Killer

SATURDAY

CHAPTER 1

Max Follett took the steps two at a time and pushed open the heavy door of the post office, his big bearlike body nearly upsetting a woman who was leaving in the same haste. As he took his place in the dwindling line before the open window, he checked the wall clock. Another five minutes and Saturday hours would have been over. Now that, he thought, would have been the final irony. My moment of triumph. The manuscript finally finished, edited, typed, packaged, in hand, and I arrive to find the post office closed—the mails totally, irrevocably inaccessible for two days.

'Next.'

He stepped forward and surrendered the package to the postal clerk. She was a sad, grey-faced woman, but she brightened as she took it. 'Oh. Mr Follett. Off to the publisher's?' Everyone in town knew he had just finished a book.

He grinned. 'Certified. Valuable property.' Standing there watching her fill out the forms—she was doing it for him, probably as a result of the grin—he had an overwhelming impulse to appeal to her, to beg her to give it back. With a dragging sense of letdown, he saw the manuscript disappear into a canvas bin.

Walking down the post office steps—more leisurely now, his appointment wasn't for another fifteen minutes—he reflected wryly that he was surely the only person in Bay Cove for whom his finishing of the manuscript produced a sense of desolation. His colleagues and his students must have reacted quite differently. Much as they admired him—and liked him, he was sure they did—they most likely were damned glad to hear the last of it.

And his neighbours, some of whom had lived through that ten-year struggle with him, obviously felt such relief that they had to celebrate. No, that wasn't fair. The party that night was one of congratulation. After a long dry period, everyone would be vying to entertain him now, just as they had after that first award-winning book ten years ago, but this gathering was different. These were friends. He squared his shoulders and strode down the tree-lined outdoor mall towards the coffee house at which he was to meet his former wife, Florence.

They had arranged to meet in a back booth of the Salt-cellar, a spot never frequented by people they knew and for the most part a high school hangout. As she greeted him, he registered with amusement that she was going to keep things pleasant; that was Florence, ever optimistic.

She smiled at him over her coffee-cup, almost flirtatious. 'How's the Great Author?'

'One book greater at least. I just mailed it.'

'That's wonderful, Max. You must be so—relieved. To have it done, I mean.'

'I am. I am. A little let down, too. I'm not sure whether that's the prospect of undertaking another or just the feeling of having lost a constant companion.' He laughed. 'Well.' He picked up his coffee-cup. 'What's this all about?'

'It's really a very little thing to ask.'

'Of an old bedmate. A discarded bedmate.' The words were out before he could check them. He had never forgiven her for leaving him.

She knew and sighed. 'Max.'

'I'm sorry. I know it's all water under the bridge. I should keep my mouth shut.' He looked at her more closely. 'You're looking tired, Flossie. No trouble at home?'

'No.' She looked away.

He reached across the narrow table and took her hand. 'Arthur's not hanging around the nursery at night, crooning to the crocuses? Maybe he's working up to some Roethkian excesses about his devouring infants.' He removed his hand. 'I don't seem able to speak of him without sounding malicious, do I?'

'No, you don't. You know, Arthur never did anything to you, Max.'

He raised his eyebrows.

'Well, he didn't. I met him *after* we separated, remember? And I don't know what you're talking about, anyway.'

'No, I suppose you wouldn't. You do look tired, though, a little pinched. Peaked, I guess we call it. Granted that Arthur never did anything to me, sometimes I think you've completely forgotten that we had our moments too, Flossie.' He smiled faintly. 'We should have gone ahead and let you have that baby. Maybe we'd still be together.' After a moment he added, 'Not that you seem to be having one with Arthur. Don't you know times's running out, babe? God knows you never had any problem with fecundity. It isn't that Arthur's—?' He stopped.

'I should have saved both of us the trouble of coming down here,' she said, her voice cold.

He thought: So that's it, and took her hands again, both of them, in his. He was surprised to find how sad for her he felt. 'I'll stop. I will. Now. Tell me exactly what it is I'm to do.'

She said nothing.

'Come on, Floss, tell me. I'll behave.'

She raised her eyes to him and drew her hands away. 'Well . . .' she began.

Listening to her, he thought: The thing that really hurts is that only Florence has really known me. Only Florence. He was aware of a yearning towards her.

*

On the way home, he couldn't resist dropping in at the nursery, admiring the new wing and exclaiming over an exotic plant. In passing, he let drop the remark. It seemed offhand, but he had got through, he knew he had. Strange he could feel pity for Florence and none at all for her husband.

Driving home, he thought about Arthur. Arthur and Florence. The three of them met often enough, had since the first bitterness was past. Civilized, adult, that was what they had been. But in part that was because Arthur had always refused to submit to his feelings about Max, as though they were somehow demeaning. But Max knew he had them, just as he had feelings about Arthur. He sighed. It was complicated, civilized or not.

By the time he pulled up before his house, he had sloughed off the mild depression he had felt since the mailing of the book. He was feeling warm towards the world and, when he saw Perry Devane and young Marcie Terpstra standing next door in front of Perry's house, even neighbourly.

He walked back towards them. 'The dead is done. The manuscript is in the mail.'

'You must be pleased,' said Marcie. 'Now you really do have something to celebrate.' In the sun, her head was like a copper penny.

He turned to Perry. 'Now if I were like you—a book a year.'

Her eyes were suspicious. 'You know that's entirely different, Max.' She extended a hand. 'Congratulations.'

'It may be different, but I envy you, really I do.' He looked away. 'It's so damned *hard* for me.'

'My books don't receive the attention yours do.'

'That may be. I'd give a good deal to be more prolific and have less attention paid.' He stopped for a minute longer. 'You're looking good, Perry. You've done something to your hair.'

She looked pleased. 'Just a different haircut. I'm surprised you noticed.'

'I notice,' he said, his eyes intent on her. She stepped back. He could see she was wondering if he was flirting with her, thinking he knew better.

'Max,' Marcie said, 'Leona's waiting for you.'

His eyes moved towards his house. 'Ah, Leona.' He turned away and then took a step back. 'May I walk you up the hill tonight, Marcie? I need moral support if I'm to be celebrated.' Remembering, he added, 'And you, Perry?'

Marcie said, 'We're going up with the Blochs. Why don't you just join us? Otherwise, we'll see you up there.' She turned back to Perry, dismissal clear in the lines of her back, the tilt of her head.

'Another time,' he said. He cast a last glance at Marcie and started towards his own house.

She had her own key and was waiting in the living-room, lying back in the big chair, the one he always sat in, her long bare legs stretched before her, her sandals off, her smooth dark head resting against the back. He never got used to her, the purity of that face above the ripe invitation that was her body. A study in contradictions. He could not escape it: she was different from anything—anyone—he had ever known. He had met no one to match her. It must have been like that with men and Marilyn Monroe, the incredible impish child-face, the rich body, the sense of having achieved the unachievable. Ah, Leona, he thought, it's a shame . . .

He dropped into the chair opposite her. 'Here to congratulate me? I just put it in the mail. My patient editor will be exulting.'

'No, I didn't come down for that, but congratulations, anyway. I came to let you know something.'

'Yes?' He felt a tug of anxiety.

'Max, I've always said we'd celebrate when the book was

finally done. I want tonight to be nice, a good party, so I want to say this before we all get together, not to cast any shadows on the evening. I did mean what I said the other night, Max. We really are finished. As lovers, I mean. We've meant something to each other and I don't want us to part with hard feelings, but I think you know as well as I do that it's pretty much over, all but the goodbyes.'

He looked at her.

She returned his glance sadly. 'Somehow, I have the feeling that none of this is news to you.'

The surge of feeling surprised him and the sense of loss. Keep things in perspective, Max, he sharply reminded himself.

To her he said, with truth, 'Not news. But maybe harder to accept than you think.'

She said nothing.

'Let's keep what's good, Leona? Friends?'

'Yes, friends.' She laughed. 'Maybe that'll be easier.' She leaned forward to slip her sandals on. When she sat up her face was suffused with rose.

'God, you're beautiful,' he said. He could have bitten his tongue.

'Thank you.' She stood up, something ironic in her smile. 'I know you do appreciate beauty.' She put out her hand. 'I would like to return this.'

'The formal final act?' But he took it from her.

'Goodbye, Max. I'll see you at the party tonight.' She bent and kissed his cheek. 'Don't get up.' She walked from the room.

He sat stroking the key. The heaviness that had overtaken him in the post office descended again. Even thoughts of his plans for the future would not dispel his sense of stinging defeat. If he had let himself, he would have wept.

MONDAY

CHAPTER 2

Detective-Sergeant Carl Pedersen backed the car out of the parking space, his face grim. This was a call he was not eager to take and his partner, Ronald Tate, was making things no easier.

'Follett?' Tate said, his tone accusing. 'Not *Max* Follett?'

'Max Follett, the writer. Our resident celebrity.'

'He's dead? You're *sure*? He's so young.'

Pedersen nodded. 'I'm afraid so.' He shook his head. 'He was about forty-eight, I think. Crazy circumstances. A hair-drier.'

'What?' The usually mild-mannered Tate scowled as though the senior detective were making a bad joke. 'That's absurd.'

'Beneath his dignity? The story is that he was in the tub, one of the enclosed kind, showering. He'd been electrocuted. The drier had fallen in the tub.'

'Follett used a hair-drier?' Tate sounded shocked. Then he said, his tone still aggrieved, 'He's just finished his second book—finally. Like Styron's second; I hear that was quite a wait, too. It was coming out in the fall.' Tate was the son of a librarian, a fact he claimed accounted for his passion for order as well as for his love of books. 'Who found him?' he said.

'The woman next door.' Pedersen turned into the boulevard that led steeply to the campus area. 'She said she knew his routine and something seemed wrong.'

'Sounds fishy. Who is she? Someone from the university?'

'No, a writer, too. Her name is Perry Devane.'

'Devane. That's that Gothic writer. Romances? There

was a big spread on her in the *Banner* a couple weeks ago. She writes bestsellers.'

Pedersen looked blank. After a moment he said, 'You know what you remind me of? Me and Camus. Freda was a lit. major when we were in college and she brought books along every time we had a date.' He smiled. 'She was broadening me. I remember we talked for hours about *The Stranger*. That was when I still had the illusion that I'd work in civil service for a while and then go back to school and study criminology or psychology. Something.' He swung the car left into a main road, climbed the hill and turned right into a side-street.

'You like what you do,' Tate said as Pedersen braked.

'I'm not complaining. You just remind me of how I felt when I heard Camus was killed in that car crash. I kept thinking, "No, it's got to be a mistake. Camus can't be *dead*."' He grinned. 'It probably hit me harder because I didn't know that many French novelists.'

Tate nodded. 'It is a shock. Follett was no Camus, but that first book was damned good.'

The side-street on which they had parked was in need of paving. Set back from street was a pair of houses, one of weathered shingle, rambling, and squat enough to be partially concealed by overgrown eugenia bushes. On its left, a matter of fifteen feet away, a second house, apparently a product of the same builder, had been given a certain elegance with putty-grey paint and black trim, but it echoed the plan of the unpainted building. Each house was flanked on its far side by an open field. In one, two horses calmly grazed in the bright sunlight.

Pedersen and Tate approached the grey-painted building. The woman who met them at the door had clipped white hair that stood on end as though she had run her fingers through it many times. The erect bearing and patrician good looks did not accord with her distraught appearance, nor did the overlay of tan conceal her pallor.

'Mrs Devane. Detective Pedersen. This is Detective Tate. It was you who phoned the police?'

'Miss. It's Miss Devane. Yes. I—found him.' She turned her head towards the house next door. 'That officer says he's dead. I thought so, I was afraid to check and see. The shower was still running.'

Pedersen raised his eyebrows. 'You were smart to be careful. Could we ask you to come next door with us so we can find out exactly what you saw?'

She nodded. 'It isn't what you think. I'm just his neighbour.'

'I don't think anything, Miss Devane. Are you all right?' He held out a hand.

She shrugged away from it. 'Fine,' she said, and pushed past to precede them to Follett's house.

Leaving her in the living-room with Patrol Officer Muller, they walked through to the bathroom. It was of the same vintage as the house, late 'fifties, unremodelled: a pair of sinks beneath a mirror along the left wall with, beyond, a walled compartment for the toilet; a tub on the far right-hand side, its sliding doors of pebbled glass. On the wall facing them, at a right-angle to the tub, was a long, narrow, high window, open half way, of frosted glass with a wide sill. The cord of the drier had been plugged into a wall socket beneath the window and led to the tub; the far shower door had been slid back just enough to accommodate the girth of the drier. The other shower door had been opened when Muller had turned off the shower.

Pedersen leaned over and peered in, touching nothing. Tate watched wordlessly. Pedersen straightened. 'Looks like an old hair-drier. I should think driers are pretty well protected against this sort of thing these days, people are so careless. Even so, it must have been some kind of freak situation.' He paused, thoughtful. 'He's down here at the faucet end, his back turned to the dryer.'

'How could it have fallen in? If he kept it on the window-sill, it'd have landed on the floor. Could it have been suicide?'

Pedersen frowned. 'Suicides by electrocution aren't common. Besides, that shower door was opened just enough to slip the drier in. If he were trying to commit suicide, would he have worried about getting the bathroom floor wet?'

Tate looked at the shower doors. 'Right. That means—'

'Let's radio a dead body call and get the crime scene boys over here.'

'We're assuming foul play?'

'Let's say the circumstances merit investigation. It's not likely to be an accident.' He shrugged. 'Any ten-year-old knows electricity and water don't mix. I think someone wanted Mr Follett not to see the publication of his second book.'

Pedersen left Tate waiting for the crime scene investigators and accompanied Perry Devane back to her house. Warm as the day was, she wrapped her arms around her body and shivered. In the kitchen, she indicated a chair. 'Coffee's still hot.' Without asking, she poured a cup for him and one for herself and sat down opposite him.

'This has been a shock for you,' Pedersen said, 'but I do have to ask you a few questions.'

She cast an oblique glance at the notebook he had taken out and sat watching him, silent.

'That's Devane—one word?'

She nodded.

'You're a writer?'

'I write for Peko Books, Gothic romances. Supermarkets sell them.' Her tone was flat.

'As another writer, you must have known your neighbour fairly well.'

'I knew him. I wouldn't say well. We were writers of . . . different breeds. He was regarded as an artist.' Almost as an afterthought, she added, 'I'm considered a hack.'

Pedersen made no comment. 'Let me ask you, what was your thought when you found him? About what had happened?'

'I thought he was dead, of course. Electricity and water . . .' She shivered.

'Did you wonder how it happened, how a hair-drier got into the shower with him?'

She shot a quick glance at him. 'I suppose—' her brow puckered—'I guess maybe I thought the hair-drier he kept on the window-sill had fallen in. But how could it have? Wouldn't it just have fallen on the floor?'

'It was his hair-drier? You'd seen it before?'

She nodded. 'One night at a neighbourhood meeting there, someone noticed it in his bathroom. They were teasing him about it. Max was rather—macho. It seemed funny his using a hair-drier. He didn't like being laughed at.'

He nodded. 'We don't. Did he strike you as being suicidal?'

'Odd way to commit suicide.' She gave a ragged sigh and he realized how tightly she was controlling herself. She was more disturbed, had been more shocked, than she was willing to let on. He could tell the effort it took her to continue. 'He was an alcoholic. His wife left him a few years ago and he joined AA. They lived around the corner so I knew him. His wife kept the house and later she remarried. You should talk to her, she'd know if he was suicidal.'

'After the divorce he stayed on in the neighbourhood?'

'Yes. The place next door was for sale, and I suppose he wanted to be near campus. He teaches.' She looked away. 'Taught.'

'He has no children?'

'None I've ever heard of.'

'You say he was an alcoholic.'

'When he first moved in he was drinking. Fairly soon after, he stopped.'

'A pleasant drunk?'

She made an ambiguous gesture. 'It wasn't like that. He held his liquor pretty well, so far as I could see. He was—morose, I guess, more than anything else. When he'd been drinking, I mean.'

'A pleasant neighbour?'

'We didn't have that much to do with each other. We were both working. Max settled down after he stopped drinking so heavily, he had a routine and stuck by it pretty closely.'

'I understand he just finished a book.'

'Yes, after ten years. There's a letdown when you finish a book, but that would hardly have made him suicidal. Now maybe you could call Max paranoid. I'd say that he always was.'

Pedersen straightened a bit in his chair. 'Paranoid?'

'In the popular sense of the word. He—' she hesitated—'I may as well tell you, somebody will, he decided Saturday night that someone was trying to murder him.'

Pedersen waited.

'We were at a party—for him, as a matter of fact. A sort of neighbourhood celebration of his new book.' She paused with an inward expression on her face as though she might be reflecting that her books were not celebrated in such a fashion. 'The party was on a neighbour's deck and the railing alongside the ravine was shaky; she'd warned us to be careful. Max must have leaned against it and knocked it loose. He seemed very shaken for the rest of the evening and later, when we were all walking down the hill together, he said in this . . . odd voice that someone had pushed him. None of us believed him.'

But you're wondering now, Pedersen thought. 'And you didn't think that was possible, that he was pushed?'

She sighed. 'Would one of us want to *kill* him?'

'Was he a man who had enemies?'

'Certainly not among the people at that party. Enemies

is a strong word. And murder . . .' She did not go on.

Yes, yes, I know, Pedersen reflected wryly. Murder doesn't happen in a neighbourhood like this—writers, artists, professors. Lady, he thought, you just don't know.

'Assuming,' he said, 'that he had been murdered—of course this is hypothetical—can you think of anyone with sufficient motive for murdering him?'

She shook her head a shade too quickly. 'No one.'

'How about this morning? Did you see anyone over there?'

'No. Only that shower going on and on.'

'Yes. Now tell me about that.'

She sighed again, that same torn sound, and got up to pour two more cups of coffee.

'I'm sorry. We're almost finished.'

'It's all right. It's just that I don't go around finding—'

'I know. This has been a strain for you.'

She shrugged. 'I'm not all that fragile. It's just—well, let's get down to it. Max's alarm must ring around seven-thirty. This morning I was at my sink when his blind went up.'

'Did you greet each other?'

'No. We glanced at each other.'

'And then?'

'There's always a little—interval. I suppose he fills his coffee-maker and plugs it in or something. Then I hear his shower begin.' She nodded towards the open window. 'He never closes his bathroom window.'

He glanced across at the house next door. He could guess that in summer with the windows open like this, sound would travel uninhibited between them. He turned back. 'What time was that?'

'When his shower started? Ten to eight. I looked at the clock before I went to make my bed. I have a routine too, in the morning—I try to be at work by nine. Anyway, I came back and changed the water in the zinnias and went into the living-room to finish picking up. I remember I stopped to watch a jogger going by. Then I came back to the kitchen. Before I get down to writing, I always have a second cup of coffee and do the crossword puzzle. As I was taking down a mug, I glanced at the clock to see how much time I had. It was eight thirty-five. And suddenly it hit me—Max had been showering for forty-eight minutes. He never did that. A panicky feeling swept over me.'

'What did you do?'

'First I called him. I could hear the phone ringing next door but nobody answered. Then it occurred to me that maybe with the shower running, he couldn't hear.'

'At that point, what did you think had happened?'

'I suppose I—I guess I thought he had fallen.'

'And then?'

'I went next door and rang the bell several times. Nobody came. So I—went in.'

'You had a key?'

'No. I turned the knob. The door was open.'

'And?'

'I walked to the bathroom—I kept expecting him to burst out and be furious with me—and knocked. Nobody answered and the shower just went on, so I opened the door. Right away I saw the wire from the wall going over to the tub and I—' she threw him a glance of appeal—'I knew what was wrong.'

'You didn't actually go into the bathroom?'

'No, I had a feeling I'd be electrocuted too—I guess that doesn't make sense but it was what I felt.'

'And then you called the police.'

'Yes, from Max's phone. That Officer Muller came.'

Pedersen turned the page of his notebook. 'That's very clear. Thank you.' He paused. 'Are you all right?'

She nodded wordlessly.

'Up to answering one more question?'

She nodded again.

'Then I'd like the particulars of that party you mentioned—who was there, where it was held.'

She relaxed a little, as though the move from talk of her discovery of Max's body eased her. But she was reluctant to answer. 'They're just his neighbours, not even close friends.' Her eyes appraised him. 'Do I have to tell you?'

Odd that she should balk over information he could easily obtain. 'Of course not,' he said mildly. 'I'm sure I can get the names from someone else. Of course I'd appreciate your cooperation.'

She frowned, considering. 'All right, I guess it doesn't matter.' She sighed. 'The party was at Leona Morgan's house, up on the hill.'

'The Morgan family that gave all that money to the university?'

'Yes. They're gone now, the parents, and Leona's big interest is the county art museum. She's on the board. Leona was Max's current . . . romantic interest.'

'I see. That's Max Follett, Leona Morgan. Who else?'

'There were, let's see, nine of us. The Smiths were there, Florence and Arthur.'

'Now who are they?'

'She's the wife I told you about who left Max. Her husband's a nurseryman. Greengrove Nursery. And there was Max's sister. Her name is Dawn Voletski. She's a potter.' She stopped. 'My God! She doesn't know.'

'I'll get to her right after I finish here. Is Voletski her married name?'

'No, the family anglicized the name. She was Doris Follett, but recently she took back the original name and at the same time changed her first one, too.'

'A legal change?'

'I have no idea. I think after her divorce she just wanted a fresh start. Name and all. It's a little silly, but she's young.' She smiled faintly.

Pedersen nodded. 'My daughter changed her first name when she was in ninth grade. Temporarily, I'm glad to say. So, who else?'

'Did I say Keith and Karin Bloch?'

'No. Tell me about them.'

'Keith teaches ed. psych. at the community college and she makes miniatures.' At Pedersen's inquiring glance, she said, 'Not pictures. These are—well, to me they look like dolls' houses, but I guess they're built to scale and accurate. Right now she's working on a Victorian mansion the art museum is going to use in connection with a fall art show. I think Leona arranged that.'

'With Mr Follett, that's eight.'

'Who did I forget? Oh, Marcie Terpstra. She rents the garage apartment behind the Blochs. Lives there with her little boy and works in the campus bookstore.'

'No husband?'

'No husband. The boy's father's long gone.'

Pedersen took down the addresses. 'I'd better see if I can locate Miss Voletski. You say down the hill on the left?'

She nodded. 'You'll find it. She's painted the door orange.'

He closed his notebook. 'You've been very helpful. You'll be all right now?'

'Of course I will.' The words were abrupt; she was still a bit sullen, resentful of being asked to cooperate with the police. He looked at her, considering. She'd have been about twenty-five in the mid-sixties when the police were 'pigs'. He smiled. The age he had been.

She caught the smile, her face suspicious.

None the less, she politely conducted him to the front door. Outside the world was untroubled. Wheatlike wild oats gilded the hills beyond just as they had done all summer. Above, a fine line of birds unravelled against the sky like a dark thread laid against blue enamel. Beyond Follett's house, the horses had moved to the other end of the field. They formed a bucolic little tableau, the small white horse and the larger dark one a pattern against the glinting green of the meadow.

It was not a scene that suggested murder.

CHAPTER 3

Karin Bloch put down the tiny piece of wood she was trimming and glanced through the open door of her studio towards the outer door beyond. 'Come,' she called. She was working on the shingled roof of the miniature Victorian house, her first real commission and one she took seriously. As a general rule, no one interrupted her during the morning hours.

It was Marcie. 'Kevin's in the sandbox. Can you walk back with me for a minute, so I can keep my eye on him? I have . . . news.'

Karin threw a hungry glance at the table spread with drawings, pots of glue, little stacks of basswood and neat rows of miniature shingles, but she rose and followed Marcie outdoors. 'What's up?' Of all her neighbours, Marcie most rigorously respected her work time. 'Are you all right? You look upset.'

'I am upset. Karin, Max is dead.'

'*Dead?* Did you say *dead?*'

'Perry just called. She sounded awful.'

'My God, what happened? Did he have a heart attack?' She glanced down at her watch. 'What are you doing here, anyway? Shouldn't Kevin be at the day care centre?'

'They phoned not to bring him. One of the kids came in with a rash and they were trying to reach his mother to take him home. I had to call the store.' She looked towards the sandbox and lowered her voice. 'It wasn't a heart attack. He was electrocuted.'

'*Electrocuted!*'

'He was in the shower and a hair-drier fell in. She found him, Perry did.'

'This gets crazier and crazier. What was Perry doing there while he was showering?'

'I don't know. She sounded so funny I didn't want to ask. The police are there—at Max's, I mean. Some detective interviewed Perry and she had to give all our names, the people at the party Saturday.'

'Why? What does the party have to do with it?'

'Don't ask me. I don't know any more than you do. There must be some reason.'

In the play yard beyond them, Kevin happily sifted sand in large shovelsful from the sandbox to the ground. For the first time it struck Karin that neither of them had expressed regret over the death. 'What a Godawful thing to have happen,' she said. 'He'll never see his new book published.' That, somehow, seemed the loss. Not Max himself but Max never seeing the book, that novel over which he had so laboured, for which he had suffered for so long.

'I know. It's terrible, and it all sounds absolutely crazy. It doesn't seem anybody'd be that careless, having a drier near—' She stopped.

'Yes.' They looked at each other. 'He had it on the bathroom window-sill,' Karin said.

'But if it just fell in the tub, why are the police interested in us? If it was an accident, I mean.'

'Maybe—'

Marcie cut her off, eyes wide. 'Suicide?'

'He was depressed often enough.'

Marcie's face puckered with emotion. 'Do you have . . . mixed feelings?'

'What do you mean?'

'Just—I don't know what I feel. Max wasn't my favourite person.'

'He probably wasn't anybody's *favourite* person.'

'Leona. He was hers, certainly. And Dawn's. Lots of people liked Max.'

Karin smiled faintly. 'Well, even though Max was hard to take at times, I doubt that anyone'll be glad he's dead.'

'Not his publisher, certainly. Or—'

'My God! I wonder if Dawn knows.'

Marcie looked stricken. 'I *never* thought. How could I not? I was just so—'

'Let me call Perry and ask. You keep an eye on Kevin.' She left Marcie looking after her, her face anxious.

On the eighth ring, the receiver was picked up.

'It's Karin. Marcie told me. Has anyone gone down to talk to Dawn, do you know?'

'That policeman. I should go, but I'm afraid I'd upset her more. I'm sort of—shaky.'

'Of course. It must have been a terrible shock. Look, Perry, why don't we go down together? I can get Dawn to come up to the house with me. She shouldn't be there alone.'

'No, you're right. What about Florence?'

'She has Arthur. Are you OK, Perry? Are you up to this?'

'Everything feels a little unreal, but otherwise I guess I'm all right. I'll meet you out front on the road.' The plan of action had a salutary effect on Perry. Her voice more normal, she added, 'Tell Marcie we'll talk later in the week about the writing. She brought some of her poetry for me to look at—that's why I called her, so she'd know not to come by today.'

Karin hung up. This was the first she had heard of Marcie's writing poetry, or for that matter, anything else. The morning had been full of news.

CHAPTER 4

Approaching the house, Pedersen spotted the crisp oblong of strong colour. The rest of the building had not seen a brush in years. Well-proportioned, it must once have been a handsome structure in the Eastlake style of the area, but the long droughts and lashing winter rains had long since stripped it of any small elegance to which it laid claim. With its flaked and blistered paint, the house had an air of desiccation. The gate in the fence that enclosed it leaned tiredly and opened with a rasping sigh.

The cramped little basement windows had also been curtained in orange. Together, the bright door and cheerful curtains lent a touch of gallantry to the whole. He sighed. In a matter of moments his message would cast a shadow over these efforts at light-heartedness.

He rang the doorbell and then slid his left hand into his jacket pocket and ran the jade worry beads through his fingers. He had bought them when he and Freda visited Greece and carried them ever since. At moments like these, he found them a solace. After a short time he could hear someone mounting the steps inside.

A small, sturdy-looking young woman wearing a denim skirt and sandals, with tights and a turtleneck shirt of bright blue and an enveloping apron, opened the door gingerly with one clay-coated hand. She had dark eyes, high colour and a tangle of brown curls. 'Oh,' she said, 'I thought—I'll wash.' She stopped as though it had occurred to her that she should question this presence.

'Miss Voletski?'

'Yes.' She said it tentatively as though it might be the wrong answer.

'Detective Pedersen.' He flipped open his identification folder.

Abruptly her attention focused on him. He was used to the stillness that gripped people to whom he announced himself.

'I need to speak to you. May I come in?'

She turned and led him into the hall and down the stairs. When she turned, her face was frightened.

'Better sit down,' he said gently.

'I—I'll wash my hands.' She turned and left the room. A moment later he heard water running.

She was postponing the moment. He looked around. A grey kitten, already half cat, was curled on the sofa-bed. The kitchen end of the large room had been partitioned off by open shelves as a cooking and work area. A large crock stood to one side, covered closely by a wet cloth, a potter's wheel occupied a small table, and on the shelves jars of glaze and various finished and partially finished pots were set. It appeared she had not yet arrived at a personal style: several finished pieces were conventional in form, bowls or vases such as he might have picked up in any shop on the mall. Others, apparently more recent, showed the first attempts at originality. He was sure his wife Freda, who had once taken a ceramics course and was more knowledgeable than he about such things, would agree they were, so far, not successful. One, still unglazed, was so wildly amorphous in shape that Pedersen doubted it would hold water. Another was boxlike with squared corners; even in his ignorance Pedersen felt sure it would present problems in the firing and would leak at the seams. The one on which she had been working seemed to be patterned after a gourd. There was something childishly appealing in the oddly assorted collection.

A door opened and she came back into the room drying her hands on a white towel. The frightened look was still on her face. 'It's my brother,' she said, 'isn't it? There isn't . . . anyone else.'

He waited for her to sit down. 'Yes,' he said, 'I'm afraid it is.'

She leaned forward. 'He's hurt? Not—'

'He's been killed, Miss Voletski. 'Instantly, it couldn't have been more than a second or two.'

Her face was slack and she let out a little exhalation of breath. The kitten, as though in response, stirred and then jumped into her lap.

He answered the question she didn't ask. 'He was apparently electrocuted—a hair-drier. He was showering.'

Her face began to crumple.

'Here,' he said impotently, 'let me have the towel.'

When the knock came and he saw her off with her neighbours, it was with relief. Walking back up the road towards the Follett house, he reflected on their conversation. She had been able to tell him nothing. She had never thought her brother suicidal. She knew of no one with whom he had had recent difficulty. No change had taken place in his life save the finishing of the book.

'There was a party to celebrate that,' he said. She nodded without words. By the time Perry Devane and her neighbour appeared, he had decided this was cruelty, trying to question her at this moment. Despite the valiant orange curtains, the dark-eyed girl struck him as defenceless, completely and utterly defenceless.

Back at Max Follett's house, he found a bustle of activity. The crime scene investigators, the coroner's deputy and Detective Ronald Tate were fully occupied.

Tate was surveying Follett's study. 'What a mess,' he said as Pedersen came in. By Tate's standards it was a mess; Pedersen, himself not compulsive when it came to tidiness, thought it looked normally, even comfortably, disordered.

'Did you alert the team? Tell them to treat it as a murder till we know more?'

'I did. I also told them to be extremely careful that nothing is carried off without meticulous documentation and to take *nothing* they don't have to. These materials—' Tate waved a hand—'will probably go to a library.'

'Good. I've told the sister. I think I'll just hie myself up the hill to see the hostess of that party before word gets all over town that Follett's dead. Will you hang around here for a while, keep track of things?'

'The *Banner*'s already been here. I told them he'd had an accident, that we'd have details later.'

'Good,' Pedersen said again. It was what he would have said. He and Ronald Tate had worked together long enough to have learned each other well.

He walked briskly around the corner to where the road began to climb. Despite the steady rain of the day before, the surface beneath his feet was almost dry. That morning there had been no fog to burn off and the sun was moving higher, warming his face. It appeared summer was settling back into its predictable pattern.

Gradually he slowed his stride, taking in what he saw. The neighbourhood had retained vestiges of its original pastoral character but now here and there raw new buildings stood, looking undressed without any of the robust foliage that surrounded the older houses. The original planning had been poorly done—he thought of the proximity of the Follett and Devane houses despite their wide flanking fields—but building had been sparse enough to lend a carelessness to the neighbourhood. The weathered houses and small pastures, the tiny graveyard, the occasional dips in the road, the little creek that ducked under an old bridge and the horses grazing close by it, together created a scene that recalled the Bay Cove of his boyhood. The medicinal tang of eucalyptus was in his nostrils. As he climbed, the feathery trees thinned and across the meadows he could catch sight of the bay. Ahead to his left a large house was set at the highest point on a broad tract of land. As he drew closer to it, he could see that beyond the house the bay glittered in the morning sun.

From this side there was no sign of the deck with the broken railing, although he caught a glimpse of an outside staircase towards the back. The house was broad-eaved and in a subtle way Japanese in feeling. He rang the door-bell.

It took one glance for Pedersen to understand Max Follett's interest in the woman who opened the door. Being chosen by Leona Morgan would have affirmed any man's sense of virility. She was slender but richly curved, with gleaming, densely black hair pulled back from a face so creamy she might never have stepped into the California sun.

She stirred under his gaze. 'Yes?'

'Mrs Morgan?'

'Miss. Yes.'

He identified himself. 'Could I come in and talk with you for a few minutes?'

She raised both hands, letting them slide back over the smoothness of the dark hair that was drawn into a firm twist at her nape. 'Talk with me? About what?' She frowned. But she stepped aside for him to enter.

She led him to a study on the left. On a huge slablike desk, papers, letters and ledgers testified to the fact that she had been working. 'Museum,' she said with an air of dismissal; she seemed to take for granted that her work was known. She waved him to one of a pair of deep leather chairs. 'Now. What's this all about?'

'It's about a neighbour and friend of yours, Max Follett.'

Something darted in her eyes. She waited.

'He's had an accident.'

'He's all right? I mean—'

'No, he isn't all right.' He chose his words. 'I'm afraid he was killed.'

'Oh no! Oh my God!' After a barely perceptible pause she shook her head. 'I always told him he drove like a maniac.'

A natural assumption, thought Pedersen. Or were they merely cleverly chosen words to show her innocence of the real cause of death? 'It wasn't an auto accident,' he said. He did not explain further, but went directly to his question. 'I'm here because I understand on Saturday you gave a party for Mr Follett.'

Her hands went up to her head again. An interesting mannerism. Did she do that when she was feeling unsure? Out of control? 'I don't understand,' she said. 'Why do you want to know about that?'

Pedersen had not expected that she would let the topic of Follett's death drop like that. 'I understand the party was for Mr Follett and that there was some sort of incident during it.'

'Oh.' Her face told him nothing. 'You mean the railing? Max leaned against it. I hadn't realized it was loose till after the party started. Then I noticed it seemed shaky, so I warned everyone. Keith says it's termite damage.'

'Anything else?'

She was beginning to look uneasy. 'I'm not sure what you mean. It started to rain. It never rains in summer, and we certainly never have thunderstorms, but we did Saturday night. But you know that. Is that what you mean?'

'I mean anything out of the ordinary.' He waited. She said nothing. 'Who came to this party?'

'Just neighbours, people from right around here. It wasn't a big affair, but I tried to make it festive, especially festive, I mean, since it was such a special occasion.' She stopped suddenly. 'Does Dawn know?'

'Yes. I was just down there. She's a friend of yours?'

'Yes.' She looked past him. 'She was here yesterday. She

came out in all that rain with zucchini, just because she'd said she'd bring some. She dropped some off at Max's and Perry's, too.' She sighed. 'That must have been the last time she saw him.'

'Miss Morgan, may I ask you a personal question? Were you just a neighbour or perhaps a—more special, let's say intimate, friend of Max Follett's?'

Without warning, the façade crumbled. She put a hand over her mouth and, without speaking, nodded. Her eyes swam with tears.

'This must be very sad news for you, then, but I do need someone to tell me something about Mr Follett. Maybe you'll do that. Most of us in the town know only the public man—I hardly have to tell you he was one of our most notable citizens.'

She nodded again. 'What happened?'

He had waited for her to ask. 'It appears to have been some sort of—' he hesitated—'accident, a hair-drier falling into the tub while he was showering.'

'Then he wasn't—' She caught herself.

'Yes? Wasn't?'

She looked at her hands. 'Responsible. But of course if it was carelessness, he was responsible.'

Pedersen wondered if it had been the word *responsible* she had been about to utter or if the word was *murdered*. He said, 'Tell me about Mr Follett.'

She sighed. 'He was a complicated, difficult, rather unhappy man. It wasn't easy having a close relationship with Max. He was rather . . . engulfing, but he himself didn't want to commit.'

'Commit? You mean commit himself to the relationship?'

'Yes. He wanted to come and go as he chose and—' she added with more fire—'with whom he chose, but he expected you—me, that is—to be here whenever the spirit moved him to see me.'

'That must have been hard to tolerate.'

'Oh—' she tossed her head and then the anxious hands checked the hair—'I didn't tolerate it. We weren't getting on at all. Not, of course, that I want to think of him—dead.' She gave a nervous little giggle. 'You know, just then I thought: He'll be in a real rage at not seeing the book published. People think strange things at a time like this.' She paused. 'Have you talked to Florence Smith yet?'

He looked at her closely. 'No. Why do you ask?'

'Oh . . .' She seemed unsure as to whether or not to go on.

'Something occurred to you.'

'Just—well, I saw them, not exactly together, Saturday. I thought that was pretty strange.'

'Not *exactly* together?'

'I was standing in the Cheese Store waiting my turn, when I glanced across the street and saw Florence come out of the Saltcellar—that's a little coffee shop. About two minutes later Max came out. That isn't a place most of our friends go, it's more a teenage hangout, so it occurred to me that Florence and Max must be having an—'

He smiled. 'Assignation?'

'Well, a meeting of some sort. Maybe she'll know something about what Max was up to.'

'You don't.'

'Not lately. We haven't seen much of each other for a week or two. Once for dinner, that's all.'

He nodded. 'Back to the party. Was Mr Follett upset or frightened at his near accident?'

'Yes, he was frightened. Out of proportion, in fact. We all went in then, it had started raining, and he was very quiet, very shaken, all the rest of the evening.'

'Did he say anything?'

'About his accident? No.'

'You started to say you planned to—what?'

She looked confused. 'Oh. We had decided not to see

each other—' she looked down—'as lovers, any longer.
Actually, I decided it.'

'But you weren't angry with him. You liked him well
enough to give a party for him.'

'That had been planned for weeks. Besides, we were still
friends. Everyone was delighted that Max had finished his
book. We all went through those birth pains.' She laughed.

'I understand he used to drink.'

'Not since I've known him. Florence would know about
that.'

'He wasn't a violent drunk?'

She gave an impatient little shrug. 'So far as I knew, he
wasn't a drunk at all. Ask Florence.' After a moment she
went on. 'I don't mean he was perfect. As I told you, he
wasn't. He'd probe and probe until he found out the one
thing you'd rather people didn't know and then he'd keep
referring to it so only you and he knew what he was talking
about. Or so you hoped. But he could be charming, too. I
suppose the inquisitiveness was just part of being a writer.'

'And there's nothing else you can tell me about that
party? How about conversational exchanges? Anything
worth paying attention to, anything you especially remember?'

'No. Really not. Talk about writing and people we knew.
Politics, zucchini recipes—Dawn's a big gardener—and,
oh, I don't know, even about TV. Nothing special.'

She was not going to tell him voluntarily; he would have
to ask. 'Did Mr Follett think he was pushed against the
rail?'

She laughed, a nervous crescendo. 'Did someone say
that?'

'Someone did.'

'Max was paranoid, but not that paranoid. Nobody
would *push* him.'

'Just suppose someone had. Who would be your nomina-
tion for pusher?'

'What a question.' Again the artificial laugh. 'You're asking me to say one of my guests had lethal intentions. I won't nominate anyone.'

Pedersen rose. 'You're right, it isn't a question a hostess, or a friend, could answer. I would like to take a look at that deck, though, if you don't mind.'

The deck was off the cathedral-ceilinged living-room, through sliding doors. Because of the house's plan, open, with the dining-room and kitchen raised a few steps above the living-room, the expanse of sun-gilded bay was visible from the entire area. The deck itself was wide and at this hour sunny and welcoming, despite the ragged rent in the bayside railing. Pausing, Pedersen laid a hand on a lounge chair. It would be good to stop right here, take off his jacket, lie back on one of these long canvas chairs and let the sun melt away all the tensions, the thoughts of unfinished paperwork, of the unmown lawn awaiting him at home, of Freda's uncharacteristically angry words the night before as she complained that he was present only in body, forever preoccupied with a case, especially when she had a problem.

He removed his hand from the chair. There was still a good deal to do back at the Follett house. On the way home that night, he'd pick up a pot of those painted daisies Freda liked, to let her know that, although his work was often on his mind at home, it was she who was on his mind during the long days. She didn't know how often. He was, as she sometimes told him in teasing, a uxorious man.

'Just how did the accident happen?' he asked.

'Well, we were sitting around, talking, eating, drinking. The sky looked threatening but we had no idea the rain would come in the way it did. Absolutely without warning there was this great splatter of raindrops and the next minute it started hard. The place was in chaos—we were all scurrying here and there rescuing food and cushions and sweaters, nobody paying any attention to anyone else, trying to get the things and ourselves inside fast. In the middle of it all, Max gave this funny shrill scream and grabbed at Arthur and crumpled forward on the deck. I suppose his clutching Arthur that way is what saved him. Several of us turned to help him up and as we did, with this sort of . . . groan, the broken railing just tumbled into the ravine below.' She shivered.

Pedersen stood visualizing the scene. In those circumstances a shove might well be accidental. What was interesting was Follett's assumption that it was intentional. Was it his 'paranoia'? Or, he wondered, was it that Max Follett had found out one uncomfortable secret too many and he knew it?

CHAPTER 5

Rounding the corner on his return from the hill, Pedersen could see the tall lean figure of Ronald Tate standing squarely before the Follett house, scrutinizing it. With his wire-rimmed glasses and corduroy jacket, he could have been taken for a sociologist down from campus doing research into the odd and wonderful ways of the local natives. Pedersen joined him.

'I've been thinking,' Tate said. 'If it is murder, the question is, could someone have got in without the interested Miss Devane noticing?' He turned to Pedersen. 'There's a little path down in back, though even that's not totally concealed by shrubbery. She could probably see anyone leaving by the front door, especially if he walked back to the main road—he'd have to go right past her. But what if it were someone she's used to seeing arrive and for that reason never noticed? His sister? A girlfriend?'

'The milkman. The iceman.' Pedersen smiled. 'Life is tough, nothing's delivered to the house any more. Cuts down on suspects.'

Tate nodded. 'Come see this path.'

Slightly overgrown, it wound off down the hill towards the main road, a little path children might have made taking a short cut. Behind the Follett and Devane houses it passed at an angle, partly masked from view by sprawling eunoymous vines. 'See?' Tate said. 'Someone could have come up by this path and then cut across the backyard to the side door. I asked the team to check the area but it seems the ground cover is too springy to take a footprint. And everything dried fast after that rain, the ground was so thirsty.'

They turned back to the house. 'I've been talking to his girlfriend—one of them, anyway.' Pedersen said, 'Trying to find out about his being pushed against the railing. I didn't learn a hell of a lot.' He frowned. 'We'd better talk to his former wife, though.'

Back in the house, the crime scene team was working room by room. The living-room had again taken on its air of drowsy neglect—couch pulled slightly askew before the fireplace, cushions piled at one end where someone, presumably Follett, had lain reading or perhaps looking into a rainy day fire. Sunday newspapers were scattered nearby. Chairs bore indentations that could have come from the day before or the week before; it appeared the room was not often subjected to a thorough going-over. The curtains, still drawn, shielded the room from the light of noonday. On a little table a sticky-looking glass had been placed in a plastic bag preparatory to being taken away; on it, Pedersen could still see the dust from fingerprinting. Probably Dawn's from the Sunday visit.

Pedersen turned into the study. 'We should check out Follett's papers, see if there's anything right at hand that might bear on this.'

Max Follett's papers could not be said to be in order nor was there anything resembling a suicide note among them. A check with the technicians confirmed that nothing had been removed. Old letters from his editor, a note from his agent, a request to speak at the university women's club, three invitations with RSVPs (Pedersen wondered if Follett had been the sort of man who bothered to respond), paid and unpaid bills, a Rollidex address file, several bank statements apparently not checked for errors in envelopes crammed with cheques, scribbled-upon pages from an old manuscript, a notebook filled with barely legible jottings related to his writing. Nothing that readily revealed anything pertinent to the death.

A large looseleaf calendar that presented a month at a time showed a notation for the Saturday night party and another unspecified one for the same Saturday marked merely '12.15'. The week to come showed entries for speaking engagements, one on campus and one in town, and a 'U meeting'. Among the papers readily at hand there was no copy of his manuscript. And no will; probably that was in a safe-deposit box.

Pedersen walked through to the kitchen and stood looking out of the window at the Devane house. 'I wonder why that door was unlocked,' he said. 'A paranoid man. You know, Ron—' He stopped.

'Yes, Carl?'

'You know, this is a little world unto itself, this neighbourhood. I've heard of them. Down in town they call them the Art Gang.'

'It doesn't sound like a term of endearment.'

'No, but not derogatory, either. Just descriptive. I've been thinking. We have to ask the right questions. If we ask the wrong ones, I have a feeling they'll draw together and protect each other.'

'You make them sound like a ring of covered wagons. Does that make us the Indians?'

Pedersen smiled. 'Not exactly. But we have to learn what they are, this Art Gang. Who is who. I think we have to proceed carefully with the bunch that went to the Saturday night party.' In a sudden lightening of mood, he swung around. 'How about lunch when they're finished here?'

Because lunch was a break before what would probably be a long, hard afternoon of work, they treated themselves to the local Chinese restaurant, which had a reputation for excellent food.

'Freda,' commented Pedersen over his broccoli and black mushrooms, 'tells me if I ever take to coming home regularly for lunch, she'll divorce me.'

'Maybe that was my trouble.' Tate's smile was wry.

'How long is it now? You must have got used to being by yourself.'

'You never get used to it. Oh, it has some good features. You make all your own plans and decisions. You don't waste a lot of energy over pointless discussions. But there's no one, no . . .'

'Significant Other?'

'Damned straight. That's it exactly. I have great respect these days for that term.' He paused. 'I guess I've never told you what happened with me and my wife. Not that there's much to tell.'

'Don't if you don't want to.'

'I don't mind.' He looked down at his plate. 'She was quite a bit younger. We met at a party the week she dropped out of college. She'd got in with a bunch who were into everything. Pot, booze, meth, coke, you name it. She couldn't get through a day without some sort of help. But we had something going, it seemed very good to me. Finally she saw it was either me or her junk. Not both. I think she really wanted out of that life, and I can be pretty uncompromising. It was tough for her—hell, for both of us—but by the time she was done, she had kicked everything. After we were married we had a couple of really good years—four, actually. She went back to school and was really excited about her work. Then she decided to go on to graduate school. After that, she outgrew me.'

'Come on, Ron. You're not that easily outgrown.'

'Maybe not. What happened was that she didn't *need* me any longer. That's what it really was. At a certain point in her life somebody like me—straight, a police detective even—well, it was as though she used me till she got free of all her hang-ups. What would the psychologists say that made me, her superego?'

Pedersen laughed. 'I think it's more complicated than that.'

'She used to ridicule me, made fun of me for not even smoking cigarettes—she never did give that up—but she wanted someone like me. Somebody who would put his foot down and say either-or to her.'

'What's she doing now?'

'She's at Berkeley, working on a doctorate. I think she's living with some law student.' He grinned. 'Same principle, but a step up.'

'You're divorced?'

'Oh, it's been final for quite a while now. Took me a little time to get over it, but I am now.'

Pedersen reached for the teapot. 'I'm glad you told me. I've wondered.'

Ronald Tate smiled. 'There's not much you don't know about me. I always think of myself as all too transparent.'

'An open book?'

'An open book.' He smiled.

Pedersen pushed his plate away and sat back contentedly. 'Well, I just wish this Follett thing were a little more like that. It looks to me as though it may be a tightly-closed book, an uncut volume. And I think—' he grinned—'we just may have trouble cutting the pages free.'

CHAPTER 6

Arthur Smith liked to come home for lunch. As a child he had had to watch the other children filing off at noon to their respective houses while he stayed behind to eat with the sons and daughters of working mothers or chronically busy ones. His mother was ill. In later life he learned the nature of her illness, but as a child he knew only that she spent whole days closeted in her room, shades drawn, unwilling to be disturbed. Occasionally she emerged, moving out of her room slowly, head down, to sit tiredly with Arthur and his father and toy with the meal her husband had prepared. Sometimes they quarrelled, or rather, his father shouted at her. But for the most part his childhood home remained in Arthur's mind a hushed place of darkness, unease, tension.

Florence understood—and welcomed him at lunch-time.

At two minutes to one he arrived. His punctuality was so reliable that Florence was drawing the quiche from the oven as she heard his car pull into the driveway. He came in, one arm full of irises, great plump bronze blossoms.

'Arthur! Where did they come from?' Arthur's nursery sold no cut flowers.

'I saw them on my way to work, right down the road in that vacant field. I stopped to pick them before someone else did and kept them in water all morning. I'll show you the place, must be the site of an old garden. Remember when I found tulips this spring?'

'Oh, there. Yes, I remember.' Florence fished a vase down from the top shelf of the cupboard and filled it with water at the kitchen sink. 'Sit down,' she called. 'It's all ready but dressing the salad.' She paused. 'You heard?'

His answer was slightly muffled; he had dropped a

napkin. 'Terrible. A shaver or something fell in the tub.'

'A hair-drier.' She returned to set the flowers at one end of the table. 'He was showering. Karin says the police are all over the place.'

'Ironic, just as he finished the book.'

'Everybody says that—Marcie called, and Leona. Dawn's at the Blochs'. I went over. Poor kid.'

Arthur raised his eyebrows.

'Well, poor woman, then. She didn't have anyone else.'

'How's she taking it?'

'Marcie says Karin's being wonderful with her. You know Karin, she should have had *ten* kids.'

Arthur rose and turned to the serving table; he began to dress the salad. His back to her, he said. 'How about you? Are you upset?'

'Of course, everybody is, but no more than if—I mean . . .'

He turned back to her, his eyes intent. 'You seem surprisingly undisturbed.' He sat down again.

'Of course I'm disturbed, but I've told you twenty times if I've told you once, Max has been out of my life for six years and that's that.'

He began to eat silently.

An edge of exasperation crept into her voice. 'Certainly *now* you're not going to be jealous?'

'I was never jealous.'

'Whatever you call it, then.'

He took another mouthful of quiche. 'Have you seen Max to talk to lately?'

'Salt. I forgot it.' She got up and went into the kitchen. 'Saturday night at the party. You know that,' she said from the other room. She returned. 'This quiche needs more seasoning.'

'It's fine. Come sit down.' He studied the face across from him. 'Just Saturday night?'

'When else would I have?' Her eyes did not meet his.

'Here, have some.' She pushed the salt and pepper towards him. 'I won't commit suicide if you add salt. Isn't that what the chef of some French emperor did?' She stopped. 'I guess that's not the best lunch-table topic right now.'

'What does that mean? Did the police say Max killed himself?'

'Apparently they asked Dawn a lot of questions that suggested he might have.'

'Now? With the book done?' Arthur shook his head. 'That's an interesting thought.'

He finished his lunch in silence. Finally Florence spoke. 'What are you thinking?'

'I'm thinking about Max as a suicide. How was Leona?'

'Shaken, I think. I've never heard her sound like that. Nervous. None of the usual airy self-confidence. I never did understand their relationship anyway, so it's hard to tell what she feels.'

'I thought it was perfectly obvious.'

'What was?'

'That they were sleeping together, had a thing going.'

'Oh, that.' She was impatient. 'I mean, was there a real relationship or was it just an occasional roll in the hay? They never talked about living together and certainly not about marriage. Besides, I thought lately he had his eye on Marcie.'

Arthur put his fork down with a clink. '*Marcie!* Her too? He wouldn't—'

'Why wouldn't he? She's darling. Any man would lust after her.' She laughed. 'Why not Max?'

'But she's so—'

'Young? Innocent? She's had one child out of wedlock, as we used to say, she was married to—or living with—a man who was a real disaster.' At his face she repeated it. 'A disaster, yes, that's what Kevin's father was. That's why she threw him out. She's a lovely young woman, I grant you, but she's not all that innocent. She's told me about some of the boys she's known.'

Arthur stood up, his face, usually so gentle, rigid with anger. 'Boys, maybe. But I can't see her with Max, not that randy, bottom-pinching, lecherous—'

Florence laughed in a sudden release of tension. 'Arthur, I don't think I've ever heard you say anything like that. Come on, he didn't do anything to her, he just looked, I'm sure. Maybe tried. Besides, why does that upset you so?'

He continued to look at her coldly.

Her smile faded. 'You aren't angry about Marcie, are you? It's me. You've been acting peculiar all weekend. Ever since Saturday.'

'I don't know what you're talking about,' said Arthur icily. 'But I will tell you one thing. I'm not sorry to see the last of Max. I'm *glad* the bastard's dead.'

After he had left the room she remained in her chair, silent. Finally she rose and began to clear the table. Passing the mirror above the sideboard, she caught a glimpse of herself, the pretty pointed face anxious. What was it Max had called it? Pinched. She thought: I look guilty. I should have told Arthur about meeting Max Saturday, told him in an offhand way so I'd have deflected his suspicions. But Max was being so sweet when I left him—and Max's bark is always worse than his bite. I didn't think he'd tell Arthur we'd met.

In a moment of sudden self-hate, she thought: It's true, all those things Max always said to me. I do talk—even think—in clichés. I am denying, manipulative, even with a wonderful man like Arthur. I can't . . . I can't . . . She began to cry, for Max, for herself, for Arthur, and because the only way her mind would finish the thought was with the words 'find a way to happiness'.

CHAPTER 7

Leona had been unable to eat lunch. Alone on her deck, the chair turned so her back was to the broken railing, she forced herself to sit still and try to make sense of the things that had happened to her in the past weeks. She no longer had the impulse to cry; it was as if not Max but something in her had died. She was numb, empty. Totally removed. The whole experience could have happened to someone else, a character in a novel she had read. She felt only this terrible restlessness. No emotion.

She knew, she had always known, why Max wanted her. The things he had said to her on that awful night and all that had happened in the weeks since had only underscored her knowledge. In all their two years it had been only in rare moments that he had allowed himself to relate to anything in her other than the surface, the way she looked, the way in which the community regarded her. Yet she had permitted their relationship to continue. She still did not understand it. Was it that she too had connected only with the surface: Max Follett, acclaimed novelist? She had never allowed herself to wonder long, yet her behaviour with him had been different from that with any other man she had known. And certainly she had never before—but no. That she would not think about.

The tranquillizer she had taken to ease her tension—she had been so jumpy she could barely stay still—was wearing off. A psychiatrist had once told her she internalized her problems. 'Let some of it out,' he had advised. 'Nobody will die.' Thinking of that now, she wanted to laugh.

She rose and went into the house. Sun spilled through the broad windows of the raised dining area and over the surface of the long walnut table. It had been her family's table—in fact, more things than not in the house had been her family's—and to Leona it was familiar beyond being seen. This morning, however, the sun unearthed buried ruddy lights and set the wood aglow; it caught even her eye. For a moment, something in her throat made her swallow. The house was lovely, yet in the midst of the loveliness that was her home, she felt only this terrible desolation, hollowness. Perhaps she had loved Max more than she thought, despite all that had happened.

She stopped pacing and walked to the window. The neighbourhood had changed since she was a little girl. When her father had moved there two years before she was born, the road and hillside were almost unpopulated. His thirty acres and the two big properties alongside them where the university now crouched against the highest hills had been pasture with redwoods beyond.

Things didn't look too different now. The university had preserved the old stone barn, kept the pastureland with a few cattle grazing, and scattered its several small colleges out of sight among the redwood forests. But there was change in the town. Filled parking lots. Long supermarket lines. Traffic jams on the freeway. Streets to be avoided alone late at night. Locks on everything. Security systems.

Except for those things, Leona liked the changes. And now that the art museum was firmly established, she found herself more and more involved with people who interested her.

Including the Art Gang. She wasn't sure how the term had arisen. They had appeared, a handful of artists and artisans, one by one buying up property that was being subdivided, telling others like themselves, building houses and studios and workshops and settling in—potters, writers, a weaver, a glassblower, an actor, a sculptor.

She had begun pacing again, so nervous she had the sensation that small things were crawling over her skin.

The bunch at her place Saturday night had not been Art

Gang people—oh, some of them qualified, all right, but she regarded them in a different way, as neighbours. But for her only one of the group had ever stood out: Max. Having him in the neighbourhood was like having Mailer or Bellow; everyone knew who he was, he was forever being interviewed and had an audience of literate readers waiting for him to give them another important book. She had known he would, too. Just being around Max was full of promise.

But promise was the word. It had always been only promise. She had waited for things to move a little, patient at first. Then she tried being offended. Making him jealous. Ignoring him. Finally she had moved to ultimatums. At one point she felt she had reached a state where all he would have to do was—what, whistle? That was about it.

She had to get out of the house. Thinking of Max had done this to her. The two years dragging on, hope immediately crushed by a kind of despair, then hope again, had left its mark on her. And then, she couldn't believe it herself—

The telephone rang. A wave of relief washed over her as she turned from her thoughts and walked briskly to her desk.

CHAPTER 8

'First,' said Pedersen, as they picked up their checks and prepared to leave the restaurant, 'we see Florence Smith. Then I think we should look at the rest of that bunch who were at the party, just to get the feel of things, how they relate to each other and to Follett. I'd like you with me, Ron.'

Tate nodded. Pedersen relied on him for the details of paperwork, the taking of statements, the tracking down of hard-to-find suspects, all the small but not incidental aspects of organizing evidence. But the discussion of a case was essential, too. That was where they did most of the real thinking through of a case.

'So,' said Pedersen, as they paid their checks, 'we start with the former wife.'

The former wife had been crying, and she greeted them with a resigned air, as though she had known she could not evade their eventual visit. Small, fair-haired, tending towards scrawniness and with the first hints on her worried little face of the woman she would be in later years, she was still pretty. She evoked in Pedersen a tenderness: his impulse was to reassure rather than to question her.

Although she submitted to his interrogation with a sort of pained passivity, most of what she told him was not helpful. Max abusive? Violent? No, he 'said things' when he was drinking, but he drank no longer. She couldn't imagine anyone's wanting to push him, although at times, like all wives, she'd have happily murdered him. Here she giggled uneasily. But, she hastened to add, he had no real enemies. And Max could be—

'Charming?' offered Pedersen, recalling Leona's words.

'Yes, when he wanted to he could be—I guess that's the word, charming.'

'And you?' Pedersen asked. 'Did you still have a—relationship.'

'Oh, when you've been married for seven years, you still feel connected,' she answered vaguely.

'An amicable relationship?'

'Amicable?' She looked from Pedersen to Tate. 'Yes, I suppose it was amicable.' She considered. 'You know, with Max and Arthur it was like night and day. Arthur's a wonderful man. He has such courage.' She glanced shyly at Ronald Tate, who had not spoken during the visit. 'Courage is the word for Arthur. I'm so lucky, and sometimes I forget and abuse my relationship with him.'

'Oh?' said Pedersen. 'In what way?'

She was vague. 'In ways.'

'I see. When did you last see Max Follett?'

She seemed surprised. 'At the party Saturday night.'

'And before that?'

'Before that? What do you mean?'

'You were both seen coming out of a coffee house Saturday.'

Alarm touched her face and was gone. She said, 'No.'

'No? You mean you weren't there?'

'I don't remember being in a coffee house Saturday.'

She wasn't a total innocent. She understood about not remembering what she didn't wish to discuss. 'You're quite sure?'

Her eyes met his, steady. 'Sure.'

She would not back down now. As he rose to leave, he said, 'You said your husband and Max Follett were like day and night. In what way was Follett like night?'

She laughed nevously. 'I meant our relationships were— different. Everything's so easy with Arthur. He's consistent. I know where I'm at with him.'

He remembered. 'Mrs Smith, did you think of Max Follett as a suicidal man?

'Max?' She laughed with a certain bitterness. 'Never. Never. That's one thing Max would never do, kill '

Keith Bloch answered the door, an amiable giant with a sheaf of papers in one hand, a pen in the other. He led the two men into the living-room and laid the papers on the table. 'I came home to do some work. My office was a madhouse today. There's something about summer school.'

'And now here we are, interrupting you,' Pedersen said. 'We won't be long. Just want to ask a couple of questions about Max Follett. Is your wife here, too?'

'Karin's in the studio with Dawn. You want me to get her?'

'Not right now.' They took the chairs he had waved them towards.

Lowering his voice slightly, Bloch said, 'I don't know a hell of a lot about Max. I may not be much help.'

'But you were friendly enough to meet now and then, as you did Saturday at the party Miss Morgan gave?'

'Oh yes. And Max dropped by from time to time.'

'What impression did you have of him?'

He grinned. 'You really want to know? Abrasive. Provocative. I think basically he was a pretty frustrated guy.'

'Frustrated?'

'Yes.'

'You mean because it took him so long to write his second book?' Tate asked.

'That too, but I meant frustrated over women.'

'Women were his major problem?' Pedersen said.

'One of them, certainly. Four bouts with marriage and God knows how many other—arrangements, and still he was a loner. And he did seem to be suffering from writer's block, too. Ten years between books is a long time.' He laughed. 'Not that I didn't emphathize. One reason I teach at the community college is that I'm damned if I'll get on that publish or perish treadmill. Writing has never been my favourite activity.' He glanced at the papers. 'It doesn't appear to be my students', either.'

'To get back to Follett.'

'Yes. All I know is that Max was a man of many problems.' He looked uneasily towards the door. 'I hope they can't hear me in the studio. Dawn would never forgive me.'

'She liked her brother, I gather.'

'Yes, she did. And he was all the family she had. He was twelve years older, probably seemed a little like a parent. This is hard on her.'

'It must be. What about this party Saturday night?'

'What about it?'

'Didn't Mr Follett have an accident? Or a near miss?'

'Oh, that. Yes. He leaned on a railing we'd just discovered was shaky. I suggested Leona barricade it, but she didn't want to spoil the way the place looked. She warned everyone.'

'You're sure he leaned on it?'

'Oh, you've been told Max thought someone pushed him. That was just Max. No one pushed him.'

'You're sure?'

Keith Bloch turned his head from one detective to the other. 'Max Follett's death was no accident. Is that what this is all about?'

'We just don't know yet. That's what we're trying to find out.'

'I see.' Bloch studied their faces.

Pedersen smiled and stood up. 'I wonder if we could leave you to your papers and join the women in the studio?'

Puzzlement crossed Keith Bloch's face. 'Sure. But if you want to talk, I can bring Karin out here.'

Pedersen waved a hand dismissively. 'I have a soft spot for workshops. I do some cabinetwork in spare moments. In fact, Detective Tate likes studios, too.'

Bloch's face changed. 'What sort of cabinetwork? I do that kind of thing too, I love to work with my hands. I do all the repair jobs around here, even electric and plumbing repairs, and I build furniture. I keep thinking I got lost en route and totally missed my calling. My path? I'm getting so I mix my metaphors as badly as the kids I teach.'

Tate smiled. 'Sometimes I think I missed my calling, too. I've always suspected it was in the cards for me to have been an accountant.'

Bloch laughed and for a moment the two men looked at one another with the simplicity and directness of friends.

And me, Pedersen thought. If I'd studied psychology— he forced his mind back to the present moment. He had mulled enough in his lifetime over his helping to put people into cages as opposed to helping save them from themselves before they needed putting into cages. God, he thought, I'm like Ron with his wife. A Messiah complex. We all want someone to save.

Bloch led them back to the studio. Off the kitchen as it was, the workshop was far enough from the living-room so they could not, Pedersen noted, have been heard.

It was a small room lined with shelves and cupboards. Along the wall opposite the door, a long pine worktable had been built under a wide window which looked directly into a lacework of roseate leaves. Heavenly bamboo. Pedersen thought of his own exuberant nandina bushes which needed pruning because he was never home long enough to clip them.

As the three men entered, two of the women he had met earlier turned from the table, on one end of which was set an impressive structure replicating a Victorian house of some substance. Alongside it was set another much smaller building done in the same style, which Pedersen recognized as a gazebo. Both appeared accurate as to scale; he could imagine a small figure in turn-of-the-century clothing standing at the door of the house with all else in perfect relationship. Pedersen thought, as he so often did: Now what would Freda think of all this?

Karin Bloch was not pleased to see him. 'Oh no—must you?' Seeing her this time, he realized she was a tall woman. With her tawny hair and her bearing, she brought to mind Vikings, princesses from northern regions. 'Does she *have* to answer more questions? I've just—we're just about to do some work. Dawn needs to get her mind off things for a little while.'

'It's all right.' Dawn's face was swollen and had lost its warm colour, but she seemed calm.

'Actually,' said Pedersen, 'I don't need to ask Miss Voletski anything more right now. I just asked your husband to let me look in on your workroom. I have a fondness for workrooms.'

Karin brightened. 'I—Dawn and I, she's helping—are working on a Victorian house, to scale, for the art museum. The September show. It's being used at the entrance, a tie-in with the show's theme.' She swung back the hinged front so he could see into the house.

Pedersen's admiration was real. 'Doesn't that work make you nervous? I could barely hold on to some of those tiny posts you've put in the—'

'Balustrade. No, I find it relaxes me. People react differently to this sort of work. Of course I can't do it for too long.'

'And you do this too?' Tate said to Dawn.

'Not the work. It does make me nervous. I've advised Karin a little. I studied architecture.' The face she turned to Tate was bleak. 'I think Karin has me working today as therapy.'

Karin was indignant. 'Working is always better than mulling, but you are helping. Really.' She addressed Tate. 'She's wonderful with all the little details—pediments and scrolled brackets and columns.'

'I can see why you need an architect,' Tate said.

'Perhaps,' said Pedersen to Karin, 'Mr Bloch could keep Dawn company for a few minutes and I could talk just with you?'

Keith Bloch picked up his cue. 'Come on, Dawn, I'll put you to work now. You can help me pick oranges for Marcie. I promised to take some up to her.' He led her out of the room.

Glancing at his partner's face, Pedersen said, 'Give them a hand, Ron. Tell him we'll carry the oranges up with us in a few minutes when we go to speak to Miss Terpstra.'

Alone with Karin, he said, 'This is a neighbourhood of artists and craftspeople, isn't it? You and your miniatures,

Dawn with her pottery, Mr Follett and Miss Devane with their books. What else do we have here?. Is Miss Terpstra an artist too? And Miss Morgan?'

'Marcie writes poetry, but I'm not sure she advertises the fact. Leona's with the art museum but only as a board member. There are others in the neighbourhood too.' She grinned. 'We're a bunch of people who like space to do things, that's why we live up here away from town. Until just lately it's been like living in the country. Not any more.' He thought of the new buildings going up.

'Your husband says your relationship with the neighbours is casual, yet a number of you celebrated Mr Follett's success with him. I gather some pretty personal exchanges took place at the party Miss Morgan gave.'

She looked blank.

'The busines of someone's pushing Follett.'

'Oh, that. That was just Max. You had to know him to understand.'

'Just Max. That's a phrase I keep running across.'

'I'm not surprised. Max was like many artists, pretty self-involved. The world responded to him, rather than it's being the other way around, if you know what I mean. He was at the centre, the focus of everything that happened. It's a sort of arrogance that's shared by many creative people. They have to be focal—or feel they are. So if Max stumbled against a railing, he'd be sure it was no accident. Someone must have done it to him, pushed him, that would be his reasoning.'

'He sounds difficult. He had friends, though?'

'Of course. All of us, and many others. And women loved him. I suppose that was sex. He had a sort of appeal. He was big, handsome in a rugged way. It flattered them to think the Great Novelist was interested in them.' She looked at him. 'You think someone wanted him dead, don't you?'

'Did anyone?'

She bridled. 'What a question. How would I know, and if I did, would I say?'

He disarmed her with a smile. 'I'm sure not. May I drop by now and then to see how your creation is coming along?'

'Oh, come now, Detective, you know perfectly well that wouldn't be why you'd drop by. You don't have that much time.'

'No,' he said, 'I don't. But I expect to have to be up here a few times until this matter is sorted out, and I do have a cabinetmaker's interest. I'm not flattering you.'

She looked unconvinced but pleased.

He glanced out of the window. 'I gather your relationship with Dawn is not as complicated as with her brother.'

'I wasn't aware I'd said it was complicated. But Dawn's great. She's been a good friend. So has Marcie. In fact all of us have good feelings about each other—maybe I misled you on that. It's just that we had to take Max as he was. Laugh him off when he was impossible. Even Dawn learned that. She's just out of a failed marriage and beginning to—' she smiled—'I guess the current phrase is "get her act together".'

'Not so current. I could give you a whole list of new phrases. Unfathomable.'

She laughed, a hearty, open-throated laugh. 'I have a couple of kids. I figure they'll tutor me as I go along.'

'They will, whether you like it or not.' He smiled. 'You and your husband have saved me a lot of busywork, Mrs Bloch.'

'Call me Karin.' She ran her fingers through her rough hair. It was the colour of the pine table. 'And come see my Victorian any time, Detective.' She stood facing him, feet solidly planted, head up, eyes on his, a Viking princess in complete possession of herself.

The orange pickers stood together, a loaded basket next to them.

'We'll take it up,' said Pedersen. He looked at the mound

of oranges. 'She'll have a time doing away with this.'

Keith shook his head. 'No trouble at all. Kevin's day care centre is having a party. She's the mother with the juice.' He laughed. 'I could have worded that better. Which reminds me. I have to get back to those papers.'

'Quite a woman, Karin Bloch,' Pedersen remarked as they carried the basket of oranges back to Marcie Terpstra's garage apartment. 'Tall.' He himself was drawn to small women.

'Very tall.'

'Impressive.'

'Very impressive.'

Pedersen looked at Tate and grinned. 'I liked her,' he said.

A slender bare-legged young woman, obviously brassiere-less under the clinging T-shirt, answered Pedersen's knock. The pattern on the full calf-length skirt was slightly a-tilt, giving it a homemade look that was not unappealing. She wore sandals. In the face under the chopped-off copper hair the teenager was not quite gone, but the smudges of purple beneath the eyes suggested the woman as well. She looked tired.

Marcie Terpstra's son was nowhere to be seen, but a framed photograph on a bookcase showed him to be an imp-faced toddler with a froth of curly hair. Tate stopped to admire the picture, while the boy's mother relieved the older detective of the basket of fruit as though policemen daily dropped in delivering oranges.

'I heard you were paying visits in the neighbourhood,' she said. 'I saw the car in the drive, so I tucked Kevin in for his nap. He's a good little kid but he can be a distraction. To put it generously.' She smiled.

The apartment was barely adequate to house two. In the living-room a box springs and mattress had been pushed into a corner and covered with a cloth that looked as though the designer had scribbled on it with coloured crayon. Pedersen liked it. In the kitchen to which she led them a blue-painted table and matching chairs had been placed next to a window, with a high chair nearby. She had set out pottery mugs.

'Well. This is thoughtful,' said Tate.

'A little self-interest involved. If we talk in the living-room we may wake Kevin. He's been asleep awhile.' She poured steaming coffee into the mugs. 'How about a cookie? Homemade.'

'Why not?' said Pedersen. 'I've never said no to a home-made cookie in my life.'

She smiled, and her face altered, became impish. Like Freda, only with Freda it was the laugh that came in a surprised little explosion, as though she were startled and delighted by her companion's wit. She hadn't been laugh-ing much in the last few days.

'What I should do is ask you for the recipe for your cookies,' Pedersen said as he started on his third, 'but I'm afraid instead I'm going to have to ask you to tell me what you know about Max Follett.'

She stirred in her chair. 'Really, Detective, I don't think I can add anything. I knew him as a neighbour and a teacher. He teaches—taught a course each quarter in fiction-writing. I took it when I first came to Bay Cove. He was terribly demanding and . . . critical. Unbelievably critical. By the time he was done with me—with most of us—we were sure we were just wasting our time. I dropped out finally and I haven't attempted any writing since.'

'But I understood you wrote poetry,' said Pedersen.

She looked annoyed. 'I don't know who told you that. I meant I haven't written any fiction since I took Max's class.'

'Was he interested in you—romantically?' Pedersen asked.

She shook her head vigorously. 'No. Somebody told you

that too, I suppose. He liked me and he flirted with every woman he saw. It was Leona he was involved with.'

Pedersen nodded. 'Let me ask something less personal. You've been in the neighbourhood for a couple of years. Have you a sense that there was enmity between Mr Follett and any of his neighbours?'

She looked puzzled. 'Oh. You're talking about his accident Saturday. His saying he was pushed? That was just Max.'

'That's a popular phrase regarding Mr Follett,' Tate remarked.

'It is?' She turned the full force of her smile on him. 'I'm not surprised.'

'So your own relationship with Mr Follett was slight. All the same, you must have—'

'No!' she interrupted with force. 'No, you don't. I'm not about to gossip about my neighbours. Any feelings they had, *they* can tell you.' Her lips folded in a firm line.

Pedersen was startled.

Tate spoke into the silence. 'You're divorced—a single mother?'

'We just lived together. When he found out I was pregnant, he took off.' She raised one hand and flicked her fingers. 'Evaporated.' No regrets, her voice said.

Pedersen cast a glance at the half-empty cookie plate and got up from his chair. 'We won't take up any more time, Miss Terpstra. If we think of anything else, we'll be in touch.'

'Yes,' said Tate. 'Thank you for the coffee. If we've forgotten something and have to come back, do we get more cookies?'

He wants her to smile too, thought Pedersen.

'I'm sorry Max is dead,' she said as she walked to the door with them. 'He could be difficult at times, but you don't want people to die for that sort of thing.'

'Not usually.' Pedersen turned back at the door. 'But if

it occurs to you that there *was* anyone who might have wanted him to die, for whatever reason, I hope you'll give us a call. Even if it's a neighbour.' He handed her a card. She accepted it, her face expressionless.

'I don't know how these single mothers do it,' Tate said as they walked around the garage and along the little concrete path. 'Imagine bringing up a kid on the pittance she must earn from that part-time job.'

But Pedersen didn't reply. He was busy with his own thoughts.

In the garage apartment, Marcie Terpstra was telephoning.

'Perry, this is Marcie. Sorry to break in on your work, but I want to ask something of you. Please don't discuss with the police what I told you Saturday.'

'You mean about Max's being after you?'

'Don't mention that, either. But I meant the other. You haven't mentioned it?'

'Of course not. I won't say anything. Although . . .'

'No, Perry. Just don't mention it. Oh damn, I hear Kevin waking up. I'll let you get back to your writing.'

She hung up and walked to the window. The detectives were getting into their car. 'Coming, Kevin,' she called.

CHAPTER 9

'I wonder why people make miniatures,' said Pedersen. They were walking slowly down the main road looking for access to the short cut that wound past the Follett property. They headed down the hill in the direction of Dawn's studio and, beyond, of town.

'Let me guess,' said Tate. 'They're childlike. Or they're threatened by big things. Or haven't the confidence to build on a large scale. Or maybe it gives them a sense of mastery—complete control over a perfect little world they've created. Am I getting warm?'

Pedersen let out a snort of laughter. 'I haven't the faintest idea. But join the Order of Armchair Psychologists—you're doing fine.'

'There's something intriguing, though, about building on such a small scale. You can grasp it. Ordinarily all sorts of things get in the way—your height relative to it, the buildings next to it, people going in and out, even the traffic. A miniature shows you the whole at a glance.'

'I wish something would show us the whole of this Follett business at a glance. Wait. I think this is our path.'

Weeds and shrubs had encroached to the point where it was barely visible, a little footpath to their left. 'Only someone who knows the neighbourhood would ever be aware of this.' Pedersen craned to see whether it led where they thought. 'Shall we?'

Concealed by eucalyptus and the low growth that bordered the main road, the path twisted back up the hill into an open area. As they reached the top, across the wide space the two men could see the rear yard of the Devane house and, beyond, that of the Follett house.

'We're not visible from the main road,' said Tate.

'No. And if we cut off along the edge of this field I think we could make it to the side door of the Follett house without being seen by Devane.'

'Yes, that hedge cuts off most of her view.'

'Of course a jogger might have gone by on Follett's street at that hour.'

'They're usually in a trance.'

They walked past the Follett house, emerged on the little side road and headed around the corner to the main one and their car. On the Bloch property, no one was to be seen.

The drove slowly down the hill, rechecking the visibility

of the path. 'Nice flowers,' Tate remarked, glancing across from the path to the other side of the road. 'What are they? Irises?'

Pedersen slowed further. 'They're like Florence Smith's. I wonder if they picked them here.' He glanced back across the road to the path, and pulled the car to a stop. 'Irises like that don't grow wild, do they? I thought only blue flags did. I'm going to pick some, Freda's crazy about that bronze colour. I'll drop them off home, maybe they'll cheer her up.' He dug his Swiss army knife out of the glove compartment. 'Come on.'

Back in the car, Pedersen laughed. 'Do you realize what we could have done to the image of the Bay Cove cop if anyone had seen us? The *Banner* would have done a spread on it. *Soft Side of a Tough Guy*, they'd call it.'

'They'd be asking us if we eat quiche.' Tate glanced behind him. 'You don't think anyone did see us?'

'No, that little patch of road is concealed. You aren't really worried about it, are you, Ron?'

'No. It's just that I'm already regarded as odd enough with my wire-rimmed glasses and my interest in books. I don't want to confirm anyone's impression that I'm not the type for the police force, especially since I have my own doubts now and then.'

'Listen, it's different now, but when I came on the force no one with a college degree was trusted, no matter what eyeglasses he wore. We were bleeding hearts—no street savvy, the guys thought. There's still some of that, of course. The town was smaller then. They gave us a map and a penal code and the keys to a patrol car and we were in business. For that, who needed an education? There wasn't even a police academy, let alone men who could waive the requirement because they were already educated.'

'That was all before the university came in?'

'Yes. The university did change things. Freda says it's all for the good, but when you think that women are afraid to walk downtown late at night now, I wonder. Attracting people to a university doesn't mean attracting just campus types. When a city grows, it grows in all directions.' He turned right, towards the heart of town. 'Well. We should be mapping out some sort of strategy where this case is concerned.'

'We're treating it as murder, right?'

'It sure as hell wasn't an accident. Suicide, maybe, but the evidence says no.' They pulled into the headquarters parking lot.

Tate unbuckled his seat-belt, his face clouded with doubt. 'That's the unlikeliest bunch of murder suspects I've ever seen.'

'You know how much that means.' Pedersen glanced at his partner. 'You liked Marcie Terpstra, didn't you?'

Tate looked surprised. 'Terpstra? Oh, she had a cute grin. Actually I kind of . . .' He looked self-conscious. 'I felt sorry for the sister. Voletski. Dawn. Poor kid.'

Pedersen laughed.

'What's so funny?'

'Oh, nothing, a thought that went through my head. Just remember, Terpstra or Voletski, keep your objectivity. Till the case is closed, at least.'

Tate's face had grown pink. 'Naturally.' He looked offended.

'I just don't want you convincing any of our colleagues that men in wire-rimmed glasses don't have their minds on their work.' Pedersen grinned as they entered the building.

Carl Pedersen hated paperwork. Like most of his breed, he was a detective who preferred work in the field to work at the desk. He had continued on as a detective-sergeant although his eligibility to compete for the rank of lieutenant, with consequent administrative responsibility, had been established; periodically he reminded himself that all he had to do was take the test. But only after the introduction of longevity pay had he continued comfortably in his present job. Now that the Powers-That-Be had seen the wisdom of keeping crack detective-sergeants in the field, he, a proven senior officer, could do what he did best without guilt over his family.

Ronald Tate was the ideal partner for him, the perfect complement. Tate thrived on detail, he had youth and education and he was assertive without being aggressive. Pedersen's suggestions and instructions magically translated themselves into neatly stacked folders of information and hard evidence. It was comforting to Pedersen to think of what he didn't have to do because of Ron Tate.

'All right,' Pedersen said, as they reached his office. 'Let's see what's what.'

Tate flipped open his notebook. 'The PM. Background checks. Prints. The university. His publisher.'

'And a statement from Perry Devane. Oh, and keys.'

'Keys? You mean to Follett's house?'

'Yes. Dawn Voletski thought she had one someplace, she thought in a bowl on the bookshelf, but while I was there, she checked. Couldn't find it.'

'Did she think it might have been picked up by someone?'

'I asked that. She said she just wasn't too careful about keeping track of things.' Pedersen smiled. 'Like me.'

'But there's a possibility someone's lifted it.'

'Yes. We should check who runs in and out of her apartment, who might have had access to the key. Maybe after you get some of the paperwork done, you can take her on.'

Tate closed his notebook. 'That should keep me busy for a half-hour or so.'

'At least.' Pedersen was suddenly tired. 'Don't try to do it all at once. It'll still be there tomorrow.' He stood up heavily. 'I need some coffee. Oh. The irises.'

*

Walking back to his car, his spirits lightened. He'd drop off the flowers, have a quick cup of coffee with Freda, see if he could smooth things out a bit between them. Arthur Smith would simply have to wait an hour for the pleasure of his company.

Freda accepted the bronze irises without comment and laid them on the kitchen table at which she was sitting. He bent to kiss her. She turned her head. This distance, the sullenness, was so unlike her that he experienced an unfamiliar hollowness in his belly.

'Freda, has something new happened?'

'Not really.' After a minute she added, 'Just another letter from Clara.' She extracted it from the pocket of her denim skirt. It had been folded and refolded many times.

He took it from her and read it. It was a bitter letter. 'Sweetie, your sister's having a hard time with your mother. You know that.'

'Go ahead, side with her.' She swung around. 'Don't you even see what she's saying? All you have to do is read between the lines. She wishes Mother were dead. *Dead!*'

'Freda!' He was shocked.

'She does. She sounds as though Mother is something used up, irrelevant. Just a nuisance, in everyone's way.'

He had never seen her like this. He became suddenly aware of how tired he was. 'Give me something to put the flowers into.'

She shook her head. 'You needn't. I'll do it.' She carried the blossoms to the sink and reached for a grey glass bowl. 'I'm sorry,' she said unrepentantly. 'You just don't understand. *Your* mother's fine.'

After a while he said, 'You heard about Max Follett?'

'Yes. What was it? An accident?'

'I doubt it.'

'Murder?' She turned to him, the bowl of flowers in her

hand. 'He got in somebody's way, too? He made somebody's life difficult?'

Later, driving to the Greengrove Nursery, he reflected on the conversation. It was not like Freda, so naturally ebullient, to be so negative, so depressed. So angry. Especially so angry with him.

He thought back to her last words. *Had* Max Follett got in someone's way? Made life unbearable for someone? It was hardly a comparable situation, but he supposed there were parallel features. He sighed. He wished the day were over and he were in bed.

The Greengrove Nursery was made up of two long low buildings between which could be glimpsed greenhouses to the rear. One building appeared to be devoted to the sale of insecticides, fertilizers, other garden preparations and ceramic containers for potting and garden tools. At one end was an open door above which hung a sign identifying it as the office. Through the open door Pedersen could see a man seated at a desk studying a scrap of paper.

He approached the door. 'Mr Smith?'

A thin, balding man with a gentle face looked up and smiled. 'Yes. Can we do something for you? I think there's someone . . .' He peered past Pedersen towards several clerks who moved among the customers.

'No,' Pedersen broke in. 'It's you I want to see, Mr Smith.' He took out his identification. 'Detective Pedersen.'

'Oh.' The man's face changed. 'Sit down. It's Max, I suppose.'

'Yes. If you have a minute.'

Arthur Smith laughed shortly. 'Oh, I have one. I was just trying to decipher this.' He thrust the half-sheet of paper at Pedersen, reading aloud as he did so:

1. That rock rose with the little red flower, the one I told you I saw in that garden in Lewistown.

2. The thing I thought was buckwheat. It begins with **P**.

3. That stuff my gardener calls society garlic. It has little lilac blossoms on tall stems. Very splashy.

'Would you think,' he finished, 'that Mrs Williams is one of Bay Cove's finest gardeners? She knows just what she wants, she just doesn't know what anything is called.'

Pedersen asked with real curiosity, 'What will you send her?'

'Oh, the first is *Helianthemum nummularium* and the lilac flower would be *Allium giganteum*, but who knows which of the *Polygonums* she wants? But you didn't come to talk about horticulture.'

'No. Although I admired your taste in irises so much I picked some for my wife.'

Arthur Smith looked up quickly. 'Irises. Oh.' His face closed as though he had drawn a curtain across it. 'You've been to my house.'

'Yes. Mrs Smith was very forthcoming. I gather from her, and from several others, that Max Follett was not a man likely to win any popularity prizes.'

'No. Of course since my wife was at one time married to him, I'm inclined to be biased.' His manner remained distant. 'What did you want to ask me?'

Pedersen, playing it by ear, decided instantly. 'I wondered what you thought about Mr Follett's near-fatal accident Saturday evening.' Smith looked blank. 'At the party for him.'

'Oh.' He paused as though deciding what to answer. 'He bumped against the rotten fence railing.'

'Hadn't you all been warned about that?'

'Leona thought there was some sort of termite damage. I don't think we took it very seriously.'

'Could someone have pushed Mr Follett? Accidentally or on purpose?'

'Either is possible. It's also possible he was just careless.'

'Did you yourself see him close to the railing?'

In an abrupt burst of impatience Arthur Smith said, 'He caught hold of me to save himself, but what difference does all this make? The man's dead. And not from falling in a ravine.' Under the thinning hair, the narrow face was flushed.

Pedersen took another tack. 'Did you find Max Follett paranoid, suspicious without real basis for suspicion?'

'You know—' Smith enunciated his words with care—'I can only say one thing about Max Follett with real authority. That is that I avoided him whenever possible.'

'It must have been a bit difficult, with his living right around the corner. Could I ask, did your wife continue to be friendly towards him?'

Smith laughed, a tart, bitter sound. 'We all went through the motions of being friendly. Florence still felt some—concern for him, they were married for years. I found him hard to take, but I never made an issue of it.'

'I see. Had either of you spoken to him recently?'

A shadow passed across Smith's face. 'We saw him Saturday.'

'I meant aside from the party.'

The ready answer surprised Pedersen. 'He came by Saturday afternoon.'

'To buy plants?'

'Follett? He had no interest in plants. He just came to talk. To needle me in his subtle fashion.' There was pain in the man's face. 'He'd just had a cup of coffee with my wife.'

Pedersen found it hard to hold his ground, his empathy with the man was so strong. 'Despite his—needling, you went to the party for him?'

'I told you, I never made an issue of my feelings. I was the only one of his neighbours who felt as I did about him, I wasn't going to flaunt my—'

'Jealousy?'

'Jealousy? It wasn't jealousy.' His eyes were cold.

'Was there something in particular he came to needle you about?'

Smith stood up so suddenly his chair tilted precariously and Mrs William's list fluttered to the ground. He was a tall man. 'Nothing I care to discuss, Detective.' It was a dismissal.

On his way out of the Greengrove, Pedersen paused beside a white azalea in a tub. Freda would like that. He checked himself. This wasn't the time. He continued on his way.

―――――

TUESDAY

CHAPTER 10

Karin woke late, her body aching as though she had been pounded all over. Beside her Keith lay sprawled on his side of the bed, looking as though he might never move again. The clock confirmed what the light had already told her. Almost eight. She had forgotten to set the alarm.

'Keith! Keith! It's late.' She shook him with all the vigour she could muster.

He moaned and rolled over, opening his eyes long enough to take in the clock. 'Five minutes.'

'Five. I'll get the kids up. *Five*, really, Keith.'

In the kitchen she plugged in the coffee-pot and switched on the radio. A dispirited young woman was announcing morning ragas on the university station; she flicked it off again.

As though they too were emotionally exhausted, the children were intolerably slow. By the time she had prodded them through their oatmeal, Karin found herself barely able to contain her irritation. Keith was no more patient. When at last he crossly nudged the children into the car and pulled out of the drive, she sighed with relief and poured herself a second cup of coffee.

Sitting over the steaming cup, sifting through the events of the previous day, she gradually felt the ache in her lower back ease. She drifted into drowsy contemplation of the bar of sunlight that lay across her hands. Capable, she thought, that's what they call hands like mine. They can do anything I want them to do. In a way it was good that Dawn had not been persuaded to stay overnight. Suddenly she was eager to get back to work.

Leaving the dishes soaking in the sink, she opened the door to her studio. What she saw took a moment to register. The Victorian structure stood in the sunlight that lay on the table, compactly elegant, awaiting further work; but alongside it the diminutive gazebo lay smashed, splintered as though someone had dealt it a crushing blow with a hammer. She stood with her hand over her mouth, incredulous, barely breathing.

Nothing else was disturbed. Tools hung neatly on the pegboard, the little stacks of wood were not an inch out of place, the house plan tacked to the wall lay flat and smooth.

She spoke aloud. 'How . . .' and heard her own voice in the empty room. Backing out of the studio as though it still held the vandal, she made for the kitchen telephone extension.

In his office Pedersen's phone rang.

'Detective Pedersen?'

'Yes,' he repeated, 'this is Detective Pedersen.' He thought he recognized the frightened voice. 'Mrs Bloch? Is something the matter?'

'Yes, we've had a break-in. Could you come?'

'I'll send—'

'No, you come. I have a feeling it has something to do with what happened yesterday.'

'I see. I'll be there in ten minutes. Are you in the house?'

'Yes.' Her voice quavered. '*I'm* all right. There's no one here now. Just come.'

She was waiting for him. 'Somebody got in.' Her face was white.

She led him through the kitchen. Around him he saw no particular disorder, no piece of furniture overturned, nothing broken.

'It's in the studio,' she explained, her voice uneven. 'Before we went to bed last night I turned out the light in there. Everything was fine then. But this morning—look!' She flung open the door.

Pedersen bent to look more closely at the debris of the tiny summerhouse.

'I don't see why,' Karin wailed. 'Why would someone ruin my work this way? What's *happening* in this neighbourhood, anyway?' He could hear that she was struggling not to cry. 'It was so little, it took days and days to build,' she cried, her voice departing.

He looked around. 'Any tools missing? Hammers?'

She calmed somewhat as her eyes ran over the pegboard. 'I don't think so. Everything's in place—I always put my tools away.'

'How about the kids?' At her expression, he went on, 'Kids do unpredictable things, sometimes for reasons we can't understand. Could it have been one of them?'

Karin crossed her arms over her chest and tipped her chin back. 'Never. Surely you can do better than that, Detective.'

'Who was in the house? Who has access to it?'

'No one. Just my family. Keith and I don't always lock doors, but we did last night, after . . .'

Pedersen leaned across the table. Without touching it, he examined the open window above the table. 'You left this open?'

She shook her head, then nodded. 'I may have. It was open yesterday. But the screen was in.'

It was no longer in.

The window opened on to a wide strip between their yard and the Smiths'. Outside beneath the window they found the screen. Stepping carefully and using the tips of his fingers, Pedersen eased the window down. It slid smoothly, noiselessly. 'You keep your house in good repair,' he remarked. 'If it was opened in the night, you'd never have heard it.'

'That's Keith. He fixed it, it used to stick.' She stood close to him between the clump of nandina and the house and reached past him to point. Splinters lay on the ground; the earth was scuffed.

'Yes. There are bits of earth among the broken pieces on your worktable. And the pieces are all heaped together.'

'That's how they did it? Broke it up out here? That must be why we didn't hear anything. We sleep on the other side of the house.'

'I'll check for fingerprints on the screen, but I doubt we'll find much.' He shook his head. 'Fingerprints are highly overrated when it comes to solving most crimes.'

They made their way back to the house, Karin Bloch oddly deflated, as though some essential stiffening of her tall frame had failed and she had shrunk.

'Do you think somebody's out to get us? All of us?' she said.

'Maybe not all. Think now. What motive could anyone have for destroying your work?'

'I can't imagine. It can't be jealousy, I don't know another soul who's doing just what I am. Dawn's going to feel awful. The gazebo was her idea.'

'Did anyone know that?'

'Know it was her idea? I should think everyone, it was in the *Banner*.' She indicated a newspaper article pinned to her bulletin board. 'They did this article on the Victorian house, used both our photographs, Dawn with the gazebo, me with the house. Everybody saw it. They were even talking about it at Max's party.'

Pedersen stood reading the article. 'Was this just one of many ideas of hers or the only one?'

'One of several, but the gazebo was the only one publicized, and it was special for her. Her family had one when she was a kid. Her parents built it for her as a playhouse. She's going to be really upset about this.'

Pedersen was silent, watching her face as she stood thinking.

'Detective,' she said suddenly, 'could it be—not me, but—' Her face was a question.

'But?'

'Dawn. Could it have been Dawn they were trying to hurt?'

'Follett's sister.'

Blankly, she returned his gaze. 'Max—and now Max's sister. *Why?*'

CHAPTER 11

Dawn was in her garden picking chives from a large clay pot, her face crinkled with concentration. She jumped when Tate spoke.

'Hi. Am I interrupting?'

She looked confused. 'Interrupting? Oh, this.'

'Can you spare a few minutes?' He looked at her face more closely. Beneath the mop of dark curls, it was pale. 'Are you up to it?'

'Yes, but can we go in? I have to put these in the refrigerator.'

Inside, Tate noted that she had been working at her pottery; an oddly-shaped piece that looked like—what? a

vegetable? a crookneck squash, he decided—sat on her
worktable as though she had just stepped out of the room
a minute and planned to return. She laid the handful of
chives on a bookcase and wandered over to the table to lay
a damp cloth over her work.

'The refrigerator?' Tate said.

She looked at him vaguely and then remembered. As she
put the chives away, he thought: Well, work is a good sign.
'Are you feeling any better today?' he asked.

'Some. I'm trying to do things. I can't not do anything,
I just cry. I called the funeral home—chapel, they call it.
Max would hate that. He was an atheist. Vehement. He
wanted cremation. The . . . body will be released today and
the chapel said they would be able to . . .' She left the last
sentence unfinished. 'I'll have to think what to do about a
memorial service.'

'Someone got through to his publisher, I see.'

'Yes, we called yesterday. Did they say something on the
radio this morning?'

'TV.'

She indicated a chair and sat down uncertainly opposite
him. 'What do you need me to tell you?' She crossed her
legs. She wore the denim skirt; today's hose and shirt were
pink. He liked the tidiness of her work outfit.

Taking out his notebook, he said, 'I need some idea of the
people who might have picked up that key to your brother's
house. Detective Pedersen says you usually keep it in a
bowl in this room.'

'I do. I haven't really searched for it, though, maybe it's
in a pocket or something. You think someone *stole* it?'

'We're wondering. Miss Voletski—'

'Dawn.'

'Dawn, have you talked with Karin Bloch this morning?'

'No. Should I have?'

'You haven't heard about the gazebo?'

'No. The gazebo?'

'During the night someone demolished it—hammered or stomped it to splinters.'

Incredulity touched her face. 'Demolished it?'

'Completely.' He removed his glasses, polished them, put them back. 'The gazebo was your idea, wasn't it?'

'Yes, but—'

'Does that suggest anything to you?'

'No. Oh dear, the gazebo.' She pulled her attention back to him. 'What should it suggest?'

'We're a little concerned that it may not just be your brother who is the target.'

'You mean *me*? You think that's what it means?'

'We don't know. Nothing else in the studio was touched.'

She considered the idea for a few moments. Then she said, her voice bitter, 'Good thing there aren't any more of us Folletts.'

He ignored that. 'We're concerned about protecting you. If your brother was murdered, the sooner we find the person responsible the safer you'll be. You see why I'm interested in that key.'

'Did the—person have a key to the Bloch's house, too?'

'No, that was done differently. Now, what about the key?'

She got up slowly as though moving were an effort. 'First let me look for it. Do you want me to do it now?'

'If you would. I have the time.'

The apartment was small but not untidy. He watched as she went through the clothes closet. Jeans and skirts made up most of her wardrobe. After she had checked jeans pockets, dug her hand into a bathrobe pocket, overturned her handbag, checked skirts and jackets, she closed the closet and began on the room. No bowl or tray or drawer or bookshelf yielded up the key.

Tate watched her as she searched. She moved neatly, efficiently. He was unsure what had made her so appealing to him, what about the small sturdy figure and earnest face roused this tenderness in him that made it hard to maintain an appropriate reserve.

Finally she spread both hands in a gesture of defeat. 'Dumb. I should have a regular place for things like keys.' She rechecked the small bowl on her worktable. 'Usually it's here. Well, I can't seem to find it.' She sat down again. 'I don't see—you want the names of the people who visit me? They'd never take it. What will you do with the names?'

He smiled. 'One thing I promise we won't do is rush your friends down to headquarters and submit them to the third degree.'

Unexpectedly she gave a little laugh. Tate's heart expanded.

'Look,' she said, getting up, 'would you like some herb tea while we talk? I have Orange Spice and Sleepytime.'

'What is Sleepytime?'

'Just a name. I'll make you some.' Her mood had lightened.

'All right,' she said after she had filled their cups. 'I don't have that many visitors and I know none of them would have taken the key, but I'll tell you. I did see that key last week, I'm sure, so why don't I tell you everyone I can think of since then?'

He pulled his pen from his pocket.

'There are the Blochs, at least Karin. I can't remember if Keith—yes, he brought me down some tomatoes. And Florence came by one morning. Perry, let me think. I guess so. Not Arthur. Marcie's in and out all the time. Leona, no. That's all the people from around here I ever see. Those are the ones you're interested in, aren't they? Any other friends of mine wouldn't know Max. Not,' she added, 'that I have all that many friends. I've sort of kept to myself—' she smiled faintly—'licking my wounds, I suppose. I was divorced recently. To my brother's delight.'

'Me, too. I mean I'm divorced too,' Tate said, warm with fellow feeling. 'It's hard.'

'You get addicted to people, don't you?' she said solemnly.

He laughed. 'I never thought of it that way. Maybe addicted to being married. How long did yours last?'

'Almost five years. My brother had his doubts it'd last five months.'

'Mine was four years. I guess I'm still not really over it.'

'Did you run?'

'Run? You mean jog?'

'No—*run*. Keep going all the time—busy busy busy? I think to keep from facing it.'

'A kind of denial. I guess I did. I know I seemed to do nothing but work, afterwards. I'd wonder where the week had gone and every night I'd fall into bed, exhausted.'

'Just as well.' They stared at each other, separately contemplating the unpartnered bed, the single setting at the table.

'Had you always lived alone before?'

She squinted at him. 'Is this a police question or a personal one?'

'Personal.' And I'd better cut it out, he thought, but he waited for her reply.

'Well, of course when I was a kid I lived at home. Max was there till I was five or six and after that it was just me and my parents. I was born late. I guess my mother thought she'd finished having children, she'd had trouble having even the first.' She stopped, then she went on. 'My folks overprotected me, fussed over me.'

'The gazebo?'

'Yes, they had it built specially for me as a playhouse. They'd built a treehouse for Max when he was little.' Her eyes filled. 'I miss him. Funny, in some ways he was terrible to me, but I adored him. I never understood him, but I know he loved me.'

'He sounds like a rather complicated man. He probably took his troubles out on you, since you were so close to him.'

'Maybe.' She mopped at her eyes with her forefinger.

'I know it's hard for you to talk about.'

'It's all right. Maybe it's even better. While I was in high school, my father died. Then, as soon as I was old enough to get out from under my mother's coddling, I went to another city to live.' She sighed. 'But she wasn't well, she died not long after that. So, to answer your question—at length—' she gave a wry little smile—'I've been on my own for quite a while. I've depended on Max a lot, though. For better or for worse.'

'He was a sort of parent?'

'A demanding one.' Her eyes had dried. 'I'd have done better to have moved somewhere further from Max, but when Will and I split up, I just reached out. Max was all I had.' She looked across at him. 'It was strange. The whole thing was strange.'

'Family relationships are. We all have . . . ambivalent feelings about our families. We need them and want them and, I don't know, want them to let go, all at the same time.'

'And your marriage?'

'It was a first marriage. We spent our whole time getting it together, and then we split.'

'People are crazy. Seems to me I've spent all my life getting it together, discovering who I am and what I want. I'm doing better, though. Or I was.'

'Seems to me you're doing just fine.'

'Working in a health food store part time?' She raised her eyebrows. Some of the rosy colour had returned to her face. 'But I've found something I love—the pottery. Max thought it was trivial, but he even felt that way when I studied architecture. I never understood why he was that way about anything I did. It was never right. You know what I mean?'

'He was probably a perfectionist—for you both.' Something in him tugged; he wanted to cross the room to her, cup the solemn face, look into the dark eyes, pull her to him. He stood abruptly and said, his voice overloud, 'I'd better be on my way.'

She looked surprised. 'Well, yes. Did you like the Sleepytime?'

He looked down into his empty cup. He had not tasted it. 'Yes, good,' he said. 'Very good. Wonderful.'

She followed him, her face puzzled, and let him out.

'If I think of any more people, I'll call you,' she said. Then: 'Where—?'

He gave her his card. 'I'm sorry about the gazebo. You watch yourself.' He wasn't sure how she could do that. 'Be careful. Lock doors.'

She nodded. 'I will.'

Tate shook his head as he walked down the path and pushed the stubborn gate open. Maybe in the future someone else should handle the interviews with Dawn Voletski.

The post-mortem revealed nothing they might not have expected. The reconstruction of events appeared accurate; however, one feature of the affair came as a surprise: the technician had discovered the hair-drier was not only old, it was defective.

The technician shook his head. 'It must have been dropped, probably on that hard bathroom tile. The wonder is the guy didn't electrocute himself long ago.' When he was reached, the manufacturer's representative explained to Tate at great length that even the older models were insulated, if perhaps not quite so thoroughly as the newer ones. The representative's voice became slightly querulous as he continued. '*Naturally*,' he said, aggrieved at the public and its deplorable behaviour, 'we expect that the appliance will be handled with care and not dropped or struck against hard surfaces. No electrical appliance will stand up to *that* sort of thing. Or to being used around water. There are warnings right on the driers.' He was clearly envisioning a legal suit that, considering the public relations quotient of Max Follett, could be devastating.

'Doesn't tell us much, all that,' said Tate after he had recounted the conversation to Pedersen. 'Who could know the hair-drier had been damaged?'

'No one. People just assume that electrical appliances in water are lethal, they've been warned so many times. Don't you assume that?'

'Well, I wouldn't experiment to find out if it's true.'

'Exactly.'

'So the person who dropped that drier just got lucky?'

Pedersen frowned. 'You could put it like that.'

Accident appeared out of the question. With the gazebo incident, suicide seemed more far-fetched than before, and since the assault on the miniature, Pedersen's sense of urgency had increased.

'What,' he said, '*don't* we know that brought someone's wrath down on both of them?'

'Something earlier?' Tate asked. 'Something someone knows about their past life? Or someone who knew them before, how about that?'

'Maybe. Of course it may be something right here and now.' Pedersen reached into his desk for a packet of peanuts. He had given up offering them to Tate. 'With Follett,' he said, 'it should be easy. His life has been examined. We can probably find out pretty much everything from Day One without trouble. The sister is another matter, and apparently she has no idea herself why she'd be a target.'

'Maybe simply because she's his sister.'

Pedersen removed another peanut from the packet and broke it in half, checking for the dwarf in the centre as he and his father had done when he was a boy. 'Maybe,' he said dubiously. 'Dawn was married. Her husband might know something. We should look him up.'

'And look into his motives, his relationship with them. Follett opposed the marriage. There must have been no love lost between them.' Tate paused. 'About Dawn.' He stopped.

'Yes?'

'Maybe—oh, nothing.'

Pedersen studied his face. 'Worried about talking with her so much while she's still upset over her brother? We have to, Ron. We don't want any more accidental electrocutions.'

'I know. It's just—' He seemed to be in some sort of struggle with himself.

'OK, then?' Pedersen looked at him for a minute and gave up. From his desk he picked up the little wire string with green beads and dropped them in the pocket that held no peanuts. 'Freda,' he remarked without humour, 'is still mad at me.'

'Oh.'

'She thinks I'm too preoccupied with work. Not paying attention to her problems.'

'A policeman's lot.'

'No. She's not like that, not usually.'

'She liked the flowers?'

'As much as she noticed them. Later on she said they were pretty but had nothing to do with the matter at hand.' He sighed.

'Women,' said Tate. It was almost a question.

CHAPTER 12

Pedersen and Tate found Dawn presiding over the counter of Hardin's Health Foods, surrounded by shelves of bottles and tins with scientific-looking labels in orange and black. She was explaining slowly and in some detail to an uncertain-looking middle-aged woman the virtues of a calcium-magnesium product.

Stacks of local give-away newspapers were piled on the floor; while they waited, Pedersen read an article on the mind's influence over gall-bladder function and looked up his horoscope in a journal dedicated primarily to astrology. The horoscope suggested that this was a fine time for him to involve himself in a new romance, and promised it would live up to his pleasurable expectations. The exhortation appeared to have overlooked some essential aspects of his character and the day ahead.

Tate stood to one side and watched Dawn. When the transaction was complete, he said, 'I'm studying your merchandising style. Soft sell, I'd say.'

She shrugged. 'I'm not convinced calcium preparations do a thing. What I'd like to sell that woman on is a long walk every day. Well, to what do I owe this visit?'

Pedersen put the newspaper down. 'I'm surprised you're back at work so soon.'

'There isn't anything else I can do. I can't go through my brother's papers yet and I can't—I decided I might as well be at work. They've been good to me here; I don't like to take their money and not work.'

Pedersen came to the point. 'Actually we aren't here to talk to you, Dawn. What we really need is your former husband's address.'

'Will's address? Why?' Her voice was cold. 'What can he possibly tell you? He barely knew Max, and he and I haven't had one thing to do with one another for over a year. I don't see any reason for your talking to him.'

Pedersen skirted a direct response. 'We need to talk to everybody connected with anyone in this affair, you must understand that.' He could see that she did not understand.

Uncharacteristically, Tate took over, more forthright. 'Look, Dawn, your former husband may still have strong feelings about the divorce. You were assaulted—indirectly, it's true, maybe only symbolically, but we should be sure just where he stands in relation to you and your family.'

'My *family*? My brother, you mean.' She looked at Tate thoughtfully. 'Will wasn't happy about the divorce, but he never in this world would—oh, all right, go talk to him.' She shrugged. 'See for yourselves.' His name was William Harner, she told them, he was a social worker with the Family Service Agency.

As they were on their way out, Pedersen turned back. 'Please don't alert him that we're coming.' She did not respond.

Walking along the outdoor mall from the health food store, Tate nodded as though Pedersen had spoken. 'Drop-in visit, that's best. He should be back from lunch.'

Will Harner had returned from lunch and had no appointment until three. He seemed unsurprised by the visit.

'Max Follett,' he announced, after they had seated themselves across the desk from him. He was a slight, sandy-haired man with a contemplative air about him. Not, Pedersen noted, the sort one would immediately fix on as a murderer. Harner smiled, something wry in his expression, as though he were reading Pedersen's thoughts.

'Yes, it is about Follett. Your former wife gave us your address.' Pedersen frowned. 'Not altogether willingly.'

Harner nodded. 'Doris and I haven't had any contact recently. I suppose she wants to keep it that way.' His words were matter-of-fact. Pedersen wondered if the subject of Dawn truly evoked so little emotion.

'What,' he said, 'were your reactions when you read of your former brother-in-law's death?'

'If you want the truth—' Harner laughed shortly—'my first thought was that it could have been predicted. The bastard only got what was coming to him.' He smiled, as if he had made the blandest of statements.

'You disliked him?'

'Not enough to do him in.' Pedersen looked up sharply, and Harner responded to the glance. 'Yesterday's newsstory suggested you think this wasn't a simple accident. Despite police disclaimers.'

'They weren't disclaimers, we're not sure yet what it was.' Pedersen leaned forward. 'Do you know of any particular enemies he had who perhaps did feel strongly enough to do him in?'

Harner shook his head. 'No. You have to realize I really didn't know the man well, even if he was my brother-in-law. And I didn't know any of his associates. Certainly not anyone who was—' he grimaced—'an *enemy*.'

'If you knew him so slightly,' Tate interjected, 'why do you refer to him as a bastard?'

Harner looked from one detective to another. 'Doris didn't tell you? He tried to break up our marriage. He didn't succeed, but he tried.'

Pedersen nodded. 'In what way did he try?'

Harner sat back. 'To begin with, he never approved of the marriage. Right at the outset Doris told me that.'

'You know,' Tate put in, 'she calls herself Dawn now.'

'I guess I did hear that. She was Doris when I was married to her. Anyway, Doris told me Max said it wouldn't last a year, I was a wimp. He saw all social workers as interfering do-gooders.' He smiled faintly. 'Not that there aren't some like that. Then when our marriage had lasted not only a year but two, then three, and finally five, I gather he gave up trying to smear me.'

'He had a lot of inlfuence over Doris?' Pedersen asked.

'Doris isn't easily pushed around, but he was all the family she had and it was hard for her to keep her interests and opinions separate from his, at least while I knew her.'

'What finally did break you up?' Tate asked.

'To tell the truth, I don't think Doris fitted into our life any longer. She'd started taking ceramics classes. She'd overcome some of her shyness and was reaching out, making friends of her own. She wasn't any longer just my wife.'

Tate frowned. 'It would be odd these days for a woman without children to be . . . just a wife.'

'It was odd. Actually it was I who tried to urge her to branch out. She was still a little girl in too many ways. Of course it didn't occur to me that my efforts would push her right out of our marriage. But, though I wasn't happy to lose her, I think she's better off now in most ways. She needs a time of being on her own.'

Pedersen grinned. 'Spoken like a true social worker.'

Harner looked doubtful. 'I've never felt like one, not with Doris.'

Pedersen sobered immediately. 'We have something else to ask you. Can you tell us anything about the Follett family? Anything in the past history of the family that could cause Max or Dawn—Doris—to be the subject of someone's anger? Or violence?'

Harner looked up sharply. 'Doris?'

'Would there have been resentment towards him—or her—*because* he was part of the Follett family?'

Harner raised his hands, palms up. 'Doris never mentioned anything, if there was anything to mention.' He came back to Pedersen's original question. 'Is someone after *Doris*?'

'We don't know. What about the parents?'

'Ordinary people, I gathered. The father sold medical supplies, the mother stayed home. They died fairly young. That left only Max and Doris. He must have taken her father's place in a lot of ways, but like all fathers and father-surrogates, he didn't like to see his little girl grow up and get married.'

'Where did Doris grow up?' Pedersen asked.

'A little town four hours north of here. Longville. I've never been there. The parents were gone by the time I met

Doris, and she and Max had already sold the house. I think she thinks of the place now and then. It always sounded very Middle America to me.'

'You're pretty understanding,' Tate said. 'I mean, considering that you didn't want out of the marriage.'

'Accepting is the word. For a long time the word was resigned. But it may all have been for the best, not only for Doris. I've met someone recently . . .' He let the sentence trail off.

Pedersen rose. 'Well, thanks for your help, Mr Harner.'

The anxiety Harner had expressed earlier resurfaced. 'Doris is all right, isn't she? No one's done anything to her?'

Pedersen avoided Tate's eyes. 'She's just fine. Hard at work dispensing health food.'

'Good.' Harner walked to the outer door with them. 'If you think of anything else I can do to help, let me know. Doris must be pretty broken up about this whole business. If you see her, tell her I'm sorry.'

'She is upset, but she's strong now, able to handle things. Just as you said.' Tate spoke with conviction.

Did Harner say that? Pedersen wondered. He glanced at Tate. Nothing in his co-worker's face told him anything.

'That didn't add up to much,' Tate said as they strolled towards the car. 'Nice guy, though.'

'He is. He seems to have recovered from the divorce. Already involved elsewhere.'

'I could take a page from his book.'

'Freda says you will when you're ready.'

'Readiness is all.' Tate sighed. 'Well, we'll see.' As they rounded the corner, Tate stiffened. 'Isn't that Mrs Bloch, loaded down with packages?'

'It is. Let's give her a hand.'

Karin Bloch turned to them with relief. 'Oh, wonderful. I'm going to drop this one for sure.' She put a huge, bulky package into Tate's arms.

'What *is* this?' he asked.

She laughed. 'It's a thirty-cup coffee-maker. I'm having a meeting at the house tonight and my old one has lost its handle. And most of its chrome, I might add.'

'What sort of meeting is that, Mrs Bloch?' Pedersen inquired. He had taken the smaller packages.

Her face clouded. 'A MADD meeting. Here's my car.' She unlocked her trunk and stowed the packages in it. 'Thanks a lot. You saved my life.' She was in the car and had pulled out before they could respond.

Pedersen and Tate looked at each other. 'MADD. Do you suppose she lost a kid to a drunk driver?' Tate said.

'I can't think why else she'd be having a meeting.' They continued to their car without speaking.

As Pedersen manœuvred the car back into traffic, he said, 'What about the will? Anything on that yet?'

'Not yet. The lawyer said Follett never had him draw up a will, despite a warning that if he had any special bequests to make he'd better get to it. The last time he saw Follett, Follett said not to worry, he'd written one himself. So there must be a holograph will somewhere among those papers in his study.'

Pedersen shook his head. 'That means if we want to see it, we're going to have to go over there and really dig. God, I dread that job. By the way, what did the *Banner* say that gave Harner the notion Follett's death wasn't accidental? Must have got past me.'

'I suppose the reference to crime scene investigators being called in.'

'Oh, that. Harner certainly picked up on it.'

'He probably wasn't the only one. Well, shall we get to those papers of Follett's?'

Pedersen and Tate stood in the doorway to Max Follett's study.

'This,' said Pedersen, 'is going to be a bitch of a job.'

From every flat surface drifts of paper confronted them. A four-drawer file cabinet was so tightly packed Tate had to tug hard with both hands to dislodge a single folder.

'I told you it was a mess,' Tate said. 'He hasn't even labelled the folders in the file cabinet. How the hell do you suppose he rounded up material to send to a publisher? Do you think he just crated it the way Thomas Wolfe is supposed to have done?'

Pedersen sighed. 'Who knows? Makes you understand why it took ten years to turn out that second book. He probably spent eight of them looking for pages of the manuscript. Well, might as well make a stab at it.'

Tate organized the task. It went better than they had expected. The stacks grew, the confusion on desk and table-tops diminished. Personal mail consisted primarily of invitations, most signed with feminine names. An occasional fan letter from some aspiring young writer turned up.

'Do you suppose he answered these notes?' Tate said.

'From the looks of it, he never answered anything. I just came across a dozen unopened letters, some of them invitations. One bill. Must have been a day he forgot to read the mail.' He picked up a notebook. 'No sign of the manuscript,' he observed.

'He wasn't totally without organization,' Tate pointed out. 'Look at this. He has one drawer just for the mimeographed material he gave out in class—course assignments, samples of edited pages, proofreader's symbols. I wouldn't have thought he'd have bothered, would you?'

'You think he'd just let the glory rub off on his students and skip the instruction? Talk about his own stuff a lot?'

'Maybe not. He was hard on students. He must have read their material.'

There was no sign of a will; however, two letters from

Leona Morgan surfaced. One, undated, had apparently been left in the house; the other had been mailed.

The first was brief:

> Max, I can't believe the *virulence* of your attack on me last night. I don't see how we can go on; what you said was an assault on the very essence of my being. How could you have gone on seeing me if you feel as you say? I can't even talk about it, I'm so so upset.
>
> Leona.

The second, its envelope postmarked nine weeks earlier, expressed an entirely different spirit:

> Max darling,
>
> After last night, I felt marvellous about us. It's the first time you've let me see that you do have a commitment to our relationship, and I agree with you that we should marry. I understand your fears. You say four failed marriages should tell a man something. I've had only one failed marriage, but I know the feeling you're describing. Maybe what the four marriages should tell you is to be more sure this time.
>
> The thing about us that's good is that we've had lots of time in which to make sure. I'm willing to take the chances you describe, although I feel you're exaggerating. The thing I won't risk is the one that's caused us all our trouble: other women. If we marry, the other women must *stop*. I mean that. This business of bedding every cute little undergraduate who bats her eyelids at you and tells you how wonderful your work is, and every matron who throws a party for you, will have to come to a halt. That's the condition if I'm to marry you. Is that agreed?
>
> I also thought about the other things you said. You said it's up to me, you're willing to go along as we are or to marry, either way. I'm not willing. Actually, until we

talked last night, I didn't realize how unwilling. At my age I need stability in my life, and at your age you certainly do. What I'm saying is that either we marry or we end things between us. I hope it will be the former.

All my love,
Leona.

'Wow! Wonder when that first note was written. They weren't secretly married, you don't suppose?'

Pedersen shook his head. 'Doesn't sound as though she's looking for anything secret. I imagine public is what she wants.' After a moment he said, 'Could be he never wrote a will at all, just said that to shut his lawyer up.'

'He could have hidden it, really hidden it. Everybody says he was so paranoid.'

'His sister says she doesn't even know whether he had a safe-deposit box. We'll have to check on that.' Pedersen stretched. He was beginning to ache all over. 'I *hate* this sort of job.'

'Hey, we're almost done. Poor Dawn has to sort through this stuff in earnest. We should probably let her get at it soon, there are student writings here, short stories he hadn't turned back.' He surveyed the room. 'Let's each take half the stuff on that little table and that should do it.'

Pedersen was thoughtful. 'We haven't found that copy of the manuscript, either. I'm going to have the publisher express me a copy.'

Before leaving the house they checked the obvious hiding-places. Pedersen unearthed a manilla envelope filled with old photographs, but no will. He put the photographs with the two letters he was taking.

'The will's in a safe-deposit box,' said Tate. 'It's got to be.'

'Or it doesn't exist.'

'You know,' Tate said, 'if it did turn out that Leona Morgan and Max Follett were married, she'd inherit. Doesn't a marriage invalidate previous wills?'

'You can be sure they didn't marry,' Pedersen said with conviction. 'The whole town would know it by now. How about if you drive?'

By the time they had locked the door and resealed the house, Pedersen's back had begun to throb and he found himself longing in the most craven way for nothing more than a hot bath. This afternoon he was aware of every one of his fifty-three years.

Tate pulled the car out, rounded the corner and started down the hill. As they passed the house with the orange door, he spoke. 'Do you think she's safe? Should we be doing something more?' His voice was anxious.

'What? Put a guard on the house? The department would love to finance that. I'll have a patrol car check regularly.'

'For what that's worth.'

'Yes.' Pedersen felt a sudden distaste for the case and everyone associated with it. He knew it was fatigue and would pass, and that he was being unfair. They all seemed decent people, concerned for each other, kind people actually. He sighed. It must be time for him to knock off. 'I'm finished for the day,' he said. 'It's four-thirty, anyway. How about you?'

Tate grinned, unaffected by their afternoon of sorting through the detritus of Max Follett's life. 'It's paperwork, always wipes you out. I don't know what you'd do without me.'

'You're right.'

'I'll work another hour. I have some things to line up for tomorrow. You haven't forgotten the little list we compiled yesterday?'

'You'll have to do it alone, Ron. I'm not going back. Just drop me at my car.' He was quiet for a moment; then he spoke. 'You know, Ron, I'm beginning to get the feeling that no one really—genuinely, I mean—*liked* this guy.'

'Yet they all went to that party for him. How do you figure that?'

'It's as though each of them thought he or she was the only one who felt distaste for the man. None of them was going to be the one who was vulnerable. And this deck business. Do you notice that they all act as though Follett had died from a fall into the ravine, rather than from a hairdrier dropped into the bathtub?'

'Yes. They took his saying he was pushed seriously, no matter how they protest.'

Pedersen sighed deeply. 'Tonight, you know, I feel like an old man.'

'You need a night's sleep.'

'Mmm.' He buried his left hand in his pocket and consoled himself by rolling the smooth surfaces of the jade between his fingers.

CHAPTER 13

Keith's response to the destruction of the gazebo seemed barely credible to Karin.

He had got back from work late, almost five; Tuesday was student conference afternoon. He was pouring himself a beer when she told him.

'Do you mean to say,' she said, rising and walking to the other side of the room so she would not have to look up at him, 'that you think it's nothing? *Nothing?*'

'Now, Karin.' His voice was infuriatingly reasonable. 'I said no such thing. I said it was good it was just the gazebo. You never intended to build one when you started this project, so it's no great loss. Now if it had been the big house—'

'Do you know how long it took me to put that little extra nothing together?'

'I do. I feel bad about it, babe. You're misinterpreting—' At her expression, he changed course. 'You're edgy and upset. How could you think I'd treat your work as unimportant? Haven't I given you every encouragement?'

'As I give *you* every encouragement. But that you take for granted,' she said, her eyes narrowed.

'Of course.' He sighed. 'We aren't going to make a women's issue of this, are we?'

That was too much for her. 'Goddamn you, Keith. You have no feeling, absolutely no feeling.' She turned and ran blindly from the room.

Keith moved to follow her; half way across the room he changed his mind. In the next room the silence was loud as the two children took in every word. Suddenly furious with Karin, he turned and slammed out of the house, banging the side door behind him resoundingly.

Half way up the hill he realized where he was heading.

Leona had been in her study; she waved vaguely at her desk and led him out to the deck. The sun hanging low beyond the still-broken railing was uncomfortably reminiscent. They glanced at each other without comment.

'So,' Leona said, seating herself and indicating a chair for him. 'What's happening down *your* way?' The question was tinged with bitterness. When he didn't answer, she went on more gently, 'I've been trying to make myself go down to Dawn's all day. She must be in a state. But then—' her voice faded a little—'I haven't been in such great shape myself.'

'I know.' Keith turned towards her. 'I never knew exactly what you and Max—' he paused, finding the right phrase—'meant to each other, were to each other, but I know this is hard on you.'

She laughed, a sharp sound in the quiet of the late afternoon. 'You aren't the only one who didn't know. Max was a strictly eat-your-cake-and-have-it man, a real bastard, if you want the truth.'

Keith's eyebrows shot up. She looked tense as a wire. One tense woman in a day was enough.

'You know,' she went on in the same taut voice, 'he was seeing or lusting after at least one other woman, usually two, ever since I've known him. Oh, the other woman changed and I remained the constant—that, I suppose, was to be my satisfaction. But this latest was too much. I'd have broken off with him altogether if he hadn't died first. Book or no book.'

That's candour, Keith thought. Being the leading lady in the script of the town's literary lion was a major consideration, and she didn't hesitate to come out with it. But it was not enough. Forthright snobbery amused him, just as covert snobbery would have turned him away from her.

'I'm surprised you had the party for him,' he said. 'Feeling the way you did.'

'We'd planned it, and I was damned if I was going to let anyone else know how I felt. I don't even know why I'm telling *you*. Besides, everyone else liked Max.'

'You felt he had it coming to him?'

'The party?' She laughed. 'I guess so. He had some other things coming to him too, believe me.'

'Who,' he asked, half caring, 'was Max's new one? Anyone I know?'

'Marcie. Miss Single Mother Struggling to Hold Things Together. If ever the phrase "Butter wouldn't melt in her mouth" was made for anyone, it was made for Marcie.'

Indignation stirred in Keith. 'Hey, that's not fair. Marcie's OK. It's not her fault that Max was horny for every woman under thirty.'

'*Is* she under thirty? I doubt it.'

'You know what I mean. She certainly seems under thirty.'

'And what do I seem?'

'I don't know what you seem.' He sighed. 'I should have stayed at home. Karin was bitching at me and now you are. What's with the women in this town today?'

'Sorry. It's all nothing to do with you.'

'You heard,' Keith said, seizing the opportunity to change the subject, 'that somebody smashed some of Karin's work?'

'She called. Thank God it wasn't the Victorian house. Exactly what happened?'

'We don't know. We also don't know what it means. Pedersen, that detective, thinks maybe somebody has it in for both the Folletts.'

'Why on earth—'

'Nobody seems to know.'

'I don't like this.' She rose and began to pace the deck nervously.

He stood up and stopped her in her tracks. 'Leona, take it easy. You're upset, aren't you, really upset?'

'Well, of *course*.' Suddenly her face twisted. She leaned her head against him and, her voice muffled, said, 'I am. More than I ever thought I'd be. And scared.'

'Scared?' He put an arm around her and with his other hand tipped her chin up. 'Why scared?'

'This is something different. The other—oh, Keith, maybe we're *all* targets.'

'That's crazy. You're just undone by all this.' He continued to look down into the smoothly perfect face, made rosy by the warm afternoon light despite its unhappiness.

'Keith,' she said, and before he thought what he was about to do, he kissed her. A second later he thought: Jesus, what have I got myself into now?

CHAPTER 14

The photographs Pedersen had taken from the Follett house spanned all but the last years of Max Follett's life. At some point Follett or someone else had arranged them in chronological order, probably in preparation for mounting in an album. Pedersen leafed through them, maintaining the order. Tate stood to one side of Pedersen's desk, looking on.

On the top was Max as a baby in the arms of his uncertain-looking mother. Then Max nude on his stomach, rearing up from a photographer's fur rug. Max as a curly-headed toddler, mother fondly looking on. A sturdy five- or six-year-old Max with lunchbox and cap, probably taken as he set off for a first day at school. A somewhat older Max and his father with fishing gear. The parents standing together before a large white frame house, the japonica bush beside them in full bloom, nervous smiles on their faces. Max, a solemn adolescent, staring down into a baby carriage.

The gap in age between the two children became more apparent as Max matured. In one snapshot Dawn stood to one side, her head ducked, her mouth set crossly, as though this undertaking most certainly was not her idea. Tate grinned.

Pedersen continued through the pictures. A professional photograph, Dawn as a pretty, shyly smiling teenager, perhaps her high school graduation picture. Max in his twenties with a young woman (his first wife?) in several shots taken at a beach, the couple intent on each other, the young woman's tilt of head flirtatious. More snapshots of them, then several of Max and another woman, Max with then a third. Finally several snapshots of Max and Florence, one taken at a party, his arm across her shoulders in an off-handedly possessive manner, a glass in his hand, in the background several people unrecognizable to Pedersen. Finally at the bottom of the packet, several professional photos of Max, perhaps taken for his first book jacket.

Nothing recent. No picture of Leona Morgan or of any of the Follett neighbours. It was as though a dozen years ago Max Follett had declared himself off bounds to friends with cameras.

Tate picked up one of the early snapshots. 'Reminds me of someone.'

Pedersen looked up. 'You know, that occurred to me, too. Probably just reminds us of Follett himself. He's been photographed so much by the press, we must know his face by heart.'

'No.' Tate put the picture down. 'It reminds me of someone else, I can't think who.'

'Dawn?'

'No. Someone else.' He picked up the picture. 'Who the hell does it remind me of?'

'Well, if you think who it is, let me know.' Pedersen suppressed a yawn. 'Sorry, I'm not awake yet. Freda put aside her . . . resentment of me for a few minutes last night and gave me a quick dinner and insisted I turn right in. She said I looked so tired it scared her. And by God, I slept right through, thirteen hours, six to seven.'

'She's still mad?'

'Not mad exactly, more depressed. Distant.' He sighed. 'Anything with the fingerprints?'

'Not a thing. A few of the girlfriend's and some of the sister's, but nothing else. Oh, a few smears, a few latents, probably the cleaning woman's. The sherry glass in the living-room was Dawn's. He gave her a drink when she dropped in Sunday.'

'Takes guts to keep alcohol around when you're a drinker,' Pedersen observed.

'I bet he'd be just the sort to pride himself on being able to do it.'

Pedersen sat thoughtful. 'I wonder about that will. From the shape of his affairs, I'd say nobody's going to come into a lot. Of course that may not be general knowledge.'

'The new book will bring something in, it's sure to be big. His death insures that.'

'You mean because he can't write another? Or because—'

'Yes, the publicity.' Tate grimaced. 'Just what every publisher hopes for, something sensational to put the book in the public eye. It'll sell like crazy.'

'Be that as it may, if he's left much to anyone other than his sister, that may give us a lead.'

'And a motive.'

'Yep. And if it all goes to Dawn, that could give her a motive. Except that she appears to be under attack as well.'

'I checked about that house patrol when I came in,' Tate said. He sat down in the room's other chair.

'You were busy this morning. I've been thinking, Ron. Florence Smith must know something about the Follett family. I'm going to drop by for a little talk with her this morning. While I'm there, I think I'll check next door and be sure things are calm at the Blochs'.'

'How about Dawn's?'

Pedersen raised his head and looked at the other man for a long moment. 'Sure, I'll stop by. While I'm out, why don't you see if you can dig up any newspaper interviews or magazine features that might tell us something?'

'If this is some vendetta, the newspapers and magazines may never have got wind of it.'

'Never can tell. They may have reported something without knowing its meaning. And Ron, just for the hell of it you might as well check and see if a marriage licence was issued to Follett in the past nine weeks.'

'You do think they might have been secretly married.'

'No, I meant what I said. I think she'd have shouted it to the world. But there's no harm in checking.'

Florence Smith was on her knees in the garden. She greeted Pedersen with something less than enthusiasm and thrust the pointed garden tool she was holding down into the earth. On the grass beside her was a little heap of dandelions she had already vanquished. 'Just let me get this, then I'll stop. Why don't you sit over there by the table?'

Pedersen eased back in the white wire chair, the early morning sun warm on his shoulders, and watched her work the weed free. Her garden reminded him of his grandmother's. In summer that had been a place of columbines and delicate nodding cosmos, massed zinnias and gaillardias; his strongest memory of his grandmother was of her dispatching him with shears and a basket and instructions to 'pick a good big bunch' for her daughter, his mother. A Freda sort of garden, it had been.

His own passion was for succulents. Tiny, slow-growing succulents were suggestive to him of some other planet, one in which the laws of nature and man were more precise, more in keeping with an order that encouraged rather than defeated life.

Small things, he had long ago recognized, attracted him. His diminutive wife, with no extra ounce of flesh, in contrast with his own bigness. The tiny worry beads. God, even the dwarfs in the peanuts.

Florence Smith washed her hands under the garden hose and pulled a chair near his. She sat down. 'Yes?' Her face was puzzled.

He smiled. 'I've been admiring your garden.'

'Doesn't look like me, does it?'

'Well—'

'Everybody's always surprised. I'm not what I look like. People just don't know me.' She looked around with satisfaction. 'And I *love* colour. But you didn't come here to talk about that.'

'Actually—you've talked with Mrs Bloch since yesterday?'

'You mean about the gazebo? Yes, she told me.'

'Any thoughts as to what that was all about?'

'Thoughts? No, not really. Karin tells me you have, though. You think somebody was getting at Dawn. I must say I can't see why, and it's a funny way to go about it.'

'That's why I'm here, Mrs Smith. We can't see why, either. We're hoping you may be able to help.'

She frowned. 'Me? How? What could I tell you that would help?'

'Maybe a great deal. You know your former husband's family, the sort of relations they had with people, whether there was someone who could have had it in for the whole Follett family.'

She threw a glance at him that indicated he had unaccountably lost his mind. 'The *whole* family, what a queer idea. Why would anyone have it in for the Folletts? It's true I never met Max's parents, they'd both passed on, but everything he ever said about them made them sound like a Norman Rockwell calendar. The only thing at all unusual was the spacing between Max and Dawn and that was accident. Max's mother had a tubal pregnancy a couple years after Max was born and the doctor thought she shouldn't have more kids. Dawn just happened.'

'How about aunts, uncles, cousins?'

'Both Max's parents were only children.'

'Did your husband ever mention any member of the community who disliked the family—or disliked him and his sister? Or even disliked just the parents? Business rivalries or personal ones that could have led to strong feelings? An old boyfriend of Dawn's that the family disapproved of? Something at school?'

'I never heard a word of anything like that. Max and Dawn both did well in school, from what he said. He worked on the school paper, she was in the Dance Club. I can't see how any of that could lead to violent feelings.' She laughed. 'Of course Max may have antagonized people. He had pretty strong opinions. But not enough to make anyone take it out on Dawn, I shouldn't think.'

'Have you ever been to Longville?'

She looked surprised at his knowing the name. 'Once. Max had to be up north one spring, something connected with his book, and I went along. While we were there, we drove to Longville—he wanted to show me the house he lived in as a kid. When we got there, he was all upset at how different it was. The family that had bought it had taken off the porch and re-landscaped. He fussed and fussed until he found that a big tree he remembered was still there and the japonica bush was alive.'

'Did you talk to neighbours? Or visit any old friends of your husband?'

'He stopped at the house next door—the parents' best friends had lived there. There were new people. We drove around town and finally stopped at a drugstore he knew. I had a cup of coffee at the fountain and he talked to the man who owned the place. He told Max most of his highschool friends had moved away. One Max was really fond of—I guess he and Max used to sit over Cokes in the drugstore and talk about all their plans for when they were grown up—was working for a newsmagazine. Billy Fitzgerald—the name just came to me. The drugstore man didn't have addresses, but Max thought maybe he'd write him where he worked.' She looked off over Pedersen's shoulder. 'He never did, though. He always thought he'd do things he never did.' She smiled. 'Like all of us.'

'You're sure he never reached him?'

'Unless he sneaked out and did it behind my back.'

'What about Dawn? Was there ever family trouble over one of her boyfriends?'

'Here? Oh, you mean back then. Max wouldn't have known about that. He'd grown up and moved out long before she began going with boys. Of course, here, Max never much liked anyone she went around with. He was like an over-protective parent. When she got married, he stopped fussing over her. She told me that, Max didn't. But he never liked her husband.' She moved her chair so the sun didn't strike at her face. 'I've learned all that since Dawn moved here. By the time Dawn was married, Max and I had broken up.'

'You and Dawn are friends.'

She looked at him for a moment. 'I like Dawn. She's much nicer than her brother. Not that she thinks so, she liked him. I think she realized he was just being protective of her.'

Pedersen studied her for a moment. 'Tell me something, Mrs Smith. How did Max Follett react to your leaving him?'

She laughed. 'Let me tell you, he reacted all right. Max is very possessive of people, he hangs on for dear life.' Engulfing, Leona had told him. 'And the older he got, the less he liked change. He wanted things to stay just the way they were, no matter how bad they were. I can tell you he didn't make things easy for me.'

'But in the end . . .'

'In the end he had no choice. But he's kept himself in my life, in some way, ever since. He really didn't let me go.' She waved impatiently. 'Let's not talk about it.'

Pedersen took out his notebook. 'What was the friend's name? Fitzgerald?'

'Billy Fitzgerald. Funny I remembered.'

Pedersen put away the notebook. 'Things straightened out with your husband?'

'You mean—about what I said? My abusing him? No.'

'You didn't tell him about meeting Max Follett on Saturday, did you?'

'No, I didn't.' She caught herself. 'Well, the cat's out of the bag now. I did lie to you. I met Max at the coffee house. I wanted to ask a favour of him and I didn't tell Arthur. I think he knew, though.'

'How was that?'

'I think from the way Arthur's acting that Max went by the nursery afterwards and told him we'd just had coffee together. He said, joking of course, that he was going to, but I didn't believe him. I thought his bark—' She stopped. 'Max was a vicious man. He probably told Arthur everything.'

'Everything. What do you mean by everything?'

'What we talked about, I mean, Max and I. He probably taunted Arthur, that's what it must have come down to.' She set her lips in a line and slid stiffly to the front edge of her chair, her feet flat on the bricks of the patio. 'We don't even know it's true.'

Pedersen had the odd feeling that somewhere he'd missed a beat. 'In what way did he taunt your husband?'

'With not being able to give me a baby.' In a rush of words, she added, 'We don't know if it's true, we've never been tested or even talked to a doctor about it. We—it was just Max being his usual vile self, but think how Arthur felt.'

'Where did Mr Follett get such an idea?'

'He seemed to think my *face* told him.' She laughed bitterly. 'Max knew how easily I became pregnant. After all, we were married for seven years.'

Pedersen looked around. 'You have children?'

'No!' Florence Smith stood up angrily. 'I don't, but it's not because I wasn't pregnant. So when Max asked me why we—Arthur and I—weren't having any, I must have looked ... funny. Anyway, he laughed and acted very knowing. And probably went to Arthur with his suspicions.' She kicked the base of the metal table, hard.

Pedersen asked, more to comfort her than for information, 'You did explain to your husband that you'd said nothing.' God, he thought, hearing himself, I sound like somebody's family counsellor. He closed off the topic. 'I'm sure he understood it was just malice.'

'No. I haven't talked with him about it. And he won't understand. Max is the one person Arthur has always been jealous of. I can't tell you the time I've spent trying to make him understand that our marriage is completely different. He feels—felt—I still thought about Max too much, that I wasn't really free of him. Do you think that's true, that even if you're having bad thoughts about somebody, you're involved with him?'

Pedersen was not about to be lured into this trap. 'It's something you and your husband will have to talk out, I think.' He paused. 'You know, when I originally spoke to you, I didn't have the impression you were so bitter about him. Why did you go to the party for him Saturday night?'

'I'm the only one that feels—felt—that way about Max. Everyone else liked him. I wasn't going to give him the satisfaction of seeing I felt that way. I never gave him that satisfaction, I was always very matter-of-fact with him.'

'But your husband. It surprises me that he'd go near the man if he was just in his shop taunting him, as you think he was.'

She sighed and looked down at her hands. 'I think Arthur must feel the same way I do. We weren't going to give him the satisfaction of thinking he'd got to us.' She looked up. 'This is a terrible thing to say, but . . .'

'Yes?'

'I'm almost glad he's dead.'

Next door the Bloch house was silent and serene. There was no sign of activity in or around the house nor was there any sign of life towards the back of the property where Marcie Terpstra lived. Pedersen circled the house. The screen had been replaced, the scuffed area beneath it raked neatly.

Although he had not planned to visit her, in fact had intended to continue directly on down the road to Dawn's, on impulse Pedersen strolled around the corner. Perry's study window faced the street; he could see her inside, bent over her word-processor, intent. He had never warmed to those machines, although by now all business was conducted on them. He wished instead that he heard typewriter keys clacking; somehow it seemed more writerly to him. But he walked up the path and rang the doorbell.

Away from the study window now, he imagined her rising with an impatient gesture. In a moment she appeared at the open door. 'Detective? You've come back for more?' Distraught when he had first glimpsed her, she now appeared contained, at ease. She was a handsome woman, he noted, with her close-cropped white hair, her aristocratic bearing.

'Just a word or two.' He followed her in. 'I'm interrupting you.'

'It'll be there when I get back.' She led him into the living-room. It was a pleasant room furnished with unremarkable, comfortably worn pieces that lent a look of easy domesticity. A bowl of fresh flowers on a table was a dash of bright colour. 'May I get something for you? Coffee? Tea?'

'No. Thanks, but I won't keep you that long. I just wanted to inquire into the—relationships, I guess you'd call them, in the neighbourhood.'

'I hate that word,' she said.

He was startled. 'Why?'

'Everybody uses it these days to suggest—oh, I don't know. It just doesn't seem to have the connotation it used to. It's like *share*. *Share* this with me,' she mocked. 'Actually, she laughed. 'I don't particularly want to share with you the nature of the neighbourhood relationships, but I suppose I will.'

'I know what you mean about *share*.' He grinned. 'Now if you'll just let me know where you're coming from . . .'

She laughed. 'That's the other one. I don't think I'm made for California.'

'I doubt that it's just California. Where are you from?'

'Michigan, the great Midwest. I suppose Michiganders are sharing things too—and having relationships.'

'Which brings us back—'

'Yes. What relationships exactly is it that you want to know about?'

'Let's start with Max and his former wife. And her husband.'

'Florence and Arthur. I certainly don't think they sought out Max, but they all got along—civilly, I'd say. They ran into each other all the time. We're a neighbourly bunch and Max was one of the neighbours.'

'Yes, I've noticed that. So you saw no particular antagonism, despite past history.'

She shrugged. 'If it was there, they handled it.'

'And the Blochs and Max?'

'They were friends. You have to understand about Max. He didn't entertain. I mean, he didn't give dinner parties or backyard barbecues or anything of that sort. He dropped in on people.'

'And they on him?'

'Well, some. Mostly Leona or Dawn. The rest of us had been given to understand that when he was writing he was strictly incommunicado. He wrote from about nine to three.'

'And after three?'

'I really think it was Max who did the after-three dropping in.'

'He came here?'

'Not often. We weren't particular friends. I don't mean

we were—what did you say the other day, enemies?—it's just that there was a professional antagonism. You can understand that. He had trouble producing; I produced, but I didn't get any critical kudos. And he didn't—' She changed her mind.

'He didn't?'

'Well, it's neither here nor there, but he wasn't too fond of the woman I lived with.' A spasm of pain crossed her face. 'She died a year and a half ago. Cancer.' After a pause she said, 'A long, dragging death.'

'I am sorry. That must have been difficult for you.'

'Awful. I thought afterwards I should have held on to her, clutched her—physically, I mean, somehow made her fight. She just lay there and—gave in.' She looked at him. 'I've thought often of Thomas's poem since.'

'Thomas's poem?'

'Dylan Thomas. "Do not go gentle into that good night." You should read it sometime.'

'I will. But I'm sure . . .'

'Oh, you're right. There was nothing I could have done, not really. And she was in pain. Terrible pain.' After a while she returned her glance to his as though she had just remembered her was there. 'What was it you were asking me?'

'You had just said Max Follett didn't like your companion.'

'He never said anything. He just looked at us as though we were something contemptible. It's hard to pinpoint, but there was no question what he was feeling.'

'Yet you liked him well enough to go to a party for him.'

'He—sort of made amends. When she got sick, I think he was really sorry he'd been so—whatever he was. He came to see her, he brought flowers and books, he tried. I got over my anger at him. Besides, I was the only one in the neighbourhood who had any bad feelings about him.

Everyone else liked him. I wouldn't have spoiled his little triumph over something from the past.' It was clear, though, that she still had feelings; her face was taut with emotion. But, Pedersen thought, looking at her, that may just be because she's been talking about her friend.

'So you were the only one who had reason to dislike him. What about the others? Leona?'

'I guess he gave her problems with other women, but she seemed to take that in stride. I'd say she was deeply attached to him.'

'And—who else is there? Marcie? Dawn?'

'He was Marcie's teacher, that's all. Her neighbour. Dawn, of course, thought he was God himself.'

'She was that attached?'

'Well, maybe not lately. She's been doing some growing up. She seems more balanced about everything, including Max. But she used to just adore the ground he walked on. I don't mean she didn't have spats with him; she had times when she'd be furious with him over something. I guess the worst was back when she was married. Max never thought much of her husband, or so I gather. But he left her alone about it after a while. I think, in all, Dawn loved her brother a lot. He was like a father to her in some ways.' She glanced towards the window. 'Probably not as difficult as some fathers.'

'Yours?'

She looked at him coldly. 'Among others.'

'So you all went to that party Saturday night feeling happy for Max. Pleased about his success.'

'I think so. Of course I was mildly jealous, but I know my limits and I've long since learned to live with them. But I think we were all quite in the spirit of the thing—really there to celebrate his success.'

As he rose to go, Pedersen reflected. How many people was it now who had said, Everyone liked Max, I was the only one who didn't? Arthur? Had Florence said it? Perry?

Somehow he had the impression that everyone at that Saturday night party had had a bone to pick with Max, everyone had thought: I'm the only one, I'll be a good sport. Or: I won't give him the satisfaction. It was a disquieting impression.

On the way down the road to Dawn's, he once again passed the Bloch house and thought how serene it appeared. Dawn was at home, but a glance told him things in this household were not serene. She opened the door cautiously, just a few inches, then when she saw it was he, swung it wide. Her face was strained.

'What is it, Dawn?'

'Oh, I'm so glad you came, Detective Pedersen! You got my message.'

'Message? No.'

'Come in, I have to show you something.' Her voice was thick.

He could see nothing in the studio that did not look exactly as it had on his previous visit. 'What? What is it you want to show me?'

'This.' She led him to the worktable and lifted a towel. It covered a crushed and twisted hump of drying clay.

'The piece you were working on? I don't understand. You dropped it?'

'I didn't drop it. I *found* it like this. I went for my morning walk and when I came back I saw it on the floor under the table. Somebody must have got in here and deliberately destroyed it. Maybe it even happened last night when I was asleep and I just never noticed till this morning.' Tears began to slide down her face. 'I'm scared. I don't know what it means.'

Pedersen walked to the door and checked the lock. 'You've got to change this. Anybody can get in, all he'd need is a piece of plastic. A credit card.' He walked back and stood before her.

'I don't know what it means,' Dawn said again, her voice small.

Pedersen looked down at the twisted lump of clay which lay on the table. It means, Dawn, he thought, that somebody's trying to get a message to you. He glanced at the white face beneath the mop of curls. And I don't like it. I don't like it at all.

'You did stay with her till the locksmith came?' Tate's question was accusing.

'No, but he was on his way. You like her, don't you, Ron?'

Tate walked to the window and stood, back to Pedersen, gazing out at the gingko tree. It was a clear, bright day; the summer fog had already burned off. 'I'm sorry for her. And all these things that are happening to her worry me.' He turned and added fiercely, 'We don't need any more accidents.'

'It worries me too, Ron. These minor assaults could precede something more serious. Before I left today, I tried to feel out whether she knew of anyone at all who could have it in for them simply because they're Folletts—Voletskis, whatever. I didn't want to scare her, so I soft-pedalled it. But she didn't seem to know what I was talking about.'

'Could Dawn be the real target? If it were her former husband, for example. Although—'

'Somehow I think it's both of them. Anything on the biographical check?'

'Just a beginning. Ordinary Middle American family. Uneventful childhood. Some wild oat sowing in college. And a lot of stuff on his many marriages.'

'Anything recent enough to refer to Leona Morgan?'

'No. Most of the stories date around the time of his first book. The later ones go into why some writers are prolific and others take forever to write each book. Discussions of

Flaubert.' He shrugged. 'Follett's hardly in a category with Flaubert.'

'Did Flaubert take a long time over his books?'

'Days over a page. A paragraph. Weeks.'

Pedersen digested the information without comment. 'And Follett's bank? Did he have a safe-deposit box?'

'They say not. Just the checking account and CDs.'

'That doesn't make sense. We didn't find the house papers when we went through his stuff. No marriage certificates or divorce papers. Not even homeowner's insurance. Where in hell could he have stashed all that stuff?'

'There are other banks.'

'But why? Why not use the convenient one, the one he deals with every day?'

'He was a queer guy. Paranoid, all his friends say.'

'He certainly was queer.' Pedersen's disgust was reflected in his tone. 'Well, we'll have to try to nose out his little hiding-places.'

Freda had left a message for him to call by noon. Instead, on an impulse, he got in his car and headed for the pizzeria. As she drove home the closed box on the seat beside him filled the car with the fragrance of cheese and mushrooms.

For the first time in several days she greeted him with a smile. 'You brought lunch! I haven't had pizza in weeks.' She transferred it to a favourite Italian platter he had given her and got out plates and tablemats. 'There's even coffee ready. You got my message?'

'Yes. What's up?' Her mood seemed too upbeat for it to be more trouble with her mother.

'You'll never guess. I was cast as Olga! Olga, remember, the interesting older woman? *Not* the mother, for a change.' Freda had bemoaned the fact that she was perennially cast as the mother in The Players' productions. She laughed with delight.

He realized how much he had missed hearing that laugh. 'Wonderful! You'll be good.'

'Of course I will. I've been telling them. It's made all this with my mother seem easier to take.' She sobered. 'I had a call from Clara today.'

'What did she say?' He helped himself to a large wedge of pizza.

She sat down opposite him and served herself. 'She says Mother's afraid to go to sleep at night. She wants Clara or one of the kids to come over and sit with her, hold her hand.' She shook her head. 'It's awful, Clara has enough without that. You know, Carl, it's just not like Mother, she's always been so independent.'

'Like her daughter.'

She was quiet for a few minutes. 'Do you think it'll happen to us? I'll be asking Carrie to hold my hand?'

That's the fear, he thought. That's why I haven't listened when Freda tried to talk to me about her mother. That's why the whole subject depresses me. I'm afraid, too.

He kept his eyes on her face. 'She was independent for a very long while, remember. But she was never eighty before. She never had cancer before. You know, you're feeling guilty again. You said you wouldn't.'

'I do feel guilty. It isn't fair, Clara's having to do it all. She's *my* mother, too. It's no wonder Clara—'

He stopped her. 'Freda. Clara doesn't want your mother dead. And we've offered to have her. She hates California and she doesn't want to leave her friends or her house. And Clara's kids. She's seen them every day of their lives.'

'We have kids. What about Matt and Carrie?'

'What are you talking about? Neither of them is here. Even if she were with us, she wouldn't see them. After all, you were with her when she had the surgery. And you help financially. What more can you do?'

Gloom had descended again. She refused to look at him. He leaned forward and took her hands. 'Look, try not to worry. Your mother's just been through a difficult period, she's scared. After this play is over, maybe we should talk about your going east to see her again. It might help you get things in perspective.'

She fixed her gaze on the table. 'Maybe.'

'Come on, sweetie.' He grinned. 'Don't pout.'

Despite herself, she laughed. 'I want to pout. It makes me feel better.' She got up and came around the table to kiss him. 'No more pizza for me. I'm off to a Players meeting.' She kissed him again. 'Thanks,' she said. 'Thanks.'

As he finished his second cup of coffee and the remains of the pizza, he thought of what she had said earlier: *Was Max Follett in someone's way, like Mother?* What then, of Dawn—was she also in someone's way? An unfamiliar pang of anxiety touched him. He had better find out, before she was no longer around to be in anyone's way.

CHAPTER 15

The phone call came in the afternoon. Dawn's voice was low. 'Detective Tate, I just wanted to tell you the key turned up. The missing key to my brother's house.'

'Oh.' He was sure the relief he felt was evident in his voice. 'Good. It was just mislaid, then.'

There was a little silence at the other end. Then, in the same laboured voice, she spoke again. 'Not exactly. I found it in that bowl, the place where I usually keep it. Remember?'

'Could you have—'

'I don't see how. Detective Pedersen and I both looked there. And I looked when you were here.'

'You've had your locks changed? Deadbolts put in?' He was shocked at the sense of panic that had arisen in him.

'Yes. Maybe it's just me. Maybe I put the key there and forgot.'

'Look.' He put aside his misgivings at his own reaction. 'I'll run out there. I have to check something else with you, anyway. You'll be there for a while?'

'Yes.' Her voice lightened. 'Thank you. I'm a little . . . frightened.'

The drive took ten minutes. The house with its cheerful, gaudy door, its warped fence, did not suggest malevolence.

She answered the door immediately, as though she had been waiting. Although she wore what he thought of as her uniform, bright tights and shirt and today a long, clay-smudged jumper, her hair was for the first time uncombed and her face drawn. Today she looked her age.

'I'm glad you're here.' She bolted the door after him. I must—' she tried for a light laugh—'be more scared than I think. I've been sleeping badly. Nightmares. People chasing me. Last night—' she shuddered—'it was a dog, a great hairy, snarling thing.'

He knew and as rapidly repressed the thought that he wanted to take her in his arms and comfort her. He brushed the grey kitten from a chair and seated himself as far as possible from her.

She was working hard to maintain calm. 'Can I get you something?' She held out her hand to the kitten. 'Here, Muffin.'

He smiled. 'Sleepytime tea? No, nothing. Now tell me, did you give anyone the key to your new lock?'

'Just my landlord, he's not going to come in. He has to have it in case of fire—you know, we have a kiln, *he* has a kiln and I use it. And he needs a key in case I drop dead or something.' She could not smile at the ludicrousness of the idea. He could hear her thinking: Or am murdered.

He walked over to the door. 'Are you *sure* you locked it?'

'I'm sure. I've been feeling a little uneasy. I double-checked.'

'And the windows?'

'I think—'

'You *must* lock both your windows and doors, Dawn.' He enunciated the word with the severity of an anxious father. 'And have your landlord put on a chain—*today*. Let's see the bowl with the key.'

The bowl was a small one. The key all but filled it. There was no possibility it had been overlooked in the original search.

'Look, if it'll make you feel better to be doing something, go ahead and make some tea. I'll talk to you while you do it. I had planned to get in touch with you today.'

She rose and went to the kitchen end of the room. Her tea-kettle was the same bright red as her skirt. It struck him that there was a sort of bravery—or bravado—in her use of colour.

'You checked the rest of the place to see if anything else was touched?' he asked.

'No. I came in from the grocery store and saw the key and phoned you. Should I have?'

'It's a good idea. While you make the tea, I'll look around.'

Nothing seemed to have been disturbed. The piece she had been working on was neatly covered. Plates and cups stood in their places. Books were on shelves. Maybe she had imagined an intruder, had somehow missed the key the first time round. He strolled to the closet, swung open the door and stopped. 'Dawn,' he said.

'Yes,' she called.

'Come here.' He heard her set down the kettle, then her footsteps as she neared the place where he stood.

'My God,' she said softly.

The clothing in the closet had been slashed with a knife or scissors. The garments hung in rags.

'My God,' she said again. 'everything I own. What'll I wear?'

The kitten rubbed against his leg and Tate jumped, suddenly furious. 'That's not the question, the question is who in hell did this?'

In a responsive anger she said, 'Well, *my* question is what I'm going to have to put on.' She walked to the dresser and opened a drawer. 'They left this stuff. Or—' she added with bitterness—'saved it for next time.'

Tate turned to her. 'Your landlord probably has insurance that'll cover you. You can buy new clothes, but— I don't like this, I don't like it at all.'

'Well, I'm not exactly wild about it myself.' She thrust a hand into the closet. 'He missed a couple of items. I may not have to go naked after all.'

'You poor kid.' Tate stood before her. 'Let's get the tea. We need it now.'

In the kitchen she removed the kettle from the little stove and reached for a box of tea. 'You wanted to ask me something.'

'Yes. Did your brother ever talk to you about a will, Dawn? Did he tell you he'd written one or give any hint as to where he kept it?'

'No.' She stopped. 'Actually, he did once. He said if anything happened to him the house would be mine, that he'd had the mortgage insured so it would come to me without any liens. His telling me was funny. You know—' she smiled—'my brother was a pretty strange guy. He never talked about things like that, never confided anything. I think he didn't trust even me. Only that once. He didn't mention a will, though.'

'He told his lawyer he had hand-written one; the lawyer was apparently worried about it. The royalties on the first book must be substantial and your brother was approaching fifty. The lawyer thought it was cavalier of him to leave the issue of the inheritance unresolved.'

'Max knew I wasn't worrying about it. And if it had been left unresolved it would eventually all have come to me, anyway, wouldn't it? Isn't that the way it works?'

'Yes, but it's more complicated and takes time.'

'Well—' she shrugged—'I thought it was good of Max to do that, insure the mortgage, but I'm perfectly fine right here. At least I was till all these things began happening.' She swung around. 'Do you think somebody's going to . . . kill me?' Her eyes on him were intent. Tate took an involuntary step towards her.

He checked himself. 'No! We'll *see* to it that nothing happens to you. Dawn, I think you should consider staying with friends for a while. Won't the Blochs or Marcie put you up?'

'Marcie? She has no space for me. No, I want to stay here. If someone's after me, it won't matter where I am. Look what happened to the gazebo. That wasn't here, that was in the Blochs' house.'

'Then you must be meticulous about locking windows and doors. And get that chain today. You hear me? I'd suggest a burglar alarm, but I suppose that would be too big an expense for you.'

'It would.' She smiled. 'Let's wait to see if I really do inherit anything from Max before I start getting big ideas.' She poured boiling water over the tea. 'You know, I keep expecting him to walk in, just to appear at the door the way he used to and say, "What are you up to, kid?"' She laughed uneasily.

'I think that's a natural reaction, Dawn.'

'Probably. But it's as if he's . . . haunting me.' She turned to him, her face puzzled.

He smiled. 'I don't think that's quite the word. But I have heard that people feel the presence of a—person long after he's gone. He'll probably be around for a while, I imagine.'

He left her holding Muffin close and looking anxious. He heard the bolt slide into place after him.

Driving away from her and back to headquarters, Ronald Tate allowed himself a few forbidden notions as to what he would do when this was over. They were the first such thoughts he had contemplated with seriousness since the day his divorce became final.

CHAPTER 16

Perry was so deeply absorbed in what she was doing that it wasn't until the second tap at the window that she turned her head. For a moment she was not just startled but afraid. Then she realized who it was and rose to go to the door.

'Leona, why are you creeping around like that?' She stood back so the other woman could enter.

'I rang and rang. Does your doorbell work?'

'Oh Jesus.' She reached to check it. 'The damned thing's been acting up, but I thought I'd fixed it.' She turned to her guest. 'This is a nice surprise. Can I fix you a cup of coffee?'

'Would you? I should stop, anyway. I've done enough for one day. Come on out to the kitchen.'

'I've meant to call,' Leona said, perching on a stool alongside the counter. 'I felt terrible about your finding Max like that. But—well, I was dealing with some feelings of my own.'

'Of course you were. I should have called you. I've thought of it, but—'

'But you knew things were pretty much over for Max and me?'

Perry measured out the coffee, filling the little plastic scoop precisely and watching the dark granules sift into the basket. She had given the same care to filling the pot. She could feel Leona's eyes hard on her. Leona was waiting for an answer.

'To tell the truth, I never knew how things were between you and Max.'

'You saw me over there often enough, you must have had some idea.' The voice was mildly resentful, as though she had been slighted by Perry.

Perry shrugged. 'I didn't pay much attention to what went on over there. Except, of course,' she added, remembering, 'in the morning. We couldn't help noticing each other then, with our windows the way they are.' She plugged in the coffee-pot.

Leona got off the stool and walked to the window that faced the Follett house. 'You can't see who goes in and out.'

'No.' Perry glanced at her back. 'I can't even see the front path from here. Those bushes cut it off, the oleanders.'

Leona swung around. 'But you probably hear things. With windows open, you must hear things.'

'Leona, I'm working most mornings—was there something in particular I should have heard?'

'Of course not. I just—you said you didn't know about Max and me.' She returned to her stool and changed the subject. 'What did you think about all that . . . interest in the party Saturday night? That Detective Pedersen came to talk to me about it.'

'They think he's been murdered.' Perry's voice was flat.

Leona looked up, startled. 'They *told* you?'

'Of course not. Why should the police tell me anything? It's obvious they don't think it was an accident.'

'But suicide . . .'

'I think they took seriously that business of Max's thinking he was pushed.' She reached into the china cupboard for mugs.

'That's ridiculous! You didn't see anyone push him, did you?'

'Not that I'm conscious of.'

'Who was close to him when he fell? Arthur, wasn't he?'

'Arthur. You were, too. And Marcie had just been talking with Arthur when the rain blew in.'

'My!' Leona pursed her lips. 'You're the regular little detective. How could you notice all that in the confusion of getting things indoors? I certainly don't remember that clearly.'

Perry looked at her levelly. 'Whatever you think of my books, I'm a writer. Writers are observers.'

'Of course.' Leona came over, picked up a mug and turned it in her hands. 'Don't be offended. And I . . . well, I haven't really read any of your books. I don't read a lot, I'm so busy, but I hear your books are good. Very good. The *Banner* certainly thought so.'

'Good within the genre. They weren't quite as unconditional as you're being.'

'Your publisher certainly sells a lot of them. You must make a lot of people happy.'

The percolator had stopped sputtering. Perry poured the dark liquid into the mugs. 'Shall I put out something? A cookie, maybe?'

Leona shook her head with vigour. 'No, I never eat sweets. I can gain pounds just looking at a piece of cake.' She picked up her mug. 'Good.'

'Not wonderful. I just don't have time to fuss with a filter pot. Now, what's on your mind, Leona? You seem to think I should have noticed something I didn't, something about Max.'

Leona set her mug down, a little shakily. 'No, no, Perry. It's just that we—that little group that was with him Saturday—we seem to be in the limelight. I understand that Pedersen has talked to every one of us. What do they think, for God's sake? That we came over here and slung that drier in his tub or something?'

'Probably that's just what they do think. It's uncomfortable, I know. And since you've brought it up, will you be put out if I ask what *was* going on between you and Max?

You've been seeing him for over two years, haven't you? I assume you haven't just been discussing literature, but what about this business of things being over between you? Why did you give that party if things were all over?'

'I don't mean we weren't speaking, nothing like that. And I was pleased, Perry. He'd worked at it so long and had such trouble with that novel. How could I not have a party for him?'

'So what you meant is that you just weren't a romantic item any longer.'

Leona's laugh was bitter. 'Romantic? There never was anything *romantic* about Max's and my relationship, believe me. But I'd had it. He couldn't decide whether what he wanted was me or me and sixteen other women. I was fed up.' She raised her hands to the smooth hair. 'I didn't have to take that, not endlessly I didn't.'

'So you gave him an ultimatum.'

Leona laughed; it was a sharp, humourless sound. 'One of many. For what it was worth. At any rate, it was the final ultimatum. He knew.'

Perry looked at the smooth face of her guest. 'Then,' she said, 'it isn't as hard for you, Max's death. You'd already . . . disengaged yourself emotionally.'

Leona's hands smoothed the dark hair and resmoothed it. 'It is hard,' she said. 'You know, I think I never stopped hoping. But I was fed up. I wouldn't have endured any more. I had to bring things to an end.' She covered her mouth, aware of what she had said. 'I don't mean—'

'Of course not.' Perry's face felt stiff. 'More coffee, Leona? How are things going with the new museum show?'

Leona Morgan thrust out her cup, her relief at the change of topic transparent. 'Fine,' she said. 'Just fine. Everything at the museum's fine.'

Tate had calculated in terms of Max's impatience. Twenty miles seemed like a reasonable distance for an impatient man to be expected to travel in indulgence of a personal eccentricity. Accordingly, Tate had dispatched a bulletin to every bank within twenty miles of Bay Cove.

The call, when it came, was from Lewistown. The switchboard put it through.

'Mr Follett did have CDs with us, Detective. And a safe-deposit box.'

Midweek was a quiet time for the Bank of Lewistown. The lines of mortgage-payers, singles dropping by for weekend spending money and workers depositing pay cheques during lunch-hours that characterized Friday's bank activities were replaced by a desultory depositor or two, a housewife urging along a reluctant toddler, a boy in jogging clothes. Tate arrived with the order to open just before three. At the entrance to the vault he was met by one of the two bank officials who were to supervise the activity. In the absence of the key the box would have to be broken into, destroyed.

The destruction took place with remarkable efficiency. As Tate and the officials watched, the bank's mechanic applied a drill. In a moment of shrill sound the box was opened.

The bank officials stood by to tabulate the contents. The box contained what Tate might have expected. Papers relating to the purchase of the house, a birth certificate, a homeowner's policy, a bundle of commemorative Kennedy dollar bills, a mortgage insurance policy on his property on Glenvale Road, three certificates of deposit. A thin rubber-banded bundle contained marriage certificates, divorce papers. There was no marriage more recent than his and Florence's. But there was a blue-bound will.

Tate unfolded it. It was not hand-written, but had been drawn up two months earlier by a Lewistown lawyer. It named Doris Follett as executor, left his house and ten thousand dollars to her. His copyrights and the balance of his estate, which appeared to be well over two hundred thousand dollars, he had left to someone else.

He had bequeathed them to Kevin Terpstra.

Once more in her own house, Leona Morgan was on the phone. 'I do think you should,' she was saying with an earnestness unfamiliar even to herself. 'I can't make it and one of us should be at that meeting tomorrow. Just to find out how they'll use your Victorian house and whether there's anything more you'll need to do. They don't even know there's to be no gazebo. Unless you've told them. I haven't.'

'If I must, I will,' Karin said. 'But you know it's Keith's free afternoon. We have half a dozen errands we were planning to run. Keith was going to take Ricky for new gym clothes and I told Ellie we'd stop at the library. And we were all going out to dinner. How late do these things run?'

'Never past four. Your kids won't be home from day camp till three, anyway, will they? You'll still have time for your errands.'

'Not all. Keith and I—oh hell, I'll go to the damned thing. You don't think they're going to ask me to start on another gazebo?'

'No, no, of course not. They never actually asked for it in the first place. It was your and Dawn's idea.'

'Is there anything I should know? Will the museum director be there?'

'Yes. You know him. He'll make you comfortable. I phoned and said you were standing in for me since they were planning to discuss the September show. You're an *angel*, Karin. Thanks.' Before Karin could protest further or follow up with additional questions, she rang off.

Of course Leona had known it was Keith's afternoon off. And there was no real obstacle in the way of her attending the meeting, none but her impatience. Since the moment Keith had stepped close and kissed her, she had thought of him. The night before, lying awake in bed with her window open to the bay air, she told herself it was a reaction, just a response to the loss of Max and the frightening emptiness that had engulfed her since then. Perhaps it was only that. Perhaps the impulse that had moved Keith to kiss her and then depart in such guilty haste had been no more than a response to her beauty. She was aware of its effect. But— or so it now seemed to her—there had been a tension, a sexual awareness between herself and Keith from the moment they had met at that first neighbourhood meeting. And she wasn't about to lure him from his wife and children, she was merely—well, she wasn't sure exactly what.

Perhaps just seeing him, confirming that what she had perceived was a fact, was all she wanted. Tomorrow afternoon would give her that opportunity.

'It means just what you think it does,' Pedersen said. 'It means Kevin Terpstra is his son.'

'But she barely knew the guy. She took his class and dropped out. That was it.'

'Not quite. That's what she *told* us. But there must have been a little something more, a visit to his house to pick up a paper, a drink after school, something. Maybe it was a one-shot affair, but I can't think of another reason for that bequest. Can you?'

Ronald Tate shook his head. 'I guess not. Funny she didn't tell us. After all, he was dead . . .'

'That's why she didn't tell us. Would you identify yourself with a man who has just died under mysterious circumstances?'

'Which means she didn't know about the inheritance. If she'd known what was in his will, she'd have known we'd find out soon enough.'

'Maybe. Why don't you go up and talk to her in the morning—and to Dawn, too? See how they react to the news. I think I'm going to take a run up to Longville—it's not more than four hours' drive. By the time I get back that manuscript should be here.'

'I will.' Tate looked at Pedersen thoughtfully. 'What are you looking for—up there, I mean?'

'I'm not sure. Someone who knew the family. Maybe just the ambience. I really won't know till I get there.'

'And this Marcie business. This adds one to our list of suspects, doesn't it?'

'*Adds* one? Everyone who was at that deck party is a suspect and has been from the beginning. This just clarifies the motive of one of them.' He looked at his partner. 'I grant you that they all seem like decent people, but they're suspects too, Ron. Don't forget that for a minute.'

CHAPTER 17

Florence Smith had never thought of her husband as a subtle man. One of Arthur's attractions for her, after seven years of a man like Max Follett, was his directness, what she thought of as his sweet simplicity.

By Wednesday afternoon of the week of Max's death she had revised her opinion. In the past three days Arthur had manifested an ingenuity at avoidance that she would never have believed possible of him had she not witnessed it. If she hadn't known him so well, known the tension he must be feeling in this unfamiliar role, she might have given up. Instead, she decided, no two ways about it, she would have to force a confrontation. She did something that in other circumstances she might never have considered: she went to the nursery and threatened to make a scene.

Arthur, for some reason—well, actually she knew the reason—detested scenes. He had told her early in their marriage that the one thing he sought was peace. Just peace. Knowing she would be there when he came home.

Knowing dinner would be served on time. Knowing the house would be bright, cheerful. 'Not,' he had explained, 'that I'm asking you to become a domestic drudge. If you want to work, you should work. If you want to study, do that. But . . .' Here he had sat quiet for several minutes. 'What I would like is a household different from the one I grew up in. I'll do anything I can, anything you want of me, I'll meet you half way, but—' She had interrupted him. After Max it was what she wanted, too. And with occasional interludes that distressed them both, it had been like that.

Arthur was in the greenhouse when she arrived. She asked one of the clerks to let him know she was there. Then she went into his office and sat down behind his desk.

She could see that he was angry, angry with a cold rage she had never before seen in him. He stood in the doorway. His voice low, he said, 'What exactly is this?'

'I came to talk.'

'Here? You came to talk here?'

'Yes. We can close the door.'

He glared at her.

'Close it, Arthur. We can't go on like this.' God, she thought, I sound like a soap opera.

He reached behind him and pushed the door shut. His lips formed a hard white line. 'Talk.'

She stiffened. 'No matter how angry you are, you needn't speak to me like that.'

With one foot through the rung, he pulled a chair towards him. He sat down heavily. '*Please* talk, then.'

'Arthur. What are you so furious about? What have I done to you?'

'Nothing. Not one single thing.'

'You act as though you hate me.'

He wiped a hand across his face. 'I don't hate you.'

'Max told you what he *assumed* about our—our ability to have a baby. I never told him anything. I wouldn't tell him anything. You know that. Max was an evil man. He destroyed people.'

'A little melodramatic, don't you think?'

'No, I don't. That is what he did. That's why he was killed.'

'That's what you think?'

'That's what I know.'

He looked at her for a long moment. 'Why did you meet him that Saturday? What was there about it that you had to lie to me?'

'It wasn't anything to lie about.' She leaned forward. 'I lied—that is, I didn't tell you about it, because you've always been so funny about Max.'

'Funny. I've been *funny*?'

'That's the wrong word. I know you hate—hated—him and were . . . jealous. I went to see him about library business, honestly, Arthur. It was my vanity. I was afraid he'd turn us down and I thought . . .'

'You could seduce him into speaking at the library.'

'Arthur. *Please*.' She held out her hands to him. 'I knew him. I figured he was a writer, after all. Writers care about libraries. I thought I could make him see what a drawing card he'd be and . . . well, we were going to rent the civic auditorium and charge for the talk. Raise some money. The library's always so short on books, equipment, everything. We thought the Friends would be making a real contribution.'

He lowered his voice further. 'Somehow all this does not seem the sort of thing to lead to a discussion of conception.'

'We didn't discuss conception.'

'You must have.'

'Well, we *didn't*.' She was angry now, too. 'You'll just have to take my word for it. He asked something—said something about our waiting so long to have a baby and I guess my face . . .' She put her head down. 'Nobody but Max would have . . .'

'And of course you had been pregnant twice by him. He knew it had to be me.'

She stood up tiredly and took two steps towards him. 'I give up. I can't fight you any more, Arthur. I love you. Nothing as good as you ever happened to me. If you can't accept it, I don't know what I can do.'

He sat looking up at her, his face sagging with fatigue. For a long moment they were locked in a silent tableau. Then in a slow movement he raised his hand and reached for hers. 'All right, I believe you, Florence. I do. I *hate* it when there's trouble between us.' He was holding her hand so hard she caught her breath. 'I *hate* it. Let's try to forget all this. Max is dead. He won't ever bother us again.'

'Yes.' She met his eyes. 'He won't ever bother us again.' Something unspoken passed between them.

THURSDAY

CHAPTER 18

Tate went out early. Too early. The bell alongside Dawn's orange door brought no response. As he rang a second time, he remembered that she walked by the water at this hour; he would have to return.

Driving up the road, he could see that someone was at home in the Bloch house; windows were open and Karin Bloch's car sat in the driveway. There was no sign of Marcie Terpstra. On an impulse he stopped. Keith Bloch and the two children were nowhere about. Karin answered the ring, a pot of glue in one hand.

'Oh, Detective Tate.' She did not sound precisely pleased.

'You're working.'

She recovered herself. 'No, no, it's all right. Come on in.'

'I will if you'll go on working. I'll just watch for a few minutes.'

She threw him a puzzled glance before she turned and led the way into her workroom. Walking behind her, he admired the rough blonde hair, the tall erect figure in its jeans and smock. This must be the sort of woman Scandinavian woodcarvers had used as their model for ship figureheads. He could imagine her with her hair blowing out behind her. When she glanced back at him, his face grew warm at his thoughts.

She was at work on some minute detail inside the building. He craned to see and then gave up. 'Tell me,' he said, 'why *do* people make miniatures?'

She laughed. 'They make such wonderful conversation pieces, that's why. I don't know how many times I've been asked that. Do you know something? I'm going to let you in on a secret, something not many miniaturists admit.'

He could not tell whether she was serious or teasing. She read the question in his face. 'This is true. It's mastery.'

His face must have expressed his confusion. She went on. 'That's right. They must have lost control over their lives, maybe never had it. Or over their bodies in some way. But over their marvellous little miniatures they have perfect mastery. They've created a little world of their own where they do have control.'

'Ah. That explains it.'

'Only partially. I don't make miniatures for that reason—in fact, there are probably lots of miniaturists like me. For us, it's an exploration, I suppose. I love doing research, finding out exactly how a building would have been constructed, what sort of details would have been included. And now that I have a commission I feel productive, I'll be able to do other museum pieces. At first, I must say—' she stopped what she was doing and looked out of the window—'it was an escape. A sort of therapy.'

'You lost a child.'

She turned back to him. 'Yes, how did you know? Oh. The MADD meeting.'

'Yes. Is it something you can talk about?'

She straightened. 'It's hard, but I can. It was my first child, a girl. She was just a little older than Ricky. We were on the road, right out here, walking along the little footpath, way over to one side.' She raised her hands in a gesture that spoke her disbelief. 'She was ahead and this car—' she stopped to gain control of her voice—'this car came tearing up the hill at us. There was no time to move or think—or anything. He hit Janey.'

'Did he stop? Did you know who it was?'

'No, he veered and went around the corner and up that hill. He must have been drunk, he was all over the road. I didn't register anything—what the car looked like, the licence number, anything. All I could see was Janey . . .' She stopped. 'We never knew who did it.'

'It wasn't—it couldn't have been Max Follett?'

She turned towards her work, her back to him. 'I'm sure if it had been Max, he'd have stopped. He was never too drunk to have stopped. But I wouldn't let him in my house after that, not till he stopped drinking. I couldn't be . . . reminded. So that's how I started working on miniatures. As a therapy of sorts.' She turned back to him. Her face was flushed with emotion.

'I'm so sorry.' It seemed inadequate beyond words. 'Actually,' he said, 'when I stopped by, all I meant to do was ask when Miss Terpstra gets back from her job. I need to see her.'

'She's back by one, unless they shop or stop off at the playground.'

'She manages well, doesn't she?' He wondered if the casual question fooled her. She was not easily fooled.

'Yes. I don't think I could do it. She's ingenious, does a lot with a little. I suppose there's a sort of challenge in that.'

'She writes, doesn't she?'

'A little, apparently. I never knew till this week. I did know she'd taken a fiction course with Max, but she said she'd dropped out.'

'She didn't consider him a good teacher?'

She looked at him as though she were perfectly following his line of questioning. She had possession of herself once more. 'Maybe too good. Critical. Very.'

'Her husband—I mean her young man—was a writer, too?'

'I don't know what he did. Not much, I gather. You'll have to ask her.'

'He did something. He made a baby.'

She did not respond.

'Were they together for a long time?'

'Not once he'd, as you put it, made a baby. He wanted no part of fatherhood.'

'Doesn't he even support the child?'

'Not a penny. The usual picture. He writes occasionally, tells her about himself, but—'

'Doesn't even ask about his son.'

'You have the picture. Now don't say anything for a minute while I get this in place.'

He watched her, the light on her hair, her intent face with its faint flush, her upper body tilted towards the Victorian house. Suddenly he was aroused. What's happening to me? he thought. I'm coming to life again.

When she straightened she turned towards him. Her eyes were amused. 'I think you've pumped me about as much as I'll let myself be pumped. If you have more questions, I think it would be a good idea to ask *her*.'

'I didn't—' He stopped. 'Right. Don't stop what you're doing. I know the way out. Thanks for letting me watch. And ask.'

She leaned against the table, facing him. 'Any time, Detective.' Her eyes were mocking.

*

By the time he got to the bottom of the hill Dawn had returned from her walk. She was in the backyard, down on her knees in jeans, her feet bare. Nearby, the grey kitten chased something not visible to Tate.

'Planting?'

She looked up, unstartled, as though she had expected him. 'Not exactly. Weeding.' She eased to a standing position. 'My garden produces more weeds than vegetables. Hi. What's up?'

He felt as though he had known her for years. She was the reason for this . . . loosening he had felt all morning, this easing of the rigidity that had enclosed him for months. He wanted to hug her, not just for her, but for helping free him.

Instead he said, his voice sounding stiff to him, 'I need to talk to you about something important. Is there some place out back here where we can sit down?'

'Sure.' She led him to an L-shaped bench in the corner of the garden. 'Here we're perfectly private.'

'You look better today.'

'I feel better. I feel *good*.' She smiled widely. 'I have to buy some clothes today and I'm going to buy a dress, a real dress. And I think shoes with heels. And black stockings.' At his face, she laughed. 'You don't know what I'm talking about, do you? It's just that I haven't done anything like that for, oh, for *months*. I've decided it's all over, those things that have been happening to me. I think that's what the key meant, the key being returned. And I decided Max wouldn't want me to go on moping about the way I have. He'd want me to do something for myself, something to make me feel better. It makes me feel . . . young to think of buying a dress.'

Tate had an almost irrepressible desire to put aside his role and say, 'I know, I know. All morning, Dawn . . .' He suppressed the impulse. 'I'm glad,' he said soberly. 'Now then.'

'Yes?'

'You know your brother left you his house, I gather.'

'Yes.'

'You didn't know anything about a will, though?'

'No.' After a moment she said, 'You found one.'

'Yes. You *were* left the house, free and clear. And ten thousand dollars.'

She said nothing. Muffin jumped into her lap.

'Did your brother have any children?'

She glanced down at the furry little creature. 'He had no children by any of his wives.'

'Or otherwise?'

'Otherwise? Would I know that?'

'You might.'

She lowered her head and contemplated her out-thrust toes. 'What are you getting at, Detective Tate?'

He sighed. 'Your brother left the bulk of his estate to Kevin Terpstra.'

She raised her head. 'Yes.'

'Yes? What does that mean?'

'It means Kevin was his son.'

'You knew?'

'Marcie didn't know I knew, but I did.'

'But how?' He reached out and took her arm as though to help brace her for what she was about to say.

'Max was twelve years older than I, so naturally I never saw him as a little boy. But my parents had lots of pictures, and my mother had one on her dressing-table, taken when he was about four. Kevin looks just like that picture.' She shook her head. 'It's funny, I never really noticed it with Kevin himself. He's so active and with his blond colouring and seeing him with Marcie, it just never occurred to me. Then one day I was up in her apartment and I looked at that picture she has on her bookcase and I thought: Max— that's exactly like Mamma's picture. It seemed crazy then that I hadn't seen it all along.'

He removed his hand from her arm and they stared at each other. 'So that's what it reminded me of, that picture of Max,' he said. 'How did you feel?' he asked. It was not a policeman's question.

'I wondered if Max knew. As soon as I had that thought, I realized it was idiotic. Of course he knew. It explained why he'd become so interested in Marcie the last few weeks.'

'Did she . . . were they . . . ?'

'No. I suppose it happened when she was up on campus. She took a class with him.'

'But you said he was interested in her.'

'I didn't say she was interested in him. She never said it to me, of course, but I think she disliked Max.'

'Your brother had a substantial estate, Dawn. Not huge, but larger than we anticipated. How do you feel about sharing the larger portion with your nephew?'

She shrugged. 'I don't feel anything. They can use it. A house and ten thousand dollars is more than I've ever had.' She looked at him with mischief in her eyes. 'I can even buy an *expensive* dress now.' He realized she had never before let him see that she had humour in her make-up.

Tate found himself at a loss for further words. 'You'll hear about this more formally from the lawyer, I'm sure,' he said. 'Oh. One thing. Let us be the ones to tell Miss Terpstra, will you?' He stood up. 'Thanks, Dawn. I'm glad for you—about the house and money.'

She said nothing. When he let himself out of the crooked gate, she was sitting on the bench looking off into space, one hand on the kitten, her face wistful.

Missing her brother? Probably she'd rather have her only family back than this small wealth. But maybe, he reflected, she was just thinking about what that difference would mean. It must be strange to struggle along on a part-time job and suddenly come into a house and money, even a comparatively meagre sum like ten thousand dollars.

Then, as he pulled the car away from the kerb, an uneasy thought struck him. He hadn't said anything to her about not relaxing her guard, even if she did think the returned key had meaning. Then he shook off the notion. She had deadbolts and a chain now and she'd been warned about not leaving windows open. He couldn't very well treat her as though she were an infant. She was safe enough.

CHAPTER 19

Pedersen ran into no traffic and was there by 10.30.

It was the sort of town one passes through without realizing a town is there at all. On a whim, Pedersen parked his car on the corner of the main street behind a bus which had just pulled up. In lieu of a bus station, a Greyhound sign had been posted and a covered bench installed. Two people debarked, one a tiny white-haired man. Before the man could go on his way, Pedersen stopped him for directions. The town hall was three blocks from the corner on which he stood. Pedersen thanked the man, locked his car and strolled leisurely along the street.

From behind every window he sensed interest. A round-backed man kneeling in the hardware store window arranging garden tools looked up, his eyes sharp. From the other side of a plate glass window bearing a coffee-shop logo, heads swung towards him. An elderly waitress, tray in hand, walked to the window and looked him over without embarrassment. Two grey-haired women walking in his direction ducked glances at him, careful not to stare, and moved closer to each other. He smiled at another passing matron and was met by a steely glare.

On the opposite side of the street, a little unpainted

shingle house with a short flight of rickety steps bore a hand-lettered sign: Public Library. Probably the volunteer effort of some booklover kept it going. He wondered if a citizen had willed a personal library to the town; often in villages such as this that was the inception of a public book collection. He was tempted to enter right then to see what the townspeople read. Maybe later. Tate would not have postponed a visit to the place.

The town hall was a small brick building with a plaque indicating its birthdate in the century before. He climbed the steps that led inside and entered. A clerk whose slightly goiterish gaze gave her a startled appearance looked up from the newspaper she was reading. The unfamiliar face brought her to attention.

Pedersen made his smile as engaging as possible. 'Good afternoon. I wonder if you can give me some help.' He opened his identification folder.

Her response was uneasy. 'Police? From Bay Cove?'

'I'm investigating a possible murder. I'm sure you've heard of the death of Mr Follett.'

Comprehension flooded her bony little face. 'Oh. Wasn't that terrible? But—was it—was he *murdered*?'

'We're operating under that assumption. What I'm particularly interested in are records you may have—marriage records, records of birth, any criminal records.'

'Criminal?' She was shocked. 'I'm sure there weren't any criminal records. Besides, the police would have those.'

Pedersen had wanted her reaction towards the suggestion of anything untoward. 'Of course. Mr Follett's sister says her parents were married before the Second World War, 'thirty-seven or 'thirty-eight. And I'd like to glance at the records of birth—Doris Follett is thirty-six, that's 'fifty-two. Her brother was nineteen-forty.'

Three-quarters of an hour later, he emerged, not much wiser. Emmeline Black, aged 20, had married Irwin Follett, aged 23, in 1937. Three years later she had borne a son,

Maxim, and twelve years after that a daughter, Doris.

The death certificates completed the picture. Irwin Follett had been born in 1914 in Rochester, New York, his parents in Poland. He had died in 1967 of a coronary thrombosis. His primary occupation was listed as salesman of medical products. Emmeline Black had entered the world in 1917 in Buffalo, New York, her parents born in the United States. She had been a housewife. She had died in 1974 of stomach cancer. He left the building. Except for the niggling thought that Black was not far afield from Bloch, he had learned nothing worth mulling over, and that was probably coincidence.

'If you want information, try the drugstore,' the clerk called after him.

Down the street, the police records offered nothing at all. The ancient clerk—no police were in evidence—shook his head vigorously. 'Not the Folletts. Respectable folk. Had a fire out their place one time. Nothing serious. But criminal? No sirree.' The records bore him out, but Pedersen lingered. 'Did you know the family?'

'Not so's you'd say know. Said 'mornin' if we ran into one another.'

'Mr Follett was never drafted?'

'Nope. He had a kid. And those eyes of his.' He grinned wickedly. 'Wore thick glasses. Like the bottom of a water tumbler. Real Four-Eyes.' With a bony finger he complacently settled his own, thinner-lensed spectacles.

'Does the town have a hospital?'

'*This* town? The nearest's up at Cruden Springs. That's where the babies get born. There's a wing for the mental ones, too. Some end up there.'

Pedersen moved to another topic. 'You knew Max Follett had become quite famous for that book of his?'

'Sure did. We had these reporter fellows all over the place one year, taking pictures of us.' He beamed amusement. 'Interesting characters, that's what we were. They liked the chief to stand out there by his patrol car, lean on it. When Matt, he's the druggist, heard they were coming, he changed his whole window, got all these old apo— apoc—' He gave up.

'Apothecary jars?'

'That's it. And big jars with coloured water. Still has 'em in his window. Visitors think we're—what'd that one lady say?—quaint. Quaint!' He snorted. 'Now my grandmother, she was quaint.'

Pedersen smiled. 'I'll have to drop by that store. What's the druggist's name again?'

'Matt Haycraft. Past retirement age, but I don't think he'll ever sell the place. Maybe he can get his son back here to take it.' He looked at Pedersen closely. 'You're a detective, you say?'

'Yes. I showed you my badge, remember?'

'The chief'll be here after dinner. He'll want to meet you if you're going to be around a while. Chief Wilson.'

'I'll try to get back, but I'm heading out for Bay Cove again this afternoon. Who would you suggest I talk to who might have really known the Folletts? It's a long time, I know.'

'Maybe the Daisches, they lived next door. Ask Matt. He'd know somebody. He knows this town inside out.'

On the pavement again, Pedersen was aware of the oppressive warmth. The morning had been warm but a slight breeze had blown; now the air did not stir. The familiar chill, faint but so often present in the air of Bay Cove at this hour, did not exist in the land-locked town. Heat did not agree with him.

Matt Haycraft's pharmacy and ice-cream parlour did exude an air of quaintness, from the handsome blue and white ceramic jars in the window to the white wire chairs at the three small marble-topped tables. At the moment the store was empty of customers except for a single teenager examining a rack of paperbacks.

'Couple of new science-fiction there, Jimmy,' Haycraft called as Pedersen entered. He turned to the detective, his manner only mildly curious. 'Can I get something for you, sir?' He was as tall as Pedersen, level-eyed, with a faint bloom on his cheek suggestive of high blood pressure.

Pedersen opened his badge-holder. 'I'm here in connection with Max Follett's death. The consensus seems to be that you're the one to help me.'

Haycraft looked doubtful. 'Help you with what?'

Pedersen looked around. The heat and the long drive had suddenly caught up with him; his eyelids were heavy. 'Do you serve coffee at your soda-fountain? Maybe I could have a cup and we could talk.'

The coffee was strong. The boy selected a book and left. Alone in the store, Pedersen and Haycraft faced each other across one of the small tables, each eyeing the other with interest. 'Now what was I supposed to help with?' Haycraft asked.

Pedersen smiled. 'Actually, I'm not sure you can. I'm investigating a death—actually a murder, we're pretty sure. Did you know Max Follett?'

Haycraft's expression changed subtly. 'I did.' He volunteered nothing.

'And the parents, I suppose? And Doris?'

'I knew them. The Folletts, the parents, weren't sociable people, my wife and I never visited back and forth with them. Their only close friends were the Daisches. They're just back from their daughter's in Arizona. What did you want to know about the Folletts?'

Pedersen settled more firmly on the unsteady wire-legged chair. 'Were they liked in the community? Was there any scandal? Any intrigue you know of?' Before the other man could speak, he raised a hand. 'I'm sure you don't deal in gossip, not habitually, but this is a murder, Mr Haycraft, and it may have its roots back here.' He grinned. 'It may not, of course, too. I may be all wrong. But, since you asked, that is what I'm trying to find out.'

Haycraft's face was puzzled. 'I never heard anything. No rumours, nothing. And in a place the size of Longville you hear rumours if there's anything to hear. They seemed perfectly respectable. He didn't have a mistress. She didn't have a lover.' He laughed. 'Even the idea seems crazy. If they did, they kept the fact well hidden.'

'What about business dealings? Property? Any struggles in those areas?'

Haycraft shrugged. 'What business? He sold medical supplies for some big house in Sacramento. Visited doctors with samples, took orders from places like mine. All on a pretty small scale. They made out all right, but I doubt they put by a lot. And the only property I know of they owned was their house.'

'Where was their house? I'd like to walk by. Pick up a sense of the ambience.'

Haycraft frowned. 'Around on Jerrold. Twenty-seven. It's just a few blocks.' He laughed suddenly, open-mouthed, easy. 'In Longville *everything*'s just a few blocks. Except the canning factory. That's a couple of miles out.'

'And the Daisches? The best friends?'

'They're pleasant folks.' He rose to help a customer. 'How are you, Mrs Stein? What can I do for you?'

Mrs Stein pondered rather longer than Pedersen thought necessary over the purchase of a box of Band-Aids and a jar of Pond's Cold Cream; then, obviously miffed that she was not to have the stranger in town explained or introduced, took herself off, her step brisk. Haycraft remained behind the counter.

Pedersen picked up his cup and strolled over. 'You did know Max Follett, you said. And his sister.'

'The sister, no. She came in for a cone or a soda sometimes, quiet little thing, cute-looking, but I never talked with her. Max was different. He liked an audience. He had all sorts of ideas, ideas about everything, and he tried them out on anybody who'd hold still. He was bright, too, he and a couple of his pals. The three of them worked on the school paper and I think they all thought they'd be writers when they finished college. One of Max's friends, Billy Fitzgerald, is a writer—he works on a news magazine now. The other one, Tom Whitaker, went to Iowa where they have some sort of programme for writers. But he went on to be a teacher. Professor. North Carolina, I think. They'd come by, buy a Coke apiece and sit there tossing their ideas around. Cocky, but bright. I enjoyed it. It was a change from all the biddies looking for a new lipstick colour.'

'Max Follett dropped in on you about ten years ago, didn't he?'

Haycraft's eyebrows shot up. 'How'd you know that? He did, it was right around the time that book of his was published. Had his wife, little blonde woman, with him. He was all upset they'd changed his old house, taken off the porch. And he wanted to hear what I knew of Tom and Billy. You'd think they'd have been in touch with him after that book came out.'

'Maybe they were. I understand Follett was drinking heavily then, maybe he wasn't aware of who was in touch and who wasn't.'

'That was it, then. I thought they must have been partying, celebrating the book. He smelled of liquor that day he came in.'

'He joined AA later. Divorced his wife, but got back to his typewriter.'

'Poor Max. Too bad about him. Mustn't have been out of his forties, and the paper said a new book was coming out.'

'It is too bad. It's especially too bad if it's murder.'

'Well—' Haycraft picked up an order book—'I wouldn't know about that. You talk to the Daisches. Want to phone them you're coming? You can use my phone back here.'

When Pedersen returned, Haycraft said, 'You know where to go? Larchmont—second corner to the right, then turn left. It's forty-two. And you needn't warn me not to say anything. I don't talk.' He chuckled. 'Not often, that is. No.' He waved Pedersen's hand away. 'The coffee's on the house. In memory of Max. I can see him there now, over at the fountain, skinny, with all that wild hair, talking so hard he almost fell off the stool.' He pursed his lips. 'The coffee's in memory of Max and all those ideas of his.'

CHAPTER 20

Given the time since his phone call to them, it was surprising: the Daisches had managed to prepare for his visit as if it were a special occasion. A table in the living-room had been spread with a cloth and on it had been placed one handsome blue-patterned plate holding slices of golden pound cake and another heaped with cookies, discernibly homemade. These kept company with a highly polished silver creamer and sugar bowl and three blue-patterned cups and saucers. The teaspoons and forks gleamed. As Mr Daisches accompanied Pedersen into the room, his wife entered from another door, carrying a silver coffee-server. Their movements seemed choreographed; they gave the impression of having worked out such details to perfection.

The room was suspiciously immaculate, as though the furnishings had been set in place years before and the room seldom entered since except for periodic ritual cleanings. The light wood, the blue and green fabric on the sofa, part of a three-piece suite, spoke of the 'forties. When he was a child, Pedersen's mother had bought a chair very like the one he was being offered; he remembered her talking to his father at dinner of the daring new colour combination. Pedersen took for granted there was some other room, perhaps once called the 'rec room', now the 'family room', in which they put up their feet and relaxed, read, talked, watched television, actually lived.

'You must be tired after your long trip,' he said. 'I understand you've been visiting family in Arizona. Isn't it hot there at this time of the year?'

'We never moved away from the air-conditioning,' Mrs Daisches confided. 'I don't know how people there *lived* before air-conditioning.'

'I never feel jet-lag till the second day,' Mr Daisches contributed. 'The first day I feel unnaturally awake. Odd, isn't it?'

Pedersen smiled. 'It's generous of you to give me time.'

'We want to help,' said Mrs Daisches. Her face was earnest.

'Yes,' said Mr Daisches. He sounded less sure. 'We don't know exactly how you want us to help, though.'

'As I said when I phoned, it's your old friends, the Folletts. I understand you were their next-door neighbours and closest friends.'

They nodded.

'You know Max Follett was found dead, electrocuted. There was evidence that it was not an accident. We are quite sure from consequent events that it was intentional.'

'Not *suicide*?' Mrs Daisches asked, disbelieving.

'No. Murder.'

'What kind of consequent events?' Mr Daisches asked.

'There have been a couple of attacks—purely symbolic, so far, she's all right—on Dawn. Sorry, Doris. She uses the name Dawn these days.'

'What a funny thing to do,' said Mrs Daisches. She did not seem to be following the essential part of the story.

'We had thought,' Pedersen said, 'that it might be not just Max who was the intended victim, but the *family*—what's left of it.'

'You mean Doris might be killed, too?' Her eyes were wide.

'We're certainly trying to prevent that. But someone appears to be trying to tell her something.'

'I still don't quite see,' said Mr Daisches, 'where we come in. Did you want her to come stay with us?'

'No, no, she'd never—she'd appreciate your offer, I'm sure, but she has a job in Bay Cove. And her other work. She's a potter.' He accepted another slice of pound cake. 'Your own? It's delicious.'

Mrs Daisches ducked her head.

'No, my feeling was that there may have been enmity. Some grudge, perhaps, that had been directed against all four of the Folletts. Something that originated way back. There seems to be no other reason for both Max and Doris being under attack, the other connections are too loose. She was not involved in Max's work in any way and he wasn't in hers. Even their friends were different. She hadn't achieved any celebrity, nothing anyone could have envied or resented.'

'I see,' said Mr Daisches. It was clear he didn't.

'I came to you hoping you'd tell me more about the family. From everything I've learned, you knew them best.'

They looked at each other. He spoke first. 'They were just ordinary people. Neighbourly, with us at least. Went to church. Kept their lawn mowed. Their kids were polite, did well in school.'

'Were they—this is hard to ask, I know you don't want to gossip—but were they people who would have confided in you if there had been anything?'

Mrs Daisches spoke. 'Emmie and I were pretty tight; we spent a lot of time together. I guess she'd have told me.'

'Perhaps what I'm looking for has to do with the children. You knew them well?'

'Well now, you know Max was older. They were more like two little families, first one with Max, then one with

Doris.' She smiled. 'I knew Doris better. She was the same age as one of my girls. But I heard about Max. They were awfully proud of him.'

'They thought the earth revolved around him,' Mr Daisches put in.

'He was talented even as a boy?'

'Yes. Always winning prizes. Of course he was an only child for twelve years. She had—' she glanced at her husband and went on—'another pregnancy and almost died. Once the doctor told her not to try again, she just . . . focused on Max.'

'That must have been hard on him.'

She looked surprised. 'Hard? Why?'

'I just mean that kids do better with a little . . . benign neglect, don't you think? Being focused on is a big responsibility.'

Mr Daisches spoke. 'He was a spoiled kid. My wife never saw it, but he was arrogant. I hate arrogance in kids.'

Pedersen smiled. 'His friends say he was a difficult man, too.'

Mrs Daisches did not like their being the source of un-flattering opinions. 'Now,' she said, her tone placating, 'you know, dear, we never knew him. Not the way we knew Doris.'

Pedersen put down his cup and settled more comfortably into his chair. 'Tell me about her. Any boyfriends her family objected to, anything like that?'

'Well now—' this seemed a favourite warm-up to the ex-pression of Mrs Daisches's ideas—'she was a sweet little thing. Pretty. And bright as a button.'

'Once she came along, *she* was her parents' pet, I hear.'

Mr and Mrs Daisches exchanged glances. 'I wouldn't say that,' she said starchily. 'Emmie and Irv were *fair*. They treated the children exactly the same.'

'No favouritism? Cute little girl born after Mrs Follett had all but given up on another child?'

'She *had* given up,' said Mrs Daisches.

'What my wife means is that she wasn't pleased when she learned she was going to have another.'

'Well now, Emil, she was scared. Remember what her doctor had told her.'

'I thought it was more than that.'

She cut him off. 'Emil, you don't know. Emmie and I talked a lot. She was pleased to have a daughter. Every mother wants at least one daughter.'

'I suppose so,' Mr Daisches grudgingly agreed. 'She didn't treat either of her kids the way you did ours.'

'He means the way I'd hug and tease and kiss our girls— You know the way you do. Emmie was different, she just couldn't be—demonstrative, I guess you'd call it. It didn't mean she didn't love them. Emmie told me things—I know. It was too bad they couldn't show it, but I'm sure the children knew, children know these things. And—' she looked at her husband with admonishment—'they were fair. They even built a beautiful little gazebo for her. They'd built a treehouse for Max when he was little and then the gazebo for her. I think Max was pleased for her, too. You know, she adored him. He was awfully good to her for a brother who was so much older. He could just have treated her as a little pest, the way some big brothers do.'

'I must say that's true,' her husband said. 'He was good. Especially when she was hurt that time.'

'Hurt?' Pedersen sat forward a little, aware that at last he had come closer to the answer he was seeking.

'Well now . . .' Mrs Daisches began.

CHAPTER 21

The meetings were always called for 1.30. At 1.45 Leona, in flat sandals and a blue-flowered cotton dress that did good things for her eyes, strolled down the road towards the Bloch house. Keith was not working in the yard, and there was no sign of Marcie or her little boy out back. She approached the side door, which faced away from the Smith house, and rang, prepared, should Florence or Marcie appear, with explanations, forgotten details for Karin to have carried to the meeting. No neighbour appeared, nor did Keith. She rang again, listening to the sound echo through the empty house, almost, it seemed, through an empty neighbourhood. Apparently Keith was doing the errands without Karin.

She turned, so angry she was close to tears, and climbed the long hill back to her house. At 2.0, impatient with pretending to work, she phoned. Still no one there. It seemed impossible that all her planning was to come to nothing. Leona had long since learned that with proper attention to detail, she could make most things happen as she wished. Today appeared to be an exception. A second call at 2.15 went unanswered. At 2.45 she made one final try. This time the phone was picked up. It was now too late: the children would be arriving home and, shortly, Karin too.

With an effort she made her tone jaunty. 'Keith? Karin back yet? She was filling in for me at a meeting.'

'I know, she left a note. She says she'll be in by four. Is there a message?'

She hesitated. 'No.' She kept her voice light. 'What's happening with you? I sort of expected you'd stroll up one afternoon or evening.'

His silence told her he was thinking that over. 'We've been busy. Up to our ears, both of us.'

'I wasn't speaking of both of you, Keith. Just you.'

His laugh was uncomfortable. 'Papers. Lecture notes. You know.'

Clearly, this was not going to be worked out by phone; it needed her presence. Max had once called her face flowerlike. Pure, he had said. She knew how men responded to her appearance and she had long since given up resenting the fact that often it was only to her appearance that they responded. It's me, she had told herself, what they find in my face is me. Why should I feel there is some shame in being beautiful? In making men want me?

Impulsively she glanced at her diary and said, 'Keith, I'd like you two to come to dinner. Would tomorrow night do? I'll ask Marcie. And Dawn too—we should do something to take her out of herself. And I'll want to hear about today's meeting.'

The return to normalcy in the conversation was met by open relief. 'Sounds fine. We don't have a thing on the diary for tomorrow. I'll talk to Karin when she comes in. She'll get back to you.'

Not even a thank-you. She had better wait until she heard from Karin before asking the others. She put down the phone conscious of an irritability such as she had not known in a long time. Perhaps she was making a mistake with Keith. But she needed someone. Someone strong. Putting all that happened in the past week out of her mind was not enough. She could push aside the events but the sense of isolation persisted. Perhaps a dinner-party would help in more ways than one. Meanwhile she had another evening to get through. She picked up the phone again. Maybe Perry could be coaxed to join her for dinner at the new Vietnamese place. Perry was alone, too.

It was after four before Tate reached Marcie Terpstra, just as he was about to give up on her for the day.

She seemed surprised that anyone had been aware of her absence. 'You've been trying to get me? Kevin and I went to a Day Care picnic. We've been swimming and building sand castles and stuffing ourselves with franks.' She sounded relaxed and merry.

'Could we talk for a few minutes, Miss Terpstra? I could

come by right now.' Tate reflected that these days he was
in that neighbourhood as much as his own.

'Well . . . Kevin would be around. My attention would
be pretty divided. I—' she hesitated—'I don't suppose
later is at all possible? He goes to bed at seven.'

Tate amended his plans for the early evening. 'That
should work. Why don't you give me a call after your son
gets to sleep?' He gave her the number. Hanging up, he
reminded himself that he was too young to be looking forward to an evening before TV with a beer and his feet up.
Being divorced had in some subtle way eroded his youth.
Maybe a little levening work would be stimulating. He
might even stop afterrwards at a bar he liked, that quasi-
Irish place, sit around a while and listen to some music.
Aside from all that, he'd like presenting Pedersen with at
least some indications of effort.

She phoned before seven. He had gone out for a hamburger and returned to his office, where he was sitting over
paperwork.

'Kevin couldn't keep his eyes open. He's *out*. It's safe to
come.'

'Fine. Give me fifteen minutes.' Once again he was
struck by what a cooperative bunch this was. He and
Pedersen had reflected less flatteringly on them at the beginning, but the impression he now had was that they were
all extending themselves in the effort to help. He wondered
if she would be so agreeable when she learned his errand:
whatever her reason, she had made it a point not to reveal
her relationship with Max Follett. It could be that she did
not realize her child was Max's and not her young man's.
If Dawn's testimony as to the photographs had been accurate, as well as the little tug of recognition on his own part
when he had seen Max's photograph as a little boy, and if
Max's wishes had been properly interpreted, the evidence
was strong that Kevin was indeed Max's child.

He found her sitting out on a little patio behind her

house. She looked pink from the sun and cheerful. 'I waited with my dessert. If you don't want any ice-cream, you'll just have to watch me eat it.' She indicated a chair. 'Isn't this great? It's Keith—he loves doing things for people. He put in the bricks and built the sandbox for Kevin, and I did the potted plants. Pretty grand for a garage apartment.' She left him sitting amid the pots of pink geraniums and blue lobelia and went off upstairs for ice-cream.

They finished eating it before they talked. Setting his empty bowl on the little table beside him, Tate said, 'That hit the spot. Now. What I have to tell you may come as a large surprise. First, though, I have to ask you a question.'

Apprehension brushed her face.

For some reason, probably his sudden sense of her vulnerability, he found it hard to ask. 'It's about Kevin's father.'

'What about his father?' Her face told him she knew what was coming.

'Is Max Follett Kevin's father?'

She grew still. 'Now why would you think that?'

'Marcie—may I call you that?—I think you should just tell me.'

'First you tell me why you think that.'

'We've had access to his will.'

She sat straight up. 'You mean he left something to Kevin?'

'Yes.'

'Well.' Her eyes met his. 'I never expected *that*.' She sat studying the geraniums. Finally she sighed and said, 'Max was his father.' She laughed shortly. 'I've just sworn Perry to secrecy about it.'

'Excuse me for having to ask this, but are you sure? You were living with someone, I understand.' As soon as he asked, he realized it was only curiosity that had fuelled the question. The will, the inheritance, perhaps even her motives, were in no way altered by his knowing the answer.

She appeared unaware that it was an inappropriate question. 'We were together, you might say, in name only. The man I was living with was pretty heavily into drugs. The last thing on his mind was sex. Around the time Kevin was conceived, I had only one—' her eyebrows went up— 'sexual contact, I guess you'd call it. One of those one-time mistakes you read about in novels that always end up in the conception of a child.' She smiled at him. 'My mother always warned me.'

'Your husband—I mean, your housemate—knew it wasn't his, then?'

'Yes.' She shrugged. 'It gave him a good excuse for leaving. I should add that I was glad to see him go, though I'd have liked a daddy for Kevin. Not that one, though.'

'You and Max Follett didn't consider marrying?'

'I never told him about the baby being his. It's just in the last few months that it seems to have dawned on him that it could be his child. Lately he's been after me to marry him, all but blackmailing me into it. He had no other kids and I guess now that he was older he wanted someone to carry on—' she frowned—'the line.'

'I don't understand. How could be blackmail you?'

'He threatened to take Kevin away from me, make me out to be an unfit mother, depriving Kevin of the life that he could have as Max's son. He seemed to think he could prove Kevin was his. You can't do that, can you? I was told you can only prove whose child it *isn't*. It scared me, all the same. And I didn't want him around, trying to bribe me, buy me, seduce me—something—all the time.'

'So you must have been quite ambivalent when you learned Follett was dead?'

'I certainly didn't feel any sense of personal loss. I didn't, however—' she looked at him levelly—'hurry him on his way, if that's what you're implying.'

'I'm not implying anything. At any rate, Mr Follett's will should make life easier for you. If you want to bring your son up as he would have been brought up as Max Follett's son, you should be able to now.'

She stood up. 'That never was an aspiration of mine. I should go up and check to be sure Kevin is OK. Are there going to be any other questions?'

'No. Yes, one. I wonder why you went to that party for Follett.'

'Party? Oh, at Leona's. I didn't want to call attention to our . . . situation. I figured the more casual I was with Max, the better. From everybody's point of view, including his. If I'd seemed threatened, then he'd have really moved in. I treated the whole thing as nonsense, as a figment of his exhausted brain. Anything else?'

'Not for now. You're probably as tired as Kevin after your day in the sun. I'll go along.'

As he walked down the drive, the thought skittered across his mind that perhaps Max *had* moved in, despite her casual handling of the matter.

Getting back into the car, he speculated on stopping at the Irish pub. It seemed less appealing than it had an hour ago and not much fun alone. No, he thought as he pulled the car out of the driveway and into the road, I'll just get along home and mull a little over this case. Or, he added, to himself as he passed the house with the orange door, watch a little TV.

FRIDAY

CHAPTER 22

Pedersen had barely entered the office when Dawn's call came. She was crying. 'Detective Pedersen, I think you'd better come up.'

'Dawn, what is it? Have you been hurt?'

'No, not me. It's my—Muffin. Can you come? Or Detective Tate?'

They both went. As though she had given up on all caution, she had left both the front door and the door to her apartment open. She was huddled in a corner of the sofa-bed, a soggy handkerchief pressed to her face. 'There.' She pointed and looked away. Lying on the worktable under a newspaper was Muffin, now a flat bundle of wet fur. 'She was in my bathtub.' She shuddered. 'I'll never be able to take a bath there again.'

'When did it happen?'

'I don't know. It was like the last time. I went for my walk and came back and found—that.' She lifted her eyes to Tate's. 'It's going to be me next.'

'Dawn!' Tate said. 'You simply have to get out of here. This stubbornness of yours *will* get you hurt. Now think. Where can you go?'

'He's right, Dawn,' Pedersen said.

'I'm not going anywhere. I'm staying here. I need the kiln, I need my clay—I'm just not going anywhere.'

'Can't you get someone to come and stay with you?'

'Who? And where would they stay? This apartment isn't big enough for me, much less for someone else.'

Tate looked at Pedersen. 'She could stay at her brother's. They've finished with the house. There's more room there.'

Dawn stuffed the wet handkerchief into her pocket in a brisk gesture. 'I'm not going anyplace. I'll go up this weekend and go through Max's things and later on I may move up there, but I don't want anyone with me. I couldn't work with someone around. I'll be all right. Or I won't. I'm sure whatever's going to happen will happen no matter how many people live with me.'

Tate raised his voice. 'Don't you care if you live or die?'

'I care.' She looked at his angry face and said gently. 'And thank you for caring. You're both nice men.'

'Did you have your chain on the door?' asked Pedersen. 'Oh no, you'd just been out.'

'Somebody has a key, that's all.'

Pedersen nodded. 'It looks that way. You had more than one key to the deadbolt?'

'Don't ask. I don't know where it is.'

Tate snorted. 'Then let's change the lock again. This time *we'll* keep the extra key.' He looked at her closely. 'Let me ask you again, Dawn. Is there anyone who would have a *reason* to be doing these things? Anyone here? Anyone you knew earlier? Anyone your brother knew?'

She shook her head impatiently. 'I told you before. I don't know why someone has it in for me. I can't think of a thing. Do you suppose they're messages for me?'

'If they are, the sender's covered just about everything by now.' He glanced at her jeans, stiff with newness. 'I see you've bought some new clothes.'

'A couple of things. Nothing much.' She looked at Tate. 'I bought the dress, then I had a dinner invitation to go with it. If it weren't for—'

'I know. It casts a pall over everything.'

'Two deaths . . .' she said.

'Let's send for the locksmith,' Pedersen said.

'I'm even beginning to suspect him,' Dawn said, after the man had tested the new lock, received her cheque and closed the gate. She sounded tired, defeated.

'Don't worry about the locksmith. Now you keep that key with you, around your neck on a ribbon or something, so no one can get at it.' Pedersen pocketed the second key. 'We'll take charge of this one.'

'I do feel safer. I guess we should have thought of this when Max's key was returned and my clothes were cut.'

'We should,' Pedersen said. 'Now, Dawn, be careful. If you have to go somewhere at night, give us a ring. We'll send a car up for you.'

She frowned. 'I can lock my car. You're making a prisoner of me.'

'Please, Dawn.'

'Oh, all right. If somebody doesn't offer to come and pick me up. Thank you, I feel better.' She glanced at the newspaper-covered hump on the worktable.

'I'll stay and help you bury Muffin,' Tate said, not looking at Pedersen.

'We'll both help,' said Pedersen. Police work included a lot of variety these days.

'Well,' Tate said, as they pulled away from Dawn's house, 'was it worth it, the Longville trip? Find out anything?'

'I found out a lot. Before I tell you, I want you to give Harner a ring, try him again.' They rounded the corner and headed down to town.

'Dawn's husband? I thought he said he didn't know anything.'

'I know. I think he's been holding out on us. Or maybe he doesn't realize that what he hasn't mentioned is important. If I tell you what I learned in Longville, you'll be tempted to lead him.'

Tate threw a puzzled glance his way. 'I'm quite able to—oh well, let's do it your way.'

Back at headquarters, Pedersen found what he had been waiting for. Lying on his desk was a fat envelope with the banners of colour that proclaimed Express Mail.

Tate indicated the envelope. 'Is that what I think it is?'

'Yes. When I called, they'd just received the manuscript themselves. Considering that, they're right on the ball.'

'You're hoping it'll give you a few clues?'

'Maybe, depending on how autobiographical it is. It may give me some ideas on the Folletts' family life.'

'Usually it's first books that are autobiographical. You going to start on it now?'

'I'd like to. Ron, why don't you try Harner now? Let him ramble, if that's what it takes, tell you everything he thinks of.'

It took several calls. Harner was at lunch, he was in conference, he had just stepped out of the office. Was the caller sure he didn't want Mr Harner to phone back?

Finally, Tate hit the right moment.

'Mr Harner, Detective Tate. You're a hard man to pin down.'

'Oh, it's you. I have a few minutes now. What's up?'

'What's up is that we're puzzled. We told you Dawn was fine, we didn't want to worry you unnecessarily, but a couple of things have happened that have made us wonder if she is fine.'

There was a short silence. 'She hasn't been hurt?'

'No, not yet, but—let me ask you the question that's on my mind. Is there anything, anything at all, that you recall her mentioning that might explain why both she and her brother are under attack?'

'You asked me that before. I should think the best source of information would be Doris herself.' He paused. 'What sort of attack?'

'Her cat Muffin was drowned. That's coming very close. You see, we thought at first maybe these attacks—the gazebo she had worked on for the museum show was destroyed, her clothing was slashed and her pottery mutilated—came *because* she was Follett's sister. It's beginning to look as though there's nothing symbolic about these— gestures. They look very real. And they're directed against her. At her, I mean.'

'My God, that sounds serious. Isn't there some way to protect her? Send her away or give her twenty-four-hour police protection?'

'She's upset, but she refuses to go anywhere else or have anyone move in with her. And we're giving her what police protection we can. Let's get back to my question. Think. What do you know about her childhood, her family?'

'You've asked her this?'

'Yes. Either she can't or—' he had had a sudden sense of disloyalty—'won't tell us.'

'I don't know anything. That is, I know she was born when her brother was practically a teenager. Her mother had some trouble and wasn't supposed to have more kids. Doris was unplanned.'

This was better. 'Her parents must have been pleased, though,' Tate interjected conversationally.

'I would have thought so, but they sounded like a pretty undemonstrative pair. Hovering, demanding, but—cold.'

'They built her a gazebo, I understand.'

'Yes, and they built Max a treehouse when he was little. I think they prided themselves on being even-handed. It's just that they sounded . . . cold, like cold people. And very hard on the kids. Expected them to be perfect. Criticized everything they did. It was hell on Doris's self-esteem, let me tell you. I guess both kids were bright and couldn't help achieving—that was just fortunate for them.'

'The gazebo was all hers?'

'It was till it burned down.'

Tate sat up. 'Burned down?'

'Oh, hasn't Doris told you? That's why she was so crazy about Max—he saved her life.'

Tate said, 'Maybe you'd better begin at the beginning.'

'It was the summer she was eight, I think. Max had come home from college to do some writing—he was writing even then. One evening the parents went to some church function and left Doris in his care. He was up in his room, writing, it was getting on towards dusk and apparently Doris decided to take a candle from the sideboard where they were stored and light the gazebo with it. The place caught fire. She was burned.'

Tate could guess. 'Her legs?'

'Yes. Not badly, but her legs were slightly scarred. The important thing is that Max looked out of the window at the right moment or something. He got her out of the gazebo in time. She could have burned to death. I guess it scared the hell out of him—after all, he was supposed to be taking care of her. He even refused to go back to college until she was out of the hospital. After that, she adored him.'

'If her parents were cold people, perhaps he seemed more like a real parent to her.'

'Maybe. Undemonstrativeness wasn't his problem.' His tone was dry.

'No, but the man takes on new dimensions the more I learn of him.' Tate was silent for a moment. 'You know, this is interesting, like a piece of a puzzle, but it doesn't explain why someone should be persecuting Dawn.'

'I know. I told you I couldn't help. But it's the only major event in her life that I know about. And she wasn't even badly burned. She's just self-conscious. Probably those parents of hers. She's not *perfect* now.'

'Nothing else about the parents?'

'They sounded like pretty conventional people. Her mother stayed home and baked, sewed Doris's clothes. She checked her homework every night. The father was the breadwinner.'

'And they're both long since dead.'

'Yes. Buried in Longville, where she lived.'

'We'll have to mull this over. But I'd like you to do the same. If you think of anything else, would you let me know?'

'I will, but what about Doris? You're going to *do* something, aren't you?'

'We'll do what we can. We'll keep an eye on her.' He looked sadly at the receiver. 'That's all we can do.'

*

Tate broke in on Pedersen's reading. 'Sorry, I know you're trying to make headway with that.'

'Did you learn anything?'

'I learned the source of her strong attachment to her brother. He saved her life when she was a kid. She set fire to her gazebo fooling around with candles and he got her out.'

'Her legs were burned?'

'Yes. I thought of it right away, too. The coloured stockings. It can't be much, though; Harner never even mentioned it the first time we spoke to him. He says she's not badly scarred.'

'But she's self-conscious about it. That's why she didn't tell us herself. I wonder if that's what she meant when she said she was being sent messages'.

'What do you mean?'

'I mean someone here in town knows about the gazebo incident and is using it to threaten her.'

'What about the other things—the clothes and the kitten?'

'Underlining. Destruction headed your way. I think the crushing of the gazebo was the big message: the next thing may be fire.'

'*Arson?*'

'Yes. The question is, what's she doing that anyone would want to threaten her?'

'But who would know? The way she keeps her legs covered, it doesn't seem like something she'd have talked about.'

'Not in general conversation. She could have confided in someone.'

'God! And this Muffin business, too. Just when she was beginning to feel better.'

Pedersen looked at him.

'I mean, she looked so exhausted the first few times I saw her and she was sleeping terribly. But when I went over yesterday to talk about the will, she seemed better, as though she were shaking it off and pulling herself together.' He sighed. 'Do you find it possible to connect anyone in this crowd with an idea like arson?'

'No, I admit I don't. They're a singularly . . . agreeable bunch.' Their eyes met. 'Agreeable people can be murderers.'

Tate indicated the manuscript. 'You finding anything?'

'I've had a lot of interruptions. I don't mean you, other things. I'm going to get down to it now.' He removed the cover sheet from the manuscript.

But he had trouble getting down to it.

He and Freda had sat over dinner late the evening before talking. The conversation had disturbed him.

Things had returned to normal between them. 'You've tuned in again,' she announced as they sat over their second cups of coffee.

'I have? I wasn't aware I'd tuned out.'

'You had. But you're listening to me again. I can see why you didn't, Carl, it's pretty discouraging.' She picked up her coffee-cup. 'What's happening with the case?'

'I'm not sure anything is. If I could work full time on it, but even then . . . Ron's been doing a lot. Talking to the neighbours, checking details.'

'You think one of the neighbours did it?'

'I do, but that's about as far as my thinking goes at this point.' With an effort he asked, 'Anything new with your mother?'

'No. I told you she's stopped reading, didn't I?'

'I don't believe it. *Your mother?*' He had heard enough family stories to know that reading had been her mother's refuge, her comfort, her life, for years. She had read while she nursed her babies, read while she sat at sickbeds, read during family crises and, after her husband's death, read almost non-stop for twenty-some years. He could not imagine Freda's mother without books.

'Yes. She says she can't concentrate, her mind just doesn't seem to be on what she's reading any more.'

'What does she do with herself, for God's sake?'

'Fusses over the house and *paces*, Clara says. Just paces, back and forth, back and forth. She seems to have this dreadful energy. Clare thought maybe she had Alzheimer's, but the doctor says no. He says those things are symptoms of senility. Arteriosclerosis, any kind of senility.'

'Freda—'

'You know what I think, Carl?' She took a big gulp of her coffee, swallowed the wrong way and sputtered until she could speak again. 'I think all those things—needing to be with someone at night, not being able to keep her mind on her book, all of it—is just part of a fear of dying. Ever since the cancer, she's been afraid of dying.'

'When you get to her age, there's reason to fear it. It's coming closer.

She looked across the table at him, her eyes a little widened. 'Have you thought what that feels like? What it would be like, not to know what happens next? Not to see the kids' families grow up? And never to see Carrie's baby learn to walk, learn to talk? Not to know who Matt will marry? Do you ever think what it's like? Dying?'

He looked across the table at her dark head and earnest face. He was filled with love for her. What would it be like never to see her again? He took her hand. 'I don't think we can grasp dying, except intellectually.'

'Oh, you're wrong. When Sylvia—' an old friend of Freda's who had never recovered after a massive heart attack—'died, I was sitting in the living-room one day thinking about her, about her never being here again. And all of a sudden I had this moment of absolute panic. For just a few seconds I grasped that someday *I* wouldn't be here, that no matter how long I held it off that time would come.

It was awful. I was just swept with *terror* at the thought of the world going on and my not being a part of it. My heart was pounding. I couldn't catch my breath. Thank God it only lasted seconds. It's never happened again.'

Pedersen nodded. '*That's* why we can't take it in, except intellectually. We have to defend ourselves. We'd be overwhelmed.'

'Then Mother must be losing that ability.'

'She may. I know it's hard for you, sweetie.'

'It is. Lately I feel like *her* mother. Sometimes she even says it, by mistake. She'll say, "Well, after all you *are* my mother," when she means "my daughter". It doesn't feel right, even though I understand.'

Pedersen reached across and took her hand. 'She was your mother all those years when it counted.'

'I know.' She sat thoughtful for a few moments. 'But she stopped being one quite a while ago. I remember realizing it when Matt went through that awful period where he wanted to drop out of school and kept running away. I was so scared and worried. I even remember one whole day when I couldn't stop crying. I kept wanting to tell Mother, I felt sure she could help, but I didn't dare. I was protecting her even then. Not letting her know either of the kids had problems or flaws, or that I was worried sick; it would have been too hard on her.'

After they had gone to bed, Pedersen kept thinking of it. His own mother, still lucid and independent, lived in the next town, and he took for granted her being there and being the same. Always. Just as he took his own being there for his children for granted. Always. Freda stirred beside him and he reached for her.

'I guess I just have to accept it,' she said sleepily.

It wasn't easy, any of it. Being a child. Being a parent. And being in these middle years, when the pull from children and the tug from parents were equally wrong.

Finally he slept.

He had his calls referred to Tate and applied himself to his reading.

About half way through the manuscript Pedersen began to understand Follett. Despite the book's length, reading it was not a difficult task. The novel was well constructed and kept him turning pages, needing to know what came next: Max Follett was a storyteller. But more impelling was Pedersen's need to understand how—or whether—the protagonist would resolve the conflicts with which he struggled. It was a novel of ambivalence and guilt. The plot was straightforward. The protagonist, Luke, a blocked writer, had in late boyhood known a young woman, the daughter of an old friend, for whom he had developed a passionate attachment. Eventually they married. The marriage was stormy, even to the point of his violently attacking her on occasion. In one of his more unbridled moments, Luke knocked her down a flight of stairs and injured her back. She could still move about but was in constant pain relieved only by an increasing use of drugs. Luke continued to live with her, hating her for holding him through her weakness and unable to break free because of his guilt and the remnants of his passion for her.

At three-quarters through the novel, Pedersen struggled not to turn to the final pages and skip all that came between. He put the manuscript aside and poured himself a cup of coffee from the Thermos he had brought against just this sort of fatigue with reading.

Clearly, he thought as he sipped the coffee, the novel had autobiographical aspects, more than Follett's first as he recalled it. That was odd: as Tate had said, first books were usually the autobiographical ones. Yet he could find no precise parallel between the attachment in the novel and those in Follett's actual life. Tate had obtained the information on three of the early wives (the fourth, he reported, lived abroad) and had left him the report. It appeared to have been, essentially, a fruitless exercise.

The wives all spoke of Follett's impulsiveness and easy anger, but all had remarried and now regarded him as no more than a dim (if illustrious) part of their histories. None had mentioned physical abuse or an injury. The first wife had met his parents on the occasion of the wedding ceremony. She was of the opinion that he had broken free from what he regarded as his parents' excessive demands and then kept his distance.

That element—the need to break free of family as a boy—was strong in the development of the character Luke. Although they were somewhat caricatured, the parents came across as sour, essentially cold people who were obsessively attached to him, yet never quite satisfied with his achievements. Luke was an only child—as Follett had been for twelve years.

A series of questions was beginning to line itself up in Pedersen's mind. The manuscript of the novel had not turned up among Follett's papers. If it had been stolen, who would need to study it when, after all, it was in the publisher's hands and on its way to becoming a *fait accompli*? For what possible purpose would anyone withhold it? Did Leona know any of what was in the manuscript? Did Dawn—and if she did, could she cast light on the strange relationship contained within the book?

He finished his coffee and once more picked up the manuscript. In the final quarter of the book, Luke struggled with his need to write a novel he did not want to write and his inability to write it. Increasingly he escaped his literary impotence in sexual encounters and alcohol. His wife bore up under the increasing burden, herself finding periodic oblivion in the drugs prescribed to ease her pain. Luke broke through and finished the book, driving himself for days without sleep at times, obsessed with saying in the book what he had to say, with writing the book in order to put it behind him. The manuscript was finished. As he sat in his study over the completed draft, free in some way in which he had never been free, his wife entered the room behind him and, with a strength born of years of pain, stabbed him.

Pedersen read the last page once more, startled. Once he had read it, the ending struck him as inevitable; the book could have ended in no other way and been as effective, yet he was amazed. Follett had predicted—or foreseen—the nature of his own death. By murder.

Pedersen had sat silent all through dinner. Finally Freda spoke. 'Something's the matter.'

'No. Just mulling. How did the rehearsal go?'

'Fine. What's wrong, Carl?'

'Nothing. That is, I don't understand something, I just can't put the pieces together.'

She stood up from the table. 'Let's go for a walk and have dessert later. Maybe if you get out, you'll come back to it fresh.'

'Maybe. I know what.'

'What?'

'Remember I told you I'd discovered a little graveyard right out of New England?'

'The first day you were up on the hill working on the case? Yes.'

'It isn't dark yet, let's go for a walk up there.' He hesitated. 'Unless—maybe that's not such a good idea right now.'

'Mother? No, it's all right. Let's go.'

He drove to a corner near the Blochs' and parked. Strolling up the road in the direction of Leona Morgan's house, breathing the damp fragrance of eucalyptus, they reached the small fenced cemetery.

As they entered, he sighed with pleasure. Graveyards were in an odd way welcoming. They offered a sharing of the past, an admission into the crises of families, into those moments of deepest feeling that forever changed the shapes of lives left behind.

Beside him, Freda said, 'It does look like New England. I didn't know there was anything like this in Bay Cove.'

'I know. It's peaceful, isn't it?'

Near the entrance the graves were new, the words on the stones clear and bright. At the far end of the cemetery were the oldest ones, many tilted askew or sunken deep. Two narrow slabs appeared to be the earliest. Grizzled with age, they bore no decipherable names or dates, merely on one, MOTHER, the other, FATHER.

They walked silently among the stones, preoccupied with their own thoughts, until Freda stopped at one. 'Look. Beloved wife and mother—this one died in 1919 when she was only twenty-six. That's Carrie's age. Oh, say, this must have been her child. And here's *another*.'

'That was the influenza epidemic. Something like twenty million people died before that was over.'

'Twenty million! From the flu?' Freda looked at her husband as though he had invented the epidemic.

They moved on up and down the little paths bordered with wide-leaved green plants. In the centre of the cemetery a small heap of rocks, perhaps someone's notion of contemporary sculpture, was ringed with flowers. A sprinkler swept the area, watering the flowers and making the grass between the graves fragrant.

'Do you notice how many babies died before they were out of their first five years?' Pedersen asked.

'And at birth. See this one. Patricia Ann Holder, born and died June 25, 1902.

'And this.' They stopped. 'He died in Korea, his Marine division is given. Robert Case Braine. 1933–1952. "Robbie".' He was quiet for a moment. 'That "Robbie" says it all. That's war for you.' Pedersen turned away, moved and disgusted.

'Matt's been lucky. He's never had to fight in any wars, he has a draft number, that's all.'

Pedersen looked at her sadly. He hoped no one would

ever walk by a gravestone with an Army Corps number carved into it and below that 'Matt'.

Towards the centre Pedersen found a pair of graves side by side, marked only by names and the dates of births and deaths. These might just as easily be the Folletts' graves—the parents. He stood before the modest headstones, their incised words invaded by moss. Unlike many of the graves, they were without flowers or a plant like the potted geranium he had just passed. He wondered if anyone ever visited this spot any longer. Did anyone ever visit the Follett parents' graves in Longville?

On their way out they passed a grave which bore a tin can, labels removed, filled with flowers that had wilted in the day's heat. They bent to read the headstone. It was the marker for a young woman deceased two months earlier: *Beloved wife of Justin, devoted mother of Stephen and Lisa.* One of the children must have left the flowers, probably that morning.

The sadness of such losses touched him. It was this that Freda's mother feared, the inevitable death that drew closer to her, the end that awaited them all. His eyes met Freda's. He guessed she was having the same thoughts. He turned and, head down, holding his wife's hand, made his way out of the little cemetery.

CHAPTER 23

Leona saw the party more as a means to check things out with Keith, to gauge his reactions, than as an opportunity for an intimate moments with him. With his wife there, that would hardly be possible. Leona was adept at judging men's reactions to her: even during her early teens, she had discerned what a boy's not looking at her often meant and what certain glances, a mere brushing of eyes against hers, hinted. She also knew how to use herself, how to move a fraction closer to a man than social custom demanded, how to touch a hand in passing or to playfully pat a face and let the hand linger. How to put up her own lips pursed for a welcoming kiss and then turn at the exact moment so the caress harmlessly skidded off her cheek and left the man still hungry.

In one sense, she sometimes told herself with regret, the problem was that she had never learned what went beyond those initial signals. Sex, of course, but there must be more. Her brief marriage had not helped her to learn. For a while, it had seemed that with Max she might be going on to understand the bond that held men to less beautiful women, the essence of that state of connectedness which she had never known. But in the end . . . She let the thought drift off.

No, she'd had few opportunities to find out, so much of what men wanted her for had been merely sexual. Nothing crude or raw, all the amenities observed, but it came down to the same thing. It was the slightly overripe body that so contradicted the angelic oval above it that intrigued them. They wanted to test the promise of that body. Since she operated at the principle that all was fair in love and war, the husbands of a number of her acquaintances had had that scientific opportunity.

Because the party for Max was still so fresh in everyone's memory, certainly in hers, she planned the dinner for a different hour, eight, which was late for the others, and indoors.

She kept it simple. A large pottery bowl filled with her special chilli, a basket of sourdough bread, a big wooden bowl holding green salad; that would be all, with as dessert a hollowed watermelon filled with fruit. A homespun cloth and napkins checked in blue, along with heavy white bowls, provided the backdrop. She stood before the set table, the fragrance of the simmering chilli in her nostrils, and minded herself that, whatever else she lacked, she did have an excellent sense of theatre.

Dawn and Marcie came first, Dawn in a black-bound white cotton dress Leona could not recall having seen before. The patterned black cotton hose and black patent pumps with tiny high heels gave her a—Leona stopped for an instant, trying for a word—grown-up look. Of course she's almost as old as I am, Leona reminded herself. She *is* grown up. Marcie, as usual, above bare legs and sandals wore a T-shirt and one of her full skirts that bore the earmarks of home sewing. Leona felt a prick of irritation. Did no invitation move Marcie to clothe herself with more attention to the occasion? Did she feel being young was all that was required of her? The face beneath the leaves of copper hair had the silkiness of a young girl's, but she wasn't even careful about that; the sunburn across her cheeks and the bridge of her nose made that clear. They sat down to wait for the other two.

'Place smells marvellous. My mouth is watering,' said Marcie.

'We'll eat as soon as they come. You can have a drink, but we're having Dos Equis with dinner; you may want to wait. I know by this time of day everyone's ravenous. But at least the kids will all be bedded down.'

'Beer sounds good. I don't drink much, but I do like a glass of beer in summer,' Dawn said.

'I like your dress,' Leona offered.

'I've been telling her she looks smashing. I'm surprised you can find anything that smart in this town.'

Dawn touched the fabric of the skirt. 'It's been a long time since I've dressed up. I was glad you gave me a reason to do it, Leona. It seems to me my life has been awfully . . . sober for a long time. Max's death has made it hard, but I'm determined to get it together now. Silly. Why does it take some people so long?'

Marcie grinned. 'Most people never get their lives in

order. I'm just happy to have a *day* where everything goes well. Kevin's a doll, but I must say he keeps things from ever settling down.'

'I don't mean settling down, that's not what I want,' Dawn said. 'It's something different. Being in control of my life, making it go the way *I* want. Maybe I'm still getting over being married.' She gave a hesitant smile.

'I think I hear them,' said Leona. 'I'll go check.'

She returned with Keith and Karin. Karin was explaining her costume. 'I don't know when I last wore a long skirt. I just decided I should. We don't have dinner out that often.'

'It looks lovely. Doesn't it, Keith?' Leona turned her face towards him.

'Karin always look lovely.'

'Ah, gallant, gallant. I was mad at him and he's trying to make up,' Karin confided.

Leona touched Keith's sleeve. 'You look very nice too, Keith.'

'Thanks.' He walked over to sit beside Marcie. 'Everybody looks good. And something smells good.'

'Yes, you must be famished. I hope you didn't cheat and nibble. It's chilli and my recipe is awfully good.'

'All your recipes are good,' said Karin. She sat down too.

'Don't get too comfortable. The dinner'll be on in just a minute. Drinks are available. Or if you want you can wait; there's Dos Equis with dinner.'

'Mmm. Let's wait,' said Karin. 'How nice you look, Dawn.'

Dawn squirmed a little in her chair. 'I'm beginning to wonder how I look the rest of the time. Everybody's commenting.'

'You look fine,' said Marcie. 'In fact, I like that little uniform you wear: the different coloured tights matched up with skirts. Even when you're working, you look assembled. Designed. Must come from being an artist.'

'I'd hardly call myself an artist.'

'Why not?' Karin and Marcie said at once.

'Let's not talk about me, please,' Dawn said, 'it makes me uncomfortable.'

Marcie laughed. 'Sometimes I think you're nine years old, not—whatever you are. We're just complimenting you because you deserve it.'

Leona had returned to the living-room. 'Food's on.'

At the table she instructed them. 'You sit here to my right, Marcie. Keith, you're on the left. Karin next to Marcie, Dawn across from Karin. This table's just too long. I put all the food down at the end to try to fill it up. Karin, will you start things around?'

They settled into their places.

'A toast, first,' said Leona, raising her beer mug. 'To us. Happier times.' She glanced at Dawn. 'To all of us getting our lives in order, just the way we want them.' She touched Marcie's glass, then Keith's, meeting his eyes above the mug.

The party broke up early. As the four made their way down the uneven road in the dark, Marcie said, 'What a funny party. It didn't feel right.'

'What do you mean?' asked Dawn. She stumbled slightly. Clearly, high heels were an unfamiliar encumbrance.

'I don't know. It was as if there were some sort of . . . undercurrent the whole time. Sometimes Leona's strange.'

'But so beautiful,' said Karin.

'How you look isn't everything.' Dawn stumbled again, and Keith took her arm.

'It doesn't do any harm to have a face like that,' said Karin.

'Or a body like that,' added Marcie. She looked at Keith, curious. 'Are men intimidated by that sort of beauty?'

Karin laughed.

Keith said, 'Is that a personal question or a psychological one?'

'I'll take both.'

'Personally, I'm unaffected, so it's hard to say. But there have been papers written on the subject of how intimidating beauty can be and how distressing for the person who's beautiful. It's easy to assume you're not being appreciated for *other* things.'

'Your brilliant mind?' Marcie said.

'And generous spirit,' said Karin.

'Maybe, in Leona's case, it's just as well that she has beauty,' Marcie said. 'No. I shouldn't have said that. It's nasty.'

'She's smart enough,' said Dawn. 'They certainly respect her at the museum.'

'I suppose,' Karin said, 'this post-mortem is unfair. The woman has just fed us extremely well and, although Leona will never be my most intimate friend, she has been decent about getting the museum interested in my work.'

'All that may be true,' said Marcie. 'But *something* was wrong this evening.'

They approached the Bloch house. 'I'll walk you down the rest of the way, Dawn,' Keith said. 'You may break your neck in those heels if I let you do it alone.'

'Good night, Dawn,' said Karin.

'You looked lovely, Dawn, funny evening or not. You should dress up more often,' Marcie commented.

'I think I will.' Dawn and Keith moved off down the road.

By the time he returned, Karin had paid the sitter. The woman was pulling her car out of the drive, Marcie's young sitter in the passenger seat beside her.

'She should practise walking in heels,' Keith said as he came in. His wife made no response. 'Good chilli, wasn't it? It always surprises me that Leona can cook.'

'Why?' Karin turned from where she was putting her cheque-book away. 'She does *other* things so very well.'

'You mean the museum?'

'No, I mean her seductive little act. What was going on tonight? I'm not blind.'

'Going on? What are you talking about?'

'Are you having an affair with Leona?'

'Of course not! What gave you that idea?'

Karin came close to him and stood looking up into his face. 'Tonight gave me the idea. Every chance she got she touched you or gazed into your eyes or slipped some little innuendo into her conversation. It's no wonder the evening felt so funny to Marcie. It was one big seduction, the whole thing.'

'Now really, Karin.' He took hold of her upper arms and squeezed gently. 'You're being ridiculous. How can you be jealous of *Leona?*'

'I've been thinking. All those times you went up there to discuss repairs of one sort or another. And earlier, when she was having the problem with the roof. Now that I think of it, you spend time up there almost every day.'

'I do not.' He shook her gently. 'I don't do anything for Leona that I don't do for Marcie or Dawn or that I wouldn't do if Perry asked me. I like to do repair jobs. I've told you, I missed my calling. I should have been a gardener or carpenter, whistling over my work. I was never meant to spend my life in a classroom.'

'That has nothing to do with what we're talking about. We're talking about you and Leona. You can't tell me there's nothing going on between the two of you.'

'I am telling you. I—' He stopped.

'You what?'

'Now if I tell you—' he held her arms till she looked up at him—'will you promise not to blow your top?'

Her face was stiff. 'That depends.'

'I'm not going to tell you I had an affair or anything, if that's what you think. Promise?'

'I won't blow my top, as you put it. I can't promise how I'll feel.'

'I kissed her. That's the sum total of it. I was pissed off at you the other day and I walked up there, who knows why, and while we were talking, I . . . kissed her. As soon as I did it, I realized what a mistake it was.'

'Mistake. That's a peculiar word for it.'

'I mean, it obviously gave her ideas, she thought I was interested in her. I've been uncomfortable ever since. I'm not interested in her. In fact my current impulse when I see her is to run in the opposite direction.'

'To escape other impulses, you mean?'

'No.' Now he was angry. He let go of her and moved to the other side of the room. 'It was stupid. I was mad at you and she was acting helpless and bereaved and . . . it just happened. For Christ's sake, a kiss isn't anything. Not if it isn't going anyplace.'

Karin sagged a bit from the rigid posture she had maintained through the conversation. 'You aren't interested in her?'

'No.' He moved close to her again. 'You're the only woman that interests me. You have plenty of confirmation of that, don't you?'

'I suppose so.' She put her arms around him and her head against him. 'But don't kiss other women. I don't kiss other men. Besides—' she pulled back—'I didn't plan to tell anyone, not even you, but I will tell you. At the party for Max . . .'

'Yes?'

'I saw her. I don't know whether it was on purpose, but it was Leona who pushed Max.'

SATURDAY

CHAPTER 24

Pedersen woke to a nagging feeling. He knew it. It meant things were beginning to fall into place. If he didn't push it, tease at it, it would happen.

It wasn't that the past couple of days had given him any final enlightenment. It had confirmed what he had known, had given him family bits and pieces, presented him with an inscrutable manuscript. But somehow things had come into focus. He knew now that the whole thing hinged on the attacks on Dawn, that understanding those would make everything else come clear.

He had meant to get in touch with Follett's old friend, William Fitzgerald, before this time. Saturday was not the best day for it, but he could begin the process, at least. He opened his morning mail and then set to work at checking major news magazines.

He was in enormous good luck. William Fitzgerald was on the staff of the third magazine Pedersen called, one to which he himself subscribed. Furthermore, the switchboard was operating. While he waited for the woman to check whether or not Fitzgerald was in, it occurred to Pedersen that he knew the name: William K. Fitzgerald. He had seen it along with two others at the end of feature articles; for some reason he hadn't remembered. Maybe because he was in Pedersen's mind still Billy Fitzgerald, school newspaper editor, sitting over a Coke with Max in a country drugstore.

Amazingly, the reporter was there. Before Pedersen could grasp that he had been put through, the man was on the other end of the line.

'Mr Fitzgerald, I'm glad I found you in. If you can spare

a few minutes now, I need to talk with you. You're not trying to meet a deadline?'

'I have the time.' The reporter's voice was impatient. 'Who *is* this?'

Pedersen identified himself. 'You've read about Max Follett's death, I'm sure. I've been told you were a close friend, at least when you were boys, and I thought you could fill me in a little.'

The response was not what he had anticipated. 'I was not a friend of Max Follett's.'

Something in the man's voice told Pedersen his impulse was to hang up. 'Wait,' he said involuntarily. 'Maybe I have the wrong William Fitzgerald. You didn't grow up in Longville?'

'Oh, I lived there. I knew Max in school.' He laughed. 'You have the right man.'

'You had some sort of falling out? You were good friends at one time, weren't you?'

'When we were kids. I didn't know any better. What is it exactly I'm supposed to fill you in on, anyway?'

'Well, I thought if you knew the family or even if Follett talked about them with you, you might have some notion as to whether they'd ever been involved in anything unsavoury, a scandal of any sort. I thought you might know if there was enmity towards the family. As a whole, that is.' Now that he had said it, it sounded feeble and far-fetched even to him.

'The only enemies they made were the people who knew what they were really up to.'

'Could you explain that, Mr Fitzgerald?'

'No, I could not.'

'You're putting questions in my mind. Is it only Max Follett you were angry with or all of them?'

'I didn't know any of them well enough to be angry with them. The only one I knew was Max.'

'You quarrelled?'

'No. I learned things.'

Pedersen considered. If he pressed, he might lose the man altogether. If he didn't . . . He made a decision. 'Look, we believe Max Follett was murdered. It's important that we know everything, anything, that might be even remotely relevant to that fact.'

There was silence on the other end.

'Won't you tell me what you learned that destroyed your friendship with Max Follett?'

Again the man laughed. '*Destroyed* it. It was never all that hot a friendship, believe me. Max just liked an audience. I served the purpose.' And the country druggist, Pedersen added silently.

'I—'

Fitzgerald broke in. 'Max and I haven't been in touch since high school, you realize. To me, Max is a dim memory, a smudged photograph in a high school annual.'

'That's a colourful description, but it's hard to believe you've been unaware of Max Follett's celebrity as a writer.'

'That. Yes. Still, it's like someone you knew so long ago neither of you would recognize the other.'

Pedersen refused to be sidetracked. 'I am appealing to you to give me any information you have.'

'Or you'll subpœna it?'

'No. I'm asking.'

'Well, I'm declining. I know for a fact that any information I have is irrelevant to Max's death. Maybe I'll give it to his biographer some day. Now *that* might be interesting. Now if you'll excuse me, Detective.'

As Pedersen opened his mouth to speak, he heard the receiver clapped down at the other end. Something in the man's manner convinced him. Short of subpœna, he was not going to reveal what it was that had so soured him on Max Follett. Or on all the Folletts, as the case might be.

*

Pedersen and Tate had sent out for sandwiches and stayed on at headquarters to talk out the findings of the past few days.

'Freda was tied up, anyway. Rehearsal. On *Saturday*. You're not cancelling any plans, are you, Ron? No need for that.' The sandwich and Coke had picked Pedersen up. He cleared his side of the desk, tossed the debris in the wastebasket and sat back. 'That's better.'

Tate shook his head. 'No plans.' He stuffed the sandwich wrapper into the paper bag and folded down the top before putting it in the basket. 'Well, I got most of the way through the manuscript this afternoon. Not careful reading, but at least we can talk.'

Pedersen leaned forward. 'What did you think?'

'Better than his last book, and that's saying something.'

Pedersen snorted. 'Come on, Ron, this isn't Book Review Hour. Save the literary criticism. Did you see any parallels that would have threatened one of our people? Or caused him or her to steal the manuscript—or, for that matter, kill him?'

'I called the two women back, the wives. They both said he'd threatened violence on a couple of occasions but had thought better of it. They'd never heard of any incidents like that with other women. Of course neither marriage lasted long, they never either of them got much past the honeymoon.'

'He didn't think better of violence when he was married to Florence.'

'No, but that was verbal. He didn't cripple her.'

'We're being too literal,' Pedersen said. 'If he was working straight from experience, there'd have to be some disguising of the material. It needn't have been a woman he *married*. I wonder if Dawn has read this manuscript. She might have ideas about it.'

'Maybe.' Tate glanced away. 'I was up there yesterday afternoon while you were busy reading. I stopped to see if everything was all right.'

'Was it?'

She said there hadn't been any more signs of anyone's disturbing things. She seems to feel that, whatever it was that set off that little spate of incidents, it's over and she's safe.'

'I wish I felt that sure. I hope to God she's still being cautious.'

Tate was immediately anxious. 'There isn't anything you haven't mentioned?'

'No. I just have this uneasy feeling that something's not right. We still don't know *why* she was a target. The destruction of the gazebo and of that piece of pottery were like warnings, alerts to us. And then the kitten—'

'And there was something—I'd say sinister if it didn't sound melodramatic—about that key being put back. As though someone wants us to know that we can put in all the deadbolts we want, but if he—or she—wants to get at Dawn, he can.'

'That's it. That's what worries me. Unless we have a full-time guard over her, she's vulnerable.'

Tate frowned. 'Maybe she's foolhardy, but *she* doesn't seem afraid any more. She was busily remaking that piece that was destroyed, the one that looked like a squash.'

'A gourd,' Pedersen said.

'Isn't a gourd a squash first?'

'Yes, but I doubt she had a squash in mind when she started shaping it.' He grinned. 'She's not doing a vegetable collection, is she?'

'She didn't have a gourd in mind, either. She said it was an amorphous piece, not representational.' As Pedersen glanced up, Tate said, 'I know, it's not Arts and Crafts Review, either. Those are her words, not mine.'

Pedersen shrugged. 'You told her the seal was off the house?'

'Yes. I finally remembered to tell her. She's up there tonight, sorting. She wants to keep mornings free for her pot-

tery and of course she works afternoons. You think—'
he hesitated—'one of us . . . You think she's safe up
there?'

'I don't . . .' Pedersen looked at the clock on the wall
opposite him. 'She'd be there now.'

'Yes. She said right after supper. Why?'

Outside a fire engine raced past.

'Fire someplace.' Pedersen sat forward, his face suddenly
rigid with apprehension. 'That pottery piece. Of course.
It's not a *gourd*. And that woman wasn't his *wife*. It fits. It
all fits. My God, we've been going at this ass-backward. I
know why Billy Fitzgerald dropped Max and what all those
attacks on Dawn were all about. I know who killed Max
Follett.' He stood up and grabbed for his coat.

Another fire truck screamed past.

'And—my God! Let's get up there—and fast! Fast!'

CHAPTER 25

They spotted it before they reached the top of the hill, the
growing smudge of crimson that coloured the darkening
sky. Ahead a fire engine gleamed red in their headlights.
Behind a siren screamed as another streaked by.

Pedersen had not yet spoken.

'What is it, Carl? Oh my God, we're too late!'

'Maybe not.' His voice was a growl. The car roared up
the hill. Sweeping around the corner on two wheels, Pedersen took the last hill and screeched to a stop before Perry
Devane's house. Beyond them, the hoses were already in
place.

'There's someone in there!' Pedersen barked.

A fireman swung around and thrust one finger towards
Perry. 'No. The lady says it's vacant.'

'I tell you!' Pedersen raised his voice to a shout. 'I tell

you! The sister of the man who lived there—she's in the house! Get her out!'

There was a moment of arrested action as the firemen turned to him in a body. Then chaos exploded. 'Try the side—you can still get in there!' someone shouted. 'Move it,' another voice shrieked.

'Let me—' Tate was struggling to reach the house.

'Get back, get back!'

'For Christ's sake, get back! We'll have to drag you out too.' Tate was shoved roughly against Pedersen.

Perry stood stricken. Pedersen took Tate's arm and firmly walked him to where she stood. 'Your house may go. If there's anything you want, better get it out.' She stood rooted. He took her arm. 'Now! Before it's too late.'

She turned her white face to him. 'Dawn's in there?'

He shook her. 'Did you hear what I said?'

Her eyes focused on him as if she were awakening. 'My manuscript. I have a book almost finished.'

Pedersen nodded to Tate. 'Give her a hand, Ron. You can't do anything here. They'll get Dawn out.'

As he spoke, a shout went up. 'There. They have her, Ron. She's walking out, she's OK. Get your manuscript, Miss Devane, and close your windows—they'll turn the hoses over here now.'

Ronald Tate threw a desperate glance behind him as Pedersen shouldered his way to a fire-fighter who was emerging from the side door of the house. Beside the fireman, Dawn was taking small, careful steps.

He said, 'She was all huddled down near the door. She must have run away from the fire. She's suffering from shock.'

'I'll take it from here.' Pedersen took her arm gently and moved her away from the building. 'Dawn,' he said, 'you found the manuscript.'

She looked up at him, her smoke-smudged face rigid with dislike. 'I was burning it. The *bastard*. He wrote it all in that book. He was going to tell everyone about me, about how he hated me.'

He waited.

'I couldn't live. I couldn't do anything. Everything I did, he hated. He laughed at me, the architecture, the pottery. My God, even at my husband. He spoiled everything for me. He wouldn't let go.' Tears began to make rivulets through the soot. 'And Sunday he told me. He set that fire that burned me. Deliberately set it.' She tipped her face back and looked directly into Pedersen's eyes. 'You can see. I *had* to do it. It was him or me. Me or him.'

'And the gazebo? The pottery? Muffin?'

She laughed, a bitter sound. 'Who knows, maybe with the gazebo I was punishing myself. But then when I saw you thought someone was after me . . .' She frowned. 'I don't even remember doing that with the clothes. But Muffin—' She turned her face towards Pedersen: it was piteous. 'I killed Muffin. How could I have done that, killed Muffin just to show you someone was after me? I'll never forgive myself for that.' Her dark eyes were filled with tears. 'That was *murder*, Detective Pedersen, it was just plain murder.'

Pedersen led her to the car.

AFTERWARDS

CHAPTER 26

A week had passed. Things had eased. Freda had, in her last midnight conversation with him, seemed to accept her mother's condition. She had settled back into her normal optimism, interpreting news from her sister in happier terms and focusing almost entirely on the production The Players was preparing. Freda was, Pedersen decided, constitutionally incapable of remaining depressed for long. He found her missing at mealtimes and in the evening, but his own spirits, as he scrambled eggs in the kitchen or ate a lonely hamburger, had risen at the change in her. Uxorious, just as she says, he thought as he waited for a frozen dinner to be ready.

He had discussed only the bare outline of the case with her, but on Sunday a rehearsal-free day had been declared and they relaxed over a late breakfast.

'Now. Begin at the beginning,' Freda commanded.

Pedersen nodded. 'You know, it's been hard on Ron. He'd begun to open up, to think maybe things would work out for him.'

'That's not the beginning.' She sounded cross. 'Don't worry about Ron, he'll be fine.'

'You always say that. All right, all right, I'll tell you.'

She sat back. Newspapers scattered everywhere confirmed their commitment to a Sunday tradition. The remains of their English muffins and an omelette sat before them on the table. The sun slanting in through the skylight touched the bits of apricot jam left on their plates. The last piece of bacon, which each had politely referred to the other, was growing cold and pale. Freda had just refilled their coffee-cups with the steaming brew.

'I've already given you bits and pieces. To put them together you have to understand what happened in the past. I've pieced together a picture from things Dawn's said and from things I finally got out of a friend of Max Follett's. I even called a druggist in Longville who knew the family. Anyway, I'd judge that the Follett parents were right from the outset a pretty tight-lipped, rigid, solitary couple. The mother—Emmeline Follett—had trouble conceiving, but after two or three years she produced Max. Of course she was delighted. She probably doted, thinking he'd be her only baby. They probably both doted. But, of course she, and her husband as well, decided if Max were going to be the only one, he'd have to be perfect.'

'Oh, of course. Right there, it sounds like an ominous beginning'.

'It would have been, but I gather he was a bright, rewarding sort of kid, so it looked as though he'd be everything they wanted.'

'If that's so, why did he turn out to be such a—didn't you describe him as a tormented man after you read his novel?'

'Yes, but wait, you haven't heard the whole story. It seems when Max was about two and a half, Emmeline discovered she was pregnant again. Except—' he paused—'it turned out to be an ectopic pregnancy. She discovered it by nearly dying.'

'Then Dawn—?'

'She came later. Emmeline was hospitalized for a while, the druggist said, and when she got out she had some trouble with Max. I gather the first trouble.'

'They used to keep people in the hospital forever, I remember my mother telling me. And Max was two and a half. Remember Carrie at two and a half?'

He gave a mock shudder. 'I do. Anyway, the doctor told her no more babies and gradually things settled down and their lives went on, except for those occasional temper tantrums of Max's that they couldn't understand and couldn't control. The druggist used to buy medical supplies from Max's father, so he got to know the family. He said he's seen a couple of those tantrums and they were real events.'

'Max was probably furious with her for leaving him, going to the hospital.'

'I imagine. At any rate it seemed to the druggist that they were harder on Max after that. Maybe they thought that was the way to handle it. But he said they expected an awful lot of him and he was a pretty little kid.'

Freda's face was set with anger. 'Three years old. Or maybe four. It's no wonder—'

'Oh, but wait.'

'Then along came Dawn. Doris.'

He nodded. 'Not, however, till Max was almost twelve. And it was a hard pregnancy, the druggist said.'

'She was probably worried she *would* die this time.'

'Probably. Anyway, she was half-sick and irritable and Max's temper grew worse about then. From time to time he'd go into a real rage. Break things. Shout. Scare them.'

'He probably hated the baby that was doing all that to his mother,' Freda said.

'The operative word is *his*. He'd been the centre of their lives. Doris was born and everything changed.'

'I wonder if by that time they really wanted another baby.'

'I don't know. If they didn't, it would have made things tougher all round. But Doris grew into a darling little girl. Apparently the parents did try to be fair in most ways. So when she was about five, they built her a gazebo—a little summerhouse to play in—just as they'd built Max a tree-house when he was five.'

'The gazebo that burned.'

'Yes. When she was going on eight, Max came home from college for a summer. He'd been working summers till then, but he was carrying a heavy programme and he wanted to do some writing and some advance work. By then, simply because he wasn't a part of the household any longer, I assume the parents had begun to focus on Doris. She was pretty and bright and *she* didn't have tantrums. Max didn't find himself totally supplanted, but I imagine there was a distinct change. His parents were probably as exacting as ever, that hadn't altered. And the druggist told me they complained about some of the habits he'd picked up at college, drinking for one. They were a very *moral* pair.'

Freda raised her eyebrows.

'Not by your definition. By theirs.'

'And then? Was that the summer—?'

'Yes. One evening Max and Doris were in the house

alone, the parents had gone off to some church affair. After dinner Doris went outside to play and Max supposedly went upstairs to write. The story was that Doris had taken a candle out to light the gazebo. She always believed that, although she couldn't remember any candles. From what we've gathered since, the truth was that in one of his moments of intense anger, Max set the fire. The day before he was murdered, he told her that. It's unclear whether he wanted to destroy his little sister or merely her gazebo; perhaps he himself didn't know, consciously at least. But she was in there, sitting on the floor out of sight and wearing overalls that caught fire. Her legs were burned. It was he who got her out and had the presence to throw something over her before she was burned worse.'

'How could he have done that? He must have been *right* there.'

Pedersen nodded. 'He probably wanted to watch it go up. But whatever he felt then, from the moment she was burned he became a devoted brother. Actually, he became more like another parent to her, only—'

'I can guess. Just as demanding as his parents.'

'I suppose it was the only way he knew to be. But you're right, she could never please him. Her study of architecture, her husband, her pottery, her friends, nothing pleased him. And of course that tied her to him. Forever seeking his approval became a way of life. It was when she divorced her husband and changed her name and took up the pottery seriously that she began to try to break free—that's what all her talk about her finding herself was about. But Max wouldn't let her break free. By then he needed her.'

'His guilt.'

'Probably. His possessiveness. His hating change. Anyway, something must have happened that Sunday before his murder, there must have been some sort of confrontation. Dawn visited Max—she delivered zucchini to him and some other neighbours—but no one knows what went on, except that Max told her he had deliberately set that fire. That put the whole thing into motion. The next morning she took the little back path up the hill where no one could see her, unlocked the side door and slipped inside her brother's house.'

'And the pottery? You said you had your first hint of the truth through realizing something about the pottery.'

'Didn't I tell you? Ron and I kept talking about this piece of pottery of hers as though it were a gourd or squash. I suddenly realized what it really resembled was a hair-drier!'

Freda laughed despite herself.

'It did. It was—' he shaped it in the air with his hands— round at the bottom with a long neckline thing extending from that. At first glance it looked like a gourd, but it wasn't that at all.'

'Why do you suppose she made it?'

'I doubt that she realized it was the hair-drier. She said she was working on an amorphous piece, non-representational was the word she used with Ron. I think she was just so preoccupied—unconsciously, of course— with what she'd done that she couldn't help shaping the clay that way.'

'And the manuscript. You said that was important.'

'I realized we were ignoring the fact that there was a person in his life who had been hurt, if not crippled. Dawn. Doris. Her being hurt had tied her to him, and his guilt had tied him to her. In the novel, it's Luke's guilt that he deals with. After I learned more about what really happened, I realized the word "crippled" may have been unconsciously ironic. They were both crippled by that event. It may have accounted for a lot of Max's inner . . . torment, his becoming the sort of twisted, self-destructive man he became.'

'He never told anyone?'

'Yes, one person. That's the man whom the druggist put

me on to, said he'd been a family friend. After Dawn was arrested, I finally got Bill Fitzgerald to tell me the whole story. He and Max got together for a drink at Christmastime when they were both home from college. Max had one too many and confessed that the reason he looked so lousy and was acting so odd was that he had nearly burned his little sister to death the autumn before. Fitzgerald said Max admitted he deliberately set the fire. He also told the friend some of what he felt about the way his parents behaved to him, and Fitzgerald ended up disgusted with the whole bunch of them. That was the end of the friendship.'

'I suppose that's understandable.'

'I suppose so. The thing that struck me as odd is that in Max Follett's book, he predicts that the "crippled" woman will kill him.'

'That is strange. And yet he really set it in motion himself when he told Dawn he had set the fire.'

'And like Luke, he had just finished his book. The human mind is a funny thing.'

'What about all those things that happened to Dawn?'

'I don't know, it would take a psychologist to figure it out. She may have been reliving the gazebo episode and at the same time punishing herself, destroying a little structure she'd put time and love into. As for the twisted piece of pottery, I suppose she was trying to get rid of the hair-drier, make the whole thing not have happened. But the other things that she explains away so glibly as intended just to mislead us—you know, Freda, I think all of it was self-punishment. Especially the kitten.'

'It sounds that way. And what happened the night of the fire?'

'Apparently she found the manuscript. God only knows where, we thought we'd turned the place upside down. She sat in his study and began to read. In an uncanny way she recognized what he was actually writing about, and she began to burn it as she read. The fact that the publisher had a copy didn't seem to occur to her. She was destroying the trapped man who, at least in part, hated the person who had trapped him, burning the manuscript so no one would ever know. She was lighting pages and dropping them in the metal wastebasket and somehow, I suppose she wasn't really paying attention, the curtains caught fire and that room with all its papers went up like a bonfire. The fireman found her huddled in the hallway.'

'The way she must have been huddled in her little gazebo when he set fire to it. Poor thing. I suppose she'll have to go to prison?'

'I don't know. But she'd have burned to death if we hadn't got there in time, the fire-fighters thought the house was empty.' He shook his head. 'I'll never forget Ron's face. You may be right that he'll be OK, but—'

'I'll tell you why I think so.' Freda reached across and squeezed his hand. 'Remember the other night when Ron was here for dinner and I asked you to go out for a bottle of wine?'

'Yes.' He looked at her with suspicion. 'Was I being got out of the way?'

She laughed. 'No. But while you were out, Ron said to me, "You know, Freda, it was the same old thing. I was all set to save Dawn. I really felt for her, I still do, but that's what it was."

'He said that? He didn't sound upset?'

'No. He went on, "Freda, you'll think this is funny, considering . . . well, just funny. But I got an invitation the other day from Marcie Terpstra." I asked what sort of invitation. He said, "For dinner, spaghetti, and you know what? I was pleased as the devil. Ever since one evening during the investigation when I sat in her yard and had a bowl of ice-cream with her, I've had her in mind—someplace, sort of not right up front, but there. See how faithless I am?"'

Carl Pedersen grinned. 'What did you say?'

'I said, "Faithless to what, Ron? A fantasy?" He laughed and said he guessed I was right.'

'Freda, you're wonderful. Well, we can wait and hope. I think he's in a state of—what would you call it, readiness?'

'I'd call it that.' She laughed. Then she added thoughtfully, 'Dawn must have been the one who pushed Max Follett at that party, too.'

'No. She says not.'

'But there couldn't have been *two* people who wanted him dead.'

'I think there could easily have been two—or more. We'll never know.'

'I don't like that. I like to know. I wonder if we'll ever know what happened that Sunday she visited him.'

'Maybe,' said Pedersen, standing up from the table. 'Maybe it will come out. Now,' he said, 'what do you say we do something that has nothing to do with the case or with The Players?' He pulled her to him and kissed her.

'What did you have in mind?' Freda's mischievous glint was back.

'Not that, you lecherous woman, you. Well—' he kissed her again, more deeply—'maybe that, first.' He grinned.

Lament For Two Ladies

For my sister, Patricia Ploughman

CHAPTER 1

Rod MacMillan shifted the folders he was carrying under his arm, balanced the styrofoam coffee-cup and reached for his key. He had come to the hospital early; none of the social workers had arrived, his secretary was not yet in. He planned to run through his notes for the meeting that day and glance over the material he had ready for Jean to type. The book was going slowly, but by evening, with Harriet's—demands, he thought, then amended it to needs—and with the two kids, he found he was too beat to put forth the effort. Maybe this business of coming in mornings would start things moving again.

Halfway through his coffee he remembered Eugénie. He had glanced into the empty room on his way down the corridor the evening before and thought he spotted her; then, carefully not looking in again, had slid the door shut and gone on his way. If the hospital needed the bed they'd evict her; till then, since the room would have to be cleaned again anyway, he might as well leave her.

He liked Eugénie. He had described her to Harriet. 'She may be a bag lady, but she has a certain elegance,' he said. 'She wears a hat, not a bad-looking one, and carries her things in this tapestry bag that must be left over from some other life, and she doesn't smell. She looks good, actually; she's straight, no osteoporosis. Maybe it's good for the body to keep moving the way she does.'

Eugénie had latched on to the notion of sleeping in an empty hospital bed some time ago. By now everyone at Bay Cove Hospital knew her. She was a sort of joke: her slyness and ingenuity at slipping in and finding just the spot where she was least likely to be discovered and her dignity on banishment from that spot. Most of the doctors regarded her with mild affection. Not Lew Mawson, of course; to him she was no joke. Of course, considering what had happened between her and Mawson, that was no surprise. Rod still felt uneasy knowing that, even though nothing would surprise him, coming from Lew. Lew had always struck him as a strange guy, very strange.

But the others would rout her out and then over coffee laugh about her and refer to her as 'our Eugénie'. No one was quite sure how they'd come to know her name. Someone or other must have talked to her.

For that matter Rod had talked to her. As head of Social Work he'd been called upon to find out what she lived on, whether she had a welfare cheque. Who she was, for Christ's sake. He had gotten no place.

Eugénie had sat in the chair opposite him, back flat, hands folded in her lap. Rod asked her name.

Eugénie.

Last name?

Just Eugénie.

Rod had straightened in his chair, aware he was slumping. Chatting her up to soften her defences seemed out of the question. He went to the heart of the matter.

Was she, that is, did she have some source of income? A monthly welfare cheque, for example?

No, no welfare cheque.

What, then, did she live on?

She smiled, a distant smile with something of self-satisfaction in it. She managed.

Nothing further could be gotten from her. She made no explanation of her need for a bed, no apology for borrowing one. After enduring a few more seconds of her silence, Rod gave up. To compensate her for his intrusiveness, he invited her to breakfast in the hospital cafeteria. Eugénie accepted and ate heartily, her manners impeccable. After she had finished a second cup of coffee she rose, gathered up her big tapestry bag, shook hands with her host and left.

Rod finished his own cup of coffee, feeling distinctly bettered.

Now, remembering her in the unused room, he crumpled his cup into the wastebasket and rose. Good idea to move her out before things got lively on the floor.

There was a moment of indecision as he determined which of the closed doors was hers. Opening the door softly, he prepared to be gentle, shake her awake and, without fuss, send her on her way. Her tall frame lay on the bed, somewhat sprawled. Quietly he moved in, then stopped dead. Projecting straight up from Eugénie's chest was a slender knife. It had been efficiently plunged into her heart, and Eugénie was no longer with them.

Ann Potter Ford Koppleman had spent the evening with her daughter. Suzanne lived ten minutes away and now that she had finally determined what her major would be, history, spent a good deal of time at her mother's, making plans for the present school year and generally talking things out. After the long period of rebellion, then the coldness, their relationship had improved. Sometimes Ann felt that if her other three children lived in Bay Cove, as did Sue, things would have gone smoother with her daughter. No matter what effort Ann put into not interfering, she found herself focused on Suzanne simply because Suzanne was the only child there. Out of sight, out of mind, had a certain truth to it.

Now, preparing for bed, Ann noted once again how much she relished her solitude. Growing up in a family of five, having four children herself, being married to Ernest, a demanding man who needed attention at every turn, had given her more than her share of togetherness. Now she relished the peace that settled over her when no one else was in the house. Even the problems that had plagued her lately seemed slighter without others around.

Not, she observed as she sat before her dressing-table mirror brushing her hair, an old-fashioned habit of which she had never broken herself, that she couldn't marry again if she wanted to. Ollie had never given up hoping. And she

was an attractive woman. She leaned forward to examine
her skin. Clear, not badly lined. True, a facelift would
improve things, but she had not yet succumbed to that
vanity. She tipped her head back and checked her throat.
That was showing signs of age, but lately she resorted to
colourful wrapped scarves and high-necked blouses with
soft distracting bows tied beneath the chin. She sighed. Too
bad one couldn't look as young as one felt.

But she was a lucky woman. Ernest had left her more
than well provided for and now with her father's recent
death, she had come into her inheritance. Actually, she had
never been anything but well cared for, surrounded by
comfort. The house in the prettiest section of town, not
extravagant in size but more than adequate for her growing
family and at present an affluence of space, still pleased her.
She could not imagine moving into something smaller, a
smart condo, for example. The children had suggested that
she might be happier in a place with fewer memories, but
now that her widowhood had advanced into its third year,
she could not say the memories were painful. No, she was
satisfied with life just as it was. She had her house, she had
her work (she warmed at the recollection of all she had done
at Marigold House and to further the University Garden
Project), she had solitude. Peace. The children were fine.
Really, all was right with the world.

She creamed her face, removing make-up, then applied
a preparation which promised to decrease signs of ageing.
She had bought a strap to encourage a lean line at the throat
but on glimpsing herself in it had abandoned it. She had
pride enough not to want to be found trussed up like that
if she died in her sleep, an unlikely event.

She stood, casting a last glance at her figure in the
lace-trimmed silk gown, and turned off all the lights except
the bedlamp. Sliding into bed, she reached for her novel. It
was a fascinating tale called *Ironweed*, with a vagrant as a
protagonist. At first she had thought she would be unable
to read it, so little identification did she feel with the charac-

ter, but gradually she had become absorbed. After a while she found her eyes closing and she reached to turn off the bedlamp. Adjusting her pillow and pulling the blanket around her shoulders, she settled down to sleep, still on the far side of the bed, just as she had slept when Ernest was alive.

Stanley Potter discovered her.

They had planned to lunch. 'Let's meet at the Pelican,' he had said, 'we haven't eaten there lately. I'm ready for cioppino again.' They set the time for 11.30 to beat the crowd.

'Outside,' Stanley announced to the hostess. It was a clear, sunny day and tables were already beginning to fill on the glass-walled patio; he had come none too soon. 'And bring me a martini. Cold.' He relaxed in the balmy warmth of the Indian summer, aware of several eyes turned his way. He was a handsome man and knew it, but he was not vain. Glancing at his watch, he leaned back and waited for his martini. When it came, it was icy. One thing the Pelican knew how to do was make a fine martini.

At noon, still alone, he signalled the waiter to ask where phones were to be found. 'On her way, I guess,' he remarked to the waiter as he reseated himself; the fellow seemed to be lingering unnecessarily. 'Bring me another martini.' By 12.30, after another trip to the telephone, he was becoming uncomfortable about holding the table. The waiter was sympathetic. Too sympathetic. 'My sister,' Stanley explained. The waiter looked unconvinced and Stanley found himself wanting to insist. 'Must've got the wrong day,' he muttered. It sounded lame. He went ahead and ordered his cioppino.

Shortly after 1.30 he backed his grey Continental out of the parking lot. He was disturbed, uneasy. Looking at his watch he decided to detour, swing past Ann's. He cut around the Yacht Harbour, driving slowly past the boats with their marine blue flags, marking the hot little breeze and reflecting that if he weren't preoccupied with his sister, he'd be thinking this was the weather in which he most liked to sail. Gliding alongside the bay, noting the full beaches, not so full as they would be on the weekend, he turned off in the direction of Ann's. It was fifteen minutes before he pulled past the manicured golf course. A singular number of men his age seemed to be out. He wondered how they did it at this hour. He wound away from the course and down the hill, descending to the little road that led to Ann's place.

Her house stood mute. Digging for his key—like his brother and sister and Suzanne—he unlocked and went in without ringing. 'Anybody home?' he shouted. No one replied.

Walking through the house, he entered the living-room, went on into the dining-room and kitchen and then turned off to the bedroom wing. Her room was the big one at the end. The door was not quite closed. 'Anybody here?' he called, his voice more tentative now. An odd chill touched him. Then he pushed the door open and saw his sister where she lay in the last posture she had known in life.

Projecting from her chest was a slender knife which had been efficiently plunged into her heart.

CHAPTER 2

At the request of the hospital administrators, Detective-Sergeant Carl Pedersen and Detective Ronald Tate and their team arrived without fanfare. The corridor on which Eugénie's room was located had been cleared; with some explanation, a number of patients had been moved. Not enough beds were free to accommodate all those on the corridor, so the decision had been made to leave in place those who were bedridden, immobile, unlikely to move from their rooms. The corridor was blocked off to wanderers by strategically placed cleaning signs; and the crime scene team, along with the coroner's deputy, moved in quietly. With surprisingly little fuss surfaces were dusted, vacuums applied, measurements and photographs taken. By the time the room was ready to be sealed, things appeared essentially restored to normal in the rest of the hospital—shocked administrators and physicians back at desks and bedsides, flustered nurses busy once more with their duties. The body had been whisked away; at the unobtrusive removal of bodies the hospital was skilled.

Pedersen, standing in the empty room with his partner, surveyed what remained and turned up his hands. 'Our first bag lady. Who knows about bag ladies? Do we go down to the mall and cosy up to the street people?'

Tate shook his head. 'Did you see that knife?'

'Yes, a steak knife straight from Carson's. Label and all—he must have overlooked that. And no fingerprints.'

'The cut looked clean. You don't suppose one of the doctors sent her on her way?'

'I certainly hope not. That would complicate things no end. I'll be interested in what the post-mortem turns up.' He moved towards the door, looking at his watch. 'It's almost two. Let's seal this place and go talk with the social worker who found her. I imagine he's keeping himself handy.'

Rod MacMillan was in his office, the door open.

'Just a word,' Pedersen said. 'You found the woman?'

'Yes.' MacMillan seemed to be making his mind up about something. 'I noticed her in there last night and decided to leave her; closed the door, as a matter of fact. When I came in early this morning, I thought I'd send her on her way, let them clean the room.'

'Did you know her at all?'

'Not really. I knew her first name and that she wasn't on welfare. Since the—this happened, I've talked with one of the doctors. Jerry Cohen. A pædiatric cardiologist. It seems he ran into her in one of the rooms he uses for his patients and got a little more out of her than I did.' He smiled. 'So much for social work skills.'

'You didn't know her surname?'

'No, nor where she kept herself when she wasn't camping here. I've never seen her on the mall. Or at the public library. A lot of them hang out there. Of course I'm not down there very often.'

'There must be a community—they must know each other.'

Rod looked doubtful. 'I have no idea how much they communicate.'

Pedersen considered. 'Did she appear psychotic?'

'No, she seemed perfectly lucid when we talked. In complete command of the situation, in fact. But she may have had lapses. Some of them are in and out.'

'And this Dr Cohen?'

'He's just finished a cardiac catheterization. I know because it occurred to me you might want to talk to him. I called up there. Third floor.'

Dr Jerome Cohen was a tall, bone-thin young man with a mop of red-gold hair. Beneath his white coat he wore clean pressed jeans and below them white jogging shoes. He greeted them with an out-thrust hand and indicated chairs. His office was tidy and book-packed. He shifted an engagement calendar to the other side of his desk and leaned his elbows on it. 'Rod told me you wanted to see me. About Eugénie, I assume.'

'Yes.' Pedersen found that he was relieved at last to sit down. 'We hear you learned something from her, made friends with her.'

Jerry Cohen laughed. 'I'd hardly call it friends, that was one wary lady. But she relaxed a bit. Told me she'd been married. I tried to get out of her where her husband was, whether she had kids, but she clammed up again. But she did say she was divorced and after the divorce she wasn't well. I figured she'd had a psychotic break or some variation of one.'

'Did she mention hospitalization?'

'No.' He looked thoughtful. 'I—somehow I got the impression she wasn't hospitalized, but she didn't say. I don't know where the impression came from.'

'And you didn't learn her surname, either?'

'No. I asked. In fact I wanted her to try to get on welfare. Rod had already talked to her about it, but she seemed to have let down her guard with me that day, and I thought I might have some success. She froze up at the suggestion that she tell me her name. You know,' he added, 'I feel bad. She had a certain air about her. We'd all become quite fond of her. All except Lewis Mawson.' He laughed again.

'Lewis Mawson?'

'Maybe I shouldn't have said that. Lew's a psychiatrist, head of division here. He considered Eugénie the scourge of the planet. It offended his sensibilities to have her crashing in his hospital. That's Lew, he owns the earth.' His tone was dry.

Pedersen noted down the name. 'Maybe I should talk to him.'

'You can't now, he's at a meeting of division chiefs. Forget what I said. That was cruddy of me. He just didn't much fancy her sleeping in our beds.'

'What about the rest of the staff?'

'They kidded about her. She was clever. Never attracted attention coming in. By now, you'd have thought we could've spotted her. That bag she carried. Her hat. But somehow she slipped in and suddenly she was just there, asleep on one of the beds, easy as you please.'

The phone on his desk rang. Pedersen stood up to go, but before he and Tate could reach the door, Cohen called them back. 'It's for you, Detective. Headquarters.'

It was the lieutenant. 'Carl, I've had one fine old time tracking you down. Didn't you tell me when we talked earlier that this woman was killed with a steak knife?'

Pedersen was puzzled. 'Yes, why?'

'Describe it.'

'Nine or ten inches long, narrow blade, black handle. The only distinguishing feature was that there was a little black Carson's marker on it. Unobtrusive, the sort of thing you'd only notice if you were washing it, I suppose.'

'Well, it seems you'd better get over to—' there was a pause—'224 Wallace Place. There's been another murder, same sort of knife, sticker still on it. There must be some nut loose with a handful of knives.'

CHAPTER 3

After he hung up on the police, Stanley phoned his sister. She had spent an aimless morning, unable to settle to anything, drifting from the examination of a newly arrived magazine on the house and garden, to the desultory preparation of a lunch with which she played but did not eat, to the attempt to remove a spot from a favourite blouse. Kay usually read when she was at loose ends, but since her husband's peculiar non-return from his business trip, she had been unable to concentrate on a book.

The spot wouldn't budge. She tried lighter fluid. Left over. These days she seldom gave in to her urge for a smoke. Lighter fluid was usually magical when it came to spot-removal, but today it refused to work. Then, cautiously, she tried soap and water, wondering if she were setting the stain rather than removing it. She was holding the blouse to the light, trying to determine whether the spot was gone or merely obscured by leftover soap, when the phone rang.

It was Stanley. She must come immediately; Ann was dead, stabbed in her bed as she slept. Listening to him, she looked at the blouse in her hand; it had begun to tremble violently.

*

For a wonder, Roy was at home when Stan tried him. He had spent the morning at the museum but had stopped off home to pick up a batch of samples he had forgotten that morning. Having skipped lunch, when Stan's call came he was seated at a table in the kitchen, eating a sliced tomato and feta cheese sandwich wrapped in pita bread, the colour samples spread around his plate. He had just decided on the grey-green—it would be a subtle backdrop for the delicate Japanese-influenced paintings he was mounting— when the phone rang. He didn't answer it immediately; in fact he considered not answering it at all. Finally its insistence became irritating and he reached across the table to pick it up.

He must come at once. Stanley had discovered their sister Ann stabbed to death in her bed.

Roy's sudden movement tipped his coffee-cup and a puddle of liquid slowly spread, darkening the greys and greens and browns of the samples. He sat staring at the squares of posterboard as though he had never before seen them.

Wallace Place was a private road, unpaved, that meandered down a wooded hill. The house, half way along the hill, had turned its back to the wood behind it, facing instead towards the vista below where careful planning had created an unstudied effect: Japanese maples, clumps of brightness that could have been wild flowers, a little dry stream, stone steps and paths. Broad living-room windows looked·out over the hill, and sliding glass doors fronted on a brick-paved patio on which several comfortable-looking chairs made of white-enamelled metal webbed with brown plastic were scattered informally as though a group of people had just risen and casually pushed them back. The house itself was low and long, one-storeyed, built of redwood that had weathered grey. It was a handsome building in a handsome setting. In its quiet and unpretentious way, it spelled money.

By the time Pedersen and Tate pulled into Wallace Place,

the family had gathered, clustered just inside the entrance hall as though unsure if they were welcome in their sister's living-room.

Pedersen took them in. Together they made a handsome group. Stanley Potter, the eldest of the lot, introduced himself. He appeared the most stricken. A good-looking man, dressed in a grey business suit, immaculate white shirt and dark tie, his face was white and drawn. In his glossiness he reminded Pedersen of some dimly remembered advertisement.

The younger brother put out his hand. 'Roy Potter.' In contrast to Stanley, he was slender and poetic-looking, with hair brushing the collar of his soft sports shirt, wearing snugly fitted jeans with a designer label over one buttock and sandals on his bare feet. He attempted a half-smile; he did not succeed.

Hovering nervously near the two men, the sister too extended a hand. 'I'm Kay Brennan, Mrs Brennan, Ann's sister. Are you . . . will you be . . .?'

'Yes. We'll be investigating.' He paused. 'This must be very hard for all of you.'

Her eyes filled with tears. Although she was certainly not out of her forties, a guess at her age was pointless. Her skilfully coloured hair was cut into a tumble of curls that appeared natural; she had removed her jacket, and her skirt smoothly emphasized the ungirdled line of her hip. Sheer dark hose and high-heeled shoes set off her fine legs. She had been crying, but the overall impression was subtly seductive. Even her face, flushed as it was with emotion, contributed to an effect of which Pedersen was sure she was unaware. He looked at her more closely. He wondered why, despite the chic clothing, the careful coiffure, the seductive façade, what came to mind was a lost little girl.

Pedersen murmured a few more words of sympathy and left Tate to accompany them into the living-room. He made his way back to the bedroom where the team was still at work. The body had not yet been removed.

He greeted Kramer, the detective in charge, and stood over the still figure. 'You know why I'm here?'

Kramer nodded. 'Harbison called. You had an identical MO on the murder of a bag lady this morning. At Bay Cove Hospital. He wants you on both cases.'

'Looks that way.' He glanced down. 'Somebody's leaving a trademark. Same type of knife. Same sticker—Carson's.'

Kramer nodded. 'I wonder if we're going to find more bodies around town.'

'He's democratic, at any rate,' Pedersen remarked. 'Picks from the social strata without discrimination.' Kramer grunted.

He looked around. Having just viewed Eugénie in her shabby blouse and jumper, with the worn tapestry bag and the tired hat the only evidences of individuality, he was struck by this body: the soft silk of the gown, now deeply stained, the rich bands of lace, the well-groomed hair and hands. And the luxury of the room. A champagne-coloured quilted satin spread had been carelessly pushed to the foot of the king-sized bed. Deep white carpeting stretched underfoot. A long dressing-table with strips of theatrical lighting was set against one wall. Jutting from another, next to glass sliding doors, stood a chaise-longue upholstered in white fur. It was the bedroom of a self-indulgent woman. He glanced back at her. A beautiful self-indulgent woman.

'How did the killer get in?' he asked.

'We aren't sure. No signs of forced entry.'

'She's alone? Was alone?'

'Well, we can't vouch for that, but she's a widow, the brother says. Widowed a couple of years ago and has lived here by herself since.'

'No alarm system?'

'There is one. Apparently she didn't turn it on at night. Only when she went out.'

Pedersen snorted in disgust. 'That makes a lot of sense. I wonder if she had a man. A lover. Someone who had a key or was here last night.'

'The bed—' Kramer began, but Pedersen nodded.

'Yes. Looks as if she was alone.' He sighed. 'Have you questioned the family?'

'Not really, yet. Maybe we'd better check and see who's in charge here. No point in my questioning them if you're going to be working on the case.'

'Right. I'll stroll in and ask about men friends while you check. I passed a phone someplace—oh, it's just out in the hall.' He paused. 'I don't think we ought to let anyone aside from the team see the sticker on that knife. Might as well keep the Carson name under wraps.'

'A lover?' Stanley was indignant.

Pedersen had put the question gently: Could your sister have been with a man at the time of her death? Stanley's reaction was that of an affronted son

Kay broke in. 'You don't know, Stan. Maybe she had someone. Do you know? Do you, Roy?'

Roy looked surprised. 'She wouldn't have discussed it with me. You'd have been the one she'd have told.'

Kay Brennan looked self-conscious. 'Maybe I'm wrong. She did say she was seeing a couple of men.'

'Ollie, I suppose,' Roy put in.

'Oh, Ollie. I didn't mean him.' She turned to Pedersen. 'Oliver Winter is an old friend of my sister's. He wanted to marry her when she was free—between marriages. I guess he'd still have liked to.'

Despite the fact that all three were distracted by shock, family relations and personalities were evident even in this small exchange, Pedersen noted. Stanley, conventional, protective of his sister, not too informed about her life. Kay, confidante of her sister, relaxed enough to be told about and accept the idea of lovers. Roy, the outsider? The detached one, of the family but not in it, the nonconformist?

'Your sister was married twice?' Pedersen asked Kay.

'Yes. She lost her first husband. The kids are his.'

'She had how many children?'

'Four. Their name is Ford.' Kay Brennan frowned. 'Suzanne lives here in town. We've called and called but we can't seem to get hold of her. Roy phoned the other kids, they're scattered all over the country. They're arranging to come.'

'Could Mr Winter have had a key to the house?'

'He might have, although I don't see why. She gave all of us in the family keys after Ernest died, and her kids, too. She seemed to feel safer knowing we could get in, I don't understand why.' She shook her head. 'It certainly didn't help. This happened.'

'Not just this,' Pedersen said. 'There was another murder today.' The thought that some killer was randomly stabbing women depressed him. 'It doesn't look good. Identical weapon and method.'

Three pairs of startled eyes turned towards him.

'Yes,' Pedersen said. 'The murders, of course, may not be connected. Or—' he paused—'they may be.'

CHAPTER 4

Pedersen located the daughter around dinner-time.

Suzanne Ford looked to be about twenty. In appearance, with her face free of make-up, her hair brushed back simply, dressed as she was in a blue jean skirt and long-sleeved white jersey, she might have been any student from the university. It was her self-possession that set her apart. She greeted Pedersen with a nod, waited for identification, then preceded him into her large living-room and indicated a chair. Her face was mildly puzzled. 'Did I park in the wrong place or something, Detective?' Her laugh was light, social.

The apartment she occupied struck Pedersen as luxurious for a college student. He accepted the chair she offered and she sat down opposite him. 'No, I'm afraid it's more serious than that,' he said gently. 'It's your mother. I'm afraid she's dead. She's been killed. Murdered.'

For a moment he thought she would faint; he half-rose from his chair. He had never grown used to telling family members of a death, never found a way, not after all his years on the police force. This girl with the open face and smooth brown hair could have been his own daughter; perhaps it was that sort of association that always troubled him.

She seemed unable to grasp what he had told her. '*Murdered*? But—*who*? Who would kill her?'

'There was another murder today with a very similar pattern. It appears to be a random killing.'

'But Mother has an alarm system. No one can get in without setting it off—it rings down at the police station.'

He nodded. 'She hadn't armed the system. It was turned off.'

She gave a little wail. 'How dumb. How could she have?' She stopped. 'Where is she? Can't I see her?'

'She—the body is at the morgue. You can see her, but you may prefer to wait till tomorrow when she's been taken to a mor—a funeral home?'

'Do my uncles and aunt know? And my brothers?'

'Your brothers were all reached. They're coming in—your aunt and uncles can tell you when they arrive. Your relatives have been trying to reach you all afternoon.'

'I was on campus.' Shakily, she stood up. 'I think . . . I'd like to call my Aunt Kay.' The surface sophistication had washed away. She was a girl in need of someone to take care of her.

'Let me ask you just a couple of things, then you can call her.' He felt cruel, deferring her phone call.

Obedient, she sat down again.

'Was there anyone you know of who felt animosity towards your mother? Anything happening in her life that we should know about?'

'Well, you see—' she looked away from him—'until

recently *I* felt animosity towards her. We were always fi— quarrelling, and I really didn't feel close to her at all. Then, suddenly, I'm not sure what happened exactly, but it sort of seemed to blow over. Lately we've had some good talks, and last night I was at the house till—oh, I don't know, eleven or so, talking to her about my plans.' She turned her face back to him. 'I'd decided on my major recently and I was pretty excited about it. History,' she added.

Pedersen glanced around the apartment. It had none of the earmarks of the usual college student housing. A long, low, black leather-covered sofa faced the fireplace; that in itself must have cost a small fortune, he observed. The bookshelves were not standards and brackets as he might have expected. Nor brick and board, certainly not that. A wall-sized walnut unit had been installed to house books and TV and, he would bet, behind some of those doors, a fancy stereo system and tape-deck. On the floor the Oriental carpet was so large that little of the hardwood floor was left revealed. Beyond, in a dining-room, stood a long walnut table flanked by matching chairs with seats upholstered in black leather and a long sideboard of some sort. Behind the pair of closed doors must lie a kitchen, at least one bedroom and perhaps a study as well. It was tidy, no clutter at all. This Suzanne must be a rare student. A recollection of his two children's college dorm rooms passed through his head; they bore no relation to this perfectly ordered apartment. Probably the girl's mother had a maid come in to clean weekly. Well, that family could afford it.

She had followed his eyes, her face blank. 'May I please call my aunt now?'

'There's nothing—no one else we should know about in connection with your mother?'

'No, I can't think . . . May I call now?'

'Yes. I'll wait till you get her.' As she began to dial, he asked one more question. 'Was your mother seeing a man? Or men?'

She put down the receiver. 'Just Ollie now and then—

Oliver Winter. He's an old family friend. Does he know? He'll be—' She left the sentence unfinished and redialled her number. 'Aunt Kay,' she said, and began to cry. 'Can you come over?' She nodded a couple of times. 'Yes. No, I'll be all right. Just come.'

She turned to Pedersen, rubbing at her face with a crumpled tissue from her skirt pocket. 'She was just on the way to my uncle's. She has to stop for a minute, then she'll come. She's been trying to find me. All afternoon.' She added, 'Oh, and Jed.'

Pedersen stared at her. 'And Jed?'

'I remembered while I was talking to Aunt Kay. Mother saw a man named Jed. It's Jedediah or something. He's younger, about fifteen years younger. I think she met him at a meeting of hospital benefactors. He works there.'

'Does he have a last name?'

'He must, mustn't he?' She hesitated. 'I'm not sure, I think it's Mason, but I'm not sure. It begins with M.'

'And she went places with him, saw him socially?'

'He sort of had a crush on her. Actually he'd be better for someone my age, but he hung around a lot. I'd run into him having drinks with her over there or they'd go out to dinner. I don't think there was anything going on. Maybe with Ollie, but not with him. It just flattered her to have a younger man so interested, at least that's what I think.'

'It won't hurt to talk to him. She may have said something to him.'

'You know,' she said, 'you don't have to wait. Aunt Kay'll be here any minute.'

'You'll be all right alone? Isn't there someone in the building you could call to come stay with you?'

'No. I'll be OK. You know, all sorts of questions keep popping into my mind and then out again. But I can wait to ask them. Oh. How was she—' she covered her mouth with her hand for a moment—'killed? You didn't say. Did you?'

'She was stabbed.'

'Was it . . . quick?'

'I imagine very quick.'

'She wasn't—' She couldn't say it.

'So far as we could see, she was undisturbed. Not raped. Of course we won't be sure till post-mortem results are in, but we think she wasn't touched.'

She relaxed slightly. 'That's good at least, isn't it?'

'Yes. It is. And I don't think she suffered.' He rose and stood hesitating. 'I guess I will be on my way then, if you're going to be all right. You'll feel better when your aunt gets here.'

She swallowed, her eyes brimming again. 'Thank you, Detective—'

'Pedersen. I'll be in touch with you again when you're feeling a little better.'

She walked to the door with him, polite to the end. This was a well-brought up girl. He nodded to her and heard the door close behind him.

Stanley came to the door.

'I can only stay a minute, Stan,' Kay said as she entered. 'I'm on my way to Sue's. That detective's told her.'

'It won't take long.' Stanley preceded her into the living-room.

Kay, pausing in the doorway, reacted as she always did in the face of the plum-coloured velvet sofas forming an L before the unused fireplace, the pair of beige-upholstered tub chairs facing the large glass-topped coffee table with its neatly aligned glossy magazines, its oversized cigarette lighter. 'You know, Stan,' she said, 'this place does look like the lounge off a board room. Why don't you have someone re-do it?' Immediately she was ashamed, both for saying such a thing at a time like this and for even noticing. Stan just needed a woman, poor guy. 'I'm sorry,' she said.

But his face grew grim. 'We are not here to discuss my living-room. It's a damn sight better than that ultra-modern pad of yours, I can tell you.'

'I am sorry, Stan. We're all edgy.' She seated herself in one of the tub chairs and changed the subject. 'Thank God Mother and Dad aren't here to know about all this.' As she said it, she felt the tug that mention of her mother always produced. Although she spoke of her familiarity, it was ever there, just as Ann had sensed. She had never known her mother, even for a day.

There was a silence. Stanley broke it. 'You're in a hurry, let's get on with it,' he said, more brusquely than he meant. 'The point is that there are certain things—family things and more recent ones—that we have to decide about. Ann didn't just die, she was—well, you know the papers'll dig up every last thing any of us has done in the past twenty years. We have to get together on this and decide what we tell them and what we don't.'

Roy spoke, his voice reasonable. 'You haven't done anything to be uneasy about.'

'You haven't done *anything*, Stan. Except in relation to your work,' Kay said. 'Isn't it enough that we have to—' unexpectedly, her voice broke—'cope with Ann's death, without all this other stuff? And you *haven't* done anything. You never do anything.'

Roy leaned towards her. 'Don't, Kay.'

'Well, I mean—he doesn't.'

'I didn't mean me,' Stan said drily. 'And I don't need an appraisal of my behaviour. You know what I'm talking about, both of you. There are just certain things we oughtn't to publish and we should get together on them.'

Roy smiled faintly. 'Get our stories straight, like a bunch of criminals?'

'I don't—' Stan began.

Roy waved a hand. 'I know. Just a bad attempt at humour. I, for one, shall be a model of brotherly caution and circumspection,' he said. He shrugged. 'Actually, I always am. No one's going to be investigating my personal affairs. And your business is doing well now, Stan—there's nothing there.'

Kay looked from one brother to the other, her face blank. 'Do you mean *me*?'

Stanley shook his head impatiently. 'I mean all of us. You know what family relationships are better left undiscussed. And I think we should all tread gently for a while, present a totally conventional façade.'

'You do mean me,' said Kay slowly.

'Now don't go away mad, Kay.' Stanley stood and walked over to her, attempting an awkward hug.

She pushed free of him. 'I'm not mad, I'm hurt. We don't all lead the same sorts of lives, but that doesn't mean—' She stopped. 'I can't—I have to go. Sue's waiting.'

'Can't one of us come with you?' Stanley asked.

'No, I'm fine.' She picked up her jacket.

'Just remember what I said. That's all I ask.' He and Roy walked with her to the door. 'You're sure—?'

'I'm *fine*,' she said. Looking at her face, Roy thought: She's not. She's showing her age. Kay doesn't handle strain well. He watched her leave, his eyes speculative.

CHAPTER 5

Freda Pedersen was avid for details. Over drinks, vermouth on ice for him, gin and tonic for her, Pedersen filled her in. He sat with his feet on the hassock of their lounge chair, comfortably established before their fireplace, which was still adorned with a large basket of dried flowers. Gradually he was beginning to feel regenerated. It had been a trying day.

'The first one,' he said, 'was a bag lady, name of Eugénie.' He discussed his cases with Freda. She hardly needed to be sworn to silence about them; for a woman with an enormous interest in people, Freda was remarkably silent about others' secrets. He told Freda about Eugénie.

She shivered. 'Was she asleep when she was killed?'

'I hope so. We don't know. It would seem so.'

Freda mused. 'A bag lady named Eugénie. She must have had imagination. And enterprise.'

'Apparently she did, she seems to have been the pet of the medical staff. But the second victim was a totally different matter, a rich woman who lives out in Galurna near the golf course. Big house tucked away on a private road. Mercedes in the garage, carpets you wade through, a fur-covered chaise in the bedroom. Even her college-age daughter is set up in a pad that would fill you with envy.'

'What makes you think the murders were done by the same person?

'The knives. Identical steak knives from Carson's, store stickers still on them.'

'Carson's? Maybe they'll remember who bought them.'

'I doubt it, but I plan to check. Surreptitiously. We're keeping the Carson name out of the papers, just mentioning that there were identifying stickers on the knives.'

'A bag lady,' Freda mused. She was intrigued. 'You know that client of mine who lives in Peter's Hotel on the mall? Maybe she'd know her just from walking around down there. She's no bag lady, but she lives on a shoestring.' Freda, whose activities included civic theatre and chronic course-taking, had added another to her list: she had become a lay counsellor with the community's Counselling Aid Centre. Lay counsellors had no professional qualifications but were specially trained to work with older people— lonely, marginal, troubled people. Freda, who had just finished her two-month training period, had taken on a client and was working under supervision, seeing her client once a week in the woman's apartment. It was at times disturbing work and often frustrating. 'But,' Freda had assured her husband, 'I'm learning a lot about *myself* from the workshops.' She grinned. 'I had no idea there was that much to learn.'

'Oh, I don't know,' Pedersen had said. 'I'd say there was quite a bit to learn.' He had returned her grin.

Now he said, 'You can't very well discuss what I've told you with your client. Once it's in the papers and Eugénie's identified by name you might mention it, but I doubt that your client will know anything. No one at the hospital, not even the social worker and one of the doctors who befriended her, was able to get anything out of her.'

'Eugénie's more interesting than Mrs—Koppleman, is that her name?'

'Certainly more mysterious.'

'Why do you suppose the two women were chosen as victims?'

He looked across at her with love, taking in the dark cap of her hair, her petiteness, her body, slender but strong. She teased him, calling him uxorious (she had been an English major in college and loved words), and it was true that around her he felt relaxed, at peace. Home was the best place on earth.

'That, Freda,' he said, rolling the glass with its dissolving ice cubes between his fingers, 'is the sixty-four dollar question.'

'Why *were* they chosen as victims? Why?' It was 8.0 a.m. and Pedersen was in his office with Tate. Pedersen admitted it to himself: he was confounded, more confused as to where to begin than with any case he'd handled. Because of the distance between the hospital and Ann Koppleman's house, the victims appeared not to have been casually chosen, but selected. The differences in the women, in their lives and economic positions, contradicted that assumption.

At least the initial findings in the post-mortems had given them something with which they could start. 'Now why in hell,' Pedersen repeated as he sat looking at the report, 'would anyone choose a bag lady to murder? Do you suppose he mistook her for a patient?'

'If he got close enough to stab her, he must have figured out that she was no ordinary patient. And if he was looking for a particular patient, he could see she wasn't it.' Tate rearranged his long, lean body in the chair and removed his wire-rimmed glasses to clean them.

'The PM set the time of death at between seven and ten. If it was on the early side, the room would still have had daylight. He could have seen what he was doing—and to whom.'

'The likelihood is that it was earlier.'

Pedersen nodded. 'Yes. Visiting hours, all sorts of people wandering the corridors, nurses not paying close attention. But was he looking for *this* woman, the bag lady? How could he know where she'd be? *She* had to check to see which room was empty. She couldn't know where she'd end up, how could he?'

'And the Koppleman murder happened sometime between midnight and three, the coroner thought on the earlier side. What did the murderer do in between? Did he have a third knife?'

'You think we're going to turn up another body?' Pedersen thrust his hand into his left jacket pocket, where he kept the green jade worry beads he had bought on his and Freda's trip to Greece.

'Maybe more than one.'

'Jesus, I hope not.'

'How about if I do what you said—cosy up to the street people?'

'Talk to them? Good idea. But change into jeans and another shirt. And get a little grime on you. Your hair looks pretty good for a street person, but maybe you can pass. Better than I would. You're younger, they might open up with you.'

Tate glanced down at himself. 'I can't do it in a corduroy jacket and flannel slacks, that's for sure. OK. I'll see what I can get.'

'I've got several places I want to hit this morning, among them Carson's. And I haven't really talked with Koppleman's family yet, I was so busy tracking down her daughter last night.'

Tate stood up and glanced at the post-mortem report. 'You know, Carl, it's interesting that both wounds were right to the heart. Done with expertise, isn't that what Rand said?'

'A doctor? A med student? Sounds pretty far-fetched even for Eugénie, who was right there at the hospital. But for Ann Koppleman? What would be the reason?'

'Well, in Eugénie's case, it sure as hell wasn't that they didn't want her cluttering up their nice neat hospital rooms.' Ronald Tate moved to the door, then hesitated. 'Could there be some point of contact between the two—a mission Koppleman was involved with that Eugénie used?'

'Could be. We can check it out, we have to check out everything she was involved in. She should be a cinch, compared with Eugénie.'

Tate raised his eyebrows. 'Compared with Eugénie, anyone would be a snap.'

Carson's opened at 10. The clerk in kitchenware called the buyer, uneasiness on her face. Pedersen had given no explanation for his interest, but she seemed intimidated by his size and air of authority.

She showed the buyer the knife. 'Didn't we discontinue this brand?'

The buyer examined the price sticker. 'Oh, this. Yes, we did. When we had that Odds and Ends sale two weeks ago I put out the last of these.' She turned to the detective. 'You want to know when it was bought, you say?' She frowned. 'It could have been brought then or earlier when we carried it as a regular part of our stock. All the knives had this same sticker, they all came from the same lot. What's the problem with it, sir?'

'No problem. I suppose there's no way of knowing who buys such things?'

She cast a pitying glance at him. 'How on earth could we know that? If it was bought at the sale and put on a charge— would it have been put on a charge, do you know?'

'I hardly think so,' said Pedersen.

'Then if it was a cash sale, there'd just be the register receipt with the department number. No way, sir, even if we went through every salescheck we ever had. Sorry we can't help you with your knife.'

My two knives, thought Pedersen. Or more? He left them looking after him, puzzled.

Pedersen had set up individual afternoon appointments for the members of Ann Koppleman's family, leaving his morning free. As he made his way from Carson's and down the outdoor mall, he detoured past the little park that had become a hangout for street people. A small statue marked it, a tribute to a local figure legendary in the town, who had dedicated himself to the welfare of others. Someone had knotted a tie around the statue's neck. Someone else had placed a bunch of flowers in a jam jar at its feet.

Passing the little cluster that populated the park, he caught sight of his partner's tall lean figure. Tate had moved in fast. Something had been done to his hair, it appeared slightly greasy, and he looked unshaven, probably from the application of grime Pedersen had suggested. He wore old jeans and a shirt that had seen better days and on his feet he wore a pair of scuffed sneakers that were both holey and dirty. Pedersen wondered where he had got them. He was lounging on a bench, whittling a stick with a pocket knife, apparently not in search of conversation. Pedersen did not catch his eye and suppressed a smile until he was past the group.

He doubled back and around the corner to the public library.

The library was beginning to be busy. Pedersen waited until the librarian at the circulation desk was free and then drew the photograph of Eugénie from his pocket, presenting his identification at the same time.

She was clearly startled. 'You want to know if I know her? What did she do?' She leaned forward to examine the photograph. 'Is she *dead*?'

'Yes, and we're trying to find next of kin. She's a street woman. Do you recall her being in here? Would you know anything about her?

'I'm not sure, she looks familiar. Did you try any of the other librarians?'

'Not yet. Just familiar? You never spoke with her?'

'I doubt it. Helen—Miss Perrine—has moved all the chairs to the back, behind the stacks. Sometimes they come in and sort of doze back there, get warm. There used to be a woman who slept in the lobby, but that's been stopped. Ask the others, maybe even Miss Perrine.'

None of the librarians placed Eugénie, yet several thought they had seen her. It wasn't until he spoke to the director, Helen Perrine, that he had results.

She was a handsome woman with an air of efficiency and good nature about her. 'Come on in my office,' she said, and closed the door behind them. 'We do get street people here. Most of them come in to get warm; they're chilled from the night. Some come to read or pass the time, I suppose. It must be a dull life.'

'I don't know.' Pedersen smiled. 'I think I'd find it pretty interesting figuring out where to get my next meal or bath or place to sleep that night.'

She laughed. 'That sort of interesting, yes. But not exactly—intellectually stimulating. Though,' she added sadly, 'most of those people are past caring much about that sort of thing. They seem reduced to a sort of primitive survival level. And of course some of them are terribly deteriorated. From drugs or just from living on the street. It's really heart-breaking.' She ducked her head in an odd little gesture. 'I'm one of those people who see a broken-down old derelict on a park bench and immediately think he was once somebody's baby boy. I suspect the truth is that many of them were once abused baby boys—or throwaways when they grew up. But I'm chattering. You wanted to know about Eugénie.'

Pedersen brightened. 'You knew her by name?'

'Yes. I make it my business to find out what I can about the regulars, the ones who come here all the time. She was an interesting woman, for one thing because she kept herself so well. She wasn't dirty and she had a sort of dignity about her.'

'Yes, several people have remarked on that. Did you learn anything about her?'

'She was a reader. Once I asked her about her schooling. She had been to college, she didn't say where. But I have the impression that she did tell me something about herself one day—what *was* it? You know, I see so many of them, especially older women. They seem to like the library. They can go into the rest-room and wash up uninterrupted. There's the public rest-room in the basement of the Kettle House building, of course, but it's always teeming with people. Mothers changing babies. Teenagers. Our rest-room is usually empty.'

'You can't remember what you learned about her?'

'Now what *was* it she told me? Or—you know—' she stood up—'you're going to have to let me mull, Detective. I'll come up with it if I don't try so hard. Give me your number.'

He handed her his card. 'You can leave a message or tell the switchboard to have me call you back. Try to remember.' He added, 'It's important.'

'Is there a reason, beyond finding next of kin, that you're so interested?'

'You haven't seen the papers today?'

'No. I never read them till evening.'

'Did you notice in last night's paper reference to a vagrant's being found murdered?'

'No, I guess it got past me. Oh.' She put her hand over her mouth. 'You mean Eugénie? She was *murdered*?'

'She was found stabbed in a hospital bed yesterday.'

'She was in the hospital?'

'She wasn't ill, she just camped there. Slept in an empty bed if she could find one. The hospital was upset that it came out that she was killed there. But some reporter got wind of it and played it up. I imagine the hospital is doing its best to keep local newspapers out of the patients' hands today. By the way, you wouldn't know her surname, would you?'

'No, she just said she was Eugénie. What a strange thing to have happened.' She shook her head. 'Strange.'

CHAPTER 6

The Mission seemed an unlikely stopping-off place for a woman who sought out an immaculate hospital room with private bath. Pedersen shelved the idea of that visit in favour of persuading Ron Tate to make it his next stop. Also, if possible, he wanted to interview Lewis Mawson—Dr Mawson, the man who so objected to Eugénie's incursions into hospital life.

A phone call produced the information that Dr Mawson would be free to see Detective Pedersen at any time within the hour. Pedersen headed towards Bay Cove Hospital.

Entering it again, he was struck by the difference in the ambiance from yesterday's visit. No nurses with alarm on their faces or administrators with apprehension on theirs. Today the brisk impersonality of the nursing staff had been re-established and none of the hospital higher-ups were apparent. He made his way to the second floor.

His first impression of Lewis Mawson was startling: the man looked Mephistophelian. The pointed beard, the ears set close to the head, the slightly tilted eyes reinforced the image. Although, come to think of it, maybe he merely looked Freudian. Psychiatrists went in for those pointed beards.

'Detective-Sergeant, is it?' Mawson rose from his chair and extended a hand. 'You're in charge of the investigation?' His tone made clear his disbelief that a mere sergeant could be in charge of anything.

'Yes, and another related case.'

'Oh, the Koppleman murder. I read that the *modus operandi* was the same in the two cases. I knew Mrs Koppleman slightly—a charming woman.'

'Ah.' Pedersen seated himself opposite the physician. 'I'm glad to hear that. Perhaps you would know whether any charity work might have brought the two women into contact. Did Mrs Koppleman serve in some capacity in the hospital itself?'

Mawson smiled faintly. 'A pink lady? No. She was a contributor, financially, I mean, to the hospital fund. She was on the premises occasionally. I would doubt that the two had met, although I suppose it's possible. What bearing would that have on their deaths?'

'Possibly none. We're just looking for a connection of some sort. The victims appear to have been chosen, not just randomly killed, so it seemed to us there might be some link. We've just begun to investigate, but so far we haven't come up with anything. This hospital affiliation of Mrs Koppleman's seems as likely as any.' He paused and then went on. 'Dr Mawson, we understand you were very much upset at Eugénie's invasion of the hospital premises. Resentful of it. More than some other physicians.'

Mawson picked up a pen and tapped his desk with it. 'I'm sure I have no idea where you got your information. I admit that I found it reprehensible, staff looking the other way as they did. It amused them—' his mouth curled— 'they took her as some sort of pet. A hospital has a specific function. It is *not* housing vagrants.'

'Of course not,' said Pedersen mildly. 'I gather they were amused—at her cleverness in slipping past them and finding a room. And once she had used a room, it would have to be disinfected. I gather some of them figured she might as

well stay the night. I understand she was not a dirty person.'
At the other man's expression, he added, 'I understand your
position, of course. There was no *particular* reason for your
resentment?'

The other man gave a bark of laughter. 'Are you suggesting that I neatly knifed . . . Eugénie—' it was apparent that
he minded referring to her in familiar terms—'because I,
as you put it, resented her?'

'Hardly. Although there is one feature of the case that is
interesting. The knifing was extremely precise, the sort of
thing a physician—or a medical student—would be capable
of doing. Have you any thoughts on that?'

Mawson looked at him for a long moment. 'None whatsoever. I must say, I don't understand your line of questioning.'

'It's spontaneous, my questioning. I'm just asking about
what's on my mind. For example, it occurs to me that interns
and residents are under a lot of pressure.'

'Interns are always under strain,' Mawson said coldly.
'They're learning to function without sleep, for one thing.
But the teaching process is such that we weed out disturbed
medical students long before they become interns. Occasionally one cracks under the pressure but that's rare, extremely
rare. I know of no one in that condition at present.' He
glanced at his watch. 'If you don't need me any longer, I
have several things I have to attend to.'

Pedersen rose. 'Just one thing. Is there a Jedediah—
Mason, I think is the surname, connected with the hospital?'

Mawson looked at him coldly. 'It's Martin. Jedediah
Martin. He's our business manager. His office is on the
main floor.'

'Thank you. Nothing further. You've been helpful. I
probably won't have to bother you again.'

'Probably?' The man's eyebrows shot up. 'Well—' he
stood—'I'm glad to have been of help. I think you should
look elsewhere than on the hospital staff for your criminal,
however.'

'I imagine so,' Pedersen said. He paused at the door. 'But

we do have to find someone who knew precisely how to strike a single blow direct to the heart.'

Jedediah Martin was available. A well-built man of medium height, casually dressed, he fixed his brown eyes on Pedersen as though he were the questioner.

Pedersen introduced himself. 'Mr Martin, we're speaking to everyone who was at all close to Mrs Koppleman. We understand you were friends.'

'Yes.' He continued to direct his gaze into Pedersen's eyes. 'What the hell happened? I could hardly believe it. I didn't know the family to call and say I was sorry—oh, I knew Suzanne a little, but I couldn't remember her last name. It isn't Koppleman.'

'No, she was the child of an earlier marriage. We aren't sure what happened, Mr Martin. There didn't appear to be a break-in. That's what I wanted to talk with you about. Did Mrs Koppleman ever say anything to you about being afraid or about anyone's having a grudge against her, anything like that?'

The man looked down at his hands, which lay flat on the desk. 'Never. Nothing like that. She was a lovely . . . easy person, a person no one could have hated.'

'Someone killed her.'

He lifted his hands and then dropped them to the desk again. 'It must have been someone who didn't know her.'

Pedersen stared at him for a moment. The man seemed genuinely upset. 'You and she were close friends? Or perhaps more?'

'No!' Martin stood up abruptly. 'I mean, we were friends, but that was all. Not that I wouldn't have liked it, but she . . . she . . . you know.' He sat down as suddenly as he had stood. 'I feel a little ill. Give me a minute.'

After a while he raised his head. 'Sorry. It just hit me again that she's gone. Really *gone*. To answer your question, we weren't lovers. Ann said she wasn't ready for anything of that sort, and she felt our age difference was an obstacle.

That was ridiculous. She was only fifty-one and as young a person as anyone I know. These days fourteen years don't matter. I told her, but she wouldn't listen.'

'What were you doing Tuesday night, Mr Martin?'

Martin looked affronted. 'I was—I was at a party, as a matter of fact. Do you want the details? Names?'

'Please.' He watched as Martin wrote them down. 'Knowing what you do of Mrs Koppleman,' he said, 'what comes to your mind as an explanation for what happened to her? Did she get along well with her family members?'

'I don't think she saw much of one brother, but she and her other brother were close and she once told me that her sister was one of her closest friends. I remember she laughed when she said it and then she said they didn't burden each other with intimacies and that was what made their relationship so good. It was an unusual view of friendship, that's why I remember it.'

'Let me ask you something else. You know about the murder here at the hospital yesterday. Do you know of any connection between the woman who was killed here and Mrs Koppleman?'

'No. I gather they were killed in the same way, same sort of weapon. I don't think that makes for a connection between *them*. I'd say the killer was just going around choosing victims at random. Their only connection would be that maniac.'

'Had you ever seen Eugénie—that's the woman's name— here in the hospital?'

'No. Some of the staff were laughing over her one day. To my knowledge, I never saw her. And I didn't consider her bedding down here a laughing matter.' His young face became severe.

Suddenly Pedersen was tired. It seemed days since he had eaten breakfast. He stood up. 'I think that's all for right now. Suzanne's last name is Ford, if you want to get in touch with her. Thank you for your help.'

The man walked to the door with him. Just as he reached

to open it he turned, his eyes filled with tears, and Pedersen saw how young and vulnerable he was. 'She was a lovely person, Detective,' he said.

CHAPTER 7

Pedersen stopped off at the hospital cafeteria for a bowl of navy bean soup and a roll, then turned his car in the direction of Stanley Potter's place of business. His appointment was for one.

He had scheduled the visits with family members separately, letting them know he needed to speak to each alone; to his surprise, no one objected. Speaking to them as a group the day before, he had noted that they reinforced each other in their reluctance to approach certain topics. Despite the fact that now they'd had time to talk together and concur on an approach to his questioning, he felt sure that, taken separately, he could persuade them towards openness.

Potter was a partner—somehow Pedersen had gathered when he phoned that he was a lesser member of the firm—in a computer software distribution firm. The building was located near the water in an area largely serving electronics manufacturers. The building was not imposing, a long rectangle painted grey with smart black trim. On the lawn before it an identifying sign handsomely lettered in black read COMPUSUPPLIERS POTTER, EGAN AND CARR. Landscaping gave the building its only character. Several flowering pears spread their shaggy umbrellas over a rich carpet of manzanita, which was broken by several clumps of rhododendron. Lantana in a calico of reds and oranges was set in boxes against the grey of the building and a basket of white azaleas hung to the left of the entrance door. The display was more relaxed than most institutional landscaping Pedersen had seen. He wondered if Egan or Carr had been responsible; somehow it didn't suggest the buttoned-down Potter he had met.

The receptionist had been alerted. 'Mr Potter is waiting for you.' She indicated his office.

Potter's desk was clear. 'Detective.' He half-rose.

'Mr Potter, how are you today?' Pedersen seated himself.

Potter let himself back into the chair behind his desk. 'In better shape. That was a terrible shock, finding Ann like that.'

'It must have been. It was nothing you could have anticipated, I gather.'

Potter looked at him as though he were mad. 'Anticipated! I should think not.' He clasped his hands as though he were about to wring them. 'Ann the victim of—who knows what? Was there a break-in after all?'

'No indications of one. Mr Potter.' Pedersen settled in his chair. 'Tell me about your sister.'

Potter seemed taken aback. 'Tell you about her? What sort of thing do you want to know?'

'Just anything that comes to mind. I need a picture of her, how she lived, what was important to her, whom she knew.'

Potter shifted in his chair. 'That's a big order. I'm not even sure I can do that.' He eyed the detective uneasily. 'I'll try. Ann was—well, a good woman. She worked for several charities and local organizations. Both financial help and time, she never skimped on time. She was a good mother. Sue's the only one of her children in town, but she has three sons away at school, living in other states. She . . .' He seemed to have run out of ideas. 'She was a good woman.' His eyes filled and he brushed his hand across them.

'What organizations?'

'Well, there was the University Garden Project, that was a special pet of hers. And—let me think. Marigold House, I think it's called. For women who are abused, I believe.'

'Did she do any mission work?'

'No, not that I know of. She had some connection with the hospital, but I think that was mostly financial. I don't think any affiliation with a mission. She might have sent a cheque now and then. You know—' he hesitated, as though the introduction of the topic might be inappropriate—'we came into some money recently. My father—he'd been sick for a long time. Parkinson's. Ann may have made some gifts from that money.' He looked around him. 'I put my inheritance into the business.'

'Ah. That must make you a very important partner.'

Potter looked vague. 'No more than anyone else. We've all invested in the business. We had a rather rough period lately, a competitor in the area seemed to be beating us out for major orders. It seemed a good time to put some money in the firm, and it seems to be working. We've picked up on advertising, have a couple more sales representatives—we're holding our own again.'

'The money was divided equally among the children? There are four?'

'Yes, four. We were five, but our sister died about ten years ago. Cancer.' A shadow crossed his face.

'So this second loss is harder, I imagine.'

Potter was still for a moment. Then he sighed. 'Harder, yes.' He returned to the original question. 'The money was divided equally among us. I imagine Ann's will now go to Sue and the boys.'

'Let's talk a little about the people in your sister's life. I understand there was a man, an Oliver Winter.'

'Oh, Ollie. We phoned him yesterday after we left you. He was quite distraught. He loved Ann.'

'Was the feeling reciprocated?'

'I don't know what Ann felt about him. I always thought she sort of kept him in reserve, in case she should want to marry again. That sounds ungenerous of me, but he'd been around for so long. From way before she married again.'

'Tell me about her marriages.'

'She was married to a professor, man named Ford.

Romance Languages. He was the father of the four kids. About twelve years ago he died suddenly from a heart attack. Ten years ago she remarried, a man named Ernest Koppleman. A lawyer.'

'Someone she had known before her first husband died?'

'There was nothing going on, if that's what you're getting at.'

'And that marriage, did it end in divorce?'

'No, Ernest died. Another heart attack. It's no wonder she hesitated to marry Ollie, she must have felt her husbands were—jinxed. She was very broken up over Ernest, maybe because she was going through it all over again.'

'You know, Mr Potter, that another woman was killed and it seems evident was killed by the same person?'

'I know.'

'Can you think of any way in which the two women could have met? We feel there might be some connection, but because of the differences in the way they lived, we can't figure out what it is. Did your sister take care of any vagrants, involve herself in anything like that?'

Potter looked at him for a long moment. 'She couldn't have,' he said, his voice uncertain.

'You don't sound too sure.'

'No. I'm sure. Ann cared about people, but . . . She— mightn't she have met this woman at the hospital where she was killed? She did go by there often. She wasn't an aide or whatever they call them, but she was interested. Gave them money.' He added, 'Especially after my sister's death.'

'We wondered about that. It doesn't sound too likely, not if she was there as benefactor and Eugénie there as suppliant. Eugénie is the woman's name, that's all we've been able to establish.'

'I saw that in the morning paper. They were appealing for information on her.'

'We asked them to do that. The trouble is that the people

who might know her probably don't read morning papers.
Or evening ones.'

'Other street people?'

'That's right. We're banking on getting something from
someone. She may have confided in someone, told them her
last name or where she's from.'

'Didn't the doctors at the hospital know her? She—the
paper said she stayed there, slept in empty rooms.'

'A couple of them talked with her. They didn't learn a
lot. She had been married, but we haven't yet discovered
who her husband is—or was. She's pretty much an unknown
quantity, at least so far.'

Potter nodded. 'Maybe the killer was just striking at
anyone.'

'He could have been, but the distance between the hospital and your sister's makes it unlikely. And your sister's
house isn't easy to spot, he'd have to go looking. No, he
seems to have chosen his victims, whether or not there was
a connection. Let me just ask a couple more questions and
I'll let you go. Tell me about Suzanne. Was her relationship
with her mother a good one?'

'You don't think—'

'No, I don't think anything. How did they get on?'

'Oh, there was the usual mother–daughter nonsense from
time to time, but I'd say fine. Fine. Suzanne is very broken
up.'

'Any enemies your sister might have had?'

'I can't think of any. Really, I can't think of a one. This
must have been someone who didn't know her.'

'Now. Just for the record, what were you doing night
before last?'

Stanley Potter's face registered alarm. 'Why are you asking *me* that?'

Pedersen shrugged. 'I imagine I'll be asking everyone
who knew your sister that question. It's nothing—' he
smiled—'personal.'

'I was—what was I doing? This business has wiped out

everything else. Oh. I had dinner downtown at Blye's and then, let's see, I came back to the office for a little while and then I went home. Watched TV all evening. Oh, I ran out of cigarettes and went to the store. That's it.'

'Hadn't everyone here gone home by the time you returned?'

'Yes, that's why I came back. I did some paperwork and then took off.'

'Do you have a night watchman, someone to check people in and out of the building?'

'Yes, I signed in and out. My God, you don't think I killed Ann?'

'And your lunch date with her? When did you make that?'

'Oh, that's another thing. I called Ann when I got home. Set up the date to meet her at the Pelican. We go there sometimes for cioppino and we hadn't been in a while.'

'Was that usual, your having lunch together?'

'Not usual, I suppose, but we did it now and then. We were fond of each other,' he added defensively, as though someone had suggested otherwise.

'No special reason for the meeting?'

Stanley Potter looked puzzled. 'Special reason?'

'You didn't get together to discuss anything special?'

'Oh no. Actually, Ann said she wanted to talk to me about Sue's plans—Sue was there when I called. But nothing else.'

'I see.' Pedersen got up from his chair and turned to go. 'Nice office,' he remarked. It was. Grasscloth covered the walls, the chairs were comfortably upholstered, against one wall sat a couch with a coffee table before it and a pair of striking prints hanging above it.

Potter's face was wry. 'It must come off better than my living-room. My sister Kay tells me that reminds her of the lounge off the boardroom.' He laughed shortly.

Pedersen smiled in sympathy. 'You said yesterday you're a bachelor. Maybe it simply looks like a man's living-room.'

'Maybe,' said Stanley. 'I hope so.' He ushered Pedersen to the outer door of the office suite.

CHAPTER 8

Oliver Winter laid the newspaper down with an angry gesture. The story was the first he had seen and he resented it. Not only did it couple Ann with a street person, a bag lady no less, but it presented her in entirely false terms. She came across as an inconsequential society woman, pretty and idle. That wasn't Ann at all. Her substance, her— he struggled for the word—integrity were lacking in the description. He sighed. He supposed it was unavoidable, this sort of thing.

The thought that Ann was gone, irrevocably gone, swept over him again. At times lately he had felt something of a clown, the faithful ever-present suitor. He had felt she was, if the term didn't seem too ridiculous, toying with him, keeping him eternally on a string as though she might turn to him if nothing better came along.

And yet that wasn't Ann. She was honest, she had told him she didn't want to marry and that if he were willing to accept the friendship—she had called it friendship, he liked that—on her terms, she would continue to see him. Seeing him, she had conceded, included sleeping with him. He had accepted, but on some of those nights, waking with her warm body close to his, he had almost wept with longing, with his wish to make it forever.

Of course marriage was seldom forever these days, but he still thought in those terms: diamonds, matched wedding rings, bridal bouquets, honeymoons. He was probably too antediluvian to be believed, a real anachronism in these days of Significant Others, casual sex, two-career families, abortion, herpes and AIDS and the rest of it. Those things, the breakdown of tradition they represented, disturbed him but did not impinge on his life. And there was nothing casual about the sex with Ann. For one thing, they were mature people who knew their own minds, and beyond that, Ann had explained that she found intimacy outside of marriage difficult; he had always been sure she was, within the bounds of their relationship, perfectly faithful to him.

All that was now beside the point. He would never see Ann again, never be greeted at the door by her, never enter her bedroom, watch her brush her hair, see her shed her negligée, feel her come into his arms. He groaned aloud. For so many years—after her first husband had died and before she married Ernest and then during her marriage to Ernest—she had been a part of his life. Of course, during her second marriage he had been made to feel a little like a loyal family pet, but that was in part Ernest's doing. Ernest wasn't the most generous person in the world, despite his kindness to Ann's children. And there was that other matter that preceded the marriage, about which none of them ever spoke; some people would say Ernest had an—he wanted to think evil, but the word wouldn't come—a cavalier side to him.

He was restless. He had decided to stay away from the university today, unable to face the questions, the surreptitious glances, the pity of his colleagues, but now he wondered if that had been such a good idea. Perhaps being in his office—he taught no classes on that day—would have been distracting, even soothing. Too late for that. Tomorrow he'd pull himself together and return to campus.

For now, perhaps he could do something for Sue and her brothers. He had phoned Suzanne the evening before and learned they were all three coming in; he could suggest dinner.

He picked up the phone and set it down again, nausea gripping his gut. He sat at the desk, his head against his fist, for a few minutes until it passed. When it was over, his forehead was damp. He reached again for the telephone.

She answered on the first ring.

'Suzanne? It's Ollie. Have the boys come in yet?' They were men, of course, but he still thought of them as boys, remembering them roaring at high school football games, swanning about in tuxedos before their first proms, finally departing, one by one excited, for their respective colleges.

'We're driving out to the airport to meet them in a little while. They'll stay at Uncle Roy's and we'll be—' she hesitated for a moment and then went on calmly—'planning the service.' She sounded surprisingly steady.

'What about you, then? How about keeping an old admirer company at dinner? It'll be a real—' his voice quavered slightly as another wave of nausea hit him—'favour.'

She must have picked up on his need. 'I doubt that I can eat much of anything, but I'd love to come along. It'll have to be early, though, I'll want to be with my brothers later.'

'That's all right, we'll avoid the dinner crowd that way. How's five-thirty? We can go out on the wharf, eat beside the water. It may soothe us.'

'Oh, Ollie.' She sounded young. 'This is hard for you, too, isn't it? I know how you felt about Mother.'

He cleared his throat. 'It's a great loss,' he said, hearing the stiffness in his voice, but unable to avoid going on, 'for each of us.' He had always retreated into formality in moments of unendurable feeling. She knew him; she would understand.

She seemed to. 'It is,' she said with a brevity that suggested to him that she didn't trust herself to discuss it further. She changed the subject. 'I'm waiting for Detective Pedersen right now. He came by last night but he wants to ask me more questions. I'll be ready at five-thirty. I—' she hesitated—'I don't have to dress up or anything, do I?'

'Come exactly as you are. Sue, I want to tell you how *sorry* I am.'

Her voice thickened. 'I know. 'Bye, Ollie.' She hung up.

He sat looking at the receiver, wondering what he would do with himself for the time till then, three and a half hours away.

*

Suzanne Ford had barely composed herself before Detective Pedersen arrived.

She was upset by Oliver Winter's call. For some reason she did not understand, she had more family feeling for Ollie than for her uncles. Fond as her mother had been of Uncle Stan, Sue had always felt his mind was somewhere else when she spoke to him. And Uncle Roy's pleasantness was mechanical, as though the moment he left the room she was wiped from his mind. Ollie, on the other hand, for all his stiffness and coolness to others, listened to her and heard her.

'Miss Ford.' The detective was taller than she remembered, bigger. His face was lined and warm. 'Your aunt got here last night?' When he smiled, for no reason tears came into her eyes.

'See here, you're still pretty upset, you sit down.'

'No, I'm not,' she said between deep breaths. 'I'm not upset. It's just—' she laughed faintly—'that I'm upset.'

He laughed gently. 'Let's just sit for a minute. Your aunt did get here?'

'Yes. She was very nice to me. My brothers are coming, too. The twins and Jason.'

'Here? To the apartment?'

'No.' She was calmer now. 'I mean here to Bay Cove. They'll be at my Uncle Roy's.'

'Ah. I'll be dropping by there later. Perhaps I'll meet them.'

She smoothed her hair and adjusted her skirt. 'Well, Detective, what was it you wanted me to tell you?'

He gave a little smile as though something she had said amused him. 'Yes,' he said, 'let's get down to business. I'm trying to find out what your mother did with her time. Did she spend a lot of it on volunteer work? Did she shop a lot? Read? Listen to music? Have parties?'

'I beg your pardon?'

Pedersen smiled. 'Just tell me about your mother.'

'Will that help you to find her—the person who killed her?'

'It might. We might figure out where your mother met her killer, how he knew her. It might also help us to find some connection between your mother and the other woman who was killed by the same person, if there is a connection.'

'You're sure it was the same?'

'Pretty sure.'

'Well.' Suzanne tried to think. All she could remember was her mother standing in the hallway of her house, smiling, and then stepping forward to hug her hard as she left Tuesday night. 'She was a good person,' she said and then turned away, embarrassed. 'You know about her work with Marigold House?'

He nodded.

'And with the Garden Project?'

'Yes.'

'The Garden's apprentices come from all over the world to learn how to garden without all those awful toxic chemicals.'

'I gather. Sounds like a good place.'

'She typed at Marigold House. My mother could type.' She could hear the pride in her voice and her face grew warm.

'What else?'

'She worried about the street people.'

Pedersen sat forward. She had his full attention. 'How do you know?'

'Mostly by the way she acted around them. When we were down on the mall last week, I noticed it. She . . . *saw* little things I never even noticed. Once she looked as though she were going to cry. She was a very *feeling* person, Mother. You know,' she added after a pause, 'I went to see her this morning. At the funeral home—they call it a chapel.'

Pedersen waited.

'When Ernest died I was in Europe and by the time I came home it was all over, even the tears. And when my aunt died, I never saw her. Suddenly one day she just wasn't there.'

'Cancer?'

'Yes. For a while she was in her house in a room upstairs with the shades drawn and Mother taking care of her. I'd go along because I was littlest and Mother didn't like to leave me so much. Mother had just married Ernest and he was very nice about her being away all the time.' She was silent for a minute.

'Yes?' Pedersen said.

'I remember it all. My aunt just lay there, very quiet, and she would turn her head away when I came in. She couldn't eat, Mother would take trays up and carry them down again with a scared look on her face. And I remember when the ambulance came to take her to the hospital.'

He nodded.

'It's funny,' she went on. 'They let me see all that and then they said I was too young to go to the funeral. I suppose they thought I ought to be protected. My brothers were allowed to go.' The long-harboured resentment was still present in her voice, she knew. 'They weren't that much older.'

'You must have minded that.'

'I did. But later Ernest described the service to me. He was very sad, naturally. He said there were simply tons of roses—she adored roses—and all her friends were there. She had lots of friends. But I don't think it was right of them.'

'Shutting you out that way?'

'Yes. You need to say goodbye, even to see the—dead person, so it's real to you. Otherwise, it's sort of, I don't know, unfinished, I guess.'

'I think you're right. Today people have a better understanding of that sort of thing, they don't protect kids unnecessarily. I'm glad you saw your mother.'

She looked up at him, knowing the gratitude on her face was transparent.

'Did your stepfather adopt you?' Suzanne had the feeling he was asking merely to change the subject.

'Not legally. I didn't change my name or anything. But he was very good to me and my brothers. He was a sweet man. He died two years ago, but I thought Mother would . . . live a lot longer.'

'It's hard on you, all these losses.'

'Well, my aunt was so long ago I don't feel it any more. And my father, too, I wasn't eight years old. But Ernest. And Mother . . .'

'You called your stepfather Ernest?'

'Yes, my real father was Daddy. I never felt right calling anyone else that.'

'I can understand that.'

'I remember him.' She looked as though she were about to cry. 'I'm an orphan, aren't I?'

'You have people that care about you, your aunt and uncles. And Mr Winter. What about Mr Winter?'

'What do you mean, what about him? Ollie's been around forever.'

'You're fond of him?'

'I am. He's like another uncle.'

'You see a lot of him?'

'Mother did. But in fact he just called. He said we'd find someplace quiet where we can be off by ourselves and have dinner tonight. He's grieving, too. He loved Mother.'

He nodded. 'Was he resentfull that she wouldn't marry him?'

She looked at him in surprise. 'Resentful? I wouldn't think so, I don't think he was pressing her. Disappointed, maybe.'

'And then disappointed again when your stepfather died?'

'Probably. But they spent lots of time together. He wouldn't have seen much more of her if they'd been married.'

She saw the question in his face. He said, 'I suppose that

living in the same house would have seemed like quite a bit more.'

'Oh—' she was surprised at the carelessness in her voice—'he stayed over often. I mean—' she caught his eye—'in the guest room, I suppose. Although it wouldn't have made any difference to me, to any of us, if it hadn't been the guest room. Mother had a right—' she stopped and smiled—'I was going to say had a right to any happiness she could get, but that's such a cliché.'

'You said you've seen your brothers.'

'Not yet. We're going to the airport to pick them up, my uncle and I. You know, I can't *believe* we're in the midst of planning a memorial service for Mother. She was the most alive person.'

'You were with her until a few hours before her death, you said. What time did you actually go home, can you remember?'

'It was about eleven-fifteen. We glanced at the news on TV and then turned it off in the middle and I left. Mother was looking tired, I guess I'd worn her out, chattering on about myself. Sometimes I'm such a *child*. Now I wish I'd given her a chance to talk. I can't remember her saying anything except "Yes" and "That's good" and "Wonderful, darling." She was a good listener and I was all full of talk about my major—I had a terrible time deciding on one—and about the boy who influenced me.' For a moment she felt brighter. 'He's in history and he makes it sound so *exciting*.'

'You must be glad at least that she knew.'

'Yes, she'd been worrying about me. I think she thought I might take a year off to decide and she didn't like that idea.' Suddenly fatigue caught up with her; she felt if she didn't lie down, she would be ill.

As though he sensed that, Pedersen rose. 'This is enough for now. You should try to lie down before you go out to the airport.'

She smiled. 'You must be a mind-reader, Detective.'

He returned the smile. 'It doesn't take a mind-reader.'

After she had walked with him to the entrance hall and closed the door behind him, she bolted it and put on the chain. She looked at her wristwatch and lay down on the couch. Fifteen minutes till Uncle Roy picked her up. As she closed her eyes she realized that she never locked and bolted the door in the daytime.

CHAPTER 9

Kay Brennan pulled one stocking taut and felt the run slide up her leg. 'Damn,' she said aloud, feeling the tears start in her eyes. It was her own stupid clumsiness, but today everything made her cry. Unsteadily she sat down, pressing her hands together to stop their shaking. After a few minutes she removed her shoes and slid the stocking down her leg, taking off the other as well. Glancing at the turn of her calf, she thought: I look good, I know I'm attractive, I can tell by the response in men's faces when they see me for the first time. Then why . . . She shook herself and went into the bedroom.

That detective was coming by. It wasn't important that her hose matched for him, but later, well, at dinner she must look her best.

Bob, her husband, was at the moment on the East Coast taking care, judging by his enthusiasm, of several kinds of business. Over the past three years she and he had moved into what might be called an Open Marriage. Actually, it wasn't much of a marriage at all; they hadn't slept together, despite her tentative caresses, her careful selection of filmy nightgowns and revealing undergarments, for nearly two years. She hated the whole arrangement. It had been Bob's idea; he said with all his travel, it was the only sensible approach.

Coming up with a pair of pantyhose in the right shade,

she shovelled the rest back and shut the dresser drawer. She must straighten those drawers. Irene, the woman who had cared for her after her mother's suicide, had been loving, although as an adult Kay had realized that it was affection born more of pity than maternal feelings, but she had also been indulgent. She had never taught her anything, how to care for her clothes or her house, how to cook, anything. She wondered if her mother would have been different, more helpful. If she was depressed, probably not, and she must have been depressed to have killed herself.

She experienced a familiar melancholy when she thought about her mother. It seemed unfair, all the others knowing her at least a little. Stan had been ten when she died and even Ann, at three, had vague recollections of her. Or thought she did. Only Kay had none. Her mother had not waited to get acquainted with her. She had never understood precisely why. She had tried to ask her father, but she was afraid of his cold grey eyes; besides, she found that all such efforts left her with the sense that it had been her birth that had precipitated the act. She felt the dull ache in her stomach beginning and shook herself free of that thought.

Her new hose on, she checked her face at her dressing-table mirror and went into the living-room to wait. The room was immaculate. Each morning a woman old enough to be her mother came in to clean. Mrs Espinosa had long since taken over complete care of the house: she decided what needed cleaning, she purchased cleaning supplies, she had her own key and went to work as soon as she arrived, even on the mornings when the mistress of the house could not drag herself out of bed. She must have observed things, with an arrangement as unorthodox as hers and Bob's, but she never said anything, nor so much as cast a critical eye in Kay's direction. Ruefully, Kay had come to recognize that Mrs Espinosa regarded the job as a job—her mind was on *her* problems, not Kay's. Another possible mother-substitute cancelled out.

As she seated herself and picked up a magazine, forcing herself to relax, she looked around her living-room. It was rather *Architectural Digest*, she decided. Stan had referred to her place as an ultra-modern pad and he hadn't been far off. But she liked the eccentrically-shaped coffee table, the post-modern pastels of the sofa cushions, the low deep furniture, the overall white look of the room and the strong colours of the two huge abstractions that punctuated the walls like exclamation marks. She had planned the room, it was something of her own, unlike so much else that made up her life. She smiled faintly as she looked around.

Settling herself against the pillows, she turned the pages of the magazine, but she could not settle her thoughts. What had happened to Ann was too much with her. Although the police had not let her into her sister's room, she had seen death, and a vivid image of Ann lying amid bloodstained sheets with rolled-back eyes and slightly protruding tongue stayed with her. The thought of Ann looking like that made her feel slightly ill. She and her sister had always maintained a special sort of intimacy, chatting about family affairs and impersonal matters and only occasionally touching on those things closest to them. She was aware of the loss in an unsettling way. Except for the unexpected moment, she was calm, self-possessed, not swamped by her grief. But it was there, nudging at her constantly. She could not escape it.

She wondered what her brothers were feeling. Roy in the last few years had increasingly distanced himself from her and Stan, she wasn't sure why, and Stan of course had been so full of the business and its vagaries that he had little left over for anything else. She wondered about Stan, not for the first time. So far as she knew, there hadn't been a woman for several years; she wondered if in fact he had someone, perhaps someone he considered unacceptable, and concealed the fact. But why should he? Neither she nor Roy would care. Unless it were Ann about whom he had been concerned.

As for Roy, she was touched each time she thought of him. Going to strangers that way—but of course recently he had developed considerably more caution—she was sure with the fear of AIDS he was not picking up any stray boy he might run into in a bar. And he must be happier than he had been in those days when he had made his try at heterosexuality. She shivered at the recollection of his ghastly marriage and the dogged battles over the child. Now that he had moved away from that, he was more relaxed in a superficial way and a lot easier to get along with. But he did not impress her as a happy man. She sighed. No question, Ann had been the best of the bunch.

She flipped over the page of the magazine and confronted an ad featuring a woman modelling a fur coat who resembled Ann. She studied the photograph, her eyes filling unexpectedly. Impatiently she turned the page and touched her eyes to check the tears. She wasn't going to be puffy-eyed from weeping when that detective arrived. Although, she reminded herself, he was probably used to that, doing the sort of work he did. Maybe he even expected it.

As she blindly turned another page, the doorbell rang. She dropped the magazine and, picking it up, knocked an ashtray off the coffee table. She had to pause to pull herself together. Then she picked up the ashtray and went to the door.

When she stood up to see him to the door, she realized she was exhausted. He couldn't have stayed an hour, yet she felt he had been with her, watching her with those canny eyes of his, silently noting every gesture, hearing the words she wasn't speaking, for hours. She couldn't recall his questions—he had been excessively interested in how Ann spent her time, but otherwise she could not remember a single particular thing he had asked. Further, she had found herself defending Ann, as though somehow Ann were responsible for her own death, a reaction on her part that she couldn't understand. But she had been discreet, she knew she had been discreet. She hadn't revealed anything untoward, any of the things about which Stanley was so worried. She knew she hadn't.

She supposed he would go on now to Roy; he had already spoken with Stanley and Suzanne. The problem with concealing information was that their stories might not precisely match; she wondered what, for example, Stanley had said about where he was the night of the murder. That was one question she remembered the detective asking of her: where was she the night Ann died? But how could she tell him where she was and what she was doing? This business of a routine inquiry was more complicated than she had imagined.

She checked the time. It was after four. She had until six before she would be picked up; she had set the time early because she knew, after her dinner engagement, she would want to spend the rest of the evening at Stan's or Roy's, seeing the boys and hearing what arrangements they had made. Now, however, she could lie down, try to calm herself.

But she was so restless she finally got up, went into the bathroom and undressed and soaked in a hot tub for a long time, trying to ease the edginess from her body. Then she re-did her make-up and changed into completely different clothing. Silly, after trying so hard to find just the right shade of hosiery to complement what she had been wearing. But the effort was worth it. When she examined herself in the full-length mirror, she recognized that she looked quite as usual, no effects of her harrowing hour with Detective Pedersen visible and none of the turmoil she was still feeling. She clasped on her little diamond-studded watch and glanced at it just as the doorbell rang.

Giving her curls a slight rumple, she turned and went to the door to let Lewis Mawson in, grateful that it was only at dinner-time and not after that they would be together.

CHAPTER 10

Ron Tate moved the newspaper that lay across his knee catching shavings from the stick he was whittling. 'Say,' he commented, glancing down at the paper in an offhand manner, 'did you read about the old woman who was killed?'

The man next to him was too strung out to answer. About him hung an odour so palpable Tate had to restrain himself from holding his breath. A young woman with a small child to whom she was feeding a bottle lifted her head. 'In the paper? Somebody you know?'

'Not me, I don't know her.' He eased a couple of inches away from the strung-out man. 'It says she holed up in the hospital at night.'

'She was one of us?' The woman looked interested. 'What's her name?'

'I don't know if it's here. I got this paper out of the basket over there, maybe the whole story's not here.' He bent over the column. 'Uh, her name's Eugénie. Pretty fancy. Know her?'

'With a hat. I know her.'

Two others moved closer. 'Shit, we all know her,' one of them said. 'You must be new in town.'

'Yeah,' Tate said, 'just came up from Lewistown. You know what they do there? They turn on the sprinklers at night. There's not a fucking place to sleep.' He wondered rather wistfully whether he came across as one of them.

Apparently he did. 'This Eugene person, she wasn't around too long,' one of them contributed. 'I talked to her one day.'

Tate restrained himself. 'Oh yeah? Wonder why somebody offed her.'

'She didn't sound like she knew anybody. She had some money, though. Bought me a hot dog.'

'No fooling? Maybe she was killed for the bread,' one of the men said.

'She didn't have *that* much. I remember she counted it out pretty careful.'

Tate held up the piece he was whittling.

'What's that going to be?' the woman asked. Her baby had fallen asleep over the bottle.

'Think I know?' Tate grinned at her agreeably. 'Well,' he said, returning to the original topic, 'if she wasn't offed for the bread, for what, then?'

'She knew something,' slurred the strung-out man suddenly.

Everyone turned to look at him.

'What'd she know?' asked one of the others. 'Where the fuckin' treasure was buried?' He laughed appreciatively at his humour.

The young woman responded. 'Maybe,' she said thoughtfully, 'she was a plant. Maybe she was working with the police.'

Tate, the plant *and* the police, avoided squirming.

'But she didn't seem like she was on anything,' the woman added. 'No, I don't think she was working with the narcs.'

'Who the hell knows? A narc can be anybody.' The man who spoke glanced around the group uneasily.

Tate turned to the spaced-out individual, who had retreated into his fog once more. 'What'd she know?' he asked.

The man looked at him vaguely. 'What'd who know?'

'The old lady. The one you said knew something.'

'Oh. What'd she know?' the man said, slight interest stirring in his face.

Tate glanced at the woman with the baby and shrugged.

'Why're you so interested?' she asked. 'You into murder mysteries?' She laughed merrily at her joke.

'No, I just figured, her today, maybe you or me tomorrow,' Tate replied.

She sobered at that. 'We don't sleep in any hospital.'

'You know,' the man for whom Eugénie had bought the

hot dog said, 'she told me something, too. I just remembered.'

The imagination of the group was caught momentarily.
All heads turned towards him.

'She said she could have all the money she wanted. She
said all she'd have to do is make a phone call.'

'Why didn't she?' asked the woman.

'I asked her that. She said, "Not yet" or "When I'm
ready". Something like that. She sounded screwy to me.
Weird.'

'Probably having delusions,' said the woman.

'Delusions?' the hot dog man said.

'Delusions, delusions,' one of the others answered impatiently. 'You know, when you imagine you see things.
You hear voices.'

'No,' said the woman, 'that's hallucinations.'

'What the fuck are you, some kind of psychiatrist?' The
man who spoke moved several feet from her.

She laughed. 'Screw you.'

Tate's curiosity got the best of him. 'I took psych in high
school,' he confided.

It drew the response he hoped. 'Me, too,' she said. 'I
thought I was going to be a psychologist.' She shook her
head. 'No shit.'

'What happened?' he asked. He was touched by this
young woman, holding her child with love, coping under
who knew what circumstances.

'Oh, I ran away from home. My mother's old man was
always coming on to me, and I figured before he raped me
I'd better get out.' She glanced at the child and sighed. 'I
liked school.'

Take looked away, afraid his feeling would show,
and there was a brief silence as the group considered her
remark.

'English? Did you even like English?' one of the younger
men asked. By now there were eight in the group around
Tate.

'Well—' she laughed—'I didn't like *English*, but I liked to read. I still go over to the library when she's—' she indicated the sleeping child—'behaving herself.'

'Nice and warm in there,' one of the older men commented. 'Got those chairs in the back.'

The subject of the bag lady had been left behind. Tate made one more attempt. 'I wonder who she'd have phoned,' he mused.

Several blank faces turned his way.

'Phoned?'

Tate found himself growing uncomfortable. 'The old lady that got herself killed.'

'Oh, *her*.' The speaker looked Tate over with more care than before, suspicion in his face. 'You're sure interested in her.'

Tate forced a laugh. 'Maybe I am a murder mystery buff,' he said, standing up and dumping newspaper and woodchips. 'I've got to take off. See if I can get some bread. I need a cup of coffee.'

'You shouldn't drink that shit,' the woman remonstrated. Then she added cheerfully, 'Good luck. See you.'

'Yeah, good luck,' offered another. 'That corner up near Kettle House where they slow down to hear the music is good. They might part with a couple of bucks.' He turned away.

Ronald Tate ambled away, aware that he had been wiped from their minds as though he had never been there.

CHAPTER 11

Closing her eyes for fifteen minutes had helped. As soon as she heard her uncle's step in the hall, Suzanne grabbed her bag and was out through the door.

'You had to do a lot of unlocking there,' he remarked. He bent to kiss her cheek. 'You all right, Sue?'

'Yes.' Her eyes filled. 'It's going to be so *good* to see my brothers.'

He opened the door of the Toyota for her. 'Great planning, their meeting in Chicago and coming the rest of the way together.'

She smiled. 'My brothers are smart.'

He laughed. 'You don't do too badly yourself.'

She relaxed as she seldom did with him. 'Seventeen should be clear at this hour.'

'Yes, we'll make it in twenty-five minutes.' He pulled out and headed towards the freeway.

'I've been thinking, Uncle Roy. Do you think it was someone she knew?'

He didn't answer for several minutes. They swung into Highway One and then cut off into Seventeen. 'Who would want to kill Ann? Who that knew her, I mean.'

'I can't imagine. She never did anything to hurt anyone. All I can think of is some abusive husband who felt she'd interfered in his marriage. Her Marigold House work. But she always said she had very little contact with the women, she spent her time there in the office. Besides, if some man were mad at Marigold House, he'd go after one of the directors.'

'So you're guessing that she was killed by someone who knew her?'

'I'm wondering. What do you think?'

'I think it's rather fruitless, this talk—it just upsets you. The police will find out what happened. We can't second-guess them, we just don't have enough information.'

'You think it upsets me to try to figure out what happened, but it upsets me more not to. You must think about it, too.'

'I try not to.'

'I—oh, damn!' She began to cry. 'It's such a mess!' She turned her head away and wordlessly studied the scenery for the rest of the drive. As they pulled up to the airport, she turned back to him. 'It's not *you*, Uncle Roy.'

'I know.' He reached over and patted her knee.

Suzanne spotted her brothers as soon as she entered the terminal. 'They're in!' She bounded across the open space between them, her handbag thumping against her body.

'Oh, Jay, Meri, El, it's so *good* to see you!' She had always been closest to Jason, the one nearest her in age. She hugged him hard now. 'Mother—it's so awful, isn't it?' She was laughing and crying at once. She blew her nose and tried to hug both the twins at once.

'Are you okay, Suzie?' Ellery asked. He sounded young and uncertain.

She smiled. 'I'm all right. Just behaving like a baby, as usual. What about you?' They picked up their bags and began to move towards the exit. 'Are you guys all right?'

'Better now,' Ellery said. 'Where's the car?'

In the car Suzanne crammed herself between Jason and Ellery and Meredith slid in up front with his uncle.

They drove for several minutes without speaking; then Meredith said over his shoulder, 'We talked a little about a service while we were on the plane.'

'Did you decide anything?' Suzanne asked.

'Small, we thought. With the . . . murder and all, we don't want to turn it into a circus.' He turned back to his uncle. 'Was there an obituary today?'

'Oh, Meri,' Suzanne said. 'It's terrible to be talking about obituaries for Mother.'

There was a little silence.

Roy spoke. 'Yes, it just said plans for a service were pending. We didn't say what day. That way we can let the people know who really cared about your mother and bypass the curiosity-seekers.'

'Will there be curiosity-seekers?' Suzanne asked.

'Of course there will.' Roy's voice took on a tinge of exasperation. 'This was a murder, for God's sake.'

The harshness of his voice silenced them all. After a while

Jason said, 'We thought chrysanthemums and autumn leaves. Would she have liked that?' He's trying not to talk about the murder, Suzanne thought.

'Yes,' she said. 'Those rust-coloured ones. And yellow. She liked colour.'

'It was easier,' Roy commented, 'with Jane. She loved roses so. Ann didn't have any special flower she liked.' He threw an uneasy glance at Meredith as though he realized he had said the wrong thing.

'She *did*,' Suzanne protested. 'She loved spring flowers, daffodils and narcissus and . . . tulips.' She began to cry. 'Oh, *damn* the flowers. I hate all this. Talking about what to do after someone's dead.'

No one said anything.

'Well, I do. When I die, I hope somebody cremates me in a hurry and doesn't say a word over me. It's gruesome.' She ducked her head, then looked up. 'There I go, acting like a baby again. I'm just so—upset.'

Ellery clumsily slid an arm around her. 'We all are, Sue. Somebody has to make arrangements. You don't have to be part of this if it's too much for you.'

'Of course it isn't!' She shook herself loose from his embrace. 'I'm just behaving foolishly. What about people to speak?'

'I thought we'd just let the minister say what has to be said,' Roy commented. 'He knew her. Unless you want to . . .'

'No.' She shook her head. 'No. I suppose that makes it less of a . . . circus.'

They were approaching Bay Cove. Roy sped towards the freeway into town. 'I thought so,' he said gently, as they rounded the last curve. 'Perhaps later, when this has all blown over, we can have a small private service in one of our homes, ask the people who knew her best to say something.'

'Yes,' Suzanne said. It seemed to her that would be worse, like reopening a wound, but she understood her uncle's reasoning. Or thought she did. They'd probably never have that second service.

'I told Ollie I'd have dinner with him tonight,' she said to change the subject. 'He sounded so forlorn.'

'Not with us?' Jason asked. He sounded hurt.

'I just couldn't say no, Jay. We'll eat early and I'll come by right afterwards. He sounded so sweet and . . . I don't know. You know how he can be, sort of severe and sarcastic, even? There was none of that when he called. He just sounded lonely.'

'He'd like to have married Mother,' Meredith said.

'Yes,' Ellery agreed. 'He's been hanging around ever since Dad died.'

'And since Ernest died,' Jason amended.

'Maybe she would have married him,' Suzanne volunteered. 'Maybe she just needed time to get over Ernest.'

Jason looked doubtful.

'Anyway, he does seem disturbed—well, of course he would, but more disturbed than I'd have expected. I thought for a minute last night that he was going to cry. *Ollie*. Can you imagine it, Jay?'

'Hard to,' Jason agreed, 'he's sort of a stick. Nice guy and all that, but not the sort you'd expect to give way to strong emotion.'

'Did you cry, Jay?' Suzanne asked.

Her brother looked around uncomfortably. 'Of course, I'm sure we all did. Not publicly, but . . .'

'I keep finding that when I'm in the middle of something altogether irrelevant to all this, suddenly I'm crying. I just don't seem to have any control, I can't tell when it'll—' Suddenly she interrupted herself. 'Oh, when you get to my place, let me out, Uncle Roy. I don't want to be at your house when that detective comes. I've had enough questions for one day.'

'Is he awful?' Ellery asked.

'No, he's nice, but enough is enough.' She looked fondly

at Jason. 'I feel so much better now you guys are in. I may even begin behaving like a human being.'

'You're enough of a human being for me just the way you are.' Jason squeezed her hand. 'See you tonight.'

The Toyota drew into the kerb. Ellery climbed out and released her. She hugged him and then stood watching as the car drove out of sight.

CHAPTER 12

Pedersen had learned to look at rooms, not just for what they told him of their owners but with an eye to description for a later session with Freda, whose passionate interest in houses had communicated itself to him. The Roy Potter house was a surprising one, unpretentious, undistinguished, not at all the house of a man who had recently come into a sizeable inheritance and had probably always been well provided for.

The living-room into which Pedersen was ushered held only some wicker armchairs, a slab with a corduroy-covered foam mattress, pine shelving and a rug made of rush squares. But as his eye moved around the room, Pedersen was startled. The works of art on the walls lifted the room out of the ordinary. One large painting done in strong shades of orange presented a woman's head with a compelling expression of deep mournfulness. Another, a huge, strongly drawn black and white print, violently distorted a spread-eagled figure. A third was a meticulously stated etching of men bound like sheaves of wheat; and a fourth, a delicate watercolour, pictured a vase of flowers; the flowers were wilted almost beyond recognition. There were more. Pedersen looked with interest at Roy Potter. He presented the same bland surface Pedersen had earlier met.

Suzanne's brothers had been waiting for Pedersen; that was apparent from the way they had arrayed themselves in the room. The 'boys', as they were called in the family, were Meredith, Ellery and Jason, three names not to be taken lightly. Pedersen suppressed a smile: Ann Koppleman had with all her children compensated for her plain Ann, un-adorned even by an *e*.

At first glance, the boys—young men—were indistin-guishable. Each had well-trimmed hair; each wore flannels and a blazer for the occasion; all gave the appearance of the prototypical well-bred young Eastern graduate students they were. Jason and Ellery, they explained, were in business programmes, Meredith in law school. As he talked with them, they began to emerge as individuals. Meredith and Ellery were not identical twins, nor were they much alike: Meredith was considered, thoughtful; Ellery more spon-taneous. The youngest, Jason, seemed most visibly affected by his mother's death, although over all the young men hung an aura of depression.

'It's terrible for the boys and Suzie,' Roy offered. 'Frankly, I can't imagine who would do such a thing to *Ann*.' Pedersen looked up sharply at the stress on the name, but Roy had moved on. 'She was a giver, you know what I mean? She gave a lot. To everybody.' He shook his head.

Pedersen looked once more at the art on the walls. This mild-mannered man had chosen drawings and paintings stark with despair, hopelessness. He looked at the black and white print. And violence.

'You're a bachelor, Mr Potter?' Pedersen settled more firmly into the chair that had been offered him. It was remarkably comfortable for wicker.

'Yes, an ageing bachelor now. One early try at marriage. I'm afraid I've missed all my chances,' said Roy Potter agreeably. Hardly the usual bachelor, thought Pedersen, glancing at the sandalled feet, the hair curling into the nape.

'And your work?'

'I'm a bit of a dabbler. A dilettante. Actually, I had a rather good training in art history. I had a little gallery for a while. Now I'm working freelance with the curator of the

Bay Cove Art Museum. If he has something he thinks I'd do well, a show to hang, for instance, he calls me in. I'm working on one now. And I still collect and deal some.'

'You and your brother and sisters came into an inheritance recently, I understand.'

'Yes.' Potter's smile was unfriendly. 'You mean that obviates the necessity of my earning a living?'

'No, I didn't have that in mind. I—' Pedersen glanced at the boys—'I want to inquire into your sister's possessions. She wouldn't have had anything of value in the house—paintings, cash, jewellery—for which she could have been murdered?'

'She had a couple of good paintings. They were still there when I was at the house after her death. And jewellery. You must have checked that.'

'We did. Nothing appeared to be missing, but of course we haven't yet obtained an inventory. She didn't have a spectacular diamond or anything of that sort?'

'No, Liz has cornered the market there.' He smiled faintly. 'She has a bedroom safe behind a picture. Has that been opened?'

It took Pedersen a moment to register that the Liz to whom Potter referred was Elizabeth Taylor. 'The safe appeared to be untouched. It hasn't been opened yet. Did she keep a lot of cash on hand?'

'I wouldn't think so. My sister was big on investments. Every extra dollar went right into stocks and bonds.' His faint amusement came through.

Pedersen changed his tack. 'Can you think how she could have come in contact with the woman at the hospital who was killed the same evening?'

'*Was* she in contact with her?' Roy Potter stood and began to pace irritably. 'I don't understand the connection you make between the two. My sister had nothing to do with vagrants —street people, bag ladies. If she'd worked at a mission or something like that, I could see it. But she had nothing to do with any place like that. Why are you linking them?'

'*We* aren't, it's the weapon that does. I suppose you know nothing of her social life, the men she saw, for instance?'

'I'm sure,' Roy said, sitting down again, 'someone in the family has told you about Ollie.'

'Yes. I have yet to meet him, but I've heard about Mr Winter.'

'That's the sum total of it, I'm afraid.'

Pedersen looked at the three young men. 'You know of anyone?'

Meredith turned his palms up. 'We've been away since college, except for summers. Ernest was alive when we left.' He looked at the others. 'Right?' They nodded.

'You've made plans for a service for your mother?'

'Not yet.' Jason spoke up. 'Uncle Roy's going to help us. None of us has had much experience with—death.'

Pedersen was startled. 'You didn't return when your stepfather died?'

'I was in the midst of exams. Ellery and Meredith made it back in time for the funeral,' said Jason.

'And your father's death, and your aunt's. You must have experienced those.'

Jason looked uncomfortable. 'Dad, yes. And Aunt Jane—' he moved restlessly in his chair—'I'd forgotten that. I was still pretty young. But, I mean, we didn't have anything to do with arranging those funerals.'

Pedersen looked at him evenly for a moment. The young man turned his face away. 'Anyway, this is different,' he said.

'Different?'

He glared at Pedersen as though the answer were obvious. 'This is my *mother*.'

'Your father's death wasn't as upsetting?' The thought disturbed him.

'Well, yes, of course. It's just that we were young and Dad was away a lot of the time, working, travelling. We've had all these years with my mother. And she was *murdered*. That's different.' He looked as though he were about to cry.

They did seem like boys still dependent on their mother rather than like men about to enter the adult world of law and business, despite their having departed the family womb years before and gone to far states for college and graduate school. Pedersen's thoughts went to his own son. Was it illusion that made him see Matt as more independent? He was sure should Freda die—or he—Matt would be responding much as these young men were, and yet—somehow, he was convinced Matt would *manage*. Well, he sighed inwardly, they were managing, with the help of their uncle.

He rose. 'Who can supply us with an inventory of your sister's jewellery? And her safe?'

Roy Potter looked thoughtful. 'She was insured by Becker and Sons, all of us are. They'd know about the jewellery. And her accountant is Terence Randall. He's in the book.'

At the door, Potter turned his cool grey gaze on Pedersen. 'You understand we'd like this cleared up in a hurry. With no fuss.'

Or else, Pedersen thought. Ridiculous. The man was just expressing the usual concern for efficiency. But the feeling that he had been gently threatened did not leave him.

The message from the head librarian was waiting for him back at headquarters: *Please call Helen Perrine*. He returned the call; she had left the library for the day. No one answered at her home. Pedersen mentally shelved the matter and phoned to see if his partner had returned. As he put down the receiver, Tate walked in, his hair restored to its normal cleanliness, grime removed.

'*That* was interesting,' Tate said, seating himself. 'I had to acquire a whole new vocabulary.'

Pedersen laughed. 'You should be more profane, it wouldn't have been such an adjustment. Or is profane the right word?'

'As a matter of fact, the Lord's name is almost never taken in vain.'

'Did you find out anything?'

'A couple of things, neither of which tells us much. Eugénie "knew something" and a phone call she wasn't ready to make would have altered her economic situation.' He explained.

'Blackmail.'

'Sounds like that. I hung around that little Bennett Park for a while and picked that up. Then I tried down in front of Kettle House. No luck there. There are a couple of true psychotics that hang around Kettle House. One guy making those strange hand movements they do. How do you imagine he connects long enough even to eat, and where does he get the money?'

'Waxy hand motions and dull smiles.'

Tate threw him a puzzled glance.

'That's how psychologists describe schizophrenics.'

'At any rate,' Tate went on, 'then I moved down to the other end of the mall, in front of the bookstore. They weren't too easy with me and they were supremely uninterested in the death of an old lady. That crowd's younger, you know, mostly high school kids. I think they hang around swapping joints.'

'And other drugs.'

'Altogether, the day's work netted very little. Funny, at one point a couple I know walked by and looked right at me—I had a moment of panic, you can believe—but they never recognized me. Or registered that I was there, even.'

'We look right through street people half the time.'

'I wonder why. They're ordinary enough. There was a girl with a baby who seemed pretty together, not at all down, taking good care of the youngster. Though—' he looked past Pedersen out of the window—'some of the little kids on the mall are pretty forlorn. Barefoot, unwashed, trailing along or being ignored altogether. It makes you want to shake the parents.' He sighed. 'Undercover work is just not my bag.'

Pedersen laughed. 'I can see that. Let's work with what

you got. Did the person who told you Eugénie knew something say what she knew?'

'He was so strung out he couldn't put two sentences together. I don't think anything he said would be reliable, he just didn't connect.'

'Blackmail.' Pedersen was thoughtful. 'If Eugénie was blackmailing her murderer, does Ann Koppleman's death somehow tie in with that? Or did the killer just have a sheaf of knives and decide to do away with anybody who annoyed him that day?'

Tate rose and walked to the window. The gingko tree outside stirred slightly in an early evening breeze. 'Could Ann Koppleman have been blackmailing the same person?'

'Sort of ganging up on him?'

'But who? Who would Eugénie know that Ann Koppleman knew?'

'I suppose,' Pedersen said, tipping his chair back dangerously, 'the answer is to find out who Ann Koppleman knew. That's a lot easier than finding out who Eugénie knew. The only name I've come up with in a day of interviewing family is Oliver Winter, the devoted Ollie. And a man named Jed.'

'We could start with Ollie.'

'We'll have to.'

Pedersen let his chair fall back to its usual position. 'I'm going to check Helen Perrine again. Head librarian. Today while you were on the mall I visited Carson's, the library, the entire family one by one and Lewis Mawson. He's the doctor who didn't like Eugénie.'

'Some people put their time to good use.'

Pedersen grinned. 'Just what I was thinking.' He reached for the receiver.

This time he was successful. Helen Perrine, sounding breathless, answered.

'Miss Perrine, Detective Pedersen. I'm returning your call.'

'Oh. Yes. I remembered. Let me put down my things, I

just got in. Couldn't get my key to work and I had to run to catch the phone.'

When she returned she was calm. 'I remembered,' she announced.

'Yes?'

'It was a funny conversation. I didn't understand it, maybe that's why I remembered it. Eugénie was writing a letter— I'd better begin at the beginning. She came back to my office. My secretary had stepped out for a minute, so no one stopped her. She just appeared at my open door, knocked on the jamb and asked if I could lend her a pen and give her a sheet of paper and an envelope.'

'Was that usual, I mean for those people to borrow or ask for things?'

'No, but I'd spoken to her a couple of times earlier and I figure she suspected I had a soft spot where she was concerned. Anyway, I said yes and gave them to her and asked if she needed a stamp.'

'The library could go broke at that rate.'

She laughed. 'It's broke already. Besides, it was the first time anybody'd asked for anything. Then I asked her, as casually as I could, if it was an important letter. She smiled in a sort of—well, with someone else, I'd have said smug way and said, yes, it was going to be a surprise for someone.'

'That's all?'

'That's all. She took the stuff and went out. I peeked later and she was at a table, busily writing. Later she came in and returned the pen to my secretary. That was a couple of weeks ago, maybe a bit more. Come to think of it, I haven't seen her since. Does that help?'

'It may help quite a bit. Thank you. If you think of anything else, please call, even if it seems trivial to you.'

'Well,' he said, as he hung up. He repeated the conversation to Tate. 'That must have been some surprise,' he finished. 'It made someone go out and buy two knives the next day.'

CHAPTER 13

Pedersen came home exhausted. Freda, impatient to tell him her news, after one glance changed her mind. 'Why don't you just sit for a while, Carl?' she said. 'I'll get you a drink. Shall I put on some Billie Holliday?'

'Sounds good.' He accepted the vermouth. 'At what stage is dinner?'

'I'm in the middle. You take it easy. I'll yell when it's ready.' She bent to kiss him.

She restrained herself until they had eaten and then, carrying her coffee-cup into the living-room, she settled for a talk. The basket of dried flowers had been removed from the fireplace and a log blazed there. In Bay Cove fashion, Indian summer had ended abruptly during the night.

Pedersen sighed with pleasure. 'I feel about one thousand per cent better. Now let's have it.'

She laughed. 'Am I that obvious? Well,' she said, 'you won't believe it. Gertrude, my client, read about the Eugénie murder this morning and it turns out she knew her.'

'Knew her? Really *knew* her?'

'I suppose not *really*. By the way, Gertrude said it was all right for me to talk to you about this. It seems it was a sort of fluke. Gertrude sits in the lobby of Peter's Hotel sometimes. You know, it has that large window overlooking the mall and couches pulled up before it? Well, one day about three weeks ago she was sitting by herself there in the lobby, working up energy to go for a walk, when this woman stopped out front. It was obvious something was wrong, she looked ill. Gertrude had noticed her before, she sort of stood out from the other women that wander the mall. Most of them seem to be psychotic, Gertrude says, muttering to themselves and fishing in wastebaskets and shouting things at people.'

'That's because half of them, the young ones too, were let out of mental hospitals when the state made that sweep.' He grimaced with disgust. 'They were going into halfway houses. Non-existent halfway houses. So what happened?' She could see that the drink or dinner or her news had set him up; he appeared quite revived.

'As I said, she'd seen Eugénie before—she didn't know her name then—and she felt sorry for her when she saw her looking faint. So she went outside and invited her to come in for a minute and sit with her in the lobby.'

'She must be an unusual woman, your Gertrude.'

'She is. She's really remarkable in several ways. I wish I could tell you about her.' She paused. 'Anyway, after a few minutes Eugénie said she had dizzy spells from time to time, it was nothing. Gertrude was worried that she might be hungry, but she didn't know how to ask.'

'She'd have alienated her right off the bat. Eugénie was a proud woman. And?'

'You want more coffee? I can get the pot.'

'*Freda*, I understand that you know all about dramatic suspense from your years with civic theatre, but tell me what your client said.'

Freda laughed. 'All right, I'll get to the point. Gertrude said they began to talk. Gertrude's been seeing me because she's been so depressed since her divorce four years ago—she said it was OK for me to mention that when I told you all this—and they began to talk about marriage and husbands. Eugénie said her husband walked out on her. She told Gertrude it was just as well, they hadn't been all that happy, but it had been a shock to her all the same. She said in fact there had been several shocks connected with his leaving, but she didn't say that. Gertrude thought he must have had another woman or got custody of the children.'

'Did she say when she was divorced?'

'No. Gertrude asked, but Eugénie just shrugged off the question. Gertrude's seen her around the mall only the last couple of years, so she figured it was around then, two years ago.'

'The autopsy showed she was in her mid-fifties. There couldn't have been any young children to fight over.'

Freda leaned back, stretching her legs on the sofa. 'That fire looks wonderful. I'm glad it's cold again. So maybe it was another woman, it usually is. I only know what she told me.' She glanced towards the window. 'It gets dark so early now. A month ago I would have been working in the garden at this hour.'

'We're not even on Standard Time yet.' He sighed. 'We're getting the same stuff over and over on Eugénie. She must have had a certain body of information she didn't mind sharing with other people and that was it. Your client didn't by any chance learn her last name?'

'No, but she did say one other thing. Eugénie told her she'd grown up in this town. She commented on how much Bay Cove had changed. Then she laughed and said she guessed she'd changed, too.'

'That's interesting. You saw we had the papers publish her photograph today, maybe we'll get something. There must be someone who'd know her if she grew up here.'

'You'd think so. Unless she's so changed. But that photograph just showed her face, she didn't look like a bag lady, she looked like just anybody. Actually, from that picture, I'd say she was pretty good-looking.'

'She was pleasant-looking. All those people at the hospital wouldn't have fallen for her the way they did if she weren't. Although I think what they liked most was her gall—her gumption. I wonder what drew her to the hospital, it'd seem there'd have to be something.'

'Maybe she went there for emergency treatment and noticed empty beds. Or was taken there. She could have had a dizzy spell and fainted. Would she have had to show ID if she were being treated?'

'No, she'd have been treated as a transient. She certainly didn't have medical insurance.'

'Wouldn't doctors who treated her have spotted her when she showed up in a bed later?'

'From Emergency? How would they? They're always in such chaos there, I doubt that they recognize anybody later.'

'I guess not.'

'There's certainly some better way of establishing her identify than counting on Emergency to remember her. But her motive for being in the hospital—maybe it was those dizzy spells, she could have wanted to be where she could get help if she needed it.' He was talking more to himself than to her. 'It couldn't have been heart, the autopsy showed her to be a little undernourished, but otherwise she was OK.' She saw him catch the quizzical expression on her face and focus back on her.

'It was probably hunger,' Freda said. 'It's hard to believe people are actually hungry. And homeless. This is such a rich country.' She sighed. 'Last names are useful, aren't they?' After a moment she added, 'People living in card-board boxes.'

He laughed. 'You lack coherence. But a social security number would be more useful. I'd know everything Eugénie did in the last ten years. Longer.'

'But she didn't have one?'

'Not that we've discovered. There wasn't a paper, a card, an identifying anything among the things in her bag. Only some money, sixty dollars.'

Freda's eyebrows shot up. 'That's quite a bit.'

'Yes, three twenties, as though she'd gotten them—been given them, stolen them—all at once.'

'Where do you go from here?'

'I have to think about that. Give us time, this is only Day Two. We'll get there.'

He believes it, too, she thought. Remarkable that he can have nothing, really nothing, and be confident that in the end he'll know. And he probably will, that's the thing.

*

With an exclamation, Pedersen woke. Freda, sleeping beside him, stirred slightly and thrust a vague hand in his direction. He had no sense of what had awakened him. Perhaps he had been mulling the case in his sleep.

He lay wide-eyed thinking of Eugénie, considering the information Freda had brought him about her. The fact that Eugénie had lived in the town all her life, yet had not been seen by the other street people until two years before suggested that something significant had happened prior to her appearance. Perhaps the break-up with her husband had occurred two years before, but wasn't it likely that it had happened earlier? She wouldn't have gone from being a wife and, presumably, a respectable home-maker to becoming a mall-dweller overnight. Wasn't the likelihood that the shocks she had described to Freda's client perhaps caused some sort of breakdown which then became the stepping-stone to her altered self? Dr Cohen had speculated on whether she had had a psychotic break.

Was it possible that two years ago she was in fact fresh out of some hospital psychiatric ward? And could that have been the reason for her attraction to hospitals? Why she found solace in a hospital bed—it was familiar?

That, he decided, is the direction we must take next. With the thought he relaxed. After a while he rolled over against Freda's warm body and settled into sleep.

CHAPTER 14

'Today,' Pedersen said as soon as Tate had seated himself, 'we start on hospitals. Hospitals and Ollie Winter are the order of the day.'

'Isn't that orders?'

Pedersen laughed. 'Order, orders, it's what we're going after. I woke up in the middle of the night with a realization.'

'A gestalt?'

Pedersen frowned with amusement. 'You're being very precise this morning.'

Tate smiled. 'I read some James last night, and I realize how imprecise we all are most of the time.' Tate, the son of a librarian, kept his reading tastes from most of the other men on the force.

'Fine. In my faltering, barely literate manner, let me outline a plan of action. But first, why do you think Eugénie chose to sleep in a hospital?'

'As opposed to what?'

'No, no, a *hospital*. Why would anyone go looking for a hospital as a place to sleep in?'

Tate considered. 'I suppose ... let's see, if she'd had a good experience in a hospital, been treated and cured of something, she might think of it as a benign place.'

Pedersen slapped the desk. 'Exactly! It occurred to me last night that Eugénie may have been in hospital. As a patient, I mean. And considering the things we've learned about her, it could have been care after a breakdown. Yesterday Freda told me something that confirmed that Eugénie had a rough time after her divorce.' He told Tate Gertrude's story. 'Anyway, I think we should check the psychiatric wards of the local hospitals for a Eugénie. It's a distinctive enough name for it to be remembered, especially if she was there for any substantial period. I don't know what time to suggest. She appeared on the mall about two years ago, so it would have to be before that. What do you think, is it enough to go on?'

Tate looked doubtful. 'We can try, certainly. What about Lewistown?'

'Yes, that too. That's near enough that she could have been there. Let's try our two hospitals first. Then we can move on to small private places. There are only two I know of in town, but once we get into those, it could be anywhere.'

'Doesn't Lewistown have some small mental hospitals, too? They don't call them that, of course.'

'Yes. You might hit a couple of those. The good ones. Probably her husband footed the bill if she went off the deep end while she was still married to him. Meanwhile, I'll see if I can reach Oliver Winter and talk to him. How about if we knock off later and have lunch somewhere?'

'Minestrone at the Italian restaurant?'

'Sounds good. Let's set it for one. We should have made some headway by then.'

'Right.' Tate rose, smiling. 'You have Freda working on the case now?'

'That was her idea. But it was useful information, especially the part about Eugénie living here all her life. I can't believe someone won't recognize her.'

'No one's called in.'

'We'll keep after it. The *Banner*'ll cooperate if we ask them to run her picture again.' He slipped his left hand into his pocket and rolled the green jade worry beads between his fingers. 'It may take time.'

'All right. I'm on my way.' The door closed behind him.

Oliver Winter lived in a smart new condominium which overlooked the hills that flanked the town to the south-east. He met Pedersen at the door, meticulously dressed and still fragrant with after-shave, a straight-backed, grey-haired man of medium height who communicated a sense of unease despite his expensive clothing and the handsome furnishings which surrounded him.

He seated his visitor and offered coffee. Pedersen declined.

'I'm here—' Pendersen began.

'About Ann's death.' The man's face twisted suddenly, as though he had been visited by a momentary pang.

'Yes. You were apparently as close to her as family; in fact, when they describe you, you come across sounding *like* family.'

'I know the children,' Oliver Winter said.

'Tell me what you think of this. Have you any thought at all about who would murder Ann Koppleman?'

'Someone who broke into the house. Ann didn't have enemies.'

Pedersen liked the simplicity of the man's statements. 'None?' he asked.

'None.'

'You've known the family—how long?'

'About twenty years. We met through her first husband. We were both at the university.'

'And you courted her—' the old-fashioned phrase seemed in keeping with this austere, courteous figure—'after her husband's death.'

'Yes. Unsuccessfully.'

'And again after her second husband's death?'

'Yes.'

'With more success, I gather.'

'She didn't marry me. She might have, someday.'

'Mr Winter, just for the record, what were you doing Tuesday night, the night Ann was killed?'

The other man looked at him without expression. 'I was here, doing some work. Alone, there's no one to corroborate that. I wouldn't have killed Ann.'

'Did you speak to her at all that evening?'

'Yes.'

Winter's taciturnity was becoming wearing. 'Can you tell me about that?'

'I called late. Her daughter had been visiting and had gone. Our conversation was brief, we just spoke of plans for the next evening and I said goodbye.'

'She didn't suggest that anyone was with her at this time—what time exactly was it?'

'Eleven-thirty or so. No, she was alone.'

'You assume.'

'She said so.' A fleeting expression crossed his face, was it dismay? 'She said, "Oliver, I don't think I'll ever marry again. I do love it so when people go, even Sue, and I'm by myself again."'

'Wasn't that rather late for a phone call?'

'I called every night around that time. That is, unless—'
He left the sentence incomplete. 'Ann never went to sleep
before midnight.'

'You were about to say unless you were there?'

'Yes.'

'This must be difficult for you. Do you know of anyone
named Eugénie?'

Winter looked puzzled. 'Eugénie? No—I, oh, that's the
other woman who was killed in the same way that night?'

'Yes. Would you know of any connection between a . . .
bag lady and your friend Mrs Koppleman?'

'No. And I've never run across the name, except for the
French empress. I can't believe Ann had anything to do
with a—' he spoke the words as though they were in another
language, and with distaste—'bag lady.'

'Mrs Koppleman worked with troubled women. She
worked at Marigold House and gave money to the hospital.'

'But those were troubled *young* women, women whose
husbands abused them. And I don't think she had actual
contact with them, she typed and gave the organization
money.'

'They weren't all young. And if she was typing at Marigold House, she had some contact with them, that would
be inescapable. But she wouldn't have met Eugénie there.
It would have had to be somewhere else.'

Oliver Winter showed the first sign of irritability. 'That's
nonsense. Ann didn't know her and that is that. The killer
must just have happened on those two victims. I refuse to
consider that Ann knew her.'

Pedersen changed the subject. 'What about the rest of
the family? The brothers, the sister? You know them. Would
any of them have had reason for attacking Ann?' He realized
he had lapsed into the use of her first name. 'Mrs Koppleman.'

'They were like families always are. There were frictions,
but nothing that would lead to murder. Ann and Stanley
were fairly close, though I think on a fairly superficial level.

They didn't share deep values. And Roy, although he wasn't much younger, she treated like a little brother. She and her sister were close, I think they confided in each other. I suppose you've spoken to her?'

'Yes, I have. So there was nothing—jealousy, money problems—nothing that could have stirred one of them up?'

'Absolutely not. And the person would also have had to kill your Eugénie, wouldn't he?'

'He would.'

Winter stood up. 'I think you're barking up the wrong tree, Detective. You should be looking for some homicidal maniac, some psychopath. Why are you wasting time visiting me?'

Pedersen met his eyes. 'We have to eliminate those close to her first. And you were close to her.'

'Yes. Well, you've eliminated me, now you can get down to business.' He paused. 'I assume you have eliminated me?'

Pedersen stood up too. 'It's early to eliminate anyone. And we're looking for a psychopath, I assure you.'

Winter stared at him. 'You make it sound as though one of us—' He broke off. 'Will that do it? I have to meet my class at eleven.'

'Your field is—?'

'Economics.' His voice was cold, as though this question were the ultimate intrusion.

Funny guy, Pedersen thought as he made his way back to his car, a very funny guy.

The final search of Ann Koppleman's apartment turned up nothing new. The inventory of her jewellery matched the contents of her jewel case. The items stored in the wall safe were those the accountant had anticipated, along with several hundred dollars in cash and a will leaving Ann Koppleman's worldly goods to her four children to be shared equally. Finished, Pedersen gave a last look around the room opulent with satin and fur. It impressed him differently

today than it had the first time he had seen it; today it did
not suggest sybaritic self-indulgence but merely pleasure in
comfort. The general image of Ann as a good woman must
be sinking in.

Turning to go, he idly picked up a book from the bedside
table where it lay face down, still gritty with grey powder.
Ironweed. A gaunt male face brooded from the cover. He
turned it over and read the blurb, conscious of mounting
excitement. The novel's protagonist was a vagrant; the novel
concerned the life of a nineteen-thirties hobo. Enlisting the
help of the officer who had accompanied him, he located
pen and paper, wrote a receipt which he left on the desk,
and pocketed the book. Coincidence? The book was the first
suggestion of a link between Ann and Eugénie; if not an
actual link, the possible interest of one in the predicament
of the other. Despite the lack of sound evidence, Pedersen
was sure Ann had known Eugénie, it was a gut feeling. He
smiled to himself. Better not make much of it with Tate
until he had more; his rational partner would raise his hands
in protest.

Back at headquarters, he put aside his impulse to begin the
novel immediately and settled down to the paperwork that
had accrued. Usually Tate disposed of that for him; paperwork was to Pedersen the least desirable aspect of the job
while Tate executed it with admirable efficiency and no fuss
at all.

Among the reports he found confirmation of Jedediah
Martin's statement: he had arrived at the dinner-party at a
little before seven, he and his hosts and their guests had
spent the evening together and then gone on to a jazz club,
staying until after two. Pedersen wondered how Martin
could work if all his weekday evenings were like that.

In the midst of the work, he was called into the lieutenant's office for a report on progress.

Pedersen liked Lieutenant Harbison. He himself had long
qualified to take the test for a lieutenancy, but as a senior

officer who preferred work in the field, he had been liberated
by the institution of longevity pay, which brought an almost
equivalent salary to some senior men. People like Harbison
were better suited than he to a desk and papers.

And Lieutenant Harbison, Pedersen had to admit, fitted
the role in more ways than one. A tall, good-looking man,
his face was tanned as though he had done nothing more
demanding than spend the summer on the beaches and his
eyes were strikingly blue with clear whites, the sort of
eyes that by their colour and clarity inspired confidence.
Pedersen gave a little inner sigh. In this man's presence, he
always felt unnaturally large and awkward, conscious of the
roughness of his own features, of his large hands and feet.
But Harbison was a good man, efficient, thorough and
completely aware of what his detectives were doing at any
given time.

'Where are you with it?' Harbison asked, indicating a
chair for Pedersen.

'Not much of anywhere yet, but I keep feeling like a
cartoon strip character with electric light bulbs going off
over my head.' He paused and shook his head. 'I think we'll
get through the maze.'

Harbison tipped his head back and laughed. 'It is a
maze all right, I can see that. Tell me some of what you've
done.'

Pedersen outlined their activity of the past two days.

'Sounds good.' He looked down at the surface of his desk.
'You're not—coming down too heavily?'

'Harassing people? No, have there been complaints?
Already?'

Harbison laughed. 'Don't worry. These seem to be sensitive souls. Stanley Potter. He's pretty well known in town.'
He hesitated. 'And I just had another call. Did you visit a
man named Winter this morning?'

Pedersen nodded. 'He's a close friend of the family. You
have to ask questions.'

'I know. He called to berate us for time-wasting. Nothing

to worry about, but it's early to be getting irate phone calls. So—' he grinned—'keep on it. Do what you have to do, but none of this time-wasting.'

Pedersen returned the grin, but he was annoyed. The briefest of interviews and already Winter was carping. He had a feeling this case was not going to be solved overnight, neither of them was. Winter had better brace himself.

At quarter of one, he knocked off and put on his jacket to go and meet Tate.

'Nothing,' Tate said after they had seated themselves and ordered. 'Not one thing.'

'You checked Lewistown Hospital?'

'All of them. I even checked out the two local small hospitals. No one by the name of Eugénie. They went back several years in their files. Those little places don't have that many patients. But no one could recall her at the two bigger hospitals. Of course, nursing staff changes, doctors come and go; they could have had her there and not been aware of it.'

'Who did you talk to?'

'Mawson, among others. Head of Psychiatry. He'd certainly remember, given his antipathy for her.'

'He's been there for some time?'

'Fifteen years. He says he's aware of every patient that goes through his service.'

'I was *sure* . . . well, so much for bright notions. I suppose we should check the local small hospitals, the Lewistown ones and the rest. But I had a feeling . . .'

'Maybe she just figured out that there would be empty beds in a hospital. What other public institution—I mean one the public can freely enter—has beds? She'd need a credit card or money to get into a hotel.'

'She had money. Some.' He glumly attacked his minestrone. 'Mawson. You didn't think he was lying?'

'He didn't appear to be, but that would be a hard thing

to determine.' Tate ate silently for a moment. 'Is there anyone else, anyone she knew, who could have been there? Maybe she went to visit a friend regularly and noticed the empty beds then.'

'What about Ann Koppleman? I wonder if she had a hospitalization. That might be a link, maybe Eugénie encountered her there.'

'You want me to check whether they have a record of Koppleman's being there?'

'Yes, probably it won't take more than a phone call.' He helped himself to a second from the tureen. 'I was so sure . . .'

Tate laughed. 'You don't give up easily. I'll check right after lunch, but I'm not sure that's going to get us any place. After we find they met, if they did, where do we go from there?'

'I don't know. Maybe the killer really did pick his victims at random. I counted on a link between the two women giving us something, but you're probably right—where will we be then?'

They continued eating in silence. Then Pedersen said, 'I'm going to phone the family members and Winter, find out if any of them received a threatening letter or any sort of letter from a stranger in the past couple of weeks.'

'If it was a blackmail letter, you don't think they'd tell you?'

'Maybe it wasn't blackmail. Or maybe they didn't perceive it as blackmail. You have the statement of the guy on the mall that she could get money by writing—'

'Phoning.'

'Same difference. I have the statement from the head librarian that she was writing a letter that would surprise someone. It sounds as though she had information she thought someone would pay to keep hushed up, but we don't *know*.'

'You'll feel better if you try calling the family.'

Pedersen threw an amused glance his partner's way. 'Let's not worry about how I feel, what we have to worry about is what Bay Cove's going to feel if we don't nail that killer.'

CHAPTER 15

Kay was preparing a salad when the phone call came. For a moment she thought it was her husband, then the speaker said a few more words and she recognized Lew Mawson's voice. 'You sound funny. Are you all right?' she said.

'Let me close this door.' He returned. 'A detective was just here, inquiring whether their bag lady was a former patient of mine.'

'Why on earth are they interested in that?' She was conscious of her acute disappointment; for a minute there, she had been sure it was her husband.

'They think she had something to do with hospitals, that's why she chose one to sleep in.'

Where *was* he? Surely she should have heard something by now. She said, 'Couldn't they have assumed she was smart enough to know there'd always be an empty bed someplace in the building?'

'They could have. They didn't.'

She sighed and focused her interest on Lew. 'Did it upset you, having detectives around again? You told them you didn't have her as a patient, didn't you?'

'Of course I did. You know, Kay, maybe till this thing blows over—'

He had her full attention now. 'We shouldn't see each other?' She was aware of a rush of conflicting emotions. No more of Lew with his peculiar requests. No more of—but then she'd be alone. Until her husband came back, Lew was all she had. She shook her curls irritably. 'Not on your life, Lew. You dump me and I stay dumped. No resumption of our activities in the future.'

'Speaking of that. You didn't say anything to the detective when he interviewed you?'

She laughed, the sound shrill in her ears. 'You think I'm out of my mind? Aside from your reputation, I have my own to protect. I go along with your little—ways, but I don't boast about them.' She could hear the irascibility in her voice. The idea that Lew thought he could conveniently strike her off his list infuriated her. The things she had done with—and for—him. And lately he seemed to be changing, wanting to do things to *her*, things which genuinely frightened her ... She had put up with all that, gone along with it, and he thought he could simply call and suggest that they not see each other until what he called 'this thing' blew over. Why, it might never blow over.

There was a silence on the other end of the line. Then, his voice constricted, Lewis said, 'Kay, it isn't *you*. You know how I feel about you. It's well, you know what it is. All I meant was that perhaps we could take it easy for a while, maybe see less of each other. Not stop altogether, nothing like that.'

'While you find some other woman to tie you up and tramp around on your chest with spike heels? Figuratively speaking, of course.'

'For *Christ's* sake, this is a hospital phone, Kay. Be careful what you say.' She could see him, sweat breaking out on his forehead the way it did when ... He broke in on her thoughts. 'Let's have dinner and talk about this. I'd better not call you from the hospital again.'

'I can be discreet when I want to. I don't want to today.' God, why *didn't* she break it off? Was she as desperate as all this? What had happened to her lately? She sometimes felt she didn't know herself at all.

'All right, all right,' he said. 'You're angry. We'll talk about that, too. I have to get off the phone now and tonight's that dinner meeting. Christ—meetings! I'll see you tomorrow night at seven. Is that all right?'

'Tomorrow night we're going to discuss not seeing each other?'

'No! We'll talk about how we can see each other and remain—discreet, as you put it.'

Despite herself, she laughed. He was really a coward. 'I'll see you tomorrow night at seven, Lew.' She put the receiver down hard. Men were all alike, her husband, Lew, all of them. Interested only in their own welfare. She went back to her salad and, invigorated by her anger, tossed it vigorously and began to eat with relish.

Before she was done, she had a second call.

'Yes? Oh, Detective Pedersen. What—?'

He was inquiring whether she had received a letter, one from a stranger, a threatening letter, anything out of the ordinary.

'No, nothing like that. Why do you ask?'

He explained that Eugénie, the woman killed the same day as her sister, had written a letter shortly before her death.

'Oh. No, it wasn't to me. It wouldn't be to me.'

Had nothing at all come from a stranger? It might not have been a letter.

'No, I just said not, didn't I?'

After she had hung up and once more returned to her salad, she thought about his question. Had the detective asked only her or had he called Stan and Roy as well? It made her uneasy. In that unexpected way she had come to know, she felt again her sister's death as a real thing. Once again, she saw her sister's face with the rolled-back eyes, the lolling tongue.

This was no time for her husband to be away. To her surprise, she found herself longing for him as a sort of anchor, a consolation, a bit of normalcy (well, she laughed as tears tightened her throat, *comparative* normalcy) in this welter of strangeness and threat.

In a flood of unfamiliar feeling, she thought fiercely: What I really need right now is a mother to turn to. Why am I the only one who never had a mother, the *only* one? She was swept by a surge of envy that left her faint.

CHAPTER 16

The budget meeting had seemed interminable. Lewis Mawson rose and looked at his watch. He had an hour free, not enough time to leave the building for lunch. As he turned to go, someone touched his shoulder. 'Lew, how about a bite together? You didn't have time to eat before all this?'

'Fine.' Might as well, he had to eat. But a moment later he blamed himself for not having thought faster, claimed a commitment. He could have had Miss Roberts bring him a tray and had an hour of quiet to think. He struggled to recall the fellow's name.

They pushed their way out of the conference room, excusing themselves as they forced their way past others who had stopped to speak to friends, and strode down the corridor.

'Godawful, wasn't it?' the other man said. 'The salient points could have been put in a memo and sent to us. These meetings come oftener and mean less all the time.'

'Division chiefs tonight,' Mawson remarked. 'We *need* a second meeting today.' They approached the cafeteria. 'God, I loathe this place. Too bad we didn't have time to go out.'

'Just as well. As I left this morning, my wife said, "Jim, if you have steak at lunch, I'll leave you. I've got a big T-bone for dinner tonight." She knows my weakness for steak. I might be tempted if we went out.' He laughed in what was for Lewis Mawson a disgustingly jovial manner.

Anyway, his name was Jim. 'Anything new in your department?' He really didn't give a fuck, it was just something to say.

'Actually, we've been doing some vision experiments that

border on your field—well, on psychology, at least. You'd be interested.' He launched into a description on which Mawson found it impossible to keep his attention. Those damned detectives were unnerving him, that was the trouble.

They took their places on line, the stainless steel of counters and of the wall containing the microwave assaulting their eyes. 'This damn place glares so, it gives me a headache,' Mawson commented. Indeed, his temples were beginning to throb. 'God, look at this line.'

It was the busiest hour. The line inched along, those further back along the counter giving suggestive little shoves of their trays against the trays ahead. Mawson glared at the person behind him.

'That beef stew looks as though it would get us through the day,' Jim remarked in his expansive manner as they were finally served.

'It'll have to.' Mawson felt his spirits dip even further. Damn! Between Kay and the detective and discussing steak and beef stew with this ophthalmologist—why in God's name had he let himself get involved with the man?

He cut it as short as he could, hastening back to his office, head down and eyes on the yellow and green lines that ran along the floor, to keep from meeting any other glance and being waylaid.

Roberts was out to lunch. He checked his watch; she must have left early. He went into the inner office, closing the door, and sank into the chair behind the desk, head in hands. This whole business was too much for him. And what in Christ's name had gotten into Kay in the past day or so; she'd bristled with hostility. Maybe it was time to cut things short, not just because of this mess at the hospital, but in general. Yet he had a soft spot for her. She could be very elegant on his arm at a staff party and the sex had been good until lately.

He did have a raging headache. He rummaged in his desk for aspirin and finally came up with a bottle in which a single tablet rattled. Fuck! When Roberts got back he'd send her to the hospital pharmacy for more, if she didn't already have some on hand. He swallowed the one pill dry, tipping back his head and nearly gagging.

Pulling a folder towards him, he opened it preparatory to concentrating on something aside from his mental state, but before he had time, there was a tap at the door. It was Brown, the Adolescent Psychiatry man. He was new and still unsure.

'Yes?' Mawson hoped he looked as though he were in the midst of something uninterruptable. But he was discovering Jay Brown was not quick at picking up cues. Grimly Mawson reflected that he hoped the man was better at that sort of thing with the adolescents he treated.

'That kid, the one I spoke to you about yesterday?'

Mentally he rummaged for the case. Something seemed to be happening to his memory these days. He supposed it was because he was distracted by all those damned fool detectives charging into his office every twenty minutes. He dredged up a recollection. 'Yes. What about him?'

'I'm meeting his mother this afternoon and I just don't know how much pressure to put on her to have the kid institutionalized. He can go someplace good; they can afford it. And he'll never stay on the lithium on his own.'

Mawson sighed. Jesus, the man was a fool. Surely by now he could figure this out for himself. 'Tell her,' he said with exaggerated patience, 'the possible consequences. Scare her a little. But let *her* make the decision.'

Brown looked relieved. 'That confirms what I thought. I'll go after it right away. I was a little uneasy about putting pressure on her.'

'Pressure's the name of the game.' He wasn't talking about Brown's patient's mother.

'I guess so. You look a little beat yourself. Are they bugging you over the woman who was murdered?'

Mawson straightened in his chair. How could the man know that? 'Why should they be?' he asked icily.

'Oh, I heard the police had been around. You're not the only one, if that helps.'

'Who else are they talking to?' He couldn't keep the urgency out of his voice.

'Oh, Jerry Cohen, Rod MacMillan, some of the nurses, I've heard.'

Mawson stood up abruptly. 'Jay, I have some work I have to get to.' He forced himself to be civil. 'You'll do fine with your client's mother.'

Brown moved to go and then turned back. 'I hear you didn't like Eugénie—that's her name. You wanted her out of here.'

'That's nonsense!' Mawson's grip on himself almost slipped. 'A hospital's no place for vagrants to be bedding down, but I had nothing against the woman personally.' Why the hell was he explaining? 'Really, Jay, I must—' He had never been so glad to see anyone leave his office.

After Brown had gone, he sank into his chair again. He wished to hell he had never let anyone know how he felt about Eugénie. For all he could tell, the whole damned hospital was abuzz with his dislike of her. He wouldn't give a shit if only Rod MacMillan didn't know what he knew about him and Eugénie. And in a weak moment he'd had to go and tell Kay all about it. Fuck it all, no wonder he was a nervous wreck.

He leaned back and massaged the stiffness in the nape of his neck. As he sat there, he heard Miss Roberts enter the outside office and pull her desk drawer out, he assumed to put her bag away.

He went out into her office. 'You went to lunch early.' He knew he sounded accusing.

She seemed unruffled. 'The calls were taken by the switchboard,' she said blandly. 'I thought you'd prefer to have me out while you were away.'

'Well, you might let me know your plans. Do you have aspirin?'

'You mean you want some aspirin?'

'That's what I said, didn't I?'

'Yes, I have some.' She opened a desk drawer. He could see that it was in perfect order. The file clerk mentality, that was Roberts.

'Can you get me a cup of coffee before that patient is brought in?'

'Of course.' She removed her bag from the desk drawer and departed. The switch of her skirt suggested that she would not be cooperative the rest of that day.

He sighed and went back into his office. He wondered if he'd make it through the evening meeting.

CHAPTER 17

At work in the museum, Roy Potter reflected that he had begun to find the boys wearing. Fond as he was of them, it was impossible not to note how unformed they were, how immature. He was working on a show that got him out of the house frequently, but when he returned they were there, three good-looking lumps. The plans for the service were complete, notes had been sent to out-of-town friends who might want to attend, flowers had been ordered and refreshments arranged for—actually there was nothing left that needed doing.

Remembering back to his own days as a graduate student, he recalled having books to read, papers to write. None of these three young men seemed burdened by such responsibilities. He had asked Meredith. The boy—man—had looked at him in a puzzled way and said, 'I'm pretty distracted right now.' It was a legitimate out, but . . . Perhaps he had been a grind and not known it. At any rate, they were hard to fathom. The glancing thought crossed his mind that perhaps they knew about him. Could that account for their unresponsiveness—apprehension? For God's sake, they didn't think . . .? He shook off the thought, but he was troubled.

He had brought along his colour samples to the museum for final consideration. The background would be important to this exhibit; the painter had been influenced by the Japanese, and his works, a softly coloured single flower in a vase, a bird drooping against a snowbank, stark yet tender works, needed precisely the right backdrop. He thought the muted grey-green would do it. For a few minutes he lost himself in contemplation of the show, forgetting the ugly death of his sister, the irritating presence of the boys, the abstinence he had imposed on himself while the case was being investigated. He walked back to the museum director's office. It was, as always, cluttered with leftovers from former exhibits: rolled posters, boxes of museum postcards, not-yet-claimed paintings from former shows. In the midst of this chaos, John Hobson, the director, sat at his huge table, intently examining slides.

'Someone trying to coax you to do a show?' Roy asked.

'Yes. He's good. Look.' He held out the little hand slide projector.

Roy pressed the button that lighted it. 'He is good.' He returned the projector. 'You have a minute?'

Hobson put down the slides. 'Sure. Have you made a decision?'

'I think this green.' Roy bent over the table to show him the colour chip. 'I used posterboard for this colour to see the effect of a larger area. It works well with the paintings.'

Hobson considered. 'It's good. More interesting than the putty colour you were thinking about, but subtle. Good. Let's go with it.'

Roy experienced the stab of pleasure that accompanied approval from someone in authority. He supposed it dated from his relationship with his father. God knows, that man had never given him any encouragement. His sisters complained that they didn't understand him, didn't know what moved him. Well, this did.

As he started out of the office, the phone rang. 'Roy,' Hobson called after him, 'this is for you.'

'For me? Must be one of my nephews, no one else knows I'm here. Don't go out, it won't be anything that personal.'

The caller was not a nephew but Detective Pedersen. Roy frowned. 'Yes. What can I do for you?'

Pedersen told him.

'No, I haven't received anything like that. Nothing threatening. Nothing from a stranger, except some junk mail, of course, and pleas for money. Have you found something?'

The detective said no, they were just checking, the woman who had been murdered the same day as his sister had written someone a letter.

'Well, it couldn't be *me*. I've never seen the woman in my life.' He hesitated. 'Could she have written my sister Ann?'

Hobson had risen and strolled into his secretary's office.

The detective explained that nothing had been found among her papers.

'Sorry, then, I'm afraid I can't help you. How'd you get my number here, anyway?'

The boys had given it to him. Irritation again swept over Roy. 'Fine. Glad you could get me. Sorry I can't help.' He hung up and Hobson ambled back in. 'That was the police.'

Hobson looked at him with curiosity. 'This must be a terrible time for you. Have they located the man who broke in?'

'They keep saying no one did break in. The police work in mysterious ways all right.'

'I imagine. You're sure you're up to working so soon?'

'It couldn't be better timed, I'd go mad hanging around my house with my three depressed nephews. I'll get back to work now. I thought the large bird right inside the entrance, by itself. What do you think?'

'Fine. I leave it to you. However you see it is OK. This is your show, Roy.'

CHAPTER 18

Pedersen had reached Stanley Potter at work and asked his question about the letter with no greater success than he had with his sister and brother. Suzanne was not at home, but Pedersen was sure that she, of all of them, would have let him know had anything extraordinary come her way. The effort had produced nothing but further frustration.

He was sitting at his desk playing with his worry beads when Tate came in. The hospital had refused to give information by telephone and he had just returned from another trip across town. It had added up to a huge zero. Well, not quite.

'What,' he said, seating himself with a self-satisfied air, 'did you say the dead sister's name was?'

'The dead sister? What are you talking about?'

'Remember the member of the Potter family that died of cancer, the sister? What did you say her name was?'

'I didn't, I never knew it. Oh, wait. Aunt Jane, that's what one of the Potter boys called her.'

'Yes, well, she didn't die of cancer.'

'What did she die of?'

'Ann Koppleman was never a patient at any of the major hospitals, but Jane Potter was.'

'We knew that. That's years ago.'

'Yes, but she didn't have cancer. She was in a psychiatric ward and she committed suicide.'

'Suicide?'

'Yes. She was admitted to Bay Cove Hospital for profound depression, stayed the maximum ten days and was transferred to a private psychiatric facility.' He consulted his notes. 'Fernwood. In Lewistown. A few months later she signed herself out. Apparently she had signed herself in, so that was all right. A couple of weeks later the hospital learned she had been a suicide. That was all they knew at Bay Cove.'

'Interesting. How did you happen to ask?'

'I was asking about Ann Koppleman and I mentioned that her name had been Ford and before that Potter. They checked all three and came up with a Jane Potter. I was sure that was her name, you must have mentioned it, so I got all the information they'd give me. Someone had scribbled in a note at the end of her file: "Suicide." Must have heard through the other hospital. The Admission person said she shouldn't, as she put it, share such information but in the circumstances . . .' He laughed.

'So much for confidentiality. And all the friends of the family assumed she had died after a bout with cancer. Amazing. They must have kept the suicide out of the papers. It does cast a different light on things. On *them*.'

'Yes. We should go out to Fernwood and see if we can fill things in.'

'We should. First thing tomorrow. Right now I have to read a novel.'

'A novel?'

'*Ironweed*. I found it on Ann Koppleman's bedside table.' He explained.

'Sounds like a pleasant way to spend the rest of the afternoon. Sure you wouldn't rather have me read it?'

Pedersen grinned. 'I'm sure. I'm curious about this book.'

Ironweed was a remarkable book. The tale of an ex-ballplayer, drunk, sometime gravedigger, roaming the streets of Albany, revisiting the scenes of past pleasure and pain, gripped him, showed him the tragedy of the alienation of this group as it had never been shown him. He wondered how far into it Ann had read by the time of her death, whether she had felt repugnance or sympathy. Or both. He had. Even empathy.

There could have been any number of reasons for her reading the book aside from a possible connection with

Eugénie. Perhaps she was merely a naturally intellectual, inquisitive woman. Perhaps she belonged to a book discussion group. Perhaps she had seen the film. Those were things he could check. But despite what reason told him, a little worm of excitement was wriggling. It was a difficult book, demanding and upsetting. How much motivation would it take to keep a person reading? The marker in the novel suggested that she was well past the middle, but the marker could have been misplaced in the fingerprinting.

He got up heavily from his chair. He had spent the rest of the afternoon and the evening reading *Ironweed* and he ached from the sitting and from the intensity of his concentration. He stretched, yawned and made his way into the darkened room where Freda, having finally given up on him, was already asleep.

CHAPTER 19

Everything about Fernwood denied its intent: the treatment of mental illness. The soft roundness of the foliage, the low building, white clapboard with brick chimneys, the casement windows, all cried out its normalcy. Surely no one could remain depressed or out of touch for long in such a benign environment, it said. Only the locked front door told them the patients needed protection from themselves.

The two men were admitted and moved past bright chintzes and bowls of fresh flowers to a pleasant office lighted by several windows. The rather severe-looking young woman who rose to greet them was presumably an Administrative Assistant; she seemed disturbed by their request that they see the director, as though her major function were to protect her against such invaders. 'I'm sure I can help you, sir,' she said with great confidence, waving them to chairs. 'She's terribly busy right now, not seeing anyone.'

Pedersen was polite as he demurred. He explained. 'The

director is the only person with the authority to give us the information we need.'

'If it's just information—'

Pedersen broke in gently. 'Will you let the director know we're here?' She studied his face for a moment and reluctantly gave up. 'I'll *see*,' she said, not totally succumbing. 'She may be tied up or—' At Pedersen's expression, she departed hastily.

'Nice place,' Tate said, looking at the green beyond the windows.

'It is. Sobering when you see what money can buy.'

The woman who entered the room and firmly closed the door on her assistant was a surprise: blonde, startlingly blonde, another Marilyn Monroe, with white skin and almost white hair wrapped smoothly around her head. She had a sensible air that belied her sensational good looks. They rose to greet her.

'How do you do. We'll stay in here, there are people in my office.' She seated herself at the Administrative Assistant's desk.

So she had been busy. 'We're inquiring,' Pedersen said, after introductions had been made, 'into a former patient of yours, a Jane Potter. She left here some nine or ten years ago. We realize records are confidential, but we'd like what information you can give us.'

'I see,' she said. 'You realize that will be very little. What is it you want to know about her?'

'First, when did she come to you and in what shape was she?'

'And second?'

'The circumstances of her leaving and her condition then.'

'You're not inquiring into the course of treatment, the therapy, the reasons she was here?'

'As much of that as you're free to tell me. I understand your position.'

'I'll have to pull her records. We have everything on computer now, even our old records, so it won't take long.

I'll have a printout in a minute. Would you care to look around the place while you wait?'

They strolled through the rooms to which she had directed them. In the dining-room bright blue tablecloths were set off by bowls of chrysanthemums. The library was amply stocked; comfortable chairs were scattered through the room.

Tate pulled a book from a shelf. 'Right up to the minute. I've been wanting to read this biography.' Reluctantly he returned it to the bookcase.

On the far side of the building the garden with paths marked by clumps of autumn flowers was walled by stone, but the walls were covered with tumbling white solanum, small-blossomed potato vine. Here and there a patient strolled, accompanied by an attendant. No white coats were in evidence.

Pedersen grunted. 'This is obviously the place to be mentally ill.'

'If you can afford it.'

'Yes, it must cost. Wonder which of them paid her bill.'

When they returned to the office, the director was ready for them. 'Jane Potter was transferred here from Bay Cove Hospital—' she gave them the date—'as a voluntary admission. You've spoken with Bay Cove?'

'Yes,' Pedersen said.

'Then you know about the suicide attempt before she was admitted there.'

Tate nodded. 'Yes,' Pedersen lied.

'Her treatment went well, she steadily improved, and we were—actually, I wasn't here at that time, you realize?— we were discussing home visits at the time she decided to sign herself out. It was against our judgement that she be discharged without any family present to see her on her way, but the rights of mental patients are protected; she had that option. There was no reason for us to put a seventy-two-hour hold on her, she seemed well. Anyway, we called a cab for her and she informed us that she was returning home.'

'To her own house?'

'It was assumed she meant that. She chose a weekend to leave the hospital and it seems that all her family was out of town—that may have been deliberate on her part. With suicide in mind, she wouldn't have wanted interference. Of course we didn't know they were out of town, we merely knew we couldn't reach any of them by phone.'

'Do your records indicate that you were afraid of suicide?'

'No, to the contrary. Her therapist made a note after her death to the effect that such an act could not possibly have been anticipated. Although,' she added, 'just leaving Fernwood could have been unsettling. And then finding none of her family around—well, it seems to *me* she might very well have felt a moment of desperation and fear. But that's my opinion, not the psychiatrist's.'

'Makes sense to me. You're a therapist yourself?'

'No.' She flushed slightly. 'It's just that being around a place like this, you pick up things. I'm strictly on the administrative end of things.'

'So she seemed well and ready for a return to normal society?'

'That's what the records say. She had plans—' she glanced at the printout—'I won't go into them, but she seemed oriented towards a productive future.'

'And she went off and killed herself.'

She looked at him sadly. 'Yes. Drowned herself.'

'Well—' Pedersen and Tate made ready to leave—'we do thank you. There's nothing else in those notes that would be of use to us?'

'Probably a lot. But I can't give that information to you. You'd have to—'

'Subpœna it, I know.'

She walked to the front door with them. She moved sensuously; it was wonderful to Pedersen that a woman who seemed the embodiment of sex could be in her manner so down-to-earth. He turned to shake her hand and take in one more glimpse of her.

'Something!' he said to Tate as they walked to the car.

Tate shook his head. 'Yes, she's something, all right.'

'And all the friends of the family assumed Jane died after a bout with cancer,' Pedersen said as they pulled out of the driveway. 'Funny. People must have come to visit her.'

'I asked about that at Bay Cove Hospital. There, she didn't have visitors, aside from family. She was just there for a couple of weeks, I suppose they figured the depression would pass.'

'But not here. She was in the hospital for the better part of a year. We'll have to check it out with someone. Stanley Potter.'

Back at headquarters, Pedersen reached for the phone.

'Oh,' said Stanley Potter with a sigh, 'you've dug up all that business. We handled it the way we did because we thought it would be Jane's wish. She made us swear before she signed herself into Bay Cove that we wouldn't tell anyone.'

'But why? Is there such a stigma attached to being depressed? Unless—it was the suicide attempt?'

'Someone's told you about that.' There was a long silence. 'We're—we've all been a bit—' Stanley Potter made a sound deep in his throat—'sensitive on the subject.' After a moment he added, his voice constricted, 'Our mother was a suicide.'

'I see. I'm sorry. But people came to see her later—at Fernwood?'

'She relented and a couple of close friends visited. Not many. After a while even they dropped off. She asked us to make clear to her friends that she needed time to herself. She'd split up with her husband a while before and . . . Anyway, when she died, we let it be known that she'd had a brain tumour. That that accounted for her depression, her odd behaviour. No one knew about the suicide. We even told the kids in the family—Ann's children—that it was cancer. No point in having suicide hanging over them.'

As your mother's suicide hung over all of you, Pedersen thought. 'Ann's children never knew the cause of your mother's death, either?'

'No,' Stanley said roughly. 'It's not a subject we talk about. I really don't understand the relevance of all this to your investigation.'

'I need the facts,' Pedersen said flatly. 'Tell me about the finding of your sister Jane's body.'

'She—' Pedersen could hear him swallow hard—'was washed up north of town. We don't know it was suicide, it could just as well have been an accident. When she was well, she loved to walk by the water and she was always sitting out on the rocks. I don't have to tell you that people are washed off.'

'How long had she been dead?'

'About two weeks. The coroner said she probably died the day she got out of the hospital. Of course none of us knew she was out. The hospital tried to reach us to tell us she'd gone, but as luck had it, none of us was available. We didn't learn for a couple of days. By then she'd simply disappeared.'

'You called the police?'

'We thought about it, but in the end we hired a private detective. We were afraid of the publicity if we called the police. We assumed she was alive somewhere. And she'd been so adamant about no one knowing.'

'How did you come to find the body?'

'The detective. He checked the morgue every day and one afternoon he phoned Roy and me and asked us to come down there.'

'You were able to identify the body?'

'It was Jane all right, but she looked . . . It wasn't easy. We didn't let the girls see her—Ann and Kay.'

Pedersen paused and then asked the question. 'Was there any sign of foul play?'

'You think she was *killed*?'

Pedersen repeated his question.

'Jesus, you—No, the coroner said not. She looked—Do we *have* to go into all this?'

'I'm afraid we do. She looked?'

'Well, battered. But the coroner said that was just from being in the water so long and being knocked around among the rocks. God! You can imagine seeing someone close to you looking like that. When she was well, she had always been so fastidious. She would have hated it.'

'So you held the service as though she had died of cancer. With a closed casket.'

'Yes. Some of her friends were angry that they had never been able to visit or say goodbye, but they felt they'd honoured her wish. They all came to the memorial service, though. And she had masses of roses. She loved roses.'

'Your sister Ann didn't let Suzanne attend the service?'

'She thought she was too young. And Sue had been very fond of her aunt. Afterwards Ann read somewhere that it had been a mistake, that it's better to let kids experience the whole thing.'

Pedersen allowed a moment to pass before he asked, 'Your mother's suicide. When did that occur?'

Stanley Potter's voice was harsh. 'Right after my sister Kay was born.' He laughed, a bitter sound, 'Post-partum depression, no doubt.'

'You were how old?'

'Ten, just ten. A very young ten. Jane was eight and Roy was—six, I guess. Ann must have been about three.'

'It must have been hard on all of you.'

Stanley said nothing.

'I'm sorry we had to stir things up, Mr Potter, but it was necessary that we have this information.'

'I'm damned if I can see why. What has a nine-year-old suicide got to do with my sister's murder? Or my mother's death? It seems to me you're going about this investigation in a most peculiar way.' His voice had become cold.

'When is your sister Ann's service to be?' Pedersen hoped the change of subject would distract the man.

'Sunday at eleven. Episcopal church.' He sounded as icy as before.

Oh God, Pedersen thought as he hung up, we're going to get another complaint about my time-wasting, hassling ways. He turned to Tate triumphantly. 'I'll lay a bet that the letter Eugénie wrote was addressed to some member of Ann's family.'

'You think she was threatening to unearth all that old stuff, the mental hospital and the suicide and the family lying to everyone? How could she have known? And why would they have cared?'

'How she knew is still a question, but I don't think she was up to anything as innocuous as that.'

'Then what?'

'I think she wrote to say she had proof of murder. And she promised if they didn't come across, she'd take it to the police.'

CHAPTER 20

'Proof of murder! That's crazy. How could she have proof of a murder committed over nine years ago, even assuming there was such a murder? Carl, I think this time you've gone off the deep end.'

'But it follows. What if Jane Potter wasn't a suicide? What if she was murdered?'

'What happened to accident? She could have gone down to visit her old haunts, been sitting on a rock and been washed off.'

'We can check the weather for that day, see whether the waves were especially high. Although there seems a little uncertainty as to the exact day she died. And we need to see that coroner's report. But I—'

'Carl, you get these notions and you ... cling to them.
Now what's wrong with the idea that Eugénie was
blackmailing the family over their shenanigans regarding
the cancer and the mental illness? Though I can't even
begin to imagine where she'd get such information.'

'That wouldn't be enough to get her killed. No one
would be concerned. And who could she have told? The
newspapers? Would the *Banner* have believed a vagrant who
came to them with a story like that? Even if they did listen,
who'd care about that stale old news?'

'The Potters and Koppleman and Brennan are prominent
enough for it to have made a bit of nasty gossip.'

'The *Banner* wouldn't have listened. Anyway, they'd be
risking a libel suit.'

Tate shook his head. 'It doesn't make sense. How, then,
are you going to account for Ann Koppleman's murder?
The murderer went after both the blackmailer *and* the
blackmailee?'

'That's true, it doesn't answer the question of why
Ann Koppleman was killed. Nothing seems to answer
that.'

'Look at what you're saying. You're suggesting that
Eugénie, a bag lady with no resources, no home, not even
a sheet of paper and a stamp, would be able to garner
information like that. Where? How?'

Pedersen grinned. 'You make me feel like an unreasonable
teenager.'

Tate laughed. 'When you get these wild ideas, you sound
like one, honest to God, Carl. At times like these, I feel
years older than you.'

'But they sometimes turn out to be right, my wild
hunches, don't they?'

'This won't be one of those times. I'll bet on it.'

'Maybe,' Pedersen said, returning to the subject, 'she was
in the hospital with Jane Potter and got to know her.'

'No one remembered a Eugénie at Bay Cove Hospital.'

'It was ten years ago, they wouldn't remember. Maybe

she was there in some other capacity, as a nurse, for example. We don't know what she did before she turned up on the streets.'

Tate sighed. 'I can see we're going to pursue this.'

Pedersen laughed. 'Come on now, Ron, don't tell me you haven't the faintest suspicion that I could be right about Eugénie.'

'I agree that blackmail seems to be in the picture. The letter she wrote at the library. The phone call she could have made. The "surprise" she was planning. But I can't see it as the uncovering of murder. Or of a murderer.'

'But if it *were* of a murderer, what an excellent motive for him to murder again. Or her to murder again. What would he or she have to lose?'

'And Ann Koppleman?'

'You know, today you depress me, Ron.'

Ron Tate laughed. 'I know. I'm so rational.'

Pedersen grunted. 'Well, let's see if we can tie in Ann Koppleman's death.'

Tate groaned.

'She could—no. What if she were the one being black-mailed?'

'Yes? What if she were?'

'No, it doesn't work. Damn it, there must be some reason for her murder. Maybe it doesn't have anything to do with Eugénie, but there must be a reason.'

'She turned down Ollie?'

'But what would Oliver Winter be doing killing Eugénie?'

'Maybe one of her brothers or her sister killed Ann.'

'Again, no connection with Eugénie.'

'Unless—no, Eugénie wrote just the one letter, didn't she? Maybe she made some phone calls, too.' Tate took off his glasses and rubbed his eyes.

'What you're saying is she got in touch with all four of them? Where does that get us?'

'I don't know where it gets us. And they all deny having ever heard *of* Eugénie, much less having heard *from* her. I think we're on the wrong track, Carl, really I do. It just doesn't fit together, any of it.'

'I know.' Pedersen swivelled around and faced the window. 'You may be right. But I think the business of Jane Potter is in some way related to the deaths. It's the only link we have—a member of the family was a patient in the hospital and Eugénie hung around the hospital.'

'There's a little gap of some ten years there. And it's one of only two hospitals in town.'

'I know. You know, Ron, you should check Bay Cove Hospital to see whether there was a nurse named Eugénie there ten years ago.'

'I'll check, but I can tell you right now that unless she was a regular employee they won't have the information. Private nurses come and go, and I'm sure those records are incomplete.'

'Regular hospital staff, that's what I meant. Of course I'd feel on solider ground if we'd found some communication from Eugénie in Ann Koppleman's house. There wasn't a thing.'

'If someone were going to the trouble of killing her because of her connection with Eugénie, he'd take the trouble to destroy it, wouldn't he?'

'*That* could be the connection.' Pedersen swivelled his chair back to face Tate. 'Ann Koppleman receives a letter and decides to pay off Eugénie. Some member of her family gets wind of that and kills her and Eugénie, thereby removing all risk of exposure. No, it doesn't make sense.'

'It sounds more plausible than some of the other things you've been saying. Although I'd think just killing off Eugénie would have been adequate.'

'Overkill?' Pedersen laughed. 'No pun intended.'

'Who do we know who is connected with this case?' Tate asked. 'Stanley, Roy, Kay—the brothers and sister. Suzanne—the daughter. Jason, Ellery, Meredith—the sons.'

'The sons weren't here. Cross them off the list. Oliver

Winter, the boyfriend. Jedediah Martin, the other boyfriend. No, he's alibied. And Lewis Mawson, the doctor
who hated Eugénie's guts and who knew Ann.'

'He knew her?' Tate asked.

'He'd met her at meetings and gatherings of benefactors.'

'That's interesting. He's the only person who's admitted
an acquaintance with both of them.'

'Jedediah Martin was at the hospital, he was aware of
Eugénie, and he knew Ann Koppleman. But he's out. His
alibi is too tight.'

'Besides, what motive could either of them have for killing
Eugénie? Or for that matter Ann? Rejection by her?'

'Mawson wasn't interested in Ann in that way, so far as
I can tell. And that's not enough to warrant a stabbing.
Ann seemed to have handled her affairs tactfully, she'd have
let the man down gently, gradually.'

'But there comes a breaking-point. Maybe Ollie—'

Pedersen scooped up his worry beads from the desk
where they lay and slammed them back down. 'Where does
Eugénie fit in? In my scenario Ann doesn't fit in. In yours
Eugénie doesn't. Let's let it lie. We've talked it into the
ground.'

Tate sighed with relief. 'Wouldn't it be convenient if it
were Lewis Mawson, an all round unpleasant person?'

Pedersen laughed. 'I'll go with that.' He dropped the
worry beads in his pocket. 'I'll go with that.'

Tate's phone call came an hour later.

'There may have been a Eugénie. Someone remembered,
an older charge nurse. She was a vocational nurse, that's
what they call the bedside care nurses, and this woman is
quite sure that was her name. She says she hasn't seen her
in ages but she remembers that it was an unusual name,
nobody could pronounce it. She couldn't recall anything
about how she looked, but she did remember that she had
worked with psychiatric patients. That could have been
when Jane was a patient.'

'And Eugénie could have learned something and kept it to herself all those years. Far-fetched but possible.'

'Yes. Maybe a couple of years ago she heard the family had come into money and decided to cash in on it.'

'It seems crazy she'd wait all that time. What could she have learned? Do you suppose it was just coincidence, someone with the same name who nursed there?'

'We have to assume it isn't, don't we? It fits so neatly. It tells us, if it's the same Eugénie, how she got her information.'

'But what information? If it was something to do with Jane's death . . .' Pedersen sighed. 'And this head nurse was sure?'

'Pretty sure. Apparently she's allergic to French names.' Pedersen grunted.

'The computer's down for repairs at the moment—'

'Of course.'

Tate grinned. 'But she said I could check the list of nurses as soon as it's fixed. We may actually come up with a *last* name.'

Pedersen grunted again.

CHAPTER 21

Rod MacMillan pushed his tray along the counter, wishing the woman at the end would make up her mind about dessert. He glanced at his wristwatch. He had scheduled a meeting for 1.30. That gave him three-quarters of an hour.

'Watch this now. She's not going to take either of them,' said a voice behind him.

He turned. 'Jerry. Isn't she something? God, now that guy's doing it. Ah, thank God, he's settled for the pie. Let's move while we can.'

'There should be separate cafeterias for patients' families,'

Jerry said as they walked away from the cashier. 'Or rather for us. Where do you want to sit?'

They found an empty table near a window.

Jerry picked up his soup spoon. 'What's happening in social work?'

Rod dumped dressing over his salad. 'The usual. Being low man on the totem pole is not a happy fate, and let me tell you, in a hospital social work is low man.'

'Physicians who don't take advantage of social workers should have their heads examined.'

'You realize you're alone in that opinion? Well, that's not true. There's such a split, though—some physicians really make use of my people but some won't let us get within feet of their patients. You've heard all this before. What's going on upstairs?'

'We have a kid who isn't going to make it. I have to tell his parents this afternoon.' He looked down at his tray. 'See how heartless we become? Eating a huge meal before giving those poor people the worst news of their lives.'

'That's rough, Jerry. If the parents'll accept help, send them down to us. I'll set them up with someone good.'

'I want to do that. I think they'll need it.' He finished his soup and began on his turkey sandwich. 'That lentil soup's the best thing the cafeteria makes.' He took another bite. 'Anything new on Eugénie?'

'I haven't heard anything. You?'

'Not much. Detectives around, I hear, checking hospital records and interviewing people. Lew was visited.'

'Mawson? No kidding. Wonder what they asked him.'

'I wonder if they know he sees Ann Koppleman's sister.'

'What? He knows that family? How do you know?'

'I know her by sight. She's Kay Brennan, a high-stepping gal who I hear has some sort of Open Marriage. She shows up here and there, usually with Lew. They're Good Friends.'

'Does he know you've seen him with her?'

'Would he care? But I doubt that he knows. As a general rule he doesn't see me, especially when I'm with my wife.

He remembers who I am at meetings. Between times he looks through me.'

Rod put down his fork and leaned forward. 'Maybe you should tell one of those detectives.'

'What? Are you off your rocker? Why would I do that?'

'Maybe he has some connection with—' he looked around and lowered his voice—'the murders.'

'Rod, what are you talking about? Just because he's making it with the sister?'

'Jerry, the rumour is that they were killed by someone with medical training. It was a surgeon's cut.'

Rod stared at him. 'You think Mawson—?'

'He's pretty flaky. And he would have had to rotate through surgery during his training.' He wondered if he should tell Jerry the other thing he knew about Mawson.

'Listen, he's a bastard, I grant you that, and a snob and supercilious and generally uncooperative, but a murderer—that's insane.'

'He's one psychiatrist that went into his field out of his own neurotic needs, let me tell you. He has all the earmarks.'

'Maybe he did, but that doesn't make him a murderer, not by a long shot.' He grinned. 'You sound a little flaky yourself on this subject.'

'I suppose I do.'

'You just hate Mawson.'

Rod mopped salad dressing from his plate with French bread. 'I don't hate him. Yes, you know I do. I don't know why I should.'

Jerry smiled. 'Maybe he reminds you of your father.'

Rod laughed. 'I liked my old man, it can't be that. Tell me, how is Mawson with a woman? I mean, how does he treat her? Is he arrogant with women, too?'

'I ran into him at this party—one of the men in cardiology had an Open House. Really open, too, all departments represented.'

'And in every corner was a group discussing its specialty.'

Jerry laughed. 'You've got it. Only not Mawson. Kay

Brennan was strictly in charge, she didn't leave his side. He was . . . very attentive.'

'Not arrogant?'

'If so, it wasn't visible. He gave the impression of being the doting lover. I *assume* lover. I can't see Lew spending time with a woman who doesn't put out.'

Rod finished his baked apple. 'I'm still hungry, I should have had some of that lentil soup. Well, that must have been something to witness.'

'It was—interesting. Made me wonder if Lew's façade conceals a totally different sort of person.'

'A pussycat? Whatever it is, it could only be an improvement. I'm going to have to take off. I've called a meeting for one-thirty. I still think you should pass on the information—' He caught Jerry's expression. 'OK, forget it. He's a pussycat, I'll remember that next time he's telling off one of my social workers.'

But, he told himself as he stacked his tray and dumped his silver into the bin, if those detectives interview me, *I'll* tell them about Kay Brennan. And maybe about the other, the time he had found him, with Eugénie asleep, touching her that way. Eugénie through some miracle hadn't wakened, probably so fagged out she didn't feel a thing, and Mawson had talked fast. The guy had seemed to him genuinely ashamed of what he called his 'impulse', and Rod had finally let him off the hook, promised him he wouldn't tell anyone. But he had never looked Mawson straight in the eye. People didn't do those things out of the blue, there was a history, but he'd never heard anything else out of line. Probably that one experience had scared him shitless.

But now, now that he realized the guy knew the Koppleman family as well, the whole thing took on a different colouration. He'd have to think about it.

CHAPTER 22

Suzanne Ford locked her car door and, conscious of how tired she was, slowly began to climb the hill from the parking lot to the building in which her class met. She didn't feel right about coming back so soon, but she'd missed the last meeting of this class and she couldn't afford two in a row. She supposed one afternoon class wasn't like coming back in earnest, all day every day. She'd do that next week after the service was over.

At the top of the hill she ran into a classmate, Mary Beth. 'Oh, Sue, what an *awful* thing,' Mary Beth began. 'I read— oh dear, I didn't mean to make you cry.' Awkwardly she fished in her pocket and dragged out a clean, crumpled tissue with which she presented Suzanne.

Suzanne scrubbed at her eyes, which immediately filled again. 'It's all right. I probably shouldn't have tried to come to class so soon. I thought it might get my mind off things.'

'Here, let me walk with you.' They mounted the steps to the second floor. 'I just—I guess you'd rather not talk about it.' But her curiosity got the best of her. 'Your place must be *swarming* with police.'

'No. A detective came by a couple of times. I know they're working on it, trying to find out—'

'Who did it? That was awfully odd, that woman at the hospital who was killed too, wasn't it? Did your mother know her? I mean, your mother was involved with some charities, wasn't she?'

'Not charities, exactly. And I don't think she'd ever met the woman, I think it was just some crazy—You know, Mary Beth, I really can't talk about it. What did I miss Tuesday?'

'That's right, you weren't in class. He talked about—

cripes, I'll have to look at my notes. You were at your mother's house?'

'No, they didn't locate me till dinner-time. I was in the library, doing some research.'

'No kidding! You mean you deliberately cut class? That must have been a first for you. You never cut classes, do you?'

'I figured it was the one time I could get at the books that are on reserve for this class, the ones we can't take out. It worked.'

'Clever, clever. I'll have to try that.'

They opened the door and seated themselves in the back of the still empty classroom. 'Now, if you'd let me see those notes, Mary Beth.'

'I guess you don't want to talk about it,' said Mary Beth, riffling through the pages of her notebook.

'That's the idea,' said Suzanne. 'That's the idea.' She began to copy the notes.

Stanley Potter, when he thought of it, marvelled that he had come such a long way. True, he was no longer young, although he was, he reminded himself, still a virile and handsome man, but none the less his progress was remarkable. Who would have guessed he'd become a major partner in a firm as substantial as this one? When he had really been young, he had been confused, directionless. All those false starts—what was the old rhyme: doctor, lawyer, merchant, chief? That had been him. Roy, on the other hand, had always had a knack with art and had settled into his field without any fuss. But he—Stanley remembered his father's anger over his indecisiveness. He sighed. He and his father had never come to terms on the subject of profession. They had never come to terms, period.

Well, he had, as the saying went, found himself when he came into business. Business, in particular the software industry, involved him as nothing else had. His partners had for a time dominated the scene, that was true, but that had ended with his investment of the inheritance. The old man had done one good thing for him, at least. And the company had rebounded; the infusion of new money had turned them around. He had seen the glances they threw his way when figures were discussed these days, and he had noticed the new respect in the way in which they addressed him. Nothing in his life had given him such satisfaction. If it weren't for Ann's death, he could be completely happy. Ann's death was constantly with him.

When he thought about himself he realized he had been unsure, always, he supposed. He sat at his desk in the new office and thought about it. He didn't know why it had been that way. As the eldest child and a boy, he must have been welcomed, but—he winced at the memory—his first recollection was of reaching out to grasp his little sister's arm and having his mother slap him hard. Immediately after, she had pulled him to her. Her face was wet. But it left a wound. That, and even more, the difference in his father's attitude towards his little sister. He still felt a slight chill when he thought of his father, even three years after his death.

His father had been a cold man, cold to him at any rate. And to Roy too, now he thought of it. Just not there for them. Absent. His father liked girls. Everything had been plummy for the girls in the family, all they had to do was look pretty and say 'yes' to their father and they could have anything. It probably accounted for their confidence, their making marriages so easily, while he and—But that was their mother's suicide, too. Objectively, he supposed he was suffering from what the shrinks would call a classic fear of abandonment, but subjectively . . . He could never think of his mother with real emotion. There was a sort of blank where filial feeling should be. You left me, I feel nothing for you, was what it added up to. It was as though something essential in him had been choked off. He guessed the same had happened to Roy.

But this new success—sometimes he felt he had spent his

life realizing his father's prediction that he would fail. Fail at studies, fail at work. He wished the old man were here now to see that he had made it, finally, that he was looked to for decisions, admired, sought out by his colleagues. It was a slightly hollow victory, as though it had come a lifetime too late, but he *had* it at last, that was the important thing.

And Martha. Now and then he thought of calling Martha, he'd heard she was widowed and alone, but something made him hesitate.

The thought of Martha damped down his spirits. He applied himself to the work at hand in an effort to put her out of his mind. But she kept popping into his consciousness, Martha with her dark eyes and gipsyish clothing. She had been a strange choice of lover for him, so different in every way, but she lent excitement to everything they did. She had an adventurousness he had never encountered, probably because women like Martha took one look at him and, buttoned down as he was, thought: Why bother? But if he had to say it himself, he had depths. There were aspects to his personality that he hadn't even known existed until he met Martha. Maybe that was what had scared him away.

On impulse, he pulled the phone towards him. Why *not* call? He could give her his condolences, rather late but still . . . He had to check her number; it had been years, literally, since they had spoken.

She answered on the fifth ring, just as he was about to give up. She must have run in from out of doors, she was a gardener. 'Yes? Let me get my breath.' After a moment she said, 'OK, I'm all right now.'

'It's Stan, Martha.'

There was a long pause, then she said, her voice low, 'Stanley. It's been a long time.'

'Yes. You—I hear you . . .'

'Yes, I lost Holman over a year ago. I'm all right,' she added as though he had asked.

Stanley felt relief. He wasn't sure how he would have

coped with an expression of grief over another man. 'Good, Martha. Good. I wondered if we might see each other, have dinner or something. Would that work for you?' He realized he had expressed himself as though he were talking with a business associate. 'I mean, would you like to do that?'

She laughed. 'Would I! Stanley, I've been thinking about you, hoping you would call. Two minds with but a simple thought.'

He was astonished at how relaxed he had suddenly become. 'Tonight, Martha?'

'Tonight's fine, Stanley. I read about your . . . trouble. About Ann. That's really dreadful. You must be so upset.'

'We are. I . . . found her.' Hastily he went on, 'The police are working on it. I'm sure they'll come up with something.' After a moment he added, his tone grim, 'That doesn't make the loss any the less.'

'No, I'm sure it doesn't. And what's this odd business of the vagrant who was killed the same day? Do the police connect the two?'

'It seems the knives—' he found it hard to talk about, even to think of—'were exactly the same, or something. The—what do they call it?—*modus operandi* matched.'

'Strange, almost as though the killer were calling attention to the connection.'

Was that what it was that accounted for the labels left on the knives? Before he had time to respond, she asked, 'Was she one of Ann's stray kittens?'

For a moment Stanley was taken aback, as though she had meant that literally. But of course she couldn't have known Ann was a collector of stray kittens as a child. 'You mean someone she worked with? No, she wasn't. Ann worked at Marigold House, that's abused women.'

'Well, it's strange all the same. What time, Stanley?'

'Tonight? Seven?'

'Fine.' Her voice soft, she added, 'It will be lovely to see you again.'

As he hung up he felt congested, positively congested

with happiness. He couldn't catch his breath properly. Everything was turning out right for him. The business doing well, his position in the firm solid, Martha eager to see him. Well, not everything. A chill touched him. There was Ann's death, that awful moment when he had entered her bedroom, it was always on the periphery of his mind.

He missed her. If he hadn't missed her so much, he wondered if he ever would have called Martha again. Maybe one good thing had come out of her murder, he thought sadly.

CHAPTER 23

'Did you catch the murderer?' Freda asked. She was smiling.

'What murderer? Oh, *that* murderer. Of course I did, that's why I'm home early.' He rummaged in his Nut Drawer for a packet of peanuts. 'How about a drink?'

She looked at him doubtfully. 'You didn't really catch him, did you?'

'Not a chance. This is going to take time. The usual?'

She nodded. 'You did find out some new things, though?'

'We found out that Jane Potter didn't die of cancer, she was a suicide.'

'Jane Potter? Did you tell me about her?'

'She, I think, is the link I've been looking for.' He handed her the drink and picked up his vermouth. 'Let's go sit for a few minutes, I'm beat.'

He swung his feet up to the hassock of his favourite chair. 'That's more like it. Want some peanuts?'

'Carl, when do I ever want peanuts? Tell me who Jane Potter is.'

'She was Ann Koppleman's sister and she died some nine or ten years ago from drowning. She had been a patient at Bay Cove and then she was transferred to a small private hospital.'

She curled her feet under her and settled into a corner of the sofa. 'That makes her a link? Because Eugénie chose that hospital to sleep in?'

'No, it's not that.' He explained what they had turned up during the day's efforts.

'Sounds pretty far out to me.'

'Freda, please. Ron spent the afternoon explaining to me that I'm totally unreasonable. I hoped for better things from you.'

She laughed. 'Know what I did today?'

'Auditioned for a new play?'

'No, there aren't any auditions this month.'

'Took on a new client?'

'You're getting warm.'

He took a sip of his drink and leaned back in his chair. 'I give up.'

'I attended a workshop. Do you know, Carl—' she leaned forward, her face intent—'I never realized I was competitive. Did you?'

Her husband put his head back and laughed. 'You, competitive?'

'Don't laugh, I'm serious. We talked about things we had done that gave us particular satisfaction and experiences that had troubled us. You know what gave me satisfaction? Beating Marilee Wilson in the ninth grade essay contest. It was the first thing that popped into my head. And what troubled me was not getting the lead in the last play. Doesn't that mean I'm competitive?'

'Or human.'

'Is it human to want to beat other people out at things?'

'We have it drilled into us, don't we? Be best. Beat them. Win, win, win.'

'Then I'm not competitive?'

'Oh, I wouldn't say that.' He looked across the room at her with a slight smile on his face. 'You like all this soul-searching you do at the Centre, don't you?'

She nodded. 'You know, I do. I think I like talking

about myself.' She darted a glance at him. 'That makes me narcissistic as well as competitive, doesn't it?'

'You know anybody who doesn't like talking about himself?'

'Some of the counsellors say they don't. They feel these sessions are intrusive. One woman left the Centre because she didn't like the workshops.'

'Just how are they supposed to help you?'

'You untangle yourself so you can be more useful to the clients. Well, to anybody, I suppose.'

'Like me?'

'I'm quite useful enough to you. Aren't I?' she added, with a little anxiety in her voice.

'What do you do for me?'

'I get dinner for you. That is, when you're rested enough to come out and help chop vegetables for the salad.'

He sighed. 'I knew there was a catch.' He studied the contents of his glass. 'I'm going to have to do more with Jane Potter.'

'Like what?'

'Go back and talk to the social worker and the head of Psychiatry at Bay Cove, see if they know anything at all about her death.'

'Why should they if she was at another place when she died?'

'I imagine when hospitals make referrals they keep in touch. Bay Cove may be more forthcoming than Fernwood.' He finished off his drink and set the glass aside. 'The last thing we did today was check the coroner's report on her. She was in perfect health, simply inhaled a quantity of water. Drowned. No signs of strangulation or beating. He noted that she'd been buffeted about during the two weeks she'd been in the water, but none of the injuries were consistent with the assumption of foul play.'

'And despite all that, you think she was killed? Why?'

'Mostly because it would be such an excellent motive for murdering Eugénie.'

'If she was blackmailing her murderer.'

'Yes. Of course that doesn't account for Ann Koppleman's death. Nothing seems to account for both deaths. If
we figure out a motive for one, it doesn't work with the
other. And vice versa,'

'It must be hard to find out about someone who's been
dead as long as Jane Potter.'

'It is. And her having spent the better part of a year
in hospitals affects things, too. If she'd been at home,
there might have been journals, writings that had been
kept. People would have noticed things. Hospitals have
records, but they're clinical, not personal. And they won't
let me have access to them, not without a subpœna.
Well—' he broke open a peanut and checked for the
dwarf as he had done with his father when he was a
boy—'let's go chop vegetables so you can be useful to
me.'

CHAPTER 24

Rod MacMillan was in conference in his office when
Pedersen and Tate arrived. Waiting under the eye of Mac-
Millan's secretary, they were silent. They had deliberately
chosen to come in without appointment, and when the door
from the office opened after ten minutes and MacMillan
and his visitor emerged, the social worker looked surprised,
almost taken aback.

He saw his visitor to the door of the waiting-room and
returned. 'More questions?' He looked at Tate with curiosity.

'A few. This is Detective Tate. He's working on the case
with me.'

MacMillan led them into his office. Empty coffee-cups
sat on his desk. 'Just had a cup, but I could stand another.
Would you care for coffee?'

Pedersen and Tate shook their heads. 'We just had some, too,' Tate said.

MacMillan pulled up a second chair, pushed the mugs aside and sat down at his desk. 'What can I tell you?'

'Mr MacMillan, how long have you been with the hospital?'

'Let's see, it's—God, it's twelve years now. I had one other job, worked for five years with a Los Angeles hospital. My wife and I wanted out of L.A. and when the assistant directorship opened up here, I applied, thinking I'd never get it. But they liked something about my résumé, my big city experience, I guess. I came on as assistant and when the director left eight years ago, I took over.'

'So you were here ten years ago, when Jane Potter was a patient?'

MacMillan threw him an odd look. 'Jane Potter? You're interested in her? I thought—'

'Yes, we're investigating two totally different lives, but we're looking for links between the two. Jane Potter was Ann Koppleman's sister.'

MacMillan looked astonished. 'She was? I never connected the two.'

'I see you remember Jane Potter, though. How is that?'

'She was a suicide, did you know that? When she signed herself out of Fernwood—that's the hospital she was transferred to from here—a psychiatric social worker I know who worked there and had seen her told me he thought she was in good shape, no longer depressed or suicidal. We'd worried about suicide right along when she was here, you see. There'd been an attempt before she came in.'

'The family didn't mention that. We learned it at Fernwood.'

'At any rate my friend was terribly upset over their misjudgement of her condition. He felt he was partially responsible. He'd had a good relationship with her, you see, and he felt if he'd made a correct assessment, he could have talked her out of leaving right then. He talked about it so much during our next few visits that—'

'It fixed it in your mind.'

'That and the suicide itself. The brother apparently made accusations, said Fernwood had behaved irresponsibly and so on. Of course, it was her perfect right to sign herself out. The family didn't try to sue, but they'd have lost if they had. The law protects mental patients these days.'

'Sometimes to their detriment, I'd say, judging by some of the people on the mall,' Tate commented drily.

'Yes, but you wouldn't want it the other way. Now what can I tell you about Jane Potter? We must have records here.'

'Good. I suppose you can't let me see them?'

'Not unless they're subpœnaed. But I can check for you, if there's something in particular, and if it isn't highly confidential.'

Pedersen's smile was disarming. 'Since I don't know quite what it is I'm looking for, maybe you'd get out the records and glance over them with an eye to spotting anything out of the ordinary.'

'Everything about a mental patient is out of the ordinary. May I ask—that is—'

'You want to know what it is that we have in mind regarding her?'

'Well—' MacMillan smiled—'it might help me to know what I'm looking for.'

'I'd prefer that you regard this as confidential, but we're considering the possibility that she was murdered.'

'She too? Isn't that a little excessive?'

Pedersen laughed. 'My partner here thinks so. But that's what interests us. Me, that is.'

MacMillan rang his secretary. 'Jean, will you dig out records on Jane Potter? That'll have been closed out about eight years ago.'

'Ten,' Pedersen corrected.

'That's ten, Jean.' He rang off.

'While we're waiting,' he said, 'I'm going to give you a piece of gossip, hearsay that may have absolutely no bearing on the case. But since you're looking for links . . .' He hesitated, as though he had thought better of the impulse.

After a minute he said, 'You know, I should have connected Ann Koppleman and Jane Potter. The name rang a faint bell, but I figured that was because her name was in the papers occasionally. Anyway, what I was going to tell you . . .'

'Yes?' Pedersen encouraged.

'Jerry'll murder me if he finds out I told you, but I feel you should know, although I'm having second thoughts— Oh, what the hell, I'm going to tell you. Lewis Mawson, the psychiatrist whom I understand you interviewed, is one of Kay Brennan's escorts. Now that I say it,' he added, 'it doesn't seem too relevant.'

'One of her escorts?' Tate said. 'I understood she was married.'

'I gather she has an Open Marriage. Remember them?'

'The O'Neills' book, yes,' said Tate. 'I thought that had gone out of style, what with herpes and AIDS on everyone's mind.'

MacMillan grinned. 'So she's old-fashioned. Anyway, for what it's worth, I've given you the information.' He hesitated. 'Something else—'

A knock at the door drew his attention. 'Ah, Jean, thank you. That was fast.'

Alone with Pedersen and Tate again, MacMillan opened the folder. 'In a general way, I can fill you in. She came to us after the suicide attempt—'

'How did she go about it?' Pedersen asked.

'The usual, sleeping pills. She was depressed, cried a lot and just sat. Brooded. Or slept. Dysfunctional for the most part, although functional enough so that she saw she needed help.'

'Her family may have influenced that,' Tate contributed.

'I'm sure they did. She had lots of family visits throughout her ten days here, but Ann was the most frequent visitor.'

Pedersen raised eyebrows. 'So they were close.'

'It seems so, although the caseworker says here that she always seemed more depressed after Ann's visits.'

'That's interesting. Anything else?'

'No, I've told you more than I should have as it is. I didn't realize the family hadn't let you in on the suicide attempt. I shouldn't have mentioned that.'

Tate turned to Pedersen. 'But it bears out the assumption that her death was by suicide.'

'Yes, it does.' Pedersen sighed. 'At any rate, thanks for your time and for what you've given us. Just before your secretary came in, you started to say something. You were going to tell us something else.'

'You're going to see Mawson again?'

Pedersen nodded. 'As a matter of fact, we are. There was something else about him?'

'No.' MacMillan looked down at the folder in his hands. 'I don't recall what I was going to say. But for God's sake—' he looked up again—'don't let on to Mawson that I told you about him and Kay. Maybe you shouldn't mention it at all, he may remember that Jerry was at some of the same parties.'

'We may have to mention it. We'll let it be assumed it came from outside the hospital.'

'I hope you convince him. I *am* having second thoughts now that it's too late. Jerry was right.'

'Dr Cohen thought you shouldn't pass the information on to us?'

'He didn't think it had anything to do with anything. And probably it doesn't.'

'No, probably not, but the links between the hospital and the Potter-Koppleman-Brennan crowd grow stronger, don't they?' Pedersen rose to leave. 'It may not be relevant, but it's interesting. And if you think of what you wanted to tell us, give me a ring.' He dropped his card on the desk.

MacMillan picked it up and said nothing.

As he and Tate left the office, Pedersen turned to his partner. 'The plot thickens,' he said. He smiled.

Tate groaned.

Lewis Mawson's secretary made clear that Dr Mawson had no time for further visits from the police. 'Didn't you see him just yesterday?' she asked, addressing Tate, her voice as pained as though they were tiresome patients making untoward and impossible demands.

'Yes. When will he be free?' Pedersen asked.

She pursed her lips. '*Really!* He'll be finished with his patient in—' she checked her watch—'five minutes, but he—'

'That's fine,' Pedersen interrupted. 'We'll wait.' He and Tate seated themselves.

After a period of time the secretary rang through to Mawson. Despite her lowered tone and turned head, they picked up the tenor of her communication: 'detectives again . . . know how busy you are . . . yes, I'll tell them.' She swung around and raised her voice slightly. 'You may go in, but Dr Mawson can give you just a *very* few minutes.'

'Isn't his patient in there?' Tate asked.

She regarded him without expression. 'The patients use the other door,' she said.

Mawson consulted his watch as they entered, controlled outrage evident on his face. 'You seem to be making a habit of this. It had better be brief, I have work to do,' he announced. He did not offer them seats.

Pedersen strolled over to the chair nearest the desk and sat down. Tate took another chair. 'Dr Mawson,' Pedersen said, once the physician had with an irritable gesture seated himself behind his desk, 'today we're here to talk with you about an old patient.'

'Jane Potter again.' His face expressed disgust. 'Someone was here, you—' he indicated Tate—'yesterday. I told you she'd been transferred out of here some years ago and I later heard she committed suicide. That's all there is.'

'Today, however, we'd like you to consult your records of her therapy sessions.'

'That's ridiculous, those records are confidential! I'm not about to share them with you.'

'We'll have to subpœna them in their entirety unless you share *some* information with us, Doctor,' Pedersen said. His voice was gentle but he knew Mawson heard the underlying resolution.

Mawson shrugged irritably. 'What is it you want to know? I don't understand your interest in a years-old suicide.'

'Jane Potter was Ann Koppleman's sister.'

'I'm aware of that—that is, your detective made me aware of it yesterday. I had forgotten.'

'Oh?' Pedersen's eyebrows went up. He let the silence extend a moment beyond comfort. 'We understood that you were a friend of the family.'

Mawson's reaction was so strong that Pedersen glanced at Tate to see if he had caught the fear that crossed the physician's face.

'You're mistaken,' Mawson said coldly.

'Then just a friend of Mrs Brennan's, is that it?'

Mawson stood up abruptly. 'I think you go beyond yourself. How do you justify inquiring into my personal affairs?'

Pedersen turned a mild face towards him. 'Inquiring into your personal affairs? I'd hardly say that. A casual remark by one of the family—'

'That's a lie! No one knows—' He stopped, his face congested by rage. 'What is it you want from me—that's within your province of inquiry? What do you want to know about Jane Potter?'

'We're interested in her last few sessions. You were the treating physician?'

'No, I wasn't, as a matter of fact.' Mawson re-seated himself. 'However, I can check her therapist's notes.' His voice was cold. 'What exactly am I to tell you about the last sessions?'

'Primarily whether she was troubled about something or

someone in particular. Maybe her sister, for example. In a word, whether her therapist regarded her as still suicidal.'

Mawson again looked at his watch. He reached for the button on the intercom. 'Miss Roberts, get out Jane Potter's record. She was discharged nine or ten years ago. That's P-O-T-T-E-R.'

They waited in silence.

The record before him, Mawson glanced down and then back at Pedersen. 'Who is your superior officer?'

Pedersen told him. As he watched Mawson note the name, he reflected with amusement that he was accumulating an extraordinary number of complaints on this case.

Mawson opened the folder, turning pages rapidly. Towards the last of the sheets enclosed within it, he slowed and read. After a time he closed the folder and looked up. 'She was not in good spirits. At the time she was transferred, she was seen as still being profoundly depressed. Any reference to specific troubled feelings, I would be unable to share with you.'

'Did her sister Ann figure in those troubled feelings?'

'Yes, but that is absolutely all I can say.'

'After her suicide, did her therapist add anything? Any addendum?'

'As a matter of fact he did. He added a note, pointing out that mood swings are common after a long hospitalization. He felt the family had been remiss in its attention to her on her return home.'

'Wasn't he aware that she did *not* return home?'

'Apparently not. We can't know everything. He did make a note expressing disapproval of Fernwood's releasing her on her own, without family there, but she was within her rights.'

'Interesting. May I have the name of the treating physician?'

'He's long since moved on.' There was triumph in Mawson's voice. 'He's working on the East Coast.' Where you can't get at him, his tone said.

'And you're sure there was no particular expression of concern or ambivalence towards anyone in those last sessions?'

'Oh, ambivalence, that's stock with patients in therapy. And I mentioned her sister. But absolutely nothing out of the ordinary. For a depressed patient, that is.'

'No hint, no clue as to her future behaviour.'

'The suicide? Nothing specific.'

'Well then, I guess that's all for now, Doctor.' Pedersen rose and Tate followed suit. 'I'm sorry I upset you with the reference to Mrs Brennan.'

'Upset me! You didn't *upset* me. It's none of your damned business whom I see and where and when. Keep your inquiries to police concerns. That's something I'd have thought you'd have learned by now.'

'It was an innocent remark, Dr Mawson. Made in passing. If I'd realized it was something you feel so strongly about, I certainly wouldn't have made it.' He stopped, one hand on the doorknob. 'Is there anything else you'd care to tell us? About yourself, I mean.'

Mawson froze. 'What do you mean? Did someone—' He checked himself.

'Anything?'

'I've no idea what you're talking about.' The physician eyed them coldly. 'Are you done? Well then, get out.'

'We're on our way. Thank you for your help.' His back to Mawson, Pedersen caught Tate's eye and winked. Then they were through the door, into the waiting-room and past the formidable Miss Roberts.

'There's something there,' Pedersen said, now sober, as they walked down the hall.

'There's always something. With everyone,' Tate said.

'Yes. That's true.' But Pedersen was quiet as they left the hospital.

'You did get his back up,' Tate remarked as they reached the car.

'Yes, Harbison's going to get another complaint. I'm

going to get myself taken off this case if I don't watch it.'

'I doubt that.'

'You caught the expression on Mawson's face when I raised the issue of acquaintance with the family?'

'Yes. Why should he be *afraid*?'

'And of what? Or should that be of whom?'

'It's crazy. There seems to be a lot more than meets the eye in this case. And the connections—here we were complaining about seeing no connections, now we can't see anything but.'

'It would be nice if we understood them.'

'Yes, it would.'

'We still don't see how Eugénie fits in,' Pedersen said. 'Except for how she got her information for blackmail.'

'If that's what it was. You don't suppose, do you, that she had Mawson on her hit list? Maybe that's why he disliked her in that irrational way.'

'Except,' said Pedersen, 'irrational seems to describe most of his reactions, it wouldn't take blackmail. Wouldn't you like to be one of his patients?'

Tate gave a mock shudder.

'If I could think what to ask her,' said Pedersen, 'I'd go see Kay Brennan.'

Tate pulled into the police parking lot. 'You could say, "What do you do to the good doctor that frightens him so?"'

'Or, "What do you know that scares him so?"'

'I suppose a fishing expedition might turn something up.'

'We could try. I doubt it, though. I have an idea she'd say, "Why, of course Lewis Mawson is my good friend. Whatever can anyone make of that?" Or words to that effect.'

'So what now?'

Pedersen turned the key in the ignition. 'Oh, what the hell. Let's go try Kay Brennan.'

CHAPTER 25

Kay Brennan was at the moment engaged in animated conversation.

She held the phone away from her ear. 'Lew, for Christ's sake, stop shouting at me. I thought you didn't want to have any personal conversation from the hospital.'

'Fuck that! Anyway, Roberts has gone off to lunch and the switchboard isn't taking calls yet.' He went on: 'You're going to be visited by the police again, I'm sure of it, and I just want to make sure you know what to say.'

'What *not* to say, you mean.'

'They sprung this friend-of-the-family bit on me and I lost my cool completely. One of us has to behave—'

'Rationally? Nonchalantly? You can count on me, I'm an expert at nonchalance.'

'You'd better be.'

'That sounds vaguely like a threat. Are you threatening me, Lewis? Because I believe I have more room to make threats than you.'

'Of course I'm not threatening you.' He paused; she could tell he was controlling his anger.

'How do you manage with your patients' problems, Lew? You get so . . . wrought up.'

'I don't get wrought up with patients.' His voice was cold. 'We've discussed this.'

'Oh yes, the Professional Self versus the Personal Self. When you get upset like this I forget that.'

'Kay, are you deliberately trying to be irritating?'

She laughed. 'Maybe. I don't like having you phone to tell me what to say and what not to say. It seems disrespectful. As though you don't trust me to make adequate judgements on my own.'

'All right. Save the sarcasm. Do you think we should still meet tonight?'

'Of course. Does a visit from the police frighten you that much?'

'It doesn't frighten me, it makes me uneasy. I'll see you at seven, then. But be careful—'

'What I say. Yes. I got the message. See you later, Lew, darling.' With amusement she heard her deliberately lilting tones. Screw you, doctor, she thought. I'll say any damned thing I please to anyone I damned please. Once all this mess over Ann's death is done, you, Lewis, will have to go. The thought was followed by an engulfing wave of relief.

The police were predictable; shortly after Lewis's alert, they arrived. This time the younger one, the one who had accompanied Pedersen that first day at the house, was along. She liked his looks: tall, thin as a blade, intelligent-looking with his wire-rimmed glasses, dressed like a young college professor. She turned to him. He looked a sympathetic sort.

'Lewis tells me you'll be asking me some questions.' She had decided to disarm them.

He was startled by her directness, she could tell. He gave her a searching look. 'Yes, we want to do that.' Pedersen had stepped back, so he went on. 'We understand you and Dr Mawson are good friends.'

'We are.' She looked up into his face. 'We are. Good friends.'

'Dr Mawson seemed disturbed that we should mention your friendship.'

She continued to gaze up at him. 'Is that a question? Or am I supposed to say something revealing in answer to your non-question?'

Pedersen spoke. 'Can you tell us, is Dr Mawson acquainted with the rest of the family? Did he know your sister Ann, by any chance?'

'He's met them all at least once. Once in a while we wind

'You've absolutely stricken out the idea that these were unrelated killings?'

'No,' Tate said. 'But we think they're related.'

Inhaling deeply, she found she was dizzy with pleasure and with the unfamiliar smoke in her lungs. The younger detective noticed. 'Are you all right, Mrs Brennan?'

'Yes. Just my first cigarette in months.' She realized as soon as she said it that it was a confession that she was disturbed. With tremendous effort, she stubbed out the cigarette. 'Guess I don't want it after all.' She felt slightly nauseated.

'Mrs Brennan,' Pedersen said, 'was there ever a suggestion of foul play in your sister Jane's death?'

'You mean someone pushed her off the rocks?' For a fleeting moment she felt the clutch of fear; she wondered if the detective had seen it in her face. 'No, no. My sister was a mental patient. Deeply depressed. It was suicide.'

Pedersen persisted. 'The records indicate that she was not depressed when she signed herself out of the hospital. In fact she seemed in high spirits when she got into a cab to come home.'

'Home?' To her ears the question sounded stupid.

'Whatever she meant by home. Didn't she have a house?'

'No. I mean yes, but she had rented it—or we had when she seemed in for a long stay at Fernwood.' At Tate's glance, she explained, 'It was rented on a monthly basis only. But she wouldn't have gone there. She wouldn't have gone there,' she repeated.

'You had anticipated a long hospitalization?'

'We weren't sure, but it was an expensive house. We rented it to cover costs.'

'Mortgage, you mean?'

'And gardener. Maintenance.'

'Did insurance cover her hospitalization?'

'Partly. She had money, it wasn't that. But she wasn't living in the house—'

Pedersen broke in. 'Let's put aside the matter of the

up at the same restaurant as one of my brothers or my sister—we *did*, that is. Lewis is hardly a friend of the family.'

They moved into the pastel and white living-room. 'This will sound odd,' Tate said, 'but has he any reason to be afraid—' he obviously didn't know how to go on—'about any aspect of his acquaintance with you or your family?'

'Afraid?' She was thrown slightly off balance. Her directness was one thing, but this policeman's was another. Did they know about Lew? If they did, she'd better align herself with them against his kinkiness. God knows, she *was* against it. She checked herself in time. That was ridiculous, they couldn't know. She repeated the word. 'Afraid? Afraid of what? What is there to be afraid of?'

'We don't know. Frankly, we were disconcerted. We couldn't tell whether or not he knew something about your sister's death—or maybe your other sister's death.'

'My *other* sister?' For a moment she couldn't think what he was talking about. 'Oh. You mean Jane. But she died ten years ago.'

'Cancer?' asked Pedersen.

Something in his face caught her up short. 'Not exactly. Although we let it be understood it was cancer. Actually, she killed herself.'

'Killed herself?'

'Yes.' Suddenly she was angry at this inquisition. This was the sort of stuff Stanley had warned them against, this sort of questioning. 'What has she got to do with anything?' she said. 'What are you doing about *Ann's* death, that's the question.'

Pedersen answered. 'Actually, we're finding the going rather difficult. We haven't a motive for your sister's death and while we can imagine a motive for the death of the other woman, Eugénie, we can't understand why someone would murder both her and your sister.'

She took a cigarette from the box on the coffee table. She hadn't smoked in months, but suddenly she needed one as she had never needed one. All this was getting to her.

house. You say your sister had money. Did she leave a will?'

'Actually, she did. We were rather surprised, she left everything to us. Of course there wasn't anyone else. She'd never had kids and she was divorced.' She felt a flicker of fear again. She leaned against the arm of the sofa, casually covering her mouth so there were no telltale signs visible. But eyes, she thought, the eyes tell. She could feel the older detective staring at her.

'Is that it?' she said brightly. 'Have I answered all your questions?'

'Not quite,' Pedersen said, taking out his notebook. 'I'd like to talk with your sister Jane's husband.'

For a moment she went blank. 'Oh, Jane's husband. I'm afraid he's dead. You know,' she went on hastily to cover her confusion, 'I find all this discussion of Jane very disturbing. I don't understand what it has to do with anything.'

He put his notebook in his pocket. She had moved him away from the topic of dead husbands. 'It's a link,' he said. 'A link with Eugénie.'

'A link with that bag lady? But what sort of link? I don't understand.'

'If Eugénie knew, say, that your sister had been assisted to her death, she'd have had excellent material for blackmail. As a blackmailer, she'd be in line for becoming a murder victim herself.'

'But that's ridiculous!' The words burst from her. 'I never heard anything so far-fetched. Jane killed herself. She was *depressed*. Besides, how would that explain Ann's death?' She was close to tears, the last thing she wanted in their presence.

'We can't answer that,' Tate said softly. 'That's what we need to know.'

'Well—' she stood up—'*I'm* not going to be able to tell you. If you don't need me any longer, I have an appointment—' she glanced at her watch—'in fifteen minutes.'

Both men got up. 'Think about it, Mrs Brennan. You never received a blackmail letter, I gather.'

'I told you I didn't. If I had, I suppose that would make

me a murderer.' She laughed uncertainly. 'I'll think about it, but I doubt that any wonderful new insights will come to me. You're the ones who are supposed to know how to find out about these things. I'd think—' She left the sentence unfinished.

At the door she glanced again at Tate. He was a pleasant young man, not too young, probably only a few years younger than she. And surprisingly articulate for a policeman. Maybe when things were cleared up and Lew was out of the picture, she'd ask him by for a drink. She sighed. If her husband wasn't back.

And where in hell *was* he? There was something ominous in his not having called. No one at work had heard from him, either. Had he thrown in the towel and gone off to an island somewhere with his latest woman? The idea of him, formal and businesslike as he appeared to the world, lying on some tropical beach in a bikini made her want to laugh, but the laugh caught in her throat.

Shaking, she sank into a chair and took out another cigarette. She was glad she had no appointments until her dinner engagement with Lewis.

CHAPTER 26

At first he didn't recognize her. When was it he had last seen her, ten, twelve years, more? He was fifty-eight so she must be close to that, but her dark hair had become grey, completely grey. And the waist he remembered clasped by bright belts was now markedly thickened. But she was still Martha, still wore a gipsylike South American-looking skirt and over her shoulder had draped a bright shawl.

And she greeted him as the old Martha had. Although, he thought, God knows she must be noticing the same things about me. Before leaving the house he had examined himself in the mirror and been pleased, but now, seeing himself through her eyes, he recalled that he had to pull back his shoulders and draw up his head to disguise the slight softness beneath his chin. But she greeted him in the old way, taking his hands and drawing him into the house, then standing on tiptoe and kissing him on the mouth.

For a moment he was startled, then she became familiar again. 'Martha,' he said, 'I've thought of you so often. I should have called months ago.'

She laughed. He remembered he had particularly liked her laugh. 'Well, we're together now. Will you have a drink or do we have a reservation for right this minute?'

'We have a reservation for eight. There's time for a drink.' He looked around the room. She had lived in this house before she was married, but it was changed. She followed his eyes. 'Holman had things, too. We combined them,' she said. 'I've grown used to it this way.' He followed her into the kitchen and surprised in himself a great sense of relief that it was unaltered from the way he remembered it. Making a move to mix the drinks, he checked himself. She had never accepted—or required—those little niceties he took for granted between men and women. Once, he remembered, she had let him mix drinks, standing watching him with a quizzical expression. When he had finished she had said, 'What was there about that you thought I couldn't do, Stanley? Lift the bottle?' He had been disconcerted and she amused. After that he hadn't volunteered. He was touched by a warm wave of pleasure at being with her once more, the person whose eccentricities and preferences he had once grown to love. How could they have quarrelled and given up all those years of companionship? But he had been a different person then, less sure, less established, less confident. Otherwise, he could never have let her go.

Settled opposite each other in the living-room, each studied the other's face. 'You look tried, Stanley,' she said. 'This business of Ann's death must have been a terrible strain.'

A flicker of anxiety went through him and for a moment he longed to tell her just how upset, bereft, he had been, but he smiled. 'I thought when I dressed today that I looked quite handsome. Hale.' She relaxed him, made it possible for him to be safely humorous. Always with his family, his attempts at humour had fallen flat. As a result, he had become increasingly staid around them. A flare of anger was struck in him at the recollection of Kay's words the other evening, her saying he never *did* anything. 'But,' he said to Martha, more seriously, 'it has been hard. The service is this weekend. Sunday. Will you come?'

She looked confused. 'I? I never really knew Ann, Stanley. But of course if you want me to, if it would make you feel better . . .'

'It would, you know. I don't—have many people.' It was true. There would be friends of Ann's, friends of Roy's and Kay's, even friends of the children there, but none of his own. The last couple of years he had let himself become absorbed in the business to the exclusion of friendship, had become what they labelled these days a workaholic. Kay had been right, except for business lunches and the occasional lunch or dinner with Ann, he didn't do anything. Hadn't, that was. He needed Martha to make him whole again.

He decided to put the business of her husband behind them. 'Was your marriage happy, Martha?'

'It was. The last couple of years Holman wasn't well and he . . . lost his sense of humour, but until then it was good. He was a fine man.'

The appropriate expression. But he found himself pleased, and mentally chided himself for it, that her marriage hadn't been perfectly smooth.

'It should have been me,' he said. 'We should never have quarrelled.'

She smiled. 'We were behaving in a pretty human way. I think you'd been alone so long you were scared to be any other way, and I was pressing you. I wanted the comfort of marriage, even though it was too late for kids. At the time, our splitting up made a lot of sense for both of us.'

'Only because I was crazy.'

She laughed. 'Not crazy. Maybe short-sighted. At any rate, it's all water under the bridge now. No point in hashing it over, no point at all.'

Her acceptance of the situation disturbed him. He wanted at least some small expression of regret from her. He could see he was not going to get it.

He finished his drink. Hers had been short and she had already set her glass down. 'Let's go, then. Let's pretend it's fifteen years ago.'

But even to that she did not respond.

Roy was still coping with the boys. Attributing their lumpishness to grief might explain it to those outside the family, but he had seen them frequently enough in their young lives to know better. Odd that they were so different from Suzanne, who seemed to him brimming with enthusiasms, commitments, plans, flightiness—the complex of contrasts he'd expect of any normal young man or woman in his or her twenties. But the boys simply sat and looked decorative. It *must* be grief, he conceded, becoming more generous as he considered the abruptness and horror of Ann's death. His notion that they were apprehensive about him was ridiculous. Impossible.

At the moment they were animated, however; they were in disagreement about dinner. Roy had suggested a quiet restaurant where at this hour—close to eight—they could find a good meal with no wait. The boys had in mind a quasi-Irish pub they had spotted. Just as he had conceded the point, the twins changed their minds and decided the restaurant was the better idea. Hastily he agreed, but the brief sputter of disagreement, even anger, among them enlivened things for Roy. With a heartier and more affectionate manner than he could usually muster, he herded them out.

At The Glade, they descended by funicular. Then, just as they were entering the restaurant, Roy spotted Stan entering with a woman—by God, that woman he used to see. What was her name? Mary? Martha, that was it.

'What luck,' he said. 'The boys were saying they'd seen almost nothing of you! Let's take a table together.' By God, he thought, I don't give a damn if I mess up his evening, I've had these clods wished on me all week, he can do his bit. 'And Martha!' He shook her hand and turned to the boys. 'Let me introduce you to Ann's sons, Martha. Meredith and Ellery, and Jason. This is Mrs—' He recalled that she had married, but went blank on the name.

'Smithson,' she prompted. 'I'm delighted to meet you. I want to say how sorry I am about your mother. I'll be at the service.'

That they turned to her with relief did not escape Roy. They're as tired of me as I am of them, he thought with amusement. Maybe they're only clods with me.

Stanley was glaring at him. He'd expected that. 'We were planning to discuss some things for which we need privacy,' he began, but it was too late. A waiter had been informed by Meredith that it was a party of six and they were being ushered to a table, Martha ahead surrounded by the boys. 'What's the big idea?' Stan managed between tight lips.

'I've had them all week, you take them on for a couple of hours.' Roy walked ahead and joined the group seating itself.

They were already deep in talk. Meredith, who had barely spoken to his uncle once the memorial service plans had been made, was excitedly describing the first year of law school. 'You wouldn't believe what being on law review means, it's everybody's goal. It makes the difference between a seventy-five-thousand-dollar a year job to start and one that begins at forty. Or less.'

'Forty sounds pretty good to me,' Martha commented. She turned to Ellery. 'You're in law, too?'

'We're dissimilar twins,' Ellery said, to Roy's amazement

attempting a joke. 'No, Jay and I are working on MBAs.' He smiled. 'I'm a year ahead of Jason, though.'

'He boasts a lot,' Jason explained. 'But he is more committed to the programme than I am,' he added.

Martha raised her eyebrows. 'Are you reconsidering, then?'

'Not really. It was just a thought.'

'Well, don't follow through on it,' Stanley put in. He seemed to have resigned himself, if grudgingly, to the company of his nephews. 'I changed my mind several times and, believe me, it set me back years.'

Jason and Ellery looked at their uncle with interest, as though he had suddenly become a valid human being to them. 'What—' Jason began, but the waiter's appearance stemmed conversation.

'You know,' Martha said, after their orders had been taken, 'I saw you all once when you were little. You won't remember, I think you were barely out of elementary school, but Stanley and I dropped by to pick up something from your mother. There was a little girl, too—your sister? Where is she tonight?'

Roy glanced guiltily at the boys. 'I never thought to call her. Did it occur to any of you?'

'Crossed my mind,' said Ellery, 'but when we asked her last time, she was going somewhere with Ollie.'

'Ollie. That rings a bell.' Martha turned to Stanley.

'Ann's friend. Her suitor for years.' Roy glanced at him. He could see Stan wished they wouldn't keep bringing up Ann. It must have been hell on Stan, finding her that way.

He noted the relief on Stanley's face as the waiter, loaded tray in hand, headed their way with the first course.

Kay Brennan and Lewis Mawson had considered The Glade but decided in favour of a restaurant seated high on a hill behind one of the town's hospitals.

'You like the proximity of a hospital,' Kay remarked as

they waited for their drinks. 'Aren't there supposed to be people who feel safer in an institutional environment?'

'There are. You're getting too wise since your acquaintance with me.' He said it good-naturedly, but she could see that he was annoyed. 'I'm *not* one,' he added. 'Ah.' He picked up the Bloody Mary that had just been brought.

'That looks a little gory for this particular week,' Kay commented, glancing at his glass.

Lewis set down his glass with a little crack. 'Are you planning to needle me all evening?'

'No.' She forced herself to relax. 'Sorry. I wasn't trying to needle you, I guess I was just expressing my preoccupations. Did you have a ghastly day?'

'Not ghastly, but not good. I didn't exactly savour that visit from the fucking police.'

'Oh yes, I forgot that. They did come by, just as you said they would. Like clockwork. Predictable.'

He leaned towards her, frowning. 'What did they ask you?'

'Whether you knew the family, particularly Ann. And whether you had any reason to be afraid of the family. I think that was it.'

'Afraid? What did you say?'

'I said, "Afraid of what?"'

'And?'

'They seemed to think you knew something about Ann's death. Or—' she raised her eyes and looked at him with calculation—'Jane's death.'

'What? Oh, Jesus—' He had upset his drink. 'I'm amazed they didn't also ask if I killed Eugénie. You didn't—?'

After the waiter had mopped up and brought another drink, Lewis went on, his voice more controlled. 'What do they know about Jane's death?'

'That's the question. What do they know?'

'Well, didn't they give any hint? Christ!'

'They know she didn't die of cancer.'

'You told them?'

'I told them she drowned herself, but that the official version was cancer.'

'They must know something, they wouldn't be bringing up this stuff otherwise. Fuck it.'

'I don't see why *you're* so upset. I should be the one.'

'I'm upset *for* you. That was it?'

'Not quite. They asked if there had ever been a suggestion of foul play, I think that's the way they put it, in Jane's death.'

They stared at each other, silent.

'And,' Kay went on after a minute, 'whether there was a will.'

'And who the beneficiaries were.'

'Yes.'

'He thought she was killed—and killed for her money, is that what he was hinting?'

Kay was suddenly irritable. 'Who knows what he thought? I told him we inherited. It wasn't much, God knows, the hospital bills had eaten up a good deal of it.'

'Was it enough to commit murder over?'

'I put him off that idea. At least I think I did. But they think something's wrong.'

'You know, Kay—'

'I know what's coming. You don't want to see me till this thing is cleared up.' Her jaw was set.

'It's just—it's just not good for me to be associated—so closely associated, that is—with a murder. That's the only reason. It's nothing to do with you. You know how I feel about you.'

'Lewis, you're just an old-fashioned courtly gentleman, aren't you? Throw the little girl to the wolves and save your own skin.'

'I'm a physician, for Christ's sake. And a psychiatrist. I can't *afford* this, visits from the police, inquiries into my relationship with the family. How the hell did they even find out we were seeing each other?'

'Who knows? We aren't secretive about it. Anybody could
have seen us.'

'It's somebody at the hospital. I've taken you to a couple
of parties. They hate me.'

'They? Who is *they*? God, you sound paranoid.'

'Never mind. And let me deal out the psychiatric jargon,
if anybody does. At least I'm qualified.' His face become
cold. 'I'm not going to see you till this is over, Kay.'

'And if I decide to share with the police some of your
little preferences? And maybe that episode with Eugénie?
That should put you right in line as a murder suspect.'

He had paled. 'You wouldn't do that. You have as much
at stake as I.'

'I wouldn't absolutely count on it, Lewis. Here comes the
waiter. Shall we order?'

At work in the museum the next morning, Roy indulged in
a rare moment of introspection. He gave the impression of
being a contemplative man, he was sure, but in fact he was
not. As a boy, aware of differences between himself and
other boys, he had gone through a long period of examining
his motives, but the process had proved too painful to
continue. In recent years he had developed a mode of
managing his life that satisfied him; he dealt with the world
on what he supposed would be regarded as a superficial
basis. He allowed himself deep pleasure in things æsthetic—
the smooth surface of a seashell, the explosion of colour in
an abstract painting, a richly textured fabric, a piece of
music. But aside from that, he functioned in terms of action
without analysis. And when it came to human relationships,
he held himself slightly apart. He had easy friendships with
people he might never see again and not feel a sense of loss,
he took lovers who satisfied his body's needs, but he kept
his distance emotionally. This all went towards creating the
bland, easy manner that he knew was assumed to be paired
with thoughtfulness.

But today he wondered. Last night Stan had been upset

at mention of Ann. Shouldn't he too be feeling *something*? The only emotion of which he had been aware in the past week was irritation with the boys. He had gone through the motions, comforting Kay and remaining steady in the face of Stan's hysterics over the family image the other night, but he hadn't *felt* anything. What did that make him, some sort of conscienceless sociopath? Or was he in shock? He had heard that people confronted by a dreadful event sometimes remained numb, unfeeling, for days, even weeks afterwards. The thing that made him suspect that this wasn't the case was the familiarity of his absence of feeling. It wasn't stunned or unnatural, it was usual.

He sighed as he lifted a painting to try it against the newly grey-green wall. Certainly this state of mind was better than going to pieces over the events of the past few days. Even Kay and Stan hadn't done that. Maybe they felt no more than he, it was possible. Maybe no one felt anything when such things happened; perhaps they just pretended they did.

Somehow that thought eased his mind. Probably that was it. This business of feeling was highly overrated. Everyone was back at work, back to the business of living his life. Even Sue, who had seemed most affected, had gone to a class, he understood. Once the service was over, they could return to normal again. Death happened. Life meanwhile, as Stan had pointed out, must go on.

Yes, he decided, the painting was right in that spot. He relaxed into pleasure at the thought that all the choices for this show were his to make.

CHAPTER 27

The phone call from Jedediah Martin came just as Pedersen arrived at his office the next morning. For a moment the strange name didn't ring a bell. Then he remembered. 'Mr

Martin. Has something occurred to you?'

'You know, it has. I thought about all your questions, about your asking if Ann was afraid of anything or anyone. I remembered a letter she got.'

Pedersen was instantly alert. 'Yes?'

'I don't know what was in it, I didn't read it or anything. But a couple of weeks before she died, we were having dinner one evening and she said, "Jed, I received a terribly disturbing letter this morning." I said, "What was that?" or "What sort of letter?" something of that sort. Then she smiled, it was a rather forced smile, and she said, "No, I'd better think about it before I discuss it with you." She changed the subject and never referred to it again. Funny I didn't remember when you came in to talk to me.'

It was funny. Pedersen said, 'That was all? She didn't say who it came from or hint at why it was disturbing?'

'No. In fact, she was so completely herself for the rest of the evening that it went right out of my head. I never thought about it till now. If I thought anything at all when she said that, it was that one of her sons was in some sort of trouble with grades, something of that sort. It may have been that, it's just that with the . . . events of the last few days, it occurs to me that it may be something related to them.'

Probably the man's explanation was an honest one; a casual remark he interpreted as school trouble might easily not remain in the memory. He thanked Martin, told him if anything further occurred to him to call, and hung up.

It certainly sounded like the blackmail letter. Yet if it accused her or some other family member of murder, would she even have considered discussing it with a younger man with whom she had a casual, if friendly, relationship? Odd, unless it was like the confidence to the airline seatmate, told to someone who mattered so little one could confide freely. But if he could take them at their words, none of the other family members had received such a letter, and surely they would have mentioned it if they had known Ann had got one. Unless, of course, it was the one accused of murder whom she had told.

With whom would she have discussed such a letter? Would there have been anyone sufficiently in her confidence? Suzanne, her daughter? No. Surely she wouldn't have burdened her youngest child with upsetting information. Oliver Winter, her lover? If she had talked to anyone outside the family, it would likely have been her Ollie, who had known the family fortunes for years and might even have been able to advise her.

Pedersen remembered the man's anger. How could he approach him? He buzzed Tate.

'Trick him,' Tate said, standing at the window.

'Trick him? What do you mean?'

'Let him think you've found the letter among Ann Koppleman's things.'

'Hmm.' Pedersen dumped the worry beads on the desk. 'It's an idea. If he actually did see the letter, he'd try to explain it.'

'And probably inadvertently tell us a lot about it in the process.'

'I think this time I'll ask him to come in. Put him on the defensive, he's too sure of himself on home ground. Of course, he may refuse. He'd be within his rights and he seems very much aware of his rights.'

'You may end up with another complaint to Harbison.'

'I may. Nothing I can do about that.' He glanced at the office clock. 'I'm going to try him now before he gets out of the house.'

Oliver Winter seemed to have undergone a change of heart. Oh, Detective Pedersen worked on Saturday, too? Yes, it was convenient for him to stop by headquarters; he'd be happy to help Detective-Sergeant Pedersen in any way he could; he was pleased the investigation was moving ahead. Pedersen hung up, puzzled.

'What the hell's come over him? Suddenly he's all co-operation.'

'Maybe somebody in the family got to him, convinced him that making waves isn't the way to go.'

'Maybe. He'll be here in half an hour. You stick around, Ron, you see if *you* can size this guy up. I found him, shall we say, enigmatic?'

Ron Tate laughed. 'That'll be the day, when I can size up somebody you haven't figured out.' He removed his glasses. 'What else do we have to go on? This case gets complicateder and complicateder, as Alice would have said, if she had.'

'Mawson. I keep coming back to Mawson. His involvement with the family and with the hospital. And the thing that we don't know about him that's bothering him. Obviously the major candidates for murder, especially of Eugénie, are family members, but I don't see them wiping out both the blackmailer and the blackmail victim.'

Tate finished polishing his glasses and put them back on. 'Do you see this Jedediah person doing it?'

'No, his alibi's rock-solid. But Mawson's an unknown quantity. So's Oliver Winter.'

Oliver Winter arrived at precisely the moment he had said he would come. Dressed as he was in an impeccably tailored suit, white shirt, black tie, he was so unlike the usual visitor to the office as to seem remarkable. It occurred to Pedersen, not for the first time, that he always took particular notice of men in suits and ties in this town, they were so rare.

Pedersen introduced Tate.

Seated, Winter smiled agreeably. 'Now what can I tell you, gentlemen?' The mockery was still there, if faint, in his voice.

'We want to talk to you about a letter Ann Koppleman received.'

A quiver of some emotion—fear?—touched his face. But he said calmly, 'A letter?'

'Yes, a letter that was intended to be very disturbing to her.'

'And undoubtedly was,' Tate added.

'What did the letter say?' Winter remained in the same relaxed posture as when he had seated himself.

'It gave her information. We think you know what it said, Mr Winter. And from whom it came.' Pedersen slid open his shallow middle desk drawer and glanced into it, then closed it.

Winter adjusted his tie. 'It was written by some crank, just to upset her.'

'What in the letter made you think that?'

'Obviously it was untrue. Completely untrue. That's what made me think it.'

'What accusations—' Although he did not know why, the moment he said the word he realized he had made a mistake. 'What things in the letter were untrue?'

Winter's eyes had narrowed. 'You haven't read that letter, have you? You just know she received one.'

'But you have, Mr Winter. It would further our investigation if you were to tell us what parts of that letter struck you as untrue.'

'Why should I? Why should I do anything to sully Ann's name?'

The old-fashioned word startled Pedersen. '*Sully* her name?'

'This is what you police call a fishing expedition. She did receive a disturbing letter. I did see it. That's all I'm going to tell you. It was filled with untruths intended to hurt and upset her, even exploit her. But I am not going to repeat them to you.'

Pedersen leaned forward. 'You realize that the person who wrote that letter may have been a real threat to Mrs Koppleman.' As he said it, he thought: Not if it was Eugénie. At least, not a threat of death.

Winter appeared about to rise. 'Is there anything else?'

Pedersen pursued his point. 'You don't care that the person who wrote the letter was a threat to Ann Koppleman?'

'Of course I care! I simply don't believe it. If I'm forced in court to discuss the letter, I will. I won't do it voluntarily.' He paused as though considering. 'I am not being unco-operative, Detective. I honestly am convinced that the letter was from a crank, someone who envied Ann or her family and had decided to be malicious. If I thought it had any direct bearing on her death, I'd tell you every word in it. It doesn't. I believe that.' He walked to the door. 'I'm sorry to frustrate you.' He sounded as though he actually were sorry. 'I'll go along now.'

'One moment. Will you at least tell us who signed the letter?'

Winter put one hand on the doorknob. 'If I told you that, I might as well tell you what was in the letter.' He opened the door and was gone.

'Well,' said Pedersen. 'It can't have been signed with Eugénie's name or he'd have tied her in with Ann's death. The other day when I talked to him, he was convinced there was no connection between the two deaths or that Ann would have had anything to do with a bag lady. So who signed it?'

'Maybe she signed it with a phrase.'

'"Out to get you"?'

Tate laughed. 'No. Something descriptive. "One who knows". Something like that.'

'Would telling us have given away the whole show?'

'If it was a phrase, it could have been extremely descriptive. "One who knows you committed murder," for instance.'

'That could be. The other thing is, did you notice the word that gave away that we hadn't read the letter?'

'No. What was it?'

'Accusations. When I started to say, "What accusations—" Winter immediately knew I hadn't read the letter.'

'That means—'

'Yes. There were no accusations in the letter.'

'Then it wasn't an accusation of murder, the way you thought.'

'You know, Ron,' Pedersen said, taking a bag of peanuts from his desk drawer, 'we may have to rethink this whole thing.'

'If that letter didn't contain threats, what did it contain? If it didn't contain accusations—' Pedersen rubbed his eyes. They had been discussing the case for an hour and they had arrived back at the main question.

'Did it occur to you that the letter might have had nothing at all to do with Jane Potter's death?'

Pedersen groaned. 'Since an hour ago it's occurred to me.'

'The one thing we do know,' Tate said, 'is whom Eugénie sent the letter to. Ann.'

'We don't know that, we assume it. All we *know* is that Eugénie wrote a mysterious letter and Ann received a mysterious letter.'

'Then you don't think—'

'Oh, I do think. I just don't *know*.'

'It's a bitch, this case, isn't it?' Tate commented. 'Nothing fits. Everybody is involved with everybody else, but not a goddamned thing *fits*.'

'You're singularly gloomy about this, Ron. Look at the positive side of things. We're being challenged.' He sighed. 'In fact, you might say we're being stumped.'

'You might.' They looked at each other.

CHAPTER 28

Freda had proposed meeting for lunch after she finished at the Counselling Aid Centre. She arrived, on her face the satisfied, slightly introspective glaze Pedersen had come to anticipate after her meetings with other counsellors. Today,

however, he had no humour about it. About anything, for
that matter.

'This case,' he said after they had installed themselves
at the outdoor café of Kettle House and ordered, 'is *impossible*.'

She looked surprised. 'Don't you always think that?'

'Jane Potter ties in there in some way and I haven't the
first notion where,' he went on, ignoring her, 'and nobody's
about to tell me, either.'

'You've tried Roy?'

'Roy?'

'That brother. Roy.'

'Why Roy?'

'I have an idea from what you've told me that he likes to
be important.'

Pedersen sat back so the waitress could set his plate before
him. 'Is this some notion you've gotten from counselling?'

She laughed. 'No. Just common sense.'

'What have I told you that led to that conclusion? *What?*'

'Oh, when you described them, he came across as someone who's always taken a back seat in that family.'

'I don't know. Sometimes I think I shouldn't discuss my
cases with you, Freda.'

She began on her salad. 'It's just an idea. You're on edge
today, Carl. It's not like you.'

'It's not, but this case is so damned frustrating. And every
time I turn around, Harbison has another complaint about
me. Maybe I need a vacation.'

'You always need a vacation, that's nothing new. I think if
you just take it easy and go about things the way you usually
do, without any fuss, you'll come up with the answers.' She
reached across the table and touched his hand.

Pedersen could feel himself let go. 'You're good for me.
Like medicine. A tonic,' he said.

She made a face. 'What a dreadful comparison. Can't I
be good for you in some pleasanter way than medicine? You
never take medicine, anyway.'

He laughed, his equilibrium mysteriously restored. 'Like a hike through a pine woods? Like a dip in the bay at noon in the dead of summer? Like sex in the morning? Is that better?'

She grinned. 'Much. Why don't you try Roy Potter? It can't do any harm.'

'I've just decided I will. I never belittle your intuitive powers.' At her expression, he added, 'Your common sense contributions, I mean.'

She raised her eyebrows. 'Now. Let's talk about me for a change.'

He found Roy at the museum. Alone in the large gallery, Roy Potter was shifting about paintings of a strange delicacy; Pedersen was struck by their simplicity. 'Mr Potter, frankly I'm stuck. I've come to you for help. Can you work and talk at the same time?'

'I can try. I'm not sure I can help you much.'

'I think so. You strike me as sensitive, aware of people and what makes them tick.' I'm slathering this on too thick, he thought, Freda's instinct about this man had better be right.

Apparently it was. Roy put down the painting he was holding and turned to Pedersen, a pleased expression on his face. 'I'll try to help. Let's sit down back there.' He led Pedersen to a bench behind a screen. 'Everybody's out of the building at the moment, we won't be bothered.'

'It's your sister Jane,' Pedersen said. He sensed an immediate tensing in the other man.

'Jane. She died ten years ago.'

'I know she did. This will seem strange to you, but I'd like you to tell me about her. You'd have been aware of the ... facets of her personality, the things that made her different from the other members of the family. That's the sort of thing I need to know.'

'But *why*? She's been dead almost ten years.'

'Let's say—let's put my motives aside for a minute. Could you do that?'

'I suppose,' Potter said, grudging. 'Jane.' His face grew soft. 'Jane was the sensitive one in the family, not me. She was—how can I describe her? When we were little, Ann rescued lost kittens, but it was Jane who became ... emotionally involved with them. She wasn't very sure of herself, Ann had a confidence that Jane never had, but Jane was intensely loyal to those people she—valued.' He looked up at the detective. 'You know, this is hard for me.'

'You were very attached to her?'

'She was two years older than I, Ann was three years younger. I was the middle child in the family. Jane sort of took care of me, she was always putting Band-Aids on my hurt knees and comforting me when she thought someone had treated me badly. She ...' An odd expression crossed his face, as though he were experiencing an unfamiliar emotion. 'She was a good big sister. She had little quirks, like all of us—she liked secrets, I remember. She wasn't exactly secretive, but she did like secrets.'

'What about her as an adult? What happened with her marriage?'

'As an adult she was over-sensitive. Easily hurt. Then her husband left her and found someone else, that really hit hard.' Pedersen glanced away and when he looked back caught a look of calculation on Roy Potter's face. It passed. 'She went to pieces. Wept and wept and wept. Finally the family saw that it wasn't just a passing thing and persuaded her to consider hospitalizing herself. By this time she wasn't crying any more, but she was ... immobilized. Just sitting. Or lying, all curled up. Not eating. It was very upsetting to all of us.'

'So she was persuaded.'

'Yes, but she didn't want anyone to know. I think she thought other people found her strange and she kept saying that we must pretend she was in the hospital for some ordinary illness.'

'And did you?'

'At first. Actually, at first we just didn't mention that she was hospitalized, but—'

'She had to go to Fernwood.'

'Yes. And after a while she saw a few friends.'

'And ultimately you did dismiss her illness as having been what one might call an ordinary one.'

'That was Kay's idea, I think. Or Ann's. They thought it might explain her being out of circulation for so long.'

'Then what?'

'What happened next couldn't have come at a worse time. She had been seeming better, we had talked to her about signing herself out. Then one weekend when all of us, *all* of us, were out of town, she did it. I think she waited for that chance.'

'All four of you away. That seems oddly coincidental.'

'I know. Ann and Kay had gone up to Mendocino for the weekend—both their husbands were tied up with meetings or were away, I've forgotten. And I visited a friend in Big Sur for the weekend. Stan was recovering from a broken love-affair and decided to take his boat out by himself. That's not a good practice, but he did it and slept on the boat for several days, just getting away, having a change of scene. By the time we returned, Jane had signed herself out and simply vanished.'

'And then?'

'We talked about going to the police, but we were afraid if she was just off someplace, recovering from the hospitalization as it were, she'd be furious. So we hired a private detective to try to find her. He found her.'

'Two weeks later.'

'Yes, but the thought was that she had died the day or within a day of getting out of the hospital.'

'You found her at the morgue?'

'Yes, the detective called us. He was pretty sure it was Jane, but he wanted us to identify her.'

'Was there any suggestion of foul play, Mr Potter?'

'You mean was she pushed, something like that?'

'Or strangled or knocked out?'

He looked shocked. 'No. The autopsy would have shown that, wouldn't it?'

'Yes. But was there any hint of that brought up?'

'No. Who could have done it? We were all away, if that's what you're hinting at. And she had been out of touch with everyone while she was in the hospital, even her closest friends. That thing about secrets I told you about, that was in full play while she was hospitalized.'

'I'm amazed that anyone could conceal such a secret for the better part of a year.'

'It was a little amazing. I suppose, to tell the truth, we weren't any of us exactly happy about having a member of the family under psychiatric care. We abetted her in her efforts to keep it quiet.' He sighed. 'It all seems like such a long time ago. I haven't thought about Jane in several years. I guess you block out things like that.'

'And you've received no communication, no letter, no phone call about her death in recent weeks?'

'No. You asked me that before. What is this all about, all this business about Jane?'

Pedersen looked at him thoughtfully. 'We're wondering if Eugénie, that's the bag lady who was murdered the same night as your sister Ann, somehow got wind that there was foul play in Jane's death. And was blackmailing a member of the family.' He thought: I persist in this notion, despite evidence. Ron's right about me, I get on a hobby-horse and ride it, even if it's going nowhere.

Roy Potter stood up abruptly. 'I never heard such nonsense.'

'Your sister Ann received a disturbing letter just before her death. Several people have told us.'

'That doesn't make sense. Why would both of them be killed then?'

Pedersen sighed. 'That's what catches us up every time.'

'And how could this bag lady get such information? She must have manufactured it.'

'She must have known about your sister Jane to manufacture it. And despite no signs of foul play, Jane *could* have been pushed off those rocks.' Of course, he thought, what I'm not telling this man is that Eugénie was a nurse and might well have known Jane. Or that this is all speculation, we don't know what the letter said.

Potter thrust his hands into his pockets. 'I don't buy it. Any of it. It sounds crazy. I think some maniac just bought a couple of knives and used them the same night.'

'That's odd, too, Mr Potter. It's almost as though he were directing us to see a connection between the murders— same knives, same price stickers on them. You can see what we're up against.'

Potter sat down as suddenly as he had stood. 'I do see. It's hard to understand. But so far as Jane is concerned . . .' He drew a hand across his eyes, a weary gesture. 'That was disturbing enough to go through, that whole business of her illness and death. We don't need to drag it all up again.'

'I don't know, Mr Potter, we may need to. One last thing, then I'll leave you to your pictures. They're—' he tried to find another word—'beautiful, those paintings. I think I'll come to your exhibit.' And bring Freda, he thought. She'll love them.

'Yes? The one thing?'

'What was your sister Jane's married name?'

A strangely resistant expression seized Roy Potter's face. 'What does that have to do with anything? The man's dead now.'

'I'd still like to know.' Now that it occurred to him, several family members had skirted answering this question.

Or had he not asked the question this directly? He couldn't remember. 'The name?'

There was a moment of silence. Then, in a low voice, Roy Potter said, 'Her name was Jane Koppleman.'

'Koppleman? You mean—?'

'Yes, Ernest left Jane in order to marry Ann.'

CHAPTER 29

This time, Stanley decided, nothing was going to spoil his evening with Martha. He would ask her to dinner at his house, broil a steak for her. She could help with the salad and he'd lay in some good wine and buy a dessert, French pastry perhaps. He'd even remember to stop off at the good bakery, though it was off the beaten track for him and he always had to line up and take a number. Their bread almost made it worthwhile.

But he might have known: Martha would have no part of it. 'Come to me,' she said; her old-fashioned phrasing was one of the things that endeared her to him. 'I'll make a roast, rare, the way you like it. You can bring dessert if you want.' At any rate, at her house they would not be interrupted any more than at his. He was elated all day.

Shortly before he was to leave work, the phone call came. It was that detective again, Pedersen; he was becoming a real nuisance. 'Yes?' Stanley said, 'I have another call waiting, can we make it quick?' That was a lie, but somehow he felt the evening to which he was so looking forward was fragile and would be spoiled if he lingered too long on the phone with the detective.

Pedersen's voice came clearly over the wire, startling Stanley with its words. 'Tell me, Mr Potter, what relationship did Ernest Koppleman have with your sister Jane after their divorce? Did he pay her hospital bills?'

'What?' For a moment Stanley couldn't get his bearings.

'Who told you about that?' He was outraged that someone in the family would have bandied about, that was the way he thought of it, Ann and Jane's private affairs. 'Who?'

'Your brother, but reluctantly, you may be sure.'

'Damn Roy! That old business! Why would you want to know about it, anyway?' He was having trouble controlling his voice. The fiction of the waiting phone call was forgotten.

'We have reasons. Did your brother-in-law pay Jane's bills?'

'Yes, most of them. That whole affair, the business of his marrying Ann after the divorce, was unfortunate, none of us liked it. But it happened and we lived with it. Is *that* going to be passed along to the press, I suppose?' His evening was ruined, he knew. He could never regain the sense of well-being that had pervaded his day.

'I don't see why the press should know anything about it unless, of course, it proves particularly relevant. What was the timing—did your sister Jane know about her former husband's involvement with Ann before the actual marriage took place?'

He supposed he had no choice but to answer. 'No. It was that that caused her depression, we thought, discovering it wasn't just some anonymous woman, but her sister that he'd been interested in all along. *Must* we go into all this?'

'I'm afraid we must. So there was the separation, the divorce and then this sudden shock, the marriage to her sister. That must have produced a lot of guilt in Ann, especially when her sister broke down.'

'I'm sure Ann felt bad about it. She didn't *plan* it, after all. She didn't do it to Jane on purpose.'

'I see.' There was a pause, no doubt while Pedersen thought up some other embarrassing question. He had. 'There wasn't any particular rivalry between the sisters, then?'

'No! Ernest comforted Ann after her husband's death—she was pretty broken up and he came around and did little things for her, helped her with finances and settling the estate, and one thing apparently led to another. I'm sure neither of them intended it. I just don't understand all this interest in Jane. She died almost ten years ago, why are you bringing her into things?' Stanley suddenly felt tired, as though the evening's plans were beyond his energies. How could he be pleasant and relaxed with Martha after this interrogation? He sighed deeply.

Pedersen must have heard him. 'I know all this is upsetting to the family. To you. We think the link between Eugénie, the bag lady, and your sister Ann may be Jane. We think Eugénie found out something about Jane's death and was trying to blackmail your sister Ann. We haven't fitted things together properly but that's the reason for the interest in Jane.'

'You found a blackmail letter?'

'No, we're hypothesizing. And we may be wrong, but we have to pursue this line till we're sure we're wrong, if we are.'

'You think there was something . . . suspect about Jane's death?'

'There could be. She could have been pushed off those rocks.'

'But you mean that some person—that Ann—?' He could hear that his voice was faint.

'Someone. We're not making any assumptions yet about who did the pushing.'

'I—Stanley felt he had handled all he could handle. God knew what bombshell the man was about to unleash next. He remembered. 'That other phone call. I have to go. Is that it?'

'That answers my questions. Thank you for your time, Mr Potter.' Pedersen rang off.

Stanley sat looking at the phone as though it had spat venom. If what Pedersen said was true, the police thought Ann had pushed Jane off the rocks. Surely they wouldn't think she'd do such a thing merely because she felt guilty over marrying Ernest? And how did they account for Ann's death, if they believed that? They were hopelessly muddled, chasing down a wrong trail, but Pedersen's suggestions had made him uneasy, uncertain. That Roy. Roiling the waters as usual, although probably he had been on the spot exactly as he, Stanley, had when Pedersen asked him about the relationship.

He began to gather up papers on his desk, preparatory to leaving. He wished the whole thing were behind him, not poisoning a day like this, one which had started out so auspiciously. Imagine suspecting Ann, gentle Ann who rescued kittens.

Well, he decided, he might as well leave, stop off to pick up dessert, go on to Martha's, down a couple of drinks and try to put behind him Pedersen's intrusion into his happiness. Easier, he thought as he closed the door to his office, said than done.

But when he arrived the house had such a jaunty air that he could not remain depressed. Martha had laid a fire which blazed brightly and set a table before it with coloured pottery and lighted candles. He recalled that she had always struck the right note of intimacy, or formality if the occasion called for it, when she entertained. Looking around the warm room, he thought: Kay's right, my living-room does look like a public lounge.

He dropped the bakery box on the kitchen counter and seated himself on a stool to watch her. She was rinsing spinach leaves and slicing a red pepper and mushrooms and papery onion rings into a salad bowl, her hands deft and graceful.

She glanced up. 'You look exhausted. Why don't you pour yourself a drink?'

Gratefully he poured himself a double bourbon, splashing a little water into it. 'I am tired,' he admitted. 'Martha, you don't know what it means to come here at the end of a day.' He took a gulp of his drink and, whether from the whisky itself or the prospect of its effects, felt himself relax. 'You're a *soothing* woman. You remind me of Ann.'

He hadn't meant to say that; to his ears, his voice sounded choked.

She smiled and poked a strip of red pepper at his mouth. 'And you're a sweet man to say so.' Her eyes were on his face. 'You miss her.'

He could not answer.

The dinner was delicious. Martha was a good cook; he could see how she had come by the extra roundness in her face and at her waistline; meals like this every night would threaten his trimness, he knew. But—a warm wave of feeling washed over him—how it would be to come home every night to a dinner like this! To Martha. For the first time since Ann's death he was drained of tension. He even considered telling Martha of his conversation with Pedersen, but he abandoned the idea. That would intrude the whole matter of the murder into their evening. What he needed tonight was to escape it.

Over coffee, he apologized. 'I'm sorry about Roy and the boys wishing themselves on us at dinner last night,' he said. 'Nothing I could do. I guess being paternal is difficult for Roy, he's had it with the three of them.'

'I didn't mind, I enjoyed meeting them. Your nephews seem so excited over their work.'

Stanley laughed. 'When we were leaving, Roy told me they hadn't shown a spark of interest in what they're doing until you showed up. You coaxed it out of them.'

'Didn't take much coaxing. The service is tomorrow, isn't it? I suppose after that they'll be going back.'

'Yes, and Roy can cease being on his good behaviour.'

'His good behaviour?'

'Ignore that, I shouldn't have said it. You've met Kay, haven't you?'

'A couple of times when we were all younger—she was in her thirties then, I think. Did they have children?'

'No.' Stanley was surprised at the question. 'Was she talking about having any? If so, you must have drawn her out, too, she's never expressed the least interest in parenthood in my presence.'

'I don't think she said anything. It just seemed to me that a married woman that age would be thinking of it, if she were ever going to.'

'You regret not having had kids, don't you, Martha?'

She met his eyes. 'I'd like to have had them. I've survived the loss.'

'Do you blame me? Keeping you hoping so long and then not coming through?'

'I never thought of it that way. I was capable of making choices. I chose you.'

'What about now, Martha? Would you choose me again?' He reached across the table for her hand.

After a moment she withdrew it. 'I don't know, Stanley. It's something I've thought about since you phoned.'

A sensation of foreboding gripped him. 'You decided something?'

'No.' She smiled. 'It's a little soon, isn't it? I haven't decided anything at all. Let's just take it a day at a time and see what we feel. Doesn't that make sense?'

'Yes, but I haven't the slightest desire to be sensible about you.'

Her laughter lightened the moment. 'Have some of this wickedly rich pastry, then. The sensible thing would be to ignore it.'

'You're avoiding the issue.'

'Not avoiding it, deferring it. No decisions for a while, Stanley. Do have some of this pastry. I'll eat it if you leave it, and I can't afford it.'

Probably, he told himself as he helped himself to a napoleon oozing with custard, she's right. We should take it a day at a time. But for the first time in his life, he felt sure. He hoped there wouldn't be too many days to live through. This was one thing in his life he was not going to botch.

CHAPTER 30

'Where are we now with the case?' Freda asked. She was standing at the stove, heating a stew she had prepared earlier in the day.

Pedersen raised his eyebrows. 'Where are *we*?'

'Where are *you*, then?' She grinned. 'You're so possessive about some things.'

He laughed. 'I'd gladly give this case away. No, that's not true. I've become fascinated with all the interrelationships. Everybody is something to someone else, but no pattern emerges from the connections.'

'What's the latest?' The stew's fragrance filled the kitchen. Freda's face was rosy from the heat.

He joined her at the stove. 'That smells wonderful. How about a taste? I'm ravenous.'

She offered him the spoon filled with chunks of vegetable and beef. 'I'm hungry, too. It's beginning to feel like fall. So, what's new in the case?'

'You won't believe it. Jane Potter was married to Ernest Koppleman before he married Ann.'

Freda stopped stirring. 'She *was*? You mean her sister swiped her husband?'

'For a lady who prides herself on her feminism, that's a pretty old-fashioned way of putting it, but it's the fact.'

'Had it been going on all the while?'

'I gather it happened after she lost her husband, her first one. Her brother-in-law became very helpful, settling the estate and all. Funny she didn't turn to her old friend Ollie.'

Freda had recommended stirring. 'Maybe she didn't want anyone outside the family to know what her husband had left her.'

'Maybe not. Anyway, it happened and Jane's depression followed their divorce and his remarriage. She must not have been a very stable person, it was clinical depression, not the usual blues a person feels after a divorce.'

Freda was indignant. 'I'm sure most people feel more than "blues". *I'd* go into a real depression if you left me and married my sister.'

Pedersen grimaced. 'Please. Make it someone other than your sister. But there's not a chance you'd go into a depression. You'd find yourself someone new on the first corner you came to. You're not the sort of woman to pine away for any man.'

She turned to face him, spattering gravy on the floor. 'What do you mean? I'm unfeeling?'

'Not unfeeling.' He reached for a paper towel. 'Just too vital to be alone for long.'

'It's not easy for a woman in her fifties to find a man, you know.'

'You'd find one.'

'Why do you assume I'd want one? You know, Carl—' her face was thoughtful—'I think you're wrong. I think if something happened to us, if you died or we were divorced, I'd live alone. Or with another woman. I'd stop worrying about dinner being on time. I'd eat when I wanted to and sleep when I wanted to and stay up all night reading or listening to jazz if I felt like it. I'd travel and—don't look so stricken. I prefer it *this* way. I just don't think I'd do it again.'

'You sound so . . . enthusiastic. As though you can't wait to try a life like that.'

She slid the stew pot off the burner, set it aside and came over to him. 'There's absolutely nothing like a Significant Other and I know it. But I don't think you'd be easy to replace. It would be a better life than just marrying someone to get married, wouldn't it?'

He kissed her. 'At least you can talk about it. I can't *think* about your not being here. I'm the one who'd go to pieces.'

She shook her head. 'You always say that. You wouldn't. You'd find someone else within a year and live happily ever after. Men need women more. Don't smile, they do. Look at any widower, they can't wait to get themselves married again.'

'What are you working from, a sampling of two?

'No. I can read. I've read things. Men can't understand a woman's enthusiasm for a life alone. You've been free in a different way from us, especially those of us who stayed home with kids. The idea of not having to adapt to anybody else's needs or schedules sounds so *restful*.' After a moment, she added meditatively, 'Actually, it's probably pretty lonely.'

Pedersen crossed to the other side of the room. 'Don't let's discuss it. It bothers me to talk about it.'

'Then—' she returned to the stove and began ladling stew into heavy white bowls—'you understand some of what Jane felt when her husband left her, why it wasn't just the "blues".' She carried the bowls to the table. 'It must have been hell, seeing him practically next door with her sister. God! She must have wanted to kill him.'

'She probably did. And he probably wanted to murder her for making him feel so guilty.' He stopped. 'Maybe that's what happened. Maybe Ernest murdered her.'

Freda slid the salad bowl from a refrigerator shelf and brought it to the table. 'That's everything. You'd better forget the case for a while, it'll interfere with your digestion.'

He reached for a thick slice of dark bread. 'Nothing will interfere with this meal.' He picked up his fork. 'But I wonder. It doesn't explain anything, though. I guess that's one blind alley I won't chase down.' He took a first forkful of stew. 'Tomorrow is the service for Ann Koppleman.' After a while he added, 'This stew is *marvellous*.'

'Well, of course,' said Freda.

The attendance was surprisingly small. An announcement of the service had appeared the evening before and firmly specified that it was being held for 'family and close friends only'; either Ann's friends had been unable to determine what constituted closeness or her close friends had been few. Held in the town's Universalist Church, a little grey-painted building of no particular pretension located near the centre of town, the service, while personal, was not a true memorial service. The young minister obviously knew Ann well; he spoke of her work with Marigold House and the hospital and even of her dedication to the University's Garden Project, in each case citing specific incidents that demonstrated her selflessness in giving. At one point he seemed about to cry. When he finished speaking, a quartet played briefly. There were no eulogies or tributes from others.

Pedersen was surprised. He had the impression the whole thing was being got over with as quickly and unobtrusively as possible, as though there were some shame in Ann's having been murdered. Nonetheless, the family seemed deeply moved. At one point Stanley openly wept; throughout the service Kay crushed a handkerchief to her mouth, above which her eyes brimmed; Roy's features bore a mournful cast that altered his face's contours. The boys sat stolidly, eyes straight ahead, obviously keeping a grip on themselves. Suzanne quietly sobbed. Pedersen was touched.

But Oliver Winter, one of the few non-family members recognizable to Pedersen, was the most interesting. His face bore an expression of disdain throughout. Several times Pedersen glanced his way; the expression was unrelenting. Immediately the service was over, he rose from where he sat apart from the others and left without a word, even to Suzanne.

Pedersen hesitated a second, then followed him out. Winter was unlocking a black Mercedes as Pedersen approached; he jumped slightly when the detective spoke.

'Affecting service, Mr Winter, didn't you think?'

'I dislike this sort of thing myself,' Winter replied, straightening and facing Pedersen.

'Oh? Why is that?'

'It's too complex to explain to you.' The subtle emphasis on the word *you* was not lost on Pedersen.

'You don't feel there needs to be . . . closure after a death?
A time to pay tribute? To, as it were, say goodbye?'

Winter looked off over Pedersen's shoulder. Pedersen was
aware that the mourners were beginning to emerge from
the building. 'I say goodbye in my own way.' Winter seemed
to be reflecting to himself. 'There are many ways of saying
goodbye.' He turned back to the car. 'I want to get out of
here before I'm placed in the position of having to say things
I don't mean to the family. Goodbye, Detective.' He climbed
into his car, started the engine and roared off.

Odd, Pedersen thought, I'd have thought he's the one
person who would be dedicated to the most conventional of
funeral services. He turned back towards the church.

Roy Potter emerged from the church with a peculiar light-
ness of spirit. After the burial of the ashes in the family plot,
it would be over. Although he still experienced a strange
distance from real grief, he thought he had conducted himself well at the service. It was true that he could not weep
on command as, apparently, Stanley could, but he had felt
the sadness of a mourner. For a second he felt irritation that
he could not weep or feel the loss as deeply as the others
seemed to. But there it was again: seemed to. Who knew
what they really felt? Or thought.

Stanley sought Martha as he turned to leave the church.
She had come as he asked, and as he approached her, he
realized she was crying. 'You seemed so upset, Stan,' she
said, using his nickname as she seldom did. She smiled
faintly, drying her eyes on a colourful handkerchief. 'It upset
me, too.' He took her hand, touched. He noted that she had
dressed with special restraint, given her wardrobe. She was
really an extraordinary woman, a caring woman. For a
moment he experienced a thrust of pain at the thought of
the missed years and the children they might have had. He
gripped her hand, hard.

Kay mopped her eyes and turned to leave the church,
reaching beside her for Sue as they both stood up. The girl's

hand was limp, as though she had been utterly enervated by grief. For a moment Kay felt an awful loneliness envelop her. She still had not had a word from her husband; he did not even know of Ann's death. Lewis seemed about to desert her completely and there was no one else at the moment. She turned and embraced Sue with a warmth unusual for her.

Pedersen, standing outside, watched them issue from the little grey building, wondering what they were feeling. As he moved towards the little family group that had stopped to one side of the door, receiving condolences, he reflected that they were a hard bunch to read.

CHAPTER 31

'I'd like it if it's here. I know it's only a Timex,' Rod MacMillan said, 'but it also happens to be the only watch I own. I must have left it upstairs when I went for my annual check-up Friday.'

The young woman behind the hospital's Lost and Found counter eyed him with doubt. 'I swear I've been through everything in the jewellery box twice. Couldn't you have left it somewhere else? Did you call upstairs?'

'Yes. They say they shoot everything down here the day they find it. Can't I look?'

She glanced around. 'Come on. I'm not supposed to let anyone back here, but since you work in the hospital, I guess it's OK.' She led him to a back room. 'Here.' She slid a box off a shelf. It appeared to be filled with pieces of costume jewellery.

'My God, *everyone* must be careless. What a collection.'

'I'll go back to the desk. You look through this, but you won't find it. There are a couple of wristwatches, but not yours.'

The assortment was fascinating. Gold predominated.

Rings, pins, watches, a bracelet, a chain and locket. He
paused over the locket to see if it contained pictures. It did,
of two children. Someone was really missing that. One
watch was a Seiko. How could anyone be that careless? He
picked up several unmatched earrings. Had the women
left wearing single earrings? Obviously the girl was
right; his watch wasn't among this assortment, although
everything else was. Even, he picked it up, a wedding ring.
That carried some significance, he thought with amusement. Had the woman taken it off and abandoned it
with unconscious intent? He smiled and looked inside
the ring. 'E/J forever,' it read. He put it down, then
in a sudden moment of recollection he saw Eugénie's
hand, quiet in her lap as she answered his questions.
She had been wearing a wedding ring; he had especially
noticed it, wondering why she hadn't long since pawned
a piece of gold like that. He looked at the ring again.
E/J? Eugénie/John? Eugénie/James? Eugénie/Jules?
He picked it up, oddly excited. Could it possibly be
Eugénie's ring?

'No watch,' he announced as he came out of the room.
'But I found something else.'

'No kidding. Something you lost?'

'No, but something I want to show the police.'

She looked shocked. 'The police?'

'In connection with that murder last week. This may
have belonged to the murdered woman.' He held out the
ring.

'I can't let you take something that belongs to someone
else.' Her face crinkled with distress.

'Then hold it aside, someplace safe, till I phone the police
to see if they're interested. Will you do that?'

'All right. I'll put it in an envelope and label it with your
name. Will the police come right away?' Her face was
anxious.

'I don't know, they may not come at all. But don't let
anything happen to it. And thanks about my watch. If it

turns up, call Social Work and leave a message for me, will you?'

Back in his office, he had Jerry Cohen paged.

Jerry remembered. 'That's right, she had a ring. When she told me she was married, she sort of waved her hand to show it to me. Gold, I think it was.'

'Yes, gold. I'm going to call Detective Pedersen and tell him about it. If it's hers, she might have left it on a bedside table or something.'

'Earlier. I'm sure they removed everything that was in the room the day she died. But you might as well tell the police, just in case. If it were hers, it might help them—'

'I know, identify her,' Rod broke in.

He could hear the amusement in Jerry's voice. 'Do you feel like a detective?'

He laughed. 'I do, it makes me want to start searching the hospital for clues. Anyway, sorry to bother you, but I wanted to tell someone. I'd better get through to the police before that girl in Lost and Found mislays it or something.'

Detective Pedersen was not in his office. The switchboard transferred the call to Detective Tate's office.

Tate sounded dubious. 'You think it's hers? All gold wedding rings look alike, don't they? And that E could be anybody.' He paused. 'Well, maybe I'll come by and take a look, I have to be over in that neighbourhood around noon anyway.'

Rod felt impelled to elaborate. 'It was coincidence, really. If I hadn't lost my watch, the ring could have lain there for months.'

'Then if it turns out to be hers, luck is on our side. But don't get your hopes up.' He still sounded unconvinced.

Rod MacMillan hung up, conscious that the papers on his desk needing his attention seemed singularly dull and uninteresting. He smiled to himself. Maybe he'd missed his calling.

*

Pedersen examined the ring doubtfully. He had just returned from a follow-up visit to Marigold House—Tate had
made the first—and had confirmed his impression that no
one having to do with that organization had the slightest
connection with either murder. Tate had meanwhile picked
up the ring.

'I suppose we could have the *Banner* run a photo,' Pedersen
said.

'Enlarge the inscription,' Tate offered.

'Yes, if it was hers, maybe someone who knew her will
recognize it. It might lead to our knowing who the hell she
was.' He sat down wearily. 'Next time we have a service to
attend, you take it, Ron. I almost didn't get up this morning.'

'Too bad she didn't put both her initials and both of his
in the ring. That might have been enlightening,' Tate said.

'Not really.' Pedersen poked in his desk drawer. 'I'm sure
I had some peanuts—oh, here they are.' He tore open the
packet. 'Supposing it were Eugénie's, which it probably isn't,
the ring tells us just one thing, the first initial of her husband.
J, that could be Jonathan, Jeffrey, Joseph—the possibilities
are endless. Endless. I suppose we should ask the *Banner* to do
something with it, but we've had no response to her picture,
why should we think we'll do better with this?'

'You do sound tired. Discouraged. That's—'

'I know. That's not like me.'

'Well, it isn't.'

'So my wife told me. I am discouraged. Usually at least
we know whom we're dealing with. This business of her
having no identity gets to me. We keep learning scraps of
things, but none of it has helped us with *her*. I don't
understand why someone hasn't come forth to say, "That
looks like a woman I once knew," or "I went to school with
a girl named Eugénie." Can she have changed that much?'
He broke a peanut in half and examined it for the dwarf.

'Did you ever think that maybe people who might know
her are uneasy about identifying themselves with a vagrant?'

'We'd give them anonymity. Maybe we haven't stressed

that enough. Tell the *Banner* when they take the ring over, will you? Tonight,' Pedersen went on, eating the halves of the peanut, 'I'm going to sit down with a sheet of paper and graph this case. Look at all the relationships and see if I can't come up with something.'

Tate smiled. 'When you turn to a paperwork solution, you must be desperate.'

'I am desperate. Don't you feel we must have enough at our fingertips to solve this, but that we're missing some obvious connection?'

'I'd—oh my God, I forgot. When I picked up the ring, Rod MacMillan told me something. He said that one time he walked in on Mawson, the psychiatrist, in the room with Eugénie. She was asleep and he was touching her. Erotically.'

'So *that*'s what he was uneasy about. Afraid about.'

'He said Mawson swore it had never happened before and would never happen again. MacMillan told him he wouldn't report it to anyone. You know, Carl, it doesn't have to mean anything.'

'Mawson.' He sighed. 'Christ, what next? Anyway, I'm going to try the graphic approach. It may lead to something.'

Tate stood up. 'And I'm going to deliver this ring to the *Banner*. Maybe they'll get something in tomorrow's paper.'

Pedersen smiled. 'I'll have it all solved by tomorrow.'

'Just in case you don't,' Tate said.

CHAPTER 32

'Guess what,' Tate greeted his partner as they entered the building together. He looked glum. They had arrived early, both of them, and parked alongside each other. 'I had a phone call last night from that nurse. The computer's been overhauled and is functioning; she said I could come by and check the lists. She was on night duty and said she'd help.'

Pedersen stopped. 'What did you find out?'

'That nurse wasn't Eugénie at all.'

'What?'

'She was Henriette, Henriette Bouchard. The nurse was in an agony of apology. Apparently she has a thing with French names. So Eugénie was not, to our knowledge, a nurse at Bay Cove.'

Pedersen laughed. 'It doesn't matter. I had a brainstorm. Come into my office for a minute.'

Tate closed the door behind him, his face troubled. 'Yes?'

'What,' Pedersen said, 'if E/J were Ernest/Jane.'

Kay put down the receiver with a crash. Now they wanted her at headquarters; what would be next? She wondered if life was ever going to return to normal.

Whatever normal was. It had occurred to her that maybe Bob, too, was having second thoughts about their arrangement. He might have settled for a more conventional relationship with some other woman; God, she hoped not. At forty-eight she did not welcome being deserted, especially if men like Lewis were all she had to look forward to. She had tried to see his kinkiness as amusing and naughty, but she had never succeeded. And the last time he had come close to hurting her—let's face it, had hurt her. She shivered.

She'd go to headquarters, humour this detective, and then maybe she'd get out of town herself, take a little trip, put all this behind her. And if her husband returned—as he must, eventually; he wasn't about to walk out on his job—she'd talk to him about another sort of marriage. After all, she had stuck to him through all they'd done together and separately because, basically, she liked him. Damn it, loved him!

Assuming, of course, that Detective Pedersen would permit her to leave town. She sighed and went into the bedroom to change her clothes. To go to headquarters, where she had been told she was needed.

*

Roy had been catching up on bill-paying, but thinking ahead to the evening. Dinner someplace pleasant, relaxed— a pot of steamers in one of the little places in the seaside village five miles out of town. Afterwards a stroll on the espla—But all plans were out. He was to appear at headquarters. The invitation had been something more, although it had no actual legal force behind it. He was needed, he had been told. Needed? For what? He wished to God the whole thing were over.

Stanley had to phone Martha to cancel dinner. 'I'm needed at headquarters,' he explained. 'It may not take long, but don't wait dinner. I'll come by afterwards.' She had let him sleep with her the night before and now she sounded soft, welcoming.

'I may have something good to tell you, Stanley,' she said, her tone seductive. He glanced down and could actually see his heart thud in response.

'Martha,' he said. He could think of no other words. 'I'll see you as soon as I can.'

Dr Lewis Mawson was furious. 'Need me for *what*? What have *I* got to do with this investigation? I can see your stopping by to ask about old patients, but I see no sense whatsoever in my coming to headquarters.' But in the end he agreed. Somehow refusing made him appear to be involved. He didn't want that.

Suzanne gave them the information they asked for, the name of the family dentist. 'We've used him forever. Actually I guess he's getting a little old, but he's still practising.'

She was puzzled but perfectly agreeable about coming in to headquarters. 'Have you new information?' She heard the fear in her voice. What was the matter with her? She wanted her mother's murderer found, didn't she? Mentally she shook herself and said brightly, 'Of course. I'll be there.'

*

Oliver Winter was the most reluctant. 'You can't need my help. I have no help to give you. You've learned everything from me that I know about Ann and about Ann's death.' He added, more severely, 'Can't you let us put this behind us? You seem to forget we have feelings about this loss.'

In the end he succumbed, actually, he supposed as he put down the receiver, because he had no choice. Maybe this would be the end of it. He so much wanted this to be the end of it.

'We've brought you all here,' Pedersen said, after the last of them had been seated in the now crowded office, 'because we have a theory and we think you can help us check it out.'

Stanley stiffened and Kay felt her stomach tighten. Roy and Ollie both shifted in their chairs. Lewis Mawson stubbornly looked away.

'Our theory is—' Pedersen paused for effect—'that your sister Jane and Eugénie were one and the same person.'

His statement was met by a shocked silence.

CHAPTER 33

No one spoke for a few seconds. Then Suzanne said, 'Aunt Jane died from cancer nearly ten years ago.'

Kay, who seemed not to have heard her, said, 'Eugénie? You mean that bag lady?' Pedersen wondered if her shock at the idea was genuine.

'Yes, the bag lady.'

'That's ridiculous!' Ollie sounded personally affronted.

'Jane died over nine years ago,' Stanley explained, enunciating as though he were talking to a retarded child.

'We know that's the story,' Tate said.

'The story!' Roy was indignant. 'Her body was identified.'

'I thought Aunt Jane died from cancer,' Suzanne said.

'Mistakes have been made in identification,' Pedersen pointed out.

'I—what on earth makes you think such a thing?' Kay's voice sounded unnatural to her.

'It explains so much. The information she had that was the basis of her letter, which she described to someone as a "surprise". Her statement to another street person that she could have all the money she wanted if she'd just make a phone call. Other things, like her writing to Ann in the first place.'

'I'm completely confused,' Suzanne said.

'Do you *know* that she wrote to Ann?' Roy's tone was contemptuous. 'Or is this just another "theory"?'

'Mr Winter—' Pedersen nodded towards him—'informs us that Ann received a very disturbing letter around the time that Eugénie borrowed paper and pen and a stamp from a librarian and wrote the letter she said would be a "surprise".' Pedersen turned to Kay. 'Didn't she discuss it with you? I understand you shared confidences.'

'Well, this was one we didn't share. She never said a word.'

'Please.' Suzanne stood up. 'Will *somebody* explain to me?'

Pedersen explained. 'You see,' he finished, 'the family originally were just honouring your aunt's wishes. Then she drowned and they couldn't very well explain that she'd been in a psychiatric hospital all along. Also they were protecting you, Miss Ford. Suicide isn't easy to live with.'

'Sue. Please. Mother never told us anything of this. But she did—I told you—act awfully odd around street people the last couple of weeks.'

'Perhaps she was trying to find out what their lives were like. The night of her death she was reading a book called *Ironweed*.'

'A book about vagrants living in the nineteen-thirties,' Tate contributed.

'Coincidence,' Stanley said.

'Which of you identified the body nine years ago?'

'Roy and I,' Stanley said, indicating his brother.

'No,' Roy put in. 'You did. I came later.'

'Well then, you came later.'

'The body had been moved by then,' Roy reminded his brother. 'Taken away.'

'Then I—' Stanley said, his mouth twisted into a wry grimace—'am the culprit. I identified her. It was Jane, I'm positive.'

'The body had been in the water two weeks?' Pedersen asked, his voice gentle.

'Yes. I—it was . . . bloated. That was why I didn't want Kay and Ann to see it. I did identify it and by the time Roy got there, it had been removed for autopsy.'

'Bloated bodies are hard to identify. Features become altered. How was she dressed?'

'She had on—God, I can't remember. It was *nine* years ago!' Stanley ran his hand over his face.

'Let's assume you identified someone you *thought* was your sister. Where do you assume your real sister would have been for the next seven years?' He looked around the group.

'I don't see why I'm here,' Lewis Mawson said suddenly.

'Nor I,' added Oliver Winter, his tone aggrieved.

'You were, respectively, the confidants of Ann and Kay. You may know more about this than you think.'

Suzanne looked at the two men with speculation. Winter shrugged, sighed deeply and turned his head away.

'If Jane was really the bag lady, I guess I mean if the bag lady was really Jane, and had told Ann, Ann certainly would have told us and welcomed her home.' Roy spoke as though that should not need explaining.

'It would seem so. But you tell me she didn't. Did she confide in any of you?'

No one said anything.

'There were other considerations,' Tate put in. 'Perhaps Eugénie wanted financial support. In fact, it would seem very likely that she did. Or some part of your father's inheritance.'

'Would she even have known about it?' Kay asked.

'She had been in Bay Cove for two years before she wrote to Ann,' Pedersen said.

'Before you *assume* she wrote to Ann,' Roy put in.

Pedersen nodded. 'Why two years? And where had she been for over seven years?'

Suzanne spoke up. 'Couldn't Aunt Jane—if it was Aunt Jane—have still been sick?'

'We think that. But we have no way of knowing. We haven't yet checked hospitals in San Francisco and San José. We wanted to talk with all of you first.'

'Why wouldn't Mother have just taken her in? Knowing my mother, I'd think that she wouldn't have been able to go another day thinking Aunt Jane was on the street.'

'She may have been suspicious, thought this person was a fraud, not really her sister.'

'Her name was different.'

'Not so very different. Jane. Eugénie. She may have liked the slightly more elegant name. Your mother never liked her name, did she?'

'How do you know that?'

'I surmised it. She named her children very differently.'

'She told me once that she'd never saddle one of us kids with such a plain name as hers. But I hate the name Suzanne. Why not plain Susan? That's why I use Sue, Suzanne sounds so—affected.'

'All right, Sue, let's get back to the topic under discussion. We haven't all night.' Roy's irritation was evident.

'Sorry.' Affronted, she retired into the background.

'So here we are, with our theory,' Pedersen said. 'The only person in the room who has seen the mysterious letter Ann received is Mr Winter.'

'If Ann wanted it kept from the rest of us, I think her wishes should be respected,' Stanley said.

Winter was looking at Pedersen, a new expression on his face. 'Where does your theory go next? How do you account for the murder? The murders, I mean?'

'Someone,' Tate said, 'didn't want Jane's identity revealed.'

'That's right,' said Pedersen. 'So he—or she—killed Eugénie. Jane, that is. And, because he didn't want Ann recognizing his or her involvement, killed Ann.'

Suzanne's gasp was loud in the silent room. 'You mean one of *us* killed Mother?'

'Or someone acting for one of you.'

'That's—' she looked at the faces around her—'that's impossible. *Why?*'

'Perhaps because of the disgrace. Your aunt was an unstable street person.'

'Or, more likely,' said Tate, 'for money.'

'But what money? You mean money to take care of her? Mother would just have taken Aunt Jane to live with her.'

'Perhaps she wanted to share in your grandfather's inheritance.'

'But he didn't know . . . Although,' she went on in a thoughtful voice, 'he said in the will—'

Kay broke in. 'Really, Suzanne, you're getting into matters that don't concern you.'

'Don't concern me? My mother's death doesn't concern me?'

'I meant—oh, go ahead. Of course it concerns you.'

'All I was going to say, Aunt Kay,' Suzanne explained in her reasonable way, 'was that Grandfather did say in his will that he left his money to "my children". Mother said he worded it that way years ago and never named them. Grandmother had her own money,' she explained to Pedersen and Tate. 'Mother thought he might even have written the will before you were born, Aunt Kay, and worded it that way in case he died before you arrived. That was all I was going to say.'

Someone in the room moved abruptly.

'Then,' Oliver Winter said, 'Jane would have been eligible to collect her fifth of the inheritance. Quite a bit of money.'

'Yes, she would,' Pedersen said. 'Are you having second thoughts about letting us in on that letter?'

'She did tell someone else about that letter,' said Oliver Winter. 'A member of her family. She told me.'

'*You* wouldn't have had a motive for murdering Ann?' Pedersen's tone was conversational.

'I? I loved her. And all I know about this bag lady is what I learned from the letter. I'd better tell you what was in it. I can't remember the exact wording, but the letter said something like this: "I'm writing you because I've come back. I ran away and then was sick for a long time, but lately I've been better and it's time for me to come home. Even though you did the worst thing anyone has ever done to me, marrying Ernest, you've always been my favourite person in the family and I'm turning to you. You needn't take me in or anything, but I just read in a newspaper that Daddy is the *late* Joseph Potter, so he must be dead. I want my share of his money and then I'll go off by myself and leave you alone. I've been living on the street. Get in touch with me under the name Jane Potter at General Delivery. Jane." Ann said she had to find a way to check whether the woman was really Jane, but she wrote her that she'd be in touch and sent her two hundred dollars in cash.'

'Why do you say Ann told someone in the family?'

'She said she did. She said she was going to, rather. She was very much upset about the whole thing.'

'Well?' Pedersen looked around the room, his face pleasant. 'Which of you was it?' He thought he already knew.

'Not me,' said Roy. 'She never said a word to me. But then she wouldn't.'

'Nor I,' added Kay hastily.

'She didn't tell me,' said Suzanne. 'Obviously.

'That seems to leave you, Mr Potter,' said Pedersen, turning to Stanley.

Stanley stood, upsetting a stack of books. 'You have only their word for it.' Then he slumped back down into his chair. 'All right. Actually, Ann did say something to me. I guess I should tell you. It was a trivial reference, really, she was mostly trying to find out if I could have made a mistake in the identification. She didn't go into the rest, the letter from Jane.'

Pedersen swung around to Lewis Mawson, who sat, lips compressed, unspeaking. 'You did a surgical rotation, I assume, as part of your medical training.'

'What—' The physician drew himself up. 'Are you suggesting that I knifed those two women?'

'No. I was merely asking a question.'

'A question! I don't like its implications. Of course I did a surgical rotation.'

Suzanne suddenly spoke. 'That seems pretty silly to me, Detective. Anyone could have . . . done that to Mother.'

'Not anyone,' said Pedersen. 'I, for example, wouldn't have known how to strike a single blow that so precisely found the heart. And two such blows . . .'

'But I mean anybody who had any medical training. Uncle Stan studied medicine. Does that make him a killer?'

Pedersen turned to Stanley Potter. 'You studied medicine?'

'It was nothing, I never did anything with it.'

'But,' Roy said levelly, 'you completed an internship.'

'So I completed an internship. I've never practised. That was years ago, one of my bad beginnings.' He turned to Pedersen, his tone light. 'I always say I'm the living illustration of that old rhyme that goes Doctor, Lawyer, Merchant, Chief. I also started a law programme. And I suppose you'd say I ended up a merchant.' He laughed. It was not a comfortable sound.

'Mr Potter, did you do a surgical rotation?'

'Yes—æons ago. It must be thirty-five years. You don't think I retained the skill to—' He broke off at the detective's face. 'For Christ's sake,' he said, 'you don't think I'd be idiot enough to leave the Carson stickers on those knives if I'd done it?'

'The *Carson* stickers? The name of the store where the knives were bought was never published.'

Everyone in the room had turned to Stanley.

'I—I'm sure I read it. Or it was just a guess. Maybe I saw it when I found Ann. You don't think I'd kill my own sister, the sister I loved—' He buried his head in his hands. 'My own sister—' her said brokenly. Tears poured down his face. 'You don't think—' He raised his ravaged face. 'I miss her so,' he said.

CHAPTER 34

'For a hundred thousand dollars? You mean he killed *two* women for a hundred thousand dollars?' Freda couldn't believe it.

They were having their evening drink. The room was darkening in the dusk, but they had not yet turned on lights.

Pedersen raised his eyebrows. 'That's so little?'

'No, I mean not to us it wouldn't be. But for a murder— *two* murders—as a motive, yes. He could have borrowed it.'

'That's true. And it does seem like little. It was what he would have had to come up with as his share of Jane's inheritance. He couldn't have taken it out of the business again; even if he could have, he'd never have been able to bring himself to do that. You don't understand, Freda, what that prestige in the company meant to him.'

'A job in a software company?'

'Come on. He was a man who had failed at everything he had undertaken for close to forty years. He had finally made it, an executive, looked up to. He panicked. But I think his motive for the murder was not so pure as all that. I think he'd hated his sisters. He'd hated his mother for abandoning him in the way she did and his sisters for so easily gaining his father's approval. Jane, especially. We'll never know whether he really believed his identification of her as the drowning victim—he says yes, but it's clear he wanted her dead, had seen her as his particular enemy all those years.'

'Why? And what do you mean, he'd been failing at everything for forty years?'

'You have to understand the background. It seems Jane was born within two years of his birth. From that day forth his father focused on her. His mother sounds pretty flaky, I doubt that she consistently focused on anything except maybe having another baby. Stanley probably felt ordinary sibling rivalry, but I suspect as one sister after the other got the approval from his father that he so desperately wanted, Jane became a sort of symbol to him—of all the rejection he felt. Then, shortly after Kay was born—the last child—his mother committed suicide. The ultimate rejection.'

Freda arranged a cushion behind her back. 'Odd that the only one to become unstable was Stanley. You'd think Kay—'

He frowned at her. 'I wouldn't say Jane was stable.'

'Of course not. That was an idiotic thing for me to say. Go ahead.'

'When Stanley reached adulthood, he went to college and finally, after much disgusted effort on Papa's part, was accepted by a medical school. He hadn't been outstanding as a student in college. He survived medical school and almost made it through an internship but he edged through all the way. Towards the end he was warned to stick to a safe specialty, nothing diagnostic and not surgery. At that point he decided he'd had it with medicine and dropped out. After an interval of soul-searching, he entered law school.'

'Where he flunked out.'

'You guessed it.' Pedersen swirled the vermouth in his glass. 'I gather rather thoroughly. Then he drifted through a number of other false starts, tried acting, then a design school. And finally ended up selling. Then he heard of a job in a big local software business, the selling end.'

'He must have been pretty old by then.'

'He was. I have the impression that he wasn't much respected there till he began to pour money into the place. Finally he dumped his share of his father's inheritance into the business. That did it. It must have been an exhilarating experience for him, being deferred to and treated as an important person in the firm. And from something he said when he made his statement, I gathered at last he had a thing going with a woman, too.' He paused. 'All down the tubes.'

'And you don't think he deliberately identified the wrong body when that drowned woman was washed ashore?'

'I don't know. He never let any other member of the family see the body, so he must have known at some level it wasn't Jane. Maybe not, though. We believe what we want to believe.'

The room had become dark. Freda reached beside her and turned on one lamp. 'What's the story on Eugénie?'

'We don't know. Maybe she just lived on the streets all those years. Apparently she spontaneously began to get better and decided to come back to Bay Cove. But not home, yet. Strange, some of them become almost . . . professional street people, if you can believe it.'

'I can. You must get so you don't want the demands of normal life.'

'I'm harbouring an incipient vagrant in my house?'

'I won't be leaving right away. But I can understand. At the same time, there must be a longing for home and all that means.'

'I think a longing and a fear. By the time you've lived on the streets for a while, especially a woman of her age, you must feel you just can't make the grade again. I don't know. I'm just guessing, but it seems that way to me.'

'Then she saw something in a newspaper about her father?'

'In the letter to Ann she said she had seen a reference to the *late* Joseph Potter. She realized he must have died. He was a well-heeled gentleman. Maybe she saw it as her chance to make a new beginning. With money, she could escape the demands of family and do it on her own terms.'

'But she was unsure?'

'Probably scared. She must have mulled over the idea for quite a while before she wrote that letter. The autopsy said she was in good health, but the fainting spells may have scared her and got her moving.'

'How did Stanley know about her sleeping in the hospital?'

'After Ann talked to him, he set out to find Jane. Most local vagrants end up spending time on the mall, so he went there, made several trips before he spotted her.'

'And followed her.'

'He hasn't filled in all the details, but I suspect he did. Either just that once or over a period of time until he learned her habits.'

'Then he set out to kill her.'

'And his other sister, yes. Ann.' He added grimly, 'I think he was poorly advised when he was a medical student. He should have gone into surgery.'

She shivered. 'But Ann was the one person in the family whom he really loved!'

'If he did. Something in the way he talked of his missing her made me wonder if he somehow had confused her with his mother. Ann, remember, for all that she was younger, was the mature one in the family, the good one. It sounds as though she may have mothered him; he certainly seems to have needed mothering. If he confused her with Mamma, well . . .'

'He thought he was the only one to whom Ann had shown the letter? He must have planned the murders; he went out and bought two knives.'

'There's something funny about that, too. Why not use a knife from his house or from Ann's? And leaving the stickers on—was that panic or was it ambivalence? Without those identical knives with their stickers, we'd never have connected the two deaths.'

'You're saying he wanted to be caught?'

'Only in so far as all killers who aren't total psychopaths want to. He did kill his sisters when they were asleep; that wasn't just convenience, at some level it was guilt.'

'And he killed Ann because she would know he had killed Eugénie?'

'Yes. Ann had said she would welcome Eugénie home, would see that she got her share of the inheritance. He felt he had to kill her, she knew he had seen the letter and would immediately guess that he had killed Eugénie. Apparently he had tried to convince Ann that Eugénie was a fraud, had tried to discourage Ann from getting in contact with her. Unsuccessfully.'

'Tragic,' Freda said severely. 'Tragic all around. But of course he *wasn't* the only one to whom Ann had shown the letter.'

'No, Winter knew, but apparently never connected Stanley or any other family member with the murders. He knew Eugénie might be Jane, but he didn't want to—besmirch Ann's memory by suggesting an association with them. So he vociferously—and snobbishly, I thought at the time—denied that Ann could possibly have known of a bag lady.'

'How did the rest of the family respond when they realized Stanley had done the murders?'

'Suzanne was horrified, but the others were strange. They sort of shrugged Stanley off, as though he were of no consequence to them. No wonder he always found it rough going in that family. I think they're *all* sick.'

'But feeling sorry for him—I mean understanding what shaped him, that's no reason for—'

'I didn't mean it was.' He looked fondly in her direction. 'You look lovely in that half-light.'

'What? Oh, you look lovely, too.'

'*Lovely?* Men are supposed to look dashing and handsome. And virile. Not lovely.'

'Well, then,' she said, rising to go start dinner, 'you look dashing and handsome and virile.' She looked at him with affection. 'And lovely. Come help.'